D1001095

Also by Anthony Burgess

FICTION

The Right to an Answer
Devil of a State
A Clockwork Orange
The Wanting Seed
Honey for the Bears
Nothing Like the Sun
The Long Day Wanes
A Vision of Battlements
The Doctor Is Sick
Tremor of Intent
Enderby
The Eve of Saint Venus
MF
One Hand Clapping

NONFICTION

Language Made Plain
Re Joyce
The Novel Now
A Shorter Finnegans Wake
Urgent Copy
Shakespeare

TRANSLATION

Cyrano de Bergerac

NAPOLEON SYMPHONY

NAPOLEON SYMPHONY

ANTHONY BURGESS

ALFRED A. KNOPF NEW YORK 1974

THIS IS A BORZOI BOOK
PUBLISHED BY ALFRED A. KNOPF, INC.

Published in the United States by Alfred A. Knopf, Inc., New York. Distributed by Random House, Inc., New York.

Library of Congress Cataloging in Publication Data

Wilson, John Anthony Burgess, date
Napoleon symphony.

1. Napoleon I, Emperor of the French, 1769–1821—Fiction. I. Title.
PZ4.W7492Nap3 [PR6073.I4678] 823'.9'14 73-20750
ISBN 0-394-47614-X

Manufactured in the United States of America

FIRST EDITION

To my dear wife, a Buonapartista, who, in her extreme youth, could never understand why the British had named a great railway terminus after a military defeat.

Also to Stanley J. Kubrick,
maestro di color . . .

NAPOLEON SYMPHONY

TALLIEN PRESSED HIS OLD ROYAL WATCH AND IT CHIMED A NEW republican nine. "An hour late already." Ventôse siffled in from the rue d'Antin and flapped the candle flames. There was a faint odor of scorched varnish from the wooden leg of the acting registrar asleep by the fire. Calmelet the lawyer, hers, in no hurry, said:

"The hours could have been longer. Or more of them to wait through. It was proposed, was it not, to decimalize the day as well as the week. Ten very long hours or a hundred very short ones. I will meet you, citizeness, at 93.55," chuckling. "The long ones could have been given names by poor d'Eglantine. Or was it Romme? No, Romme was no poet. They're both dead, anyway."

"There have been some fantastic ideas presented to the Directory," Barras said. "Someone wrote somewhere that revolutions are best left to the conservative."

"That was somebody else who died," Tallien said. "And somebody else said that the Goddess of Reason is proud of her ten fingers."

"The man who said that is still alive," Barras said, "and intends to remain so."

"Witty," Calmelet giggled. "Dinaire. Dormial. Amorôse. How about those, eh? For the hours. The hour of Amorôse was striking."

Barras tickled four fingers with the trinity of plumes on his directorial hat. A man in love with the senses, Tallien thought yet again. He would sell anything for the senses. To be watched. "Total consistency," Barras said, "is to be avoided as inhuman."

"You mean Jacobin," Tallien said.

"Let five and three dance together in amity. There is a sort of classical poem in which twelve syllables alternate with ten."

"Elegiac, I think," Calmelet said. The registrar, acting, snorted in his sleep. "It is not appropriate to speak of elegies. Epithalamia, perhaps. A pity that the names of the months are so, shall we say, local? Foggy, Snowy, Rainy, Windy. In Madame's country these names do not apply."

"There are rain and wind and mist." But they sounded as languorous as her vowels.

"Yes yes, what I mean is that as terms of mensual designation—"

"It's right that our tropical French should be reminded of the weather in Paris," Barras said.

"But in Madame's country it will always be Thermidor."

"It seems a long time ago," Tallien said. "Thermidor."

"Yes yes yes, you braved it, you were very brave." Barras stroked the tip of his nose with the tip of a plume. He hovered voluptuously on the promise of a sneeze but, a strong man, would not yield. Sniffing, he looked at Madame, petulant in her chair. He knew the body under the muslin dress, or rather he had a memory of its knowledge. You could know a book but you could only remember knowing a body. It was not the body that changed so much as the fingers that touched it. And it would not be long before he could think the same about the gorgeous, as it was now, body of Tallien's wife. The electric charge failed, something like that. Science. *The Revolution has no need of scientists.* Nonsense really. She said:

"I might as well go home."

"You and he will go home together," Barras said. "Courage, patience. He has much to do."

"There were longer waits," Tallien said. "No waits should be hard for us any more." She looked at him, posing on his chair as for a painter. Past glory caught in a cadence. Oh, make an alexandrine of it. Tallien on the stage, tumbrils rumbling in the wings. Shed then the tyrant's blood that blood be shed no more. And, from the window of the Carmes prison, she had seen that old woman dancing in toothless joy, a pierre in one hand, the dirty end of her robe in the other.

"Courage, patience, amity," Calmelet smiled, admiring her elegant neck, "for your new republic in which the month shall ever be Floréal." She was tricolored in flowers, she loved flowers. There had been a time when necks like hers had been ribboned in red for what they called survivors' dances, usually ending in hysterics. Suddenly the acting registrar called a name from his sleep.

"It sounded like *Joseph*," Tallien said. "One of your names. The name he has feminized and diminutized for you."

"The name perhaps of an old comrade-in-arms," Calmelet said. "That is very interesting, what a man will call in his sleep. Or perhaps a son or a brother. It is of course also," he said, "the name of your new brother-in-law. Titular head."

"I do not have him as a brother-in-law yet. I begin to wonder if I ever will."

"If he calls the name Catherine," Barras said, "then we shall know that his sleeping mind is troubled about an imposture. Very ironic. There have to be certificates of birth. Those are lodged in their respective islands. Both islands are in the hands of the British enemy. Very ironic."

"Not forever," Calmelet said.

"So he must use his brother's and she her sister's. A harmless enough imposture."

And, she thought, elder brother and younger sister, it brings our ages closer together, is he thinking that? We are made to be but a year apart. She felt her age as she felt Ventôse nip in again through the window crack that had been healed with some old ill-printed proclamation beginning *Citizens.* I have passed through too many hands. "If we must go on waiting, what shall we do? If I'd brought my tarot I could be telling all our fortunes. That passed the time once."

"We know our fortunes," Tallien acted. "We survived, and that's enough. Now there's a bigger—"

"Yes yes," Barras said. "That is what all the waiting is about."

"Joseph," Calmelet said, "had a coat of many colors and saved Egypt. He would not be seduced by his employer's wife. In France he's always been derided for that. And of course there's the other one, the holy cuckold." Nobody smiled. Barras said:

"We've abandoned religion but not, I hope, good taste."

"Oh, very aristo," Tallien said. Barras looked at him. Survival.

"I stand rebuked, Citizen Director," Calmelet said, though with no tone of abashment. "Myths, nevertheless, that have misled a whole country and kept them in slavery."

"These slogans ring hollow in a small room," Barras said, "when people are waiting for a wedding. True, yes, but they ring hollow. We must start thinking of new modes of taste and propriety. We are the custodians of civilization."

"Survival first," Tallien said.

"It's civilization in the bigger sense that has to survive." He kept to himself, as tasteless, the image of wagons rolling north, full of meltable plate from whipped monarchies. The registrar abruptly changed his position but went on sleeping. He uttered irritable sounds, but they were not words.

"That wooden leg is almost in the fire," Calmelet said. "Would there be, perhaps, a sort of memory of feeling as it were associated with the missing extremity? Ah yes, see, he's moved it away." The registrar shifted grumbling and seemed about to wake. "Sleep on," Calmelet soothed. "The bridegroom himself will awaken you." He looked cunningly around to see if any had caught the biblical echo, but there was the sound of two pairs of feet outside, approaching. They all cocked to it, but the sound passed on. Barras began to feel that, after all, apart from that special courtesy due to the bride, the general courtesy due to representatives of the state and the law, there was something deeper and, as it were, reverent due to himself as, so to speak, patron as well as powerful finger of the hand of authority, the ruling—

"What do you call a group of five, Calmelet?"

"A quincunx? No, a quinquevirate."

Monsieur Goodpart could have sent a message from his headquarters. There was a disquieting whiff of insubordination here, as of a man too insolently aware of the authority of cannonballs. And then (but this had to be quickly dismissed) the head-swimming doubt whether he would come at all, having taken fright like other bridegrooms before him. No, the man palpitated with adolescent love, he practically spasmed into his breeches on very sight of her. The electricity was in him to excess. And did not the way to the Alps lie (this was coarse, he admitted) between her legs? Take it another way and be calm: they were all three of them aristocrats, though those two from disregardable island colonies, speaking very provincial French, language with no kiss in the vowels. They all three had, in a sense, to cling together in a world ruled by the middle-class. A cast-off mistress settled in a reasonable marriage, a friendly man who took deep breaths and had a brain clever with cannonballs. The two were, so to speak, engines of his own survival.

Calmelet, trying to amuse the pouting bride, was fantasying about the acting registrar's wooden leg. "Neither a royal nor a revolutionary tree but a tree of France—simply that. Giving up a fragment of its being as he, this sleeping one here, gave up a fragment of his. In what war? For what cause? Like trees, such beings are insentient or indifferent."

"Write an elegy on it," Barras half-sneered. "Ode to a patriot's wooden leg. From that same tree came wood pulp for a new edition of Rousseau. Come on, Calmelet. Amuse us."

"Well, then," chortling:

"This son of France, shoeless, without a shirt,
Played in the royal highway's royal dirt.
Monseigneur's carriage rolled right over him.
He gained a louis when he lost a limb.

How about that then, eh?" Barras improvised:

> *"That tree provided a gavel or two*
> *For when the Declaration of Rights went through.*
> *Its bang healed many an intellectual schism*
> *At the confirmation of the Abolition of Feudalism."*

"Oh no," Calmelet said, "with respect, that is inadmissible prosodic license. Too revolutionary." Tallien tried:

> *"Truncheons for the Paris bread riot.*
> *Sawdust for the bread to keep them quiet."*

Calmelet cut in with:

> *"It might have been a tree made confiscate*
> *Along with Crown or Church land where it sate.*
> *It yielded a strong cane for Mirabeau,*
> *And gave him paper, half a ton or so,*
> *For him to pen his constitutions on."*

Tallien quickly rhymed:

> *"Perhaps he lost that leg there at Verdun."*

"Well," Calmelet now prosed. "They'll never be back on French soil. Madame's belated bridegroom will see to that."

Tallien pressed his old royal watch and it chimed a new republican ten. "Yes," he said. "The kinsmen of that bitch with a crown but no head."

"We fervently hope," Barras said. "We fervently pray, if we're so minded."

"To the Supreme Being," Calmelet said piously.

"Well," Tallien said, "the cult of the Supreme Being served its turn. It held the Convention together, among other less spiritual innovations. It led to Thermidor and the end of—"

"The incarnation of the General Will," Barras said. "A book can be a stick in the hand of a liberator. The same book can be a tyrant's weapon. Who can say that the truth lies here or there?

The Girondins were inspired by the finest Jean-Jacques motives. They declared war on everybody and they killed a king."

"They paid for it," Calmelet said, nodding.

"We go on paying for it. Survival is something that lies in the future. Sieyès said that to me. He wants his epitaph to be: *He survived.*"

"Oh, this is absurd," she said. "How much longer—?"

"Ah." Calmelet's quick ears heard first. Feet approached in urgent marching. The door was thrust open. Lemarois, aide-de-camp, the fourth witness. And then. "*Lui,*" Calmelet said.

He strode in. "Wake up. Get your leg out of the fire." He gave her two excruciating love-pinches, one on each lobe, and cried:

"Begin!"

I

Germinal in the Year Four, but in this opening of our own Year One the seed throbs and frets in frustration. Ah, how I should love to believe that what you have already of mine is at work deep within you. Albenga is on the coast halfway between Nice or Nizza and Genoa or Genova, and I am busy with maps and protractor and chief of staff. Looking up that volume on Piedmont and its topography, I swear I caught the scent of your body from it. It is strange and magical that about those dull tomes with which I encumbered our so short honeymoon your glow and odor should hover. Oh, how I slaver at the thought of you, hunger to chew your very toes, to munch your delta of silk in the valley of bliss—now but a delirious memory and a long promise. Oh, to fill you again with myself as I am filled now to overflowing with your sweetness. The bees, I swear, will buzz around me when we reach the honeylands. It is cold here and the troops grumble still. Kiss after kiss after kiss begins to abrade the crystal of your portrait.

Massena took it from Augereau who had taken it from La Harpe and handed it back. "As I said last time, very handsome."

"Handsome? *Handsome*? Life, ecstasy, the goddess of spring, the inspiration of battles. Come along then, Berthier." Berthier spluttered over his bread and followed him as he strode out into the morning, kissing before stowing.

"This bread tastes of very stale chestnuts," Augereau said. "Look at him after his night of wet dreams, ready to come in his breeches. Barras's stale chestnut, that's what she was, you know that. That's good, you see that? Chestnut hair, a bit dyed I should think now. Getting on in years, glad to marry that fucking scarecrow out there."

"We're all fucking scarecrows," Massena said.

"It tastes of very stale chestnuts," Kilmaine said, "because it contains very stale chestnuts."

"I saw a rotten potato yesterday," La Harpe said.

"You know what it is I'm going to tell you?" Kilmaine said. "We have horses there, real ones. Talking about chestnuts, I could cry when I think of—"

"That's the humanity coming out," Massena said. "You want to watch that Rousseau stuff. They're things, that's all, that have got to be used. You can fatten those that survive when we get down there in the plains. Good rich country. Irish."

Outside, in the raw morning, they saw Saliceti riding a fat nutmeg. "It's a funny thing," Augereau said. "About the Revolution, that is. You see that one there, with his feathers a mile high and those boots cost plenty, I can tell you. Well, that's the spirit of the Revolution, supposed to be. There's the old gap coming back, as in the old days. The men in rags and straw wrapped round their toes, and there you have gold and silver and perfume stinking to heaven."

"It would be crying stinking fish to go to Genoa looking otherwise," Massena said. "He went to raise this loan, you see. For the army."

"He didn't get it," La Harpe said.

"He got boots."

"And that fucking chestnut stuff."

"Look at it another way," Augereau said. "You and me, we got out of the ranks by election. The democratic way. Right, lads, vote for old Sergeant-major Massena and make him a colonel. Right?"

"I don't quite see what you—"

"There's a limit to democracy. *We're* not running this campaign. It's Wet Dream doing that. Who elected him? Fat womanizing Barras in Paris. Influence again. Intrigue, womanizing. It's no accident, I tell you—his chestnut mare in one hand and his roll of maps in the other. He got his kissing mixed up the other day. Smacked his big fat Corse smackers on a map of the Po Valley."

"He did all right at Toulon," Massena said. "That new man Murat will tell you all about the Tuileries business. Saved the Directory, not that it's worth saving, guzzling bastards. Cannon, he got this lot of cannon in. It was Murat brought them, on the double. You'd have had worse than the Directory. King's men howling round the Tuileries. He saw them off, bang bang bang."

"King's men howling in the Alps. Austrian bastards."

"A lot of them. He'll have his work cut out."

"Well, we'll see. In the old days we weren't encouraged to ask questions. But now I'd like to know what all this is about. Wet Dream says we're going to take them fraternity and equality —a right fucking recommendation we are, all rags and tatters. You can see how that Saliceti looks at it—gold and silver and loot for those Paris bastards. What's it all about? If a man believes in the Revolution is he just a fucking idiot?"

"First things first," La Harpe said. "The Austrians will have things back as they were if we don't shoot the balls off them. In Turin where the king goes to sleep all the time—"

"Old Dormouse."

"He woke up just enough to bring back racks and thumbscrews for the unbeliever. Fat priests gobbling fat pork and giggling when they have some poor bitch who ate meat on a Friday lying there with her tits ready to be cut off in nomine domine. Tossing themselves off under their whatyoucalls."

"Surplices."

"They'll be back," Augereau said, "if we don't watch it. Wet Dream was quick off the mark there. Those two, forgotten their names, who shouted God save the king on parade. Court-martial on the double. Bang bang bang, as you said."

"He's got no cannon here but he's got some things," Massena said. "He's got these big eyes and they're good on terrain. I should know. We'll see how it goes and judge later."

"He looks bigger with his hat on," Augereau said. "He doesn't sit a horse too well. You know, I don't really like to say this—"

"Look at that troop there," Kilmaine said. "There's not one poor nag that's not sagging in the middle."

"What?"

"I can't understand it, really. I lay in bed last night trying to, you know, work it out."

"What?"

"There are times when that little bugger scares the shit out of me."

"Ah. Let's see if he can—" Massena rubbed his beak, grinning sadly. He looked north towards, say, Cairo.

BUONAPARTE turned himself into Bonaparte. When they took Milan he could perhaps juggle with that u, conquering French or fraternal Italian as the occasion dictated. As he dictated the occasion. He finished dictating his letter to the Directory and said to Berthier:

"The days of the minuet are over. These are the days of the waltz. Not, mind you, that I necessarily approve of this frank embracing on the ballroom floor. Still, the speed is too great for lasciviousness." As Berthier had expected, he took the portrait from his inside pocket and gave it a quiet smiling smack, as to sanctify, by particular application, the beatings of lust. "Speed." Having restored the portrait to its nest he kept his hand on it. "The application to the art of warfare should be obvious. Let's have more red pins."

Berthier handed him the pins one at a time and watched him pierce the enemy positions. The positions seemed, like pricked thumbs, to start to well blood. Better him than me, Berthier thought. Back in Paris they both want and don't want victorious generals. If they're dangerous in the field they're dangerous back home. And it's a youngster's game these days. The old, such as have been kindly allowed to live, can't be trusted. Doubtful loyalty. Old heads trundled off in market-carts like cabbages. As for me, born into what they used to call the officer class, forty-three and looking it, loyalty not really in question. Fought in a revolutionary war before their Bastille fell, a citation at Philipsburg. Let the bloodletting civilians, if their blood hasn't been let, stuff that into their revolutionary pipes. But keep me out of the victorious general's role. Better off as I am. Bonaparte said:

"As we expected, no reply from the Genoese."

"They'll have told Bbbeaulieu, be sure of that."

"Now look here." He fisted the map. "If Italy's a leg, then we're midway between the navel of Nice and the genitals of Genoa. Right? Put it to the troops that way, humanize your geography. Beaulieu, dodderer that he is, will think we intend the march through Genoa. He'll bring his lot down from Alessandria, which is the sort of inner recesses of the genitals, Italy being a woman. Right?"

He's soaked in it, they should have given him a longer honeymoon.

"Schérer tttook that ffforce to Vvvoltri before you before you—"

"We'll give Beaulieu something substantial to play with at Voltri. Play on, rather. La Harpe, ha ha."

"Not a ddd—"

"Not a division, no. But enough to give Beaulieu confidence. He'll move too far south from his Piedmontese, we can crack his right wing up in the hills there. There—Carcare. The top of the pubic hairs."

Has the whole thing worked out.

"Close that gap. Massena's division there, Augereau's there. Very foul-mouthed, Augereau, by the way. Risen from the ranks, it shows."

"His dddiscipline's all right."

"Sold watches in Constantinople, didn't he? Must ask him about Constantinople, have to look ahead. Used to give dancing lessons. Let's see if he can use a watch as well as sell one. I want all divisional commanders to put the hour on their messages as well as the date. Speed. Timing. No more minuets. Augereau knows all about the waltz. We'll waltz them back to Vienna. But first knock Piedmont off the dance-floor. They'll welcome a little liberation."

"Ccc—"

"*The French Army has come to break your chains.* I must work something out. In Italian as well."

CITIZENS Carné, Thiriet, Blondy, Tireux, Hubert, Fossard, Teisseire, Carrère (Jacques), Carrère (Alexandre), Trauner, Barsacq, Gabutti, Mayo, Bonin, Borderie, Verne, Chaillot, Barrault, Brasseur, Dupont, Salou, sixteen thousand others, went forward in their washed-out blue rags and old revolutionary caps or rotting shakos, but boots boots, mark that, boots most of them, to engage. Easier, lads, if you remember what it's all about. Those Austrian bastards can't forgive us because we're free and they're in chains and we claimed the right of free men to whiz the head off that bitch of a queen we had that was an Austrian herself, and now they want to bring stinking kings and unholy bishops back and more, wanting their revenge as you can understand. Who we're attacking is Argenteau, Austrian in spite of his name or says he is, there must be some French traitor's blood there somewhere, who's pounding away at our thousand men specially set up for him in the fort over there and we'll get him in the flank and rear while General La Harpe's lot goes for him in the front. Any questions? Yes, when do we get some fucking leave, how about our back pay, I've got this pain in the balls citizen sergeant.

Drizzle fell coldly on Montenotte, then thickened to proper rain.

Bonaparte watched from a thousand feet up. It is in some way, my own heart's darling, an emblem of love, this engaging of armies. My ADC Marmont says it is to do with atomies of electricity crackling between the male and female poles, or some such thing, but I feel it is the quality of the beating of the heart, which is the same for both love and war. The priests in Ajaccio used to say that the Song of Solomon in the Bible was a metaphor of the marriage of Christ and his church, but now we know better: it is plain or not so plain love between a king and his chosen handmaiden, and I am struck by the phrase which makes this love terrible as an army with banners. I take out your image and rain weeps on the crystal. I kiss the rain away and look down to see the interlocking of the blue and white ants. Three blue to two white, hand to hand, mostly bayonet-fighting, we have no problem. Your slim white back, I must imagine, is turned against the musket-puffs and the thin noises that rise from below. I lock you again in the warmth of my breast, out of the rain and slaughter. This is our first victory and I must go on to others. I see Austrian banners in French hands and whole blocks of white now as still as snow-patches. Prisoners are always a nuisance.

"WHAT does he say?"

"I can't read his writing." And she threw the letter like a bone to the pug Fortuné, who sniffed at it and then began to chew it.

"But it's important to know when he'll be back. My angel. Mmmmmm." Lieutenant Hippolyte Charles, First Regiment of Hussars, at present in undress, munched at her right, or left, nipple.

"Paul Barras is excited. About victories. Can you read those names there?"

He tussled with the dog a moment. The dog let go Millesimo, Ceva and Dego, though with an ill grace. "It's a lot of marching," he said. "All those foothills. That's why it's called Piedmont."

"I never thought of that."

"And why should you, you little bundle of deliciousness? Mmmmmm." He munched lower. "Does he ever do that to you?"

"He tried. He's always in such a hurry about everything. Oh, sweetheart, what are we going to do?"

"Now? I'll show you. Get that damned dog off the bed. I'll have no toes left."

"Stays here, don't oo, precious? Mummy's little messenger when horrid men kept mummy in prison and were going to cut mummy's head off."

"Don't look too far ahead is what I say. He's a long way to go. There's Milan and Vienna and Venice. Lots of time. It would be nice to be in Venice."

"He's always so quick about everything. Do that again. Keep on doing it. Oh, sweetheart, I'm so unhappy. Oh, that's lovely."

"You're too moderate," Saliceti said. Bonaparte, half-dressed and unshaven in the cool spring dawn of Cherasco, looked with no liking on the Government Commissioner of the Army of the Alps. All that red white and blue, including red white and blue plumage a mile high. And yet a sort of magpie really, ready to peck at anything bright and stow it.

"Look," Bonaparte said, "Citizen Commissioner, or whatever you like to be called. I know precisely what's in your mind. Loot loot loot."

"They need money in Paris. This is partly—not wholly, I never said that—but partly what this war is about. To finance the new order. Look at this damned palazzo, for a start. Whose is it?"

"Count Salmatori's. You want to finance the new order out of that bit of porcelain there and those damask curtains? That silver Neptune would fetch a few hundred francs. You, citizen, would like a little loot for the palazzo Saliceti that is to be, and I'm not going to have any looting. We're here to make friends and respect property. I know what the Directors want to do with Italy—ransack it and then exchange it for the Rhine frontier. Have you ever considered that it might be a sort of duty to bring the Revolution here? Or is that too naïve a notion?"

II

Saliceti felt the coffee pot and found it cold. "Send for some more, will you? Victor Amadeus is the enemy still. He's priest-ridden, tyrannical, bigoted. He's also father-in-law of the Count of Provence. The man they call Louis the Eighteenth. He's got to be thwacked and punched and throttled, which means he has to vomit up gold and silver till it hurts."

"Oh, that will happen. But it will all happen officially and legitimately, with papers signed and countersigned and damned great seals on them. But if I catch you, sir, citizen, encouraging the acquisition of loot, then I come down with the chopper."

"Do you realize that I represent the Government in Paris? Do you realize that you're a mere salaried employee whose task is to win battles for your masters? Do you realize that the chopper can come down for you on the squeak of a pen?"

"Oh, Christophe, if I may still call you that—We used to be friends before you got this liking for feathers—Oh, don't you see that times are changing? Those old Representatives to the Armies—all of two years old—where have they gone to? They didn't work. You, and the rest of the new Commissioners, represent a step down. A good revolutionary general doesn't need orders, he only needs supplies. Nobody ever had a monopoly of the Revolution, though some of them thought they did. Let me put it simply and say that I am in charge here. No looting. And, if I were you, I'd dress more like a revolutionary. All those feathers, God help us."

"We'll see who's in charge. We'll see."

CITIZENS Carné, Thiriet, Blondy, Tireux and the rest, not forgetting the flame-headed giant Dupas, the wine and meat of Mondovi working in their bodies, listened to him as he performed his big scene from his white horse, riding up and down the ranks, the great tail swishing (more flies here, more dung, fertile plain, thank Christ we're finished with those fucking mountains). ". . . And we outflanked them, we're over the Po, and we're only a few miles south of Milan . . . And they're across that river there, the Adda, and it breaks my heart that you can't do it . . . Because you can't, you've got cunts between those jelly-shivering legs of yours, there's not one of you here willing to follow your commanders over that bit of a bridge there . . . Frightened of victory, that's what it is, scared of the responsibility of showing these cringing Italian bastards that you're better than they are because you'd got the guts to throw off your chains . . . Well, a time for courage comes once, and it's been and gone for you . . . There's a gate there, you see, and all I have to do is give the order to open it and send brave citizen soldiers shouting and screaming to get at the Austrians as they go over, but you're not the ones to do it, oh no . . ."

A good act, Dupas thought, it works up the growls in them. Come on, growl, you bastards, I'm tired of just standing here.

They roared, not growled. The drums rattled and the flutes screamed *O come ye children of the motherland the sun of glory fills the sky* and they started to clatter over, some of them going splash over the sides in the press, there being no parapets, and the Austrian guns flaming at them, bloody murder. A few yards from the end some jumped into the Adda and tried to wade ashore, and then the cavalry came at them, sabers and great whinnying horsemouths, and there was not one Frenchman on the further bank, but they still poured across, Massena yelling and Berthier forgetting his stammer and no sight of our cavalry, why the hell couldn't he wait till he knew our cavalry was across?

And then, by Christ, there they were, Kilmaine and his bony nags and the screaming men on them, right onto the Austrian flank, stopping the guns, until you could hear the thumping and trundling of the feet of the Savoy infantry coming over the bridge over the Adda.

God almighty it was a near thing, Bonaparte was thinking, God almighty it wasn't planning this time, it was taking a chance, it was impossible gambling that came off, and it tastes like brandy, it feels like that delirious flying moment when you spend into her thighs, now that I know I am a living spirit and a very special one as well as a military library and a craftsman and a machine as modern as a semaphore telegraph or a hydrogen balloon. And suppose the cavalry had not been able to ford that river? They almost did not, almost, *almost.* It is in the region of Almost that the blood sings. We won, my love. Sixteen guns and nearly two thousand prisoners. Prisoners, my love, are such a nuisance. War feeds on war; what do prisoners feed on?

And he took his love's miniature from his inner pocket to kiss, against a background of bivouac fires, the fried-bacon reek of cannon-smoke fading. Raising it to his lips he nearly staggered. Marmont was concerned.

"Look, Marmont—the glass is broken."

"Well, then," smiling, "our first task in Milan must be to—"

"No no no. It means she is very sick or very unfaithful. Oh God God God."

"Don't believe it. We shall be in Milan in a day or so, and she will not be many days after. Murat should be in Paris by now. He will bring her, you will see."

"You will be receiving a letter," Saliceti said. "Meanwhile I am empowered to tell you of the Directory's intentions."

Bells bells bells, but now it was merely angelic noontime in Milan.

"The Directory would have made no difficulty about preparing a passport for her," Bonaparte said. "As for a letter, Murat has written—she is a bad letter-writer, God bless the girl. It seems I am to be a father. You must put off that stern look and have some wine. This absconding archduke kept a good cellar. There's a fine bin of—"

"I refer to different business altogether."

"—Chambertin. Business?"

"It is the Directory's intention to split the command. General Kellermann of the Army of the Moselle—"

Bonaparte sat down on a magnificent uncomfortable chair. He noted a quick irrelevance: mouse-dirt under the escritoire.

"—to continue the northern campaign against the Austrians. You to fight Austria's southern allies."

"Kellermann is sixty-odd. He lives on his reputation at Valmy. I am, in effect, demoted." He picked up the keys of Milan, very heavy, very solid. "Set in his ways, thinks he's God. I'm not having it. I'll resign first. Where's their sense, let alone their gratitude? No, forget the gratitude. Nobody has a monopoly of the Revolution. Said that before, didn't I? All I say now is that joint command ruins everything. You need the single voice. The fools. One bad general is better than two good ones. Tell them that from me. I'll tell them myself, I'll be writing a letter."

"You mean that about resignation?"

"That's my duty to the army, not that anybody in Paris cares much about duty. Or should I say it's all one-way duty with them. I told the army all about the Directory's confidence in them through me. They're simple men, they believe in these things, they need them. Now they're going to have this stuck-up swine with the Austrian name barking at them."

"Alsatian. I see. You're just *threatening* resignation."

"Dirty politicians. You need the single voice."

"That sounds like a threat too."

THEY were sitting in an alcove, taking a sorbet. The swish of the ball-gowns and the clink of the medals came through, along with the sweet and lively violins.

"There was another thing I heard. *General Bonaparte has got off the Po and is now busily wiping up.*"

She laughed, taking care to hide her teeth. Bad teeth or not, he was thinking, she has this very rare thing, can't quite think of the word. Grace? That sounds religious. Hair covered with roses for her real name, the high-waisted silk sheath made to cling with Cologne water to her breasts, the most delicate instep, the delicious pose of languor. Bonaparte sent letters full of extravagant desires ("feed off your throat, bite off your nipples and watch new ones grow like rosebuds, wear out your little cunt with kisses"), but he, Lieutenant Hippolyte Charles, had the pleasure of real fulfillments, neither poetically extravagant nor Corsican coarse. Call it vicarious, a subaltern's duty to a general. That she would not find funny, she talked too much of love. And money. She needed money for flowers and gowns and shoes. There were so many victory balls these days. He himself was not doing too well for money.

"How much longer," he said, "do you think you can put it off?"

"You live one more day, just like in the Carmes prison. Besides, I'm ill, or pregnant—I'm not sure which."

"Not well enough to make the journey. But Junot and Murat are still waiting. And still writing, presumably. There are also the newspapers, which undoubtedly *lui* sees. Interesting that our poor sick Lady of Victories should be the belle of the Luxembourg ball."

She looked at him puzzled. "Do you *want* me to go?"

"The poets write of the world well lost for love. True love, as true lovers know, is built on caution. Besides, my own General Leclerc will do anything for Madame Victoire. We could both go. There are some pleasant things to be picked up in Italy these days, so I hear. The fruits of conquest. And Venice is very lovely."

"Oh, you're mad."

"Not really. Too many ears and eyes and noses in Paris. Better to have one pair of eyes, his. All for you and none else."

"Why do you say Venice? Venice is a long way from Milan."

"Not for *lui*. You're always saying how quick he is. One of his big faults, you always say."

DAPPLED Tuileries summer sun, mad with motes, danced on the map and on Barras's ringed finger. "If we gave in, events have proved that we were right to do so. See what he's done with his unified command. Look. The tricolor all over Lombardy. Florence. Leghorn—one in the snout for the English. Ah, I forgot." He stuck a toy flag on a Mediterranean island.

"Where's that?" peered Moulins.

"Corsica. Another one in the snout. That was the Leghorn Corsicans. Back in the fold, anyway. Apart from the actual occupations, there are the various invasion threats. Tuscany, Naples, the Pope. Good hard cash there. He's already paying his men in silver."

"Is that wise?"

"Half silver, the rest paper."

"And all these damned works of art, as they're called," Reubell said. "I'd rather see more money."

"Paris," Barras said primly, "is the great new center of culture. Revolutionary culture. Revolutions aren't just decapitations and screaming women with no drawers on. Beauty and light—aspects of our republican policy."

"Cramming the museums with saints and the rest of the superstitious garbage," the hunchback Larevellière snarled. "Beauty, indeed. We have a solemn mission, and that is to keep the state Godless. If I had the Pope here now, I'd—"

"Yes yes, your well-known zeal continues to be well-known."

"I admit the cleverness," Moulins said, "but what worries me is the high-handedness. Look what he said about Saliceti."

"He has a strong objection to what he terms looting," Barras said. "He draws a perhaps over-nice distinction between the wholesale and retail varieties of er spoliation. Ethically, that is. Saliceti has, apparently, been engaging in simony."

"A man's tastes are his own," Reubell said.

"Let's have that plain," Larevellière said. "I'm a plain man."

"Saliceti has been looting churches, selling chalices and ciboria and other godless trappings of godliness. Sometimes ciboria with the consecrated wafers in them."

"And right too," snarling. "Show those priest-ridden cretins what superstitious wickedness it all is."

"You," Barras said, "are a responsible man and a Director. Do think carefully. Consecrated hosts cannot be desecrated overnight. The priest-ridden cretins are quite capable of turning on their er liberators. There is such a thing as discretion, diplomacy."

"I think I have a right to object to that. I always think carefully. I would ask you to withdraw—"

"A little more discretion and diplomacy towards the Directory would be in order," Moulins said.

"He lives and dies," Barras said, "by the Constitution. That is, in a sense, touching. But there is a word hovering on my tongue, and undoubtedly on yours. Ambition. A word made rather fiery by the days of the Terror."

"What you mean is," Reubell said, "that we don't want him back in Paris."

"Oh, he can be controlled, I think," Barras said. "But he will not be in Paris for a long time yet. He talked of compassionate leave, but his wife—his bride, I should say—is already on her way to Milan. A wife can be a great solvent of ambition. In the honeymoon phase, that is. Let him carry on with his wholesale spoliation."

"And the politics?"

"Let him preach fraternity and equality and so on. Sister republics? I'm not quite sure about sister republics."

Some of them knew what he meant, though not Larevellière.

"Time to worry about that later," Barras said.

SHE turned herself into a thing. He was not heavy though he was very active. The guns and fireworks of Turin were now a steady headache, and they flashed through the pitch dark. And the dinner, with Joseph Bonaparte there. The whole family soon, Corsican claws. Oh, the cold greasiness of that main meat dish. The Palazzo Serbelloni, rose and crystal candy granite, nothing too good for her.

He floods in me like a river, she thought. Like urine.

"Oh my God oh my. Angel oh my own heart's. Blood. How I've been able to. Sustain this. Long time of waiting only God.

And the angels know. And even now, my celestial vision, it is. As it was at the beginning. A snatch of heaven in your arms and then. Back to it."

"To what?"

"The war, Würmser, the Austrians. But we won't think of the Austrians today or tomorrow, my seraph. We won't move out of this bedroom."

"Do we have to have it so dark? I like the moon and the sun to follow. This is like being blind."

"And blind is what I am except for this light in the center of my soul. My fingers must learn your beauty by night. Blasted. Damn that. I won't have that dog in here, I'm not going to share a bed with a. Damn. Right on the shin."

"My precious. Mmmmm. Mother's brave little pug. Tomorrow," she said with relief, "is Bastille Day. A gala performance at La Scala and a ball after."

"Oh." And then: "There've been a lot of balls in Paris. And you at every one. That was courageous. Take that dog's nose away."

"He can't see in the dark, can you, angel? Why courageous? Oh, I see what you mean. It was duty, really. They couldn't have you so they wanted me."

"Ah. All that dancing—could it have possibly—"

"It was a false one. It sometimes happens. But it made me very tired. Oh, Eugène and Hortense send their love."

"We must have children of our own. *We will.*"

And, straight to the target again, as ever, pushing the snarling bundle away, the reserves pouring in fast and joyful, he was back on to his angel and heart's blood. She tried to think of Charles, but it was difficult. The one did not fit easily into the other's body, not even in the dark.

And then: "Where will you be going, and for how long?"

"Mantua. We're besieging the Austrians there. If it looks like being a long business, then, core of my innermost heart of light, I shall send for you."

"Oh no."

"Is you scared then of the nasty blood and noisywoise, sweetheart?" For a moment she thought he was talking to Fortuné. "But you was so brave in Paris. Besides," he said, lopping the baby-talk clean off, "you'll be a long way from the noise of the guns. They'll be just summer thunder, the cannon. The muskets will go ping ping." One ping for each nipple.

"Ow. Oh no."

IN her dream her husband was trying to take her naked on the terrace, in the presence of the servants who were clearing the table: she distinctly saw a spot of coffee fall from the lifted pot on to the marble pavimento. Oh no, oh no. But he kept laughing that this was the town of Romeo and Juliet. Then they both saw white specks like ash drifting slowly down the mountains. "Good God, they got through," he said. Then the Austrians were climbing by vine-ropes on to the terrace itself, and she tried in vain to cover her nakedness.

Her maid Louise woke her, sleeping in her clothes. "Colonel Junot, madame. And a lot of soldiers." There were whinnyings and clompings outside on the cobbles. This was Peschi something. Peschiera. She could hear General Guillaume talking in the next room: responsibility patrol boats on the lake advised her strongly strongly insisted responsibility.

There was bad coffee and yesterday's bread. "We set up," said Junot, "a command post at Castelnuovo."

"He told me to wait for him here. Where's Castel—?"

"Inland. On the road to Verona. You must have passed it last night."

"This sounds to me as if the Austrians are everywhere."

"A brief defensive interlude call it." Junot smiled, very tired, with his unshaven bristles catching the laky light. "Our first, or very nearly."

Her pout was a woman's unreasonable rebuke for *lui*: you

said I'd like this play and I hate it; you said it would be fine and it's rained all day.

It was Louise who pointed at the shining boat on the beautiful lake as big as a sea, so lovely in the Italian summer morning. Then smoke puffed with great cracks and whines, the coach swerved and sidled and tilted and stopped, with Junot shouting, Louise going oh oh oh, and the noise of thuds and mad hooves, then the sight of two horses threshing and foaming as they tried to die between the shafts. A dragoon was dead with one foot in the saddle, being dragged by his frantic horse, a cheek ripped open and the back of his head scraped raw along the road. Junot had them out of the coach and, using it as a shield from the firing, made them crawl into a shallow dry ditch, then he whipped the lead offside horse with his sword and had all four trundling the empty coach off with the patrol boat guns still cracking away at it.

Louise wept in the ditch. "Quiet, girl, quiet, this is an adventure, this is something to tell them back in Paris, this is war."

"Waaaaaaaar." That started Fortuné barking.

She had not seen Lieutenant Charles at Verona, there had been some talk of his doing well in battle, he would not now be concerned about the quality of cloth and the sit of a cravat, but she shut him out of her needs, lying there as the sun mounted, hearing the flies around the corpses: she did not want now to be in a Paris drawing room with Charles witty and saying my dear what a delightful foulard. She wanted the protection of her General. Later, of course, she knew, it would be different. One does not move straight from a ditch to a drawing room.

"There's a farmer's cart there," Junot said later.

They jolted in flea-leaping straw past more war: buzzing mounds of horse and man flesh, the acrid smoke a solvent of the foul sweetness. She was half-asleep when rough hands pulled her out of the cart. Having missed death in war it seemed that she was now to meet it in love. His love, all howls and tears, tears she joined in, was confused with desire to strike at once at the renegade French swine Field Marshal von Würmser, leader of the attacking Austrians. *He shall pay dearly for your tears.* "Waaaaaaaar," howled Louise, joining them. He got her and her dog to bed in a rough room of his headquarters, and she could hear the rustle and thumping of maps as she fell into sleep dug deep as a pit, gun-crumps, shadows in lantern-light, his words: *local disorganization disorganization of the entire front.* Bbbest make the atttack southeast of Bbbrescia?

Mark how the Alexander of our age
Bids soldier's skill fulfill a lover's rage.
His numbers far inferior are found:
Too many ring resistant Mantua round,
Too many languish in the fevered swamp,
Too many through the restive boroughs tramp
With freedom's flag unvocal to convince
Men long enslaved to prelate and to prince.
Though Würmser's roll take twice the time to call,
Yet is he tardy in unrolling all.
Our general is impetuous to fling
His total force upon a single wing,
Then on the other, then he splits the spine
In center of th' attenuated line.
At Castiglione see the guns advance
And tricolor of liberating France.
The double-eagled banner dips and droops,
And Würmser whines, then growls, and then regroups.
But at Bassano, Rovereto, Trent,
His front is fractured and his rear is rent.
He spies th' encircling trap that soon awaits
And refuge seeks in Mantua's battered gates.
Ah, Mantuan Virgil, could but time re-roll
And from th' Elysian meadows pluck thy soul,
A greater than Augustus would inspire
A mightier chord upon the trembling lyre,
And verbal flames might match that swift
reverberant fire.

. . .

"But it was terrible," she said, in his arms in bed in Brescia. "Pushed along like that. Parma, Florence, and that other place. I told him that a battlefield was no place for a woman. I'd told him before."

"My precious." He did not smell so fresh as he had in Paris. Nor perhaps, she thought, did she. They both had gunsmoke in their skin. And he was quicker, more urgent, as though infected by *lui.* He was no longer the boudoir soldier; he had been mentioned in dispatches.

"He's mad," she said. "He doesn't love me—he *worships* me. I tell you, it's not civilized. Oh God, if only we were back in Paris."

"And I worship you too. More than he does, angel."

"Don't say that, for God's sake. I don't want to be worshipped. I want everything to be calm and pleasant and *sane.*"

"Love isn't sane. Love's a madness. Pagan, elemental, dark. Feel that." It felt like a weapon, something that would go off.

"Oh Hippolyte, he says these things as though he means them."

"I mean them too, my treasure."

"No no, as though he means them as he means, you know, the other things. Like taking over all Italy and then marching to Vienna and then invading the English. He writes a battle order about turning flanks and so on and then he writes about stripping the skin off me and possessing me wholly and then he goes back to his dispatches about enveloping the left wing or whatever it is. I'm frightened."

"You'll always have me, precious angel. Always have me to turn to. I don't frighten you, do I?"

"His brother knows, I'm sure. Joseph. He has another brother here now on his staff. He'll have the whole family here soon, if he wins all his battles. And Joseph will talk to his mother and his mother will talk to him and. Corsican jealousy. He'll have you court-martialed and shot. Me too perhaps. He's mad enough."

"No, precious treasure. Not yet. Mmmmmm."

"Oh, don't joke. I'm serious."

"Mmmmmm."

"Ious." The word *diversify* came, for some reason, into her head. Skirmishes, feints, confusing the enemy. Then everything became confused, transfused, fused.

At last, adorable, adorable, behold me reborn. Death no longer in my eyes, glory and victory in my heart. We defeated the enemy at Arcola, six thousand killed, five hundred prisoners. Mantua will fall to us in less than a week. Then then then I shall be back in your arms.

AND on her lap, a flag in his hand, her arms holding him still, fidgety because Mantua had not yet fallen. Young Antoine Gros, favorite pupil of David, was painting him in the after-breakfast light, hero of the Arcola bridge. Bonaparte was saying:

"An old woman in Ajaccio said it. She said that the earth would be my friend and the water my enemy. It was, I confess, a very unpleasant experience—all that swampy mud right up to my shoulders. And my poor shot horse screaming and writhing. No, I must not descend to pity for animals. A horse is an instrument, no more."

"Do keep still," she said.

"I've finished the passage," Gros said. "It will be you, madame," smiling, "who needs the rest."

"He's not heavy." And he wasn't, all skin and bone, pared down with fever. Bonaparte jumped up and walked round to the canvas.

"Hm. Who am I to say whether it is a good likeness? It is more like some character out of myth. Perhaps the face of Ossian?" He gave Gros an acutely painful pinch of affection on the lobe. "You have some good young men about you," he said to her. "Collect more, we need good young men. Like that young Charles of yours, a very promising soldier."

She tried not to show the change in her breathing.

"How would you," he said to Gros, "like to take over the art commission? I know what I like, but I'm not well able to judge of masterpieces. Italy's grateful tribute to her liberators. How would you like that?"

"I would be greatly—"

"Water," he said. "These Italians are water. Water must be controlled, made to work mills, be tamed into canals, have bridges thrown over it. I'm not afraid of water."

They did not quite understand.

THE first full moon of the new year, as the dead régime would see it. But it was really Nivôse, still in the Year Four. To his right lay that fearful river, now tamed. He shivered again; the warm greatcoat seemed too big for him. And that old woman had said that he must also beware of the moon. Why? The moon pulsed out now like a lake in the sun. He was with Joubert on the plateau of Rivoli. He saw camp fires all about, far below: five camps, each signifying an enemy column. To the north, beyond his vision, on the slopes of Monte Baldo, General Alvintzi planned, he knew, a six-column advance, but, in that terrain, so complex a strategy would be difficult. The columns of Liptay, Koblos and Ocksay would find it impossible to deploy cannon. To the west and east of the plateau the columns of Lusignan and Wukassovitch waited to fall on the French rear. But it would be a hard passage to besieged Mantua, that they knew. Then there was General Quasdanovitch, ready to roar up the gorge of Osteria to the east. It was all too much, he hoped, for Alvintzi to coordinate. He said:

"That village, San Marco, is one of our keys. Take it, and you split their advance. A great deal depends on our reinforcements."

"When?"

"I expect Massena before dawn. He will precede his division. You, Joubert, are to hold the eastern side of the plateau with one brigade. That should secure the gorge and Ocksay's column. For a time, that is. Your two other brigades must hold off Koblos and Liptay in the northern sector." He seemed to feel Mantua raying out its dangerous heat behind him.

When Massena arrived, he ordered him to hold the valley of the Tasso (ah, noble name) on the left flank, using a single brigade, and to mass the rest in readiness around the plateau. The moon moved to setting. At dawn they began.

In blissful nescience of the[1] *drift of man,*
Fulfilling only its[2] *Creator's plan,*[11]
The wide[3] *plateau*[9] *extends its windy plain,*
A rarity in that engorg'd terrain,[4]
Where eagles wheel[8] *about the mountain-wall,*[6]
Soar to the height then like a plummet fall.[7]
{*Th' Italia of the poet's lay is far:*
{*A cold land sleeps*[5] *beneath a colder star,*
{*Indifferent to the*[10] *transient flags of war.*

1. Joubert advances with ten thousand men, eighteen cannon (six from Massena) to engage Austrian twelve thousand.
2. Koblos's column checks.
3. Liptay's proceeds toward flank of Joubert's most westerly brigade. Eighty-fifth half-brigade in disgrace: collapses, flees. Massena's reserve moves in.
4. Austrians mount batteries on eastern bank of Adige, begin to dominate Osteria gorge.
5. Lusignan's column appears on southern ridge of plateau. French line of retreat and reinforcement cut off. Eighteenth half-brigade, newly arrived from Lake Garda, ordered to attack column.
6. Austrians have advantage in gorge. Joubert brigade exhausted. Koblos and Liptay adjudged temporarily harmless. Joubert's westerly brigades moved east. Light artillery devastates

close-set Austrian column. One chance shot hits two Austrian ammunition wagons. Carnage, disorder.

7. Five hundred infantry and cavalry take advantage of Austrian panic and drive the enemy from the gorge. Eastern sector now cleared.

8. 9. All forces shifted northward to meet Koblos and Liptay, now revived and regrouped. Main Austrian army split. Flanks harried.

10. Rey's reinforcement arrives, pincering with Massena's brigade on Lusignan. Three thousand prisoners.

11. (Bonaparte and Massena move south to engage Provera.) Rivoli now in Joubert's hands. Three Austrian columns flee for La Corona. Murat and Vial seize gorges. Joubert to Bonaparte: "Followed your plan. Success beyond all hopes. Three guns, four thousand to five thousand prisoners. Alvintzi himself precipitated down rocks and fleeing up Adige valley." Last great Austrian offensive over.

Citizens Thiriet, Carné, Blondy, Fossard, Teisseire, Hubert, Tireux, Carrère (Jacques), Carrère (Alexandre), Trauner, Barsacq, Gabutti, Mayo, Bonin, Borderie, Verne, Chaillot, Barrault, Brasseur, Dupont, Salou and all the thousands and thousands of others wondered how the hell they had done it. Marched all night, then fought all day at Rivoli, marched all next night, all next day, then smashed Provera at La Favorita. Mantua, a snarling great fortress ringed with fever lagoons, was quick to fall. It was full of skeletons, some of them still alive, and there was a powerful stink of decaying horsehides.

"The view of the Directory," Bonaparte said, "is that you are a Frenchman who has taken up arms against his own people." He kept hitting his left palm hard with his riding crop.

"I see," Würmser saw. "It's not enough merely to fight for the monarchical cause against the republican. I take it that they want me for the guillotine."

"No. Shot. By my immediate orders."

"They ordered you, did they? Do they *order* you?"

"I won't do it, of course." The sugary fecal reek of the dead city pierced even here, the palazzo set about with deformed trees, stripped of bark and leaves for hopeless ragouts. "You naturally escaped from me. I consider that you're a good brave commander."

"But not as good and brave as a republican one, yes? So. The long cold road to Vienna."

"Not so long." He saw the map very clearly in his mind. How many available for guarding the Tyrol? It was the Austrians on the Rhine that were the trouble. Snow still at this season, and he dared not wait. Spilimbergo, San Vito, Laybach, Klagenfurt, Marburg, Gratz. As for the Papal States, they were as good as subdued. He smiled and said: "You would have been in very holy company. One of our Directors wants the Pope shot too. The Goddess of Reason told him in a vision."

"And what do *you* want?"

"I don't want the Bourbons back in France. I share that view with my army. I stand for the Constitution."

"Yes. What hypocritical nonsense: a Frenchman taking up arms against his own people, indeed. You and I appreciate the metaphysical aspects of this struggle. And it will be a long struggle, we both know that. How can you win? You can't garrison the whole world."

"Education. Spreading the truth. The republican clubs in Milan are already powerful and enlightened. The people have to be made to be free."

The eyes, Würmser was thinking, are remarkable. The eyes are a whole Haydn orchestra. "Your Directory, if I may say so, seems to contain some rather giddy men."

"I stand for the Constitution."

"You have to hand it to her," Massena said. "She shows the other women up. Look at old Mother Goodpart there, blazing. Can't keep her eyes off her tits."

"Not the only one." The victorious generals took fresh

flutes of champagne from the flunky with the silver tray. They kept together, awed by the aristocratic company and the creamy splendor of Mombello. Pauline Bonaparte, Pauline Leclerc as she had just become, was, as the Paris papers would say, radiant, but the Creole matron knew all about outshining. "It's the eyes," Joubert said.

"Whose?"

"The whole damned family of them. Sexuality. That little bitch there couldn't wait to have it from Leclerc. *Lui*— What does his mother call him?"

"It sounded like Nabuliune."

"He found them fucking behind a screen. But he didn't turn on old Charles Victor, oh no. He knew where the fault was, if you can call it a fault."

"So now it's benefit of clergy," La Harpe said. "Back where we were before. Incense and communion and the whole butcher's shop. Still, this is Italy." Summer Italy, gorgeous, sun and fireflies and fountains and sexuality. "Nabuliune is going to make a speech."

It was in Italian, and they could not understand it all. They caught certain key abstractions—victory, democracy, tyranny, republicanism—but they missed the jokes, which seemed to be unsoldierly, positively intellectual. He seemed to quote from an Italian poet, and then from a Latin one. Some of the old and distinguished smiled and nodded at each other. You had to hand it to him. Then he said how delighted he was to have *tutta la famiglia* there with him, including Joseph, Giuseppe, his elder brother, to whom he apparently apologized for taking over from him his elder brother's function, but he saw himself, if he might so put it, as *Giuseppe in Egitto*. Everybody applauded.

"What's that word?"

"Egypt."

A lot of the Italian dignitaries present seemed to know French very well, and one of them, very old, said something about the remarkable son of a remarkable mother, quoting Racine or somebody.

"You see what he means about family," Kilmaine said. "He wants to have everything in the family. He'll bring in more sisters and cousins and try to have us married to them. It won't make any difference if you're married already. Bills of civil divorcement. Family everywhere. Nothing's right for a Sicilian unless it's in the family. The *clan*, so to speak."

"He's a Corse."

"Where's the difference?" He looked benevolently at old Berthier, smarter these days, spluttering less, hardly biting his nails at all any more, as he spoke halting but worshipping Tuscan to the Visconti married woman, a beauty. *Lui* would soon have the poor devil married to that little Caroline there, only a child, or somebody.

Lui was somewhat flown with wine and water: this, after all, was his sister's wedding. "No," he was smiling, "that is one toast I will not propose. *Not* peace. Not on the terms of a restored monarchy. I know all about Pichegru's intrigues. Augereau should be in Paris by now, ready to save the republicans, more cannon round the Tuileries. I stand for the Constitution."

"Whose constitution?" Miot de Melito asked.

"Ah." He gave him a warm cold complicated look. "An excellent question."

Pauline, even though she was now a married lady, put out her tongue at her sister-in-law, bitchy little jealous madcap as she was. Chatterbox too, all about Giuseppina and her *young men.* Madame Letizia, a handsome hard-eyed ramrod, dowdiness a virtue, gave the deep décolletage and the willow body, Grecian high-waisted silk seemingly pasted to it, a fine look of hate. Neither chit nor child yet, where was his sense, seduced by Parisian wickedness, Joseph should have asserted his authority, inherited too much of his poor father's weakness. Then she smiled at some who bowed, a happy mother though unhappy among these Greek columns and pagan pictures, cherubim writhing on the ceiling. Little Caroline and Jerome were playing a hitting game with *her* son, Eugène. Children by her first, but none by *lui.* There had been time, there had been urgency. A curse from somewhere, God's curse? There *was* a God, and a punishing one, despite or because of the Paris wickedness. Time would show a lot, but not a child.

"The whole province of St. Mark," he was now saying. "Well, it's useful for bargains. The Austrians can have it, the Venetians know who the real masters are." He suddenly grabbed and hugged his wife with bedroom relish, despite all these eyes. Real masters are. "And my dove shall be fêted by the Doge, so you shall, my pigeon, and ride in a gondola." She saw herself stepping into one, Charles's warm hand sustaining her. Lights lights. Then *lui* became Alexander again. "It's one gate to the East. It's in the East where the scheming foxes of Albion will be hounded and torn. Those watery kings, those kings of water. India." He looked round the family, including his generals, all brothers-in-law really, with bright scheming eyes. Sarees and turbans and their fingers afire with spill of sapphires. "If only father were alive," he said. Then the dancing began.

In the name of Allah the all-powerful, all-merciful, all-knowing, know that it is by his holy will that we come to free the peoples of the Nile from their immemorial and most cruel bondage to the Turks and the Mamelukes, free men of Frankistan bringing freedom, respecting Islam and the tenets of the holy prophet, may his name be praised and the holy name of Allah most high exalted for ever more.

The disembarkation was a fucking shambles and we only took Alexandria as quick as we did to get a fucking drink somewhere, because we were near dead with the thirst. There he sat watching, on a mess of old ruins called Pompey's Pillar, slashing away at old bits of pot with that whip of his. The town was full of a lot of half-starved blacks, near-blacks you could call them, in filthy rags, raising their hands to the bloody burning heavens when they saw us come in, shouting Allah Allah and so on. Some old bints with veils on gave us fucking filthy water to drink, but filthy or not it was like elation and ecstasy and so on. There was hardly a solitary fucking thing worth having in the whole town, all half-starved goats and so on, and talk about the fucking heat and the smell. Anyway, what they called sheikhs came and gave him the keys, and the officers did all right with like knives and scimitars with jewels on, but then we had to move on to Damanhur and Rahmaniya and so on, near dropping with the fucking heat.

The trouble is, Carné said, all the fucking lies. First we were sailing to England, and then it was Malta we took, and now we're here, and Christ knows why. The fucking heat and the flies and scorpions and all this fucking sand. On on on, loaded with fucking equipment, only dry biscuits to eat and no water bottles, not that there'd be any water to put in them. Thiriet went mad, crying out ha ha ha I see you mother stop swirling about in the air with all that water pouring out of your tits, then she seemed to call out shoot yourself son, better that way, and by Jesus he did. Blondy and Tireux saw what they swore was the Nile just over the next sandhill, and Hubert said it was what they call a mirage, then he wanted to peel down his breeches to shit but we were told on on on on, got to get there before the Nile floods, wherever the fucking Nile is, so he shat all the time in his breeches like the rest of us. *The sun of glory fills the sky*, but it was a big baker's oven up there with the doors wide open. Fossard screamed out that he'd gone blind, and so did Teisseire a bit later on, and later on Jacques Carrère. These fucking great swarms of black flies had plenty to drink, which was the sweat on our necks and faces. In a way you could see that a man could laugh at the extremes of the misery of it, for misery could not easily go any further, three days of it, stumbling through all this white sand like hot snow, the dried shit in our breeches, and knowing we were marching on on on on only to get cut to pieces with fucking axes and scimitars at the end of it. Man is born free but is everywhere in chains, as that bastard said. Once or twice we came to villages, but they were all empty or full of dead that the Bedouins had left to the flies and the ants, and the wells had been filled in with stones. Soon it was Alexandre Carrère that went mad and shot himself and nobody stopped him. We were like silent ghosts going through that sand, and the only sound was the buzzing of these fucking great black flies. The sky was pure metal, pewter or brass or something, clanking down on your head with no noise, and the sun was like a great round arse shitting fire.

"WHAT I hear," Bonaparte said in his tent, whisking at the flies with his whip, "sounds very like mutiny. I gave General Mireur a chance which he dredged up enough honor to take, but there will be no more suicides on my staff. I will shoot General Dumas with my own hand."

"There's a lllimit—"

"I will set an example. At the same time let it be known to all ranks that their troubles are nearly over. Temporarily, of course. We shall soon be in Cairo. Murad and Ibrahim are frightened. Now you can tell Croisier to come in." He took a draught of Italian wine unmixed with water. Captain Croisier almost tottered in, young, scared, pale, sweating. Bonaparte said:

"Your military conduct shows you unfit to be an aide-de-camp. You are a trained soldier leading trained soldiers. It was inexcusable of you not to wipe out that band of Bedouins. They penetrated some of the outer tents. They killed, they stole, they got away."

"It was a very large band, sir. I had only a handful—"

"Don't interrupt. To think that an officer of the French Army, an officer moreover entrusted with so high and intimate an appointment—I am ashamed. A ragged troop of marauding Moors, flea-bitten, disease-ridden—"

"As I said, sir, we were outnumbered."

"Outnumbered? We are always outnumbered. Numbers are nothing, as I showed again and again in Italy. You're a stain, you're a blot, a cowardly travesty of a soldier of the Republic. Do you hear me?"

"I can hardly do otherwise, sir."

"Insolence." And he cracked Croisier on the body with his whip.

"That, sir, is surely inexcus—"

"Don't. You. Tell. Me. What." This time the blow was on the left cheek. In almost no time the flies were feeding. "I hope, sir, you will know how to make amends."

"Have no fear of that, general. If you want a sacrificial victim, you shall have it."

"I don't want a suicide. I don't want that sort of cowardice again. You'll have your chance. Now get out. *Out.*" And the whip swished.

Nerves, Berthier was thinking, nerves. Is it worth it, any of it? He had forgotten, in his own exhaustion, what precisely they were supposed to be doing here. Doubts crept: *his* youth, the mess of the disembarkation, the encumbrance of scientific civilians, the worst possible season of the Egyptian year. It was something to do with modernizing this country and something to do with India and Africa and British trade. And saving the Republic, in all this sand, miles from anywhere. Berthier said:

"On bbbehalf of the savants, Monsieur Monge wishes ttt—"

"Soft civilians. No time for them now, let them suffer like the troops. Conquer first, civilize after."

THEY could hardly believe it, the retreating arses of all that Mameluke or Turkish cavalry, heathen anyway, crying heathen words as they cantered off in gunsmoke and dust-clouds, dropping spears and jewels and good Birmingham pistols. And soon it was water water water, a world of blessed water, the muddy stinking welcoming mother Nile near Rahmaniya. The citizen troops threw themselves into it like crocodiles and soaked and swilled and gorged, champing the water like solid food, inhaling it like air. Trauner and others burst like blown frogs; others, luckier, vomited up gallons like public fountains. Then Barsacq yelled *watermelons*, and soon they were all gouging and bayoneting and tearing with sore teeth. They lay like babies, sucking succulent pulp. Gabutti got through eight in a single sitting, then the dysenteries started. Mayo and Bonin lay moaning while their entrails pumped out through their anuses. Borderie died wondering what those big pointed things were, staring through the mist, the Holy Trinity perhaps, come to get him.

Defiling their shadows, infidels, accursed of Allah, with fingernails that are foot-long daggers, with mouths agape like cauldrons full of teeth on the boil, with eyes all fire, shaitans possessed of Iblis, clanking into their wars all linked, like slaves, with iron chains. Murad Bey, the huge, the single-blowed ox-beheader, saw without too much surprise mild-looking pale men dressed in blue, holding guns, drawn up in squares six deep as though in some massed dance depictive of orchard walls. At the corners of the squares were heavy guns and gunners. There did not seem to be many horsemen. Murad said a prayer within, raised his scimitar to heaven and yelled a fierce and holy word. The word was taken up, many thousandfold, and in a kind of gloved thunder the Mamelukes threw themselves onto the infidel right and nearly broke it. But the squares healed themselves at once, and the cavalry of the faithful crashed in three avenging prongs along the fire-spitting avenues between the walls. A great gun uttered earthquake language at them from within a square, and, rearing and cursing the curses of the archangels of Islam onto the uncircumcised, they wheeled and swung toward their protective village of Embabeh. There they encountered certain of the blue-clad infidel horde on the flat roofs of the houses, coughing musket-fire at them. But then disaster sang along their lines from the rear as shell after shell crunched and the Mamelukes roared in panic and burden to the screams of their terrified mounts, to whose ears these noises were new. Their rear dissolving, their retreat cut off, most sought the only way, that of the river. They plunged in, horseless, seeking to swim across to join the inactive horde of Ibrahim, waiting for action that could now never come. Murad Bey, with such of his horsemen as were left, yelped off inland to Gizeh.

"LIKE a great big meaty stew," Gallimard of the 32nd kept saying. In the sauce-colored Nile blown corpses floated gently seaward, to be fished out with bent bayonets. There were good pickings here, since each Mameluke carried his gold about him. On the shore lay ornate pommels, daggers, pistols, all encrusted with pearl and jewels, worth a fucking fortune. "Just no end to it," Gallimard said, fishing. They all laughed to see him got up like one of these Mamelukes, flashing in the sun with forty centuries of history behind him. Verne and Chaillot snarled at each other, tugging like dogs at a belt with what looked like an English guinea mounted on the clasp. "Stop that, lads," Gallimard smiled. "Whole river's shining like farm butter with them. Look." And he started to harpoon out a sogged and bloated dreaming Mameluke or Turk or whatever he was. "Poor bugger's in paradise now, drinking sherbet, poor bugger." But where the rest were looking was to the north, all fire and smoke rising. "Ships. That'll be that Abraham. Wonder he doesn't burn up Cairo too. I bet he's had his Marmedukes shit in the wells. Not that it makes any difference." They were all plump and sleek with Nile mud.

THE paperwork was beginning and it was all in Arabic. The Mameluke palace was loud with boots, the music of order. He would have thought: like a ship, clean and trim on a dirty sea of pox and camel-dung. But a ship was not a good symbol these days, not after the horror of the news from Aboukir Bay. Water. The Sphinx kept having a look of Nelson, the pyramids took on in dreams the shape of monstrous advancing hulks. He dictated to young Legrand, who had worked for the Egyptian branch of the Propagation of the Faith: "Why, O people of Cairo, is your city poor and ragged when it should be blazing with health and prosperity? The answer is simple: absentee rule from Constantinople, the presence of a haughty and alien military caste that consults not the welfare of the population but only its own aggrandizement."

Legrand scratched his cheek with one of Conté's lead pencils and started to Koranize: I say unto you that you have been brought low by kings who lie with houris on the fat sofas of Stamboul and by those that were once among you and came from lands of the sunset, men pale but warlike, to steal your camels and women and snatch the bread from your teeth, in no wise to raise you high among the peoples of the earth. Meanwhile the C-in-C got on with other things—gunpowder factory, street-lighting, Paris-style café, accommodation for laundresses, a balloon demonstration.

"Done that?"

"Yes, general. General, that case of Arabic type isn't complete. No toks, not enough nuns."

"Improvise. Surely you can make a tok out of a combined saad and alif. I leave the details to you."

"If we could send to Paris—"

"There will be no sending to Paris." Legrand wondered why. "We must learn to make everything ourselves. Even lead pencils. Monsieur Conté himself is with us. That is something to go in a later proclamation perhaps. Bullets melted down to make lead pencils."

"There are not many here who use lead pencils."

"They will learn, we shall teach. Have we kept those dignitaries waiting long enough?"

"The eyes of the eternal are blind to time."

"Is that in the Koran?"

"It's the sort of thing they say." They left the office with its sweating clerks and clomped down a long corridor to a sort of council chamber. Imams and muftis and kathis sat here on cushions, turbaned elders who had risen above the squalor of the flesh. The heat was tamed by wide-eyed boys with feathery fans. One of the muftis much admired one of these boys, and he stroked his buttocks with a gentle hand. The smell of the holy was wafted toward entering Bonaparte, who said with care:

"*Salaam aleikum.*"

They nodded at that and waited. Bonaparte sat on a kind of throne. Young Legrand did his best, but it was a long slow business.

"We believe in Allah, we take the Koran as a sacred book. In our land we broke the power of infidel Rum, in his own land we struck down her Sultan whom men call the Pope, in Malta we slew the Knights, sworn enemies of Islam. Inform your people that we are sent by Allah to geld the evil Turk and raise high the people of the Nile."

"How can slaves be sent by Allah? You all have hairless faces, the mark of the bondsman."

"That can be put right, with time and God's holy help. My men shall grow mustaches. The point I would now make is that we French are children of Islam like yourselves. Where lies the difference, save in things of the surface? We believe in brotherhood under one God, the reward of heaven and the punishment of hell, the power of prayer—"

"You drink wine, you have foreskins. These things have been observed."

"It was not seemly to raise your flags on the minarets."

"That was a mistake. We were too eager to show that our cause and the cause of Islam are one. They have all been taken down."

"As for your circumcisions, the chief modin can arrange all. Your wine must return to the earth whence the grape came. *Haram.*"

"Yes yes yes, later. For now I would ask you to proclaim next Friday from the mimbar in the masjid that the French are protectors of the faith and friends of the Prophet."

"What the people have so far seen is godless slaves who tear at the veils of our women and have stolen gold dangling from their belts."

"What you will see is justice. Justice. You will see printed books, from which the people will learn—"

"There are afrits and shaitans in books."

"Houses where the sick shall be healed. With us are learned physicians."

"Allah disposes sickness and health. All is in the hands of Allah."

"Look," he said. "I've heard about these afrits and shaitans before. Some of your holier citizens said that my soldiers were shaitans and afrits. You know what they did. Holy slaughter. I was strongly advised to wreak vengeance. One of my staff went on his knees to me, imploring that I burn your mosques and hang some of you. As an example. Some of you here, that is. I did not. I was merciful."

"Only Allah is merciful."

"But I am quite capable of not being merciful."

Legrand translated that, making them mumble among themselves. But he perceived, a little too late perhaps, that the C-in-C was thinking of other, more privy, areas of justice and mercy.

"Why *you*, why do *you* tell me this?" This was the first moment, the refusal to believe what he knew he was all too ready to believe, because that would be an end of doubt, and the turning on the teller of the incredible believable. But it couldn't be, they were cut off, there were no letters from France.

"This," Junot said, showing it. "Some got through." Bonaparte froze him to a picture, the sort of thing that her young man Gros would paint, the sand-swirls frozen behind him, the merciless blue that the sun rent. The thing to remember, the terrible thing that was not so terrible.

"My brother Joseph," he said. "Said something. I took little notice. To humor him. I had the man posted." The sun and desert drank his rage like a mere tear, unimpressed. The Sphinx, Nelson, was couched at ease. "The whole damned race of ladies' men, fops and damned coxcombs, effeminate dandies, playing at soldiers. Oh God." And then at Junot: "Why *you*, why do *you* have to tell me? Jealousy, is that what it is? You've ridden in coaches with her, you've stayed in inns."

"I don't under—"

"There was a certain champagne breakfast you gave and the punch you made from what you called a Creole recipe—"

"That was not—"

"Given to you by a Creole lady, wink wink. She put you off, is that it? One of the few she didn't fancy?"

"It was General Murat, not I."

"Murat too. Let us have them all in. Bourrienne! Bourrienne!" And Bourrienne his friend and secretary came stumbling over the sand. "Do you know, does everybody know?"

"Know?"

"That your commander-in-chief is a damned cuckold. The cuckold is always the last to know, isn't he? Can you imagine anything more more more *bizarre*? The Sphinx and the pyramids and the leagues and leagues of emptiness are witnesses to the dénouement of a Paris farce. Buonaparte the cuckold. Oh Christ, oh Jesus." He had gone back to the old form of his name.

"You had to know," Junot said, "sooner or later."

"Sooner or later, yes, when there's no action to be taken. There's no running to get a divorce here. But I'll be back, by Jesus. The faithless bitch. But I'll kill the lot of them, the impotent Paris swine of bastard pansies. I'll lead the army in, I'll make a man's town out of it. Oh God, oh God God God."

"Women," Bourrienne said gently, "are more open to calumnies than men. With a man it is never a calumny. A married lady with her husband at the wars—she has to have an escort. We don't have purdah in a country where we boast of equality. Who has seen Madame Bonaparte with more than a mere escort?"

"Don't you give me a sermon, Bourrienne. The world cries cuckold and the world's right. You know this, Bourrienne, you told me nothing. Is that loyalty, is that friendship?"

"It's not my duty to retail calumny. Even if it were a duty, I'd not choose a moment when you're six hundred leagues from France."

"If that," Junot said, his voice thickening, "is meant to be a stab at myself—"

"It is you, if I may say so, who do the stabbing."

"I insist that you retract that. My motive was one of love, of duty, my heart bled—"

"This is the end, what more is there?" Bonaparte shouted to the Nelson-Sphinx. "This is a great lesson, about the true meaning of honor and glory. Well, if she can fuck, I can fuck too." Bourrienne wrinkled at the coarseness. That was his race, but it was also in his race to take the knife to her, swim the Mediterranean with the knife in his teeth. But he had read *Othello*, he had sometimes written laughing letters to her about the jealousy of Othello, he would not now be Othello. Enlightenment, reason, that sort of thing. "I loved her. Too much." He was reasoning, sorting; he did not say not wisely but too well. "You don't know what it's like, you damned womanizers, to love a woman like that. I gave her my youth, everything. And now she gives her her—" Delicacy like a sudden breeze. "—to these mincing coxcombs with their sweet red tongues. I worshipped the bitch. But that's the only way to take them—bitches. Take them as a dog takes a bitch. Fuck and fuck off." He turned again on Junot. "True, is it? You're sure it's true? Let me see that letter."

"With respect, it's a personal letter. What it says is that she went to Plombières—"

"The waters are great for pregnancy, that's the damned silly superstition. Go on, go on."

"And they stayed at the same inns on the way back. And she had him several times staying the night at—the address is here, you see—6 rue Chantereine."

"Divorce," he nodded. "A stinking great divorce. But first I'll show her. I'll show the whole of Paris."

"We're cut off from Paris," Bourrienne said.

"I want a woman. I want women. Not these pox-ridden bints. I'll have that one who shouldn't be here. That dragoon's wife. No wives—that was the order. Well, he must take his punishment." He saw that he must seem already to be more cheerful, so he cried out: "Betrayal, betrayal—the pattern of history. Read Plutarch, read Suetonius. But men must accept their destiny and, in a sense, glory in it. There is a great lesson here in Egypt, with Antony and the wiles of that snake of a woman. And there is that martyr of Alexandria, named, like myself, Napoleon. But it was not a woman who betrayed him, it was the stupid, the faithless, the mob. We cling to our faith, all of us." It was as if Junot and Bourrienne also had recently been betrayed. "The faith of the disregarded maker, the builder of civilizations. That bitch, that unutterable wretched treacherous harlot. Oh, I'd give anything for it not to be true. But I won't be the laughingstock of Paris. I'll write to my brother Joseph. I'll tell him to have the divorce pronounced."

"Blockade. Interception. Cut off."

"Some things go through. Like this dagger, this letter of Junot's. But treachery has wings, that's well known. Wings, wings."

He conquers first, then seeks to civilize.
With speed he bids an Institut *arise.*
Where once the perfum'd houris of the Turk
Seduced to play, the savants set to work.
Forgotten now the jeer that flaw'd the air:
"Let ass and scholar to the midst repair
And skulk and shiver in th' embattled square."
Dogs of Pekin *the soldiers term them now,*
Pets of a general with a scholar's brow.
See how these dogs are swift upon the scent
Of Egypt's lore, on tempting tracks intent.

Berthollet broods upon the natron lakes
And tomes upon their chimick wonder makes;
Saint-Hilaire snatches at the crocodile,
The ostrich, and the fishes of the Nile,
Whence the polypterus he brings to view:
A finny monster but mammalian too.
See Caffarelli wooden-legg'd advance
(The homesick sigh: "He has one foot in France")
Seeking upon the Rouge Mer's *littoral*
The ghost of an impossible canal.
By hot Rosetta Lancret finds a stone
Variously inscrib'd, which may, he thinks, make known,
Spite of the pedant's scoffs, th' unlearned's sniffs,
The secrets of the Pharaohs' hieroglyphs.
Meantime the workshops buzz with useful toil.
A lighted city drinks a cleaner Nile.
Conté's balloons the turban'd mob astound,
And the sharp surgeon probes the fetid wound.
{Extortion wilts to hear clear Justice call,
{Her cannon breach the tyrant's crumbling wall,
{And keen-eyed Alexander watches all.

"Sultan El Kebir," he announced himself, coming into her room in robe and turban. "If they call me Sultan, I must dress like one. Tallien says not in the streets or at the Divan. I must be a sober Frenchman, he says. But here, with my little houri—"

Bellitote, little houri, was at once briskly assaulted by her Sultan, whose dagger, loose in its sheath, clanked gently up and down in time to his action. Well, if he had been slower, more expertly and considerately amorous, the situation would have called out another dagger, and not in play, when Fourés strode in. When Fourés strode in, she was decently covered with a sheet and he, Sultan El Kebir, gaped under his turban. "No," he said. Fourés did not at first recognize him and was ready to say something about filthy natives, then he saw who it was. He said sarcastically:

"So sorry to intrude on the Citizen General's fancy-dress party."

"How dare you, sir! Out! Knock!"

"I didn't realize a man had to get his commander-in-chief's permission to enter a room where his wife is. In bed. Sir."

"You," Bonaparte said, "should be in Paris. I entrusted you with urgent dispatches to the Directory. Report at once to your company commander and, with my compliments, request him to make out the charge." He was in control, despite the absurd costume and the naked woman in the bed.

"Urgent dispatches my bottom. Your David and Bathsheba plan misfired, Citizen General. The British Navy captured our ship and kindly brought us back to Egypt."

Only Bellitote saw the humor of that. Her laughter shook gold hair over her shoulders. Her husband cried out: "False little whore." That did not stop her laughter. Nor did Bonaparte rebuke the intemperate language; instead he spoke metaphysics. He said:

"Your wife is not officially here. No wife is officially here. You smuggled your wife aboard at Toulon dressed as a drummer boy. This is a gross breach of discipline. You merit cashiering. There is a shameful ceremony attached to cashiering. It is performed in open square, before the entire regiment. Then, with your badges of rank cut off and your sword surrendered, you are automatically re-enlisted. But this time as a private soldier."

"You're threatening me, Citizen General."

"The official becomes the real." He shivered as he uttered the word, but he knew this would not be seen under the loose silk: "Divorce. Retroactive divorce. The papers can be made out tomorrow morning. Suitably backdated. That makes everybody free. Madame Fourés free to come on board at Toulon as an army laundress. You free to continue in what, I'm sure, will be a highly successful military career."

Lieutenant Fourés swore without pause for two minutes. Bellitote tut-tutted but Bonaparte listened with respect. At the end he said:

"I'll give you a brief free lesson, Lieutenant. In generalship. Good generalship is a matter of choosing, not of having to submit to the choice of others. You choose when to attack and where. Sometimes you also choose whether a thing actually happened or not. Time is a terrain whereon certain things can be eliminated. By choice. There. Don't you think that's a good lesson?"

Fourés just stood there, seeming to sulk. Then he smiled. "Poor bugger," he said, adding: "With respect, that is. Sir. Suppose it gets into the newspapers? You can't wipe out what it says in the newspapers, can you? Well, it's in the English newspapers. I learned that on board the ship."

"What is in the English newspapers? What are you driveling about?"

"The British Navy captures everything. Everything that tries to get across the Mediterranean they just take. Like a letter you wrote. It was about—you will know, Citizen General, who it was about. To your brother, they said it was. Try choosing not to have let that happen. Sir."

"Out out out get out—"

"Just going. Sir. Not forgetting *madame*."

Talleyrand had dinner alone with Paul Barras. "This saltcellar," Talleyrand said, admiring it under the bright candles, "looks vaguely ecclesiastical."

It was Friday and they had begun with a thick soup of pork kidneys. They had now been served with ham slices poached in Madeira. There was a dish of smoking spinach with croutons stuck in it like little golden gravestones. "*Credite experto*," Barras said. "From Bologna. Saliceti told me the name of the church, but I've forgotten. I have one or two nice little things. I'm disappointed," he joked, "that I have nothing opulent from Constantinople. You failed me there."

"Did he honestly expect me to go?"

"He honestly did. On assback and camelback and quinquereme or however one gets to the Sublime Porte, if that's the right name. A good thing for you you didn't go. They'd be presenting your ballocks, nicely mounted, to Sir Smith there."

"So that's the end of Egypt. A pity in a way. A Gallicized Cairo would have been pleasant for a winter holiday. Apéritifs in the sun."

"And the smell of camel-dung. No, Egypt won't do. No ecclesiastical saltcellars there. It's mad. All that comes out of Egypt is letters screaming about divorce. Has there ever been anything like it before in the whole history of the world? The British press prints evidence that our friend's a cuckold, and the intended recipient gets his letter by courtesy of London, Frankfurt and the Paris press. Well, this is perhaps the end of a promising career. It's hard to survive that kind of laughter." He took a draught of burgundy from a delicately wrought chalice. Talleyrand seemed to murmur words of consecration over his before drinking:

"*Gloria mundi, gloria mundi.*" And then: "How long will it be, do you think, before the Directory sees what has to be done? And the Elders and the Five Hundred and all the rest of the nonsense."

"When they're thoroughly frightened they'll listen. And nod. And say yes yes yes."

"I suppose history will say it was an interesting experiment. Useful too. Confirmatory. The bottoms of the monarchs will feel their thrones securer than ever."

"That isn't what happened in England. No more absolutism after Cromwell. Nothing in history is a mere parenthesis."

"Did you make that up?"

"It's not too soon to start getting a speech ready. I have a number of little maxims of that kind. Purged and cleansed, we return to the ways of light. Would *interregnum* be better than *parenthesis*? That partridge you have seems over-crisp."

"I like crisp things."

"Armies," Barras said, when they got to the roast beef stage, "are very expensive."

"They brought you some pleasant things from Italy. Don't you think that Tiepolo is hung a little too high?"

Bonaparte thrust from his head the biblical associations of Gaza, but the image of gouged-out eyes kept recurring. The Turks would do anything with a captured screaming infidel body—make it chew its own penis, thrust the testicles up the anus, saw the noseless earless head off with slow delicacy. There were so many of the skeletal or bloated who had survived the Sinai march, now torpid under the limes and lemons and olives, who might welcome the ultimate atrocity—at least on others—as the fitting artistic completion—a nod of satisfaction as the concluding horror prepared. Some were sick in their sleep as they remembered, in some dream fantastication that could hardly outdo hard fact, the tearing at raw donkey-flesh, the fetidity of sliced dromedary hump, the salt acid abomination of camel-piss. Some had fallen dead in the burning snow with the taste of crushed limes almost in their leather mouths. Of the living, furred teeth could hardly engage the golden skins, eyes swooned up in pain at the released zest. With the orchards stripped in a blue locust-swoop, the goats butchered and eaten to the very caecum, what was there to feed the two thousand prisoners on? Quartermasters snarled, with right jealousy, over the dwindling store of army biscuit. The Turks expected head-lopping but they were given freedom, what was called parole: your war is over. They did not understand: this was holy war, holy war was never over. Bonaparte dragged his men to Jaffa and whipped them to another victory, what time the fifes cried:

Let extortion and tyranny tremble:
Now the blood-red flag is on high.

This time they took four thousand Turks. Some of them were parolemen of Gaza. None could be fed, none could be freed. The field officer said from caked lips:

"But I promised quarter. It was the condition of their surrender."

"On whose authority?"

"I assumed—"

"Never assume in war." And, after two days of discussion with his staff, he strode up and down, boots softly crunching, a fluent parcel of red and shadow in the night-fires. "Anything, some have said, but that to which we are, I am, ineluctably led. We freed the Gaza prisoners and they considered it weakness. Djezzar Pasha and his friend Sir Sidney Smith are watching. What would Djezzar Pasha do if he took four thousand Frenchmen? What, in fact, has he done, or encouraged to be done, to the Greeks they hold in the bondage of terror? I need not answer. He fights with the British but he fights in his own way." He was puzzled at the image of a kind of French savant he knew of, a cousin of Paul Barras, a gross-bellied man in a madhouse. What was his name? "We have to decide now how to execute a regrettable duty, putting out of our minds the humane philosophies on which our Revolution is based, thinking only, as soldiers should, of the technic or method." A man full of dreams of slaughter and earthquakes, frotting his yard with glee as he dreamed. "So how? Split the entire corpus into forty centuries, conducting each century without the walls for an entire infantry company to dispatch with ordered rifle-fire. The task could be completed in a day."

An anonymous deputy aide started to retch.

"Take that officer away. Give him cognac. Unfortunately, we are not rich in ammunition. Spent cannonballs, as you have been informed, may soon have to be collected from the field, a nominal money prize awarded for each retrieval. Steel, however, iron, points and edges, are not spent as bullets are. How many heads has our guillotine in Paris shorn?" One or two staff officers thought of the guillotine for an instant with homesickness that threatened tears: a cup of coffee, a cognac (and not for nausea), a stroll by that killer, trapezoid of light in the air, Paris.

"Iron, steel, gentlemen. They that live by the etcetera etcetera. Practicable would be a narrow egress in the outer wall—our engineers could blast one speedily, the prisoners to walk as to freedom through it, an endless file with gaps of several meters to obviate panic, two men to grasp the emergent Turk, one to fell him with a club, the executioner to perform his office—executioners in shifts, a roster can be drawn up, two men to drag the body away. The technic of execution. The axe? That means the grotesquerie of thousands of severed heads, always more frightening to the squeamish than a corpse minimally mutilated by some entering instrument. The bayonet? Our men are, ha, well-used to the bayonet. Perhaps I might depute the choice of actual mode of dispatch. General Berthier would welcome volunteers."

"Bbb—"

"Think about it, gentlemen." He took on a visionary look that the fires made devilish, angelic. "Conceivably a thesis might be written, a considered conspectus drawn up. The army's functions expand, we have our *Institut*, we need theory, thought, speculation, philosophy, all within the army. Consider, for instance, the efficient annihilation of a whole disaffected city. The unventilated room crammed with subjects—we must not think of victims, prisoners, the terms being emotive—and the introduction, by a simple pumping device, of some venomous inhalant. Our army chemists may work on such things. New methods, gentlemen, for new wars. We are done with dancing minuets."

THEY sarabanded to Acre. Captain Croisier and the rest saw a crusaders' castle white in the glare beyond a wide ditch and the great groins of ramparts. Sea-glare and sand-glare. Nearly three hundred cannon and jolly English tars under Sir Smith, known to the Commander-in-Chief from his days at Toulon. And the Turks. Hornpipes and dervishes. Beer and sherbet. *Ashkurak*, mates. *Fackyou*, effendi. The French guns sent by sea and, inevitably, the English had captured them. They had twelve guns, twelve, mark that. It was mad, but Croisier was glad of the madness. *I don't want that sort of cowardice again.* Cannot too much emphasize gentlemen the importance of taking Acre vital British naval base take it way clear to Damascus and Constantinople: words filtered down from army to brigade to division to company to platoon. And so they pounded, the guns loosing their twenty-four-pounders, pounding, while the infantry waited. Out of the smoke, incredibly, a wound gaped in the wall. They charged and met scimitars. Croisier saw one of his men converted to a prodigy: a bayoneting pair of hands beneath a rich arterial fountain. Another cursed as he slithered in the blood of his fellows, dancing, groping, running-on-the-spot his way out. Turks went down with shocked beard-framed open mouths, ringed fingers holding in spilling guts. Croisier saw with surprise his own legs splashing out *don't want that sort of* to safety, scrambling over corpseless heads, headless corpses, *cowardice again,* in coughing gun-fog and thunder. But, on the last hopeless plunge into that wound, he found atonement. He watched with a sort of interest as the Turk, one eye bleeding, his mouth full of words he had a passionate and hopeless desire to understand, swung with a grunt with the scimitar. Sorry for his body, not for himself, he saw for an endless second that body spurt out its crimson gallons, *himself* in his head that flew and spun, the body only just about to buckle at the knees as his light went out, still in the air.

At Mount Tabor thirty-five thousand Turks roared and slashed at the right flank under Kléber, and Bonaparte rushed in and slashed back with his four-and-a-half thousand and sent them off screaming. But Acre would not yield and disease crept through a frustrated army. Monge moaned with the dysenteries, Caffarelli died of gangrene, Bonaparte wept. "Max, Max, my dear friend Max, his heart shall go back to France with me, never leave me, cut it out tenderly, Larrey, we shall have it embalmed and kept in a fine box, there is no friendship like the friendship between men, comrades-in-arms, comrades in ideas and hopes and aspirations, women are nothing, women are treacherous toys, that wooden leg of poor dead Max Caffarelli is worth more to me than all the perfumed flesh in the Grand Turk's seraglio, all the proffered bosoms of the stinking Paris salons, when I think what that bitch bitch did to me and she lives, lives, fornicates, grins, glories in her infidelity, and as for those fucking idiots in the so-called Fighting 69th, the number is right, 69, they suck cocks, no, they have no cocks, they're a load of simpering treacherous pansies, they won't take Acre, oh no, I'll have their breeches off and dress them in skirts, cunts they have not cocks, poor poor dead Max, a scholar, a fighter, a man." A time-bomb fired from Acre fell at his feet and he was dragged back by two grenadiers. A shell struck the gun-fascines where he peered through his telescope and knocked him back so as nearly to knock Berthier over. He cursed women, the cruel fates that had taken Caffarelli, cursed Berthier, the 69th, the bubonic plague, the foul water, the weeviled biscuit. He saw thirty ships sailing in proudly from Rhodes, an Anglo-Turkish fleet full of fresh and ready marines. Now or never, he ordered a blistering attack and the jollies and tars were ready for him, yare me hearties so much for the Frenchies, and drove him out. He danced before the 69th, tore off his buttons, out his hair, had an untimely accession of micturition after dysuria and stained his breeches, raged and dithered so that it was a great and memorable wonder.

"That's what I'll do," he screamed, "I'll have your fucking trousers off and parade you as prickless creampuffs, you ungrateful and cowardly effeminate bastards, not one decent cubic millimeter of man's sperm in the fucking lot of you, I'll turn you over to the Turks to have great men's rods stuck up your wincing sweet little arseholes, that's what I'll do, I'll paint and powder you and sell you in the market, not that you'd fetch more than two cunting Turkish piasters, the sweet-breathed girly-wirly mincing and primping lot of you, a load of perverts and bloodless bastards of bitches' gets, get out of my nauseated line of fire before I spew, you filthy cockless unsoldierly ingrates."

And then there were the sick to be transported back to

— …ere already the holy war might have spread like the bubonic and smiling beards above gelders' knives be waiting at the gates), and how in the name of filthy castrating Allah did you march men back through the Sinai who couldn't even sit a mule? He reviewed the sweating patients in gloom, all distorted with buboes, and if you could kill prisoners, breaking one rule of war, you could. Put them out of their misery, you did it with animals.

"Out of their misery." To Desgenettes, in charge of medical services. "A strong dose of laudanum. I think you know what I have in mind."

"An overdose? You mean, you suggest, you would order that I give an—?"

"I did not use that word, *you* did. A strong dose, I said. An unusually strong dose. That's not the same as an overdose."

Desgenettes gave the cold-blood Turk-slayer a look of special awe: killing your business, mine save lives. "It may act as an emetic. Painful in their weakened—"

"They'll vomit the plague up, they may vomit the. What do you want, eh, what are you after?" He double-rayed onto the groom, a good obsequious man, disproportionate lightning. "What horse, you say, which horse do I choose, do I hear aright, *horse*? Horses only for the incapacitated, do you hear me, everyone else on his own two feet or one foot or whatever he has. Poor Max, poor poor Max. Including me, yes, me, yes, me, me, me." And he laid into the groom with his whip. He likes it, Desgenettes thought, he likes to be cruel.

"Can I go now, sir?" the smarting groom said.

"Go, go, go." And a couple of whip-strokes on his back. "Who asked you to come in the first place?"

A good question to ponder as they trudged. Out of Syria with. Yelling fly-swarms of rear-harriers and. Marauders. *He* did, *lui*, but he would, would he not, proclaim himself no more than the agent of the goddess of republics, reason, humanity, knowledge, scientific progress, the goddess being encharged with many portfolios. A book of many volumes, all about Egypt, was being paid for by that man roped to a mule, vomiting endlessly into the sand, the vomit punching a transitory hole into the dense mob of black flies that fed on him, that man in multiplicate. And the British flag flew in the Acre wind and, on the Mediterranean, British warships flaunted like whores in the Place de la Concorde.

"The laudanum worked, the excess dose."

"What?"

"Some of them expelled the activating organism. Praise God, or *lui*, or something."

Sand and sand and everywhere was sand,
Sand and sand and sand on hand and hand,
The Holy Land I understand is sand.
Expand the planned command that planned the sand,
With blue too true a blue too blue to view
Garagorigrawninfieryfieryflaw
And blue to you who blew the few that flew.
Then band and bland and brand and gland and grand
And hand and land and rand and strand and sand
And then remand the band in ampersand
And overland and reprimand the sand.

From Murat: They fell on such fleshpots as were, and *lui*, hardly pausing for a bath and a change of uniform, fell on his little blonde from Carcassonne. It was a matter of watching the sea, and the expected Turkish fleet was sighted making, it was evident, for Alexandria, or rather the peninsula they name Aboukir. We gave them a whole fortnight to encamp and to rest and reinvigorate our men. Report spoke of some ten thousand Turks, many of them of the new militia or, in their language, *yeniceri*, *yeni* meaning new, and frenched to janissaries, colorful in their red and blue and well-trained in the employment of musket, saber and pistol. When *lui* observed their formation—one line on flat ground and another on Mount Vizir—he said vigorous cavalry charge into the very heart of these Mussulman worthies. It was on this occasion that your servant lost his good looks. I was honored to be confronted by the Turkish general himself, a fine if ancient fellow named Mustufa or Mustafa, the Mussulman being uncertain as to his vowels, who fired straight at my jaw with some inevitable disordering of both bone and dentition, whereupon I slashed at my assailant's hand, driving to the ground in one saber-stroke both the pistol and two of his fingers. The pain in my lower jaw was slow in declaring itself, and I was able to share in the ensuing victory. The gallant victor must ever have some measure of compassion for the vanquished, especially when they are rendered pitiable by forces beyond the scope of the attacker. Thus, the sight of thousands of terrified janissaries plunged to certain drowning is not one I would willingly witness again. The two thousand or so who lay, transformed speedily to garishly attired cadavers, were of the general order of the fairly slain, and the shivering prisoners foiled of more severed French heads, were worthy of the contempt that the lower ranks lavished upon them. It would seem that the Turkish threat has been lifted from Egypt, but the British ships continue to parade their power in the Middle Sea, and Acre remains a blot and a humiliation. Sir Smith compounds the humiliation with the foxy subtlety of his race, ensuring that certain packets reach Alexandria for transportation to headquarters at Cairo, these being exclusively made up of newspapers that report sad things of the *patrie*, which I for one would be glad to believe pure English slander, though I fear there may be all too much truth in the uneasy reports.

. . .

"Stop reading those old magazines or whatever they are," she pouted.

"Eh? Who?" And he went on frowning at the six-weeks-old copy of the *Gazette Française de Francfort.* It all seemed hardly credible, what with the English and the Russians in Holland and the Austrians and the Russians in Zürich and the Turks and the Russians in Corfu, and Naples, where that royal bitch was, joining in the anti-French alliance. He had not reckoned with the Russians, who had a watery diffused kind of country. He had a sudden hunger, which chimed in with a dyspeptic jab or might have been somehow cognate with it, for some maps of Russia. Instead he had the pink and gold map of this houri here, spread over the bed and swiping languidly with a feather fan at the flying insect life. Outside the palms whistled in the night breeze.

"Away all this time fighting your stupid wars and now you sit there with your uniform buttoned up to your chin and not a single word for your little—"

"Very well." He sighed and put the newspaper down on a camp stool. She had, he now noticed, tacked some engravings to the walls—fat allegorical nudes by nameless and disregardable artists. She did not have the taste, this one, of that traitorous whore in Paris. And that too, another confrontation, along with those Directory swine. Oh yes, the time had come, and the Egyptian scheme must fall in abeyance since no money was available and, anyway, inflation had filled good French cash full of air. He suddenly shouted in agony:

"And they sell comfits in the streets and snigger *eighteen for a louis.*" The fifes were playing outside, a detachment marching in from somewhere:

Like the wild roar of the waters
The guns of the soldiers advance
Who rip the bleeding heart of France
And will slay our wives and sons and daughters.
To arms—

Monge? Berthollet? Berthier? Yes, those for a beginning. He must get some paper and make a list.

"You're returning to France, is that not true?"

"Who said that? Who is saying so? Who spoke of this?"

"You're tired of me, of course. Nevertheless, I'm going back with you. Sick of Egypt, why should I have to stay? Cleopatra, indeed. They call me Cleopatra, do you know that? Well, Cleopatra desires to see Paris."

"Who puts these rumors about? I return to Paris when I'm ordered to return. Not before. A soldier must follow orders."

"It's you who make the orders, that's well known. Lack of orders won't stop you." She squashed a mosquito against the carious wall. "*Anthony*."

And Lannes and Murat and Duroc and Lavalette and Merlin. And *her* son, flesh of her flesh, Eugène Beauharnais, good boy, promising aide, he must not be smirched further by her rottenness.

"Anthony was a *great* lover. He lost a kingdom for love."

Bourrienne, of course. And my servant, a man needs his servant, my genuine Mameluke, all to show Paris for the whole adventure, no no, no call for despondency, work has been done, work is still to do, Turkey and India to take, I will be back when France is reordered. Those villains, those libertines, gluttons, incompetents.

"In bed he made a woman desirous. Your skill is not there. Not in bed." She slammed with her whisk at a great booming winged beetle.

Andréossy, Marmont, Bessières, a couple of centuries of the Guides. Her, no. Very much no. Kléber can look after things, the calm, the republican, the efficient.

"Not in bed."

"Yes yes, I will be back there with you in a moment."

GENERAL KLÉBER's mouth opened and remained open. Hot breath emerged in a gust and discouraged the flies. "But," he said. "I mean, this is a shock. The lack of preparation. I am not sure whether it's possible to. This is, to say the least, a."

"Surprise, eh, surprise?" He was cheerful and brisk. "Well, peace as well as war can have its surprises. You are more than equal to surprises, Kléber."

"I had not realized that orders. I was aware of no courier."

"The Turks will not annoy us further, be sure of that. You have an ordered republic here to rule. Be stern in the Divan, parade armed might occasionally. More than equal to it. As for France, must we let these rogues ruin all we have made? I know where my place is, Kléber."

"But." And then he crashed his resentment out. Bonaparte listened patiently, smiling sidewise occasionally at Roustam, his Mameluke, who was impressed by the noise and flying spittle. Thousands of men sick and homesick, a whole fleet sunk, here forever in this land of flies and camel-dung, the treasury seven million francs down, those savants to be responsible for, here till we die, I will write to the Directory, make no mistake about it, flagrant disregard of duty.

"There, Kléber, I know how you must feel. You never said those hard words, they will go unrecorded. Rest assured I will do all in my power to effect your repatriation. It will take time, undoubtedly, but you shall not be here forever. It has been a great adventure, ah yes. The world will be enriched by a new science, what may be called Egyptology. Doesn't that awaken pride in you? We shall be kings of the East yet, but the *patrie* is in danger, it calls me. Look after the little blonde, will you,

And we were at sea full forty-seven days, the key
To the seas not ours but theirs, fleeing the
Fleet free of the sea, we, in ennui not glee, greeting
Each sun's levee, each evening, thee, O sea,
Seeing in sea the sheen of evergreen of damascene
Of fellahin of guillotine of wolverine machine
Foreseen nectarine josephine intervene contravene
Thirteen ravine gabardine and spleen and preen and
Queen and teen, cheek bleak beak clique oblique
Mystique pique physique, antipodes, antitheses,
Hippocrates, parentheses, cleave, achieve, conceive,
Believe believe believe
That Bonaparte will kiss the soil of France.

"THE point is," Gohier said, "that he will now have become aware of the official order of Fructidor. But he did not receive that letter before embarkation. Nevertheless the letter existed, he was authorized to leave Egypt even though he did not know of the authorization. A nice metaphysical point."

"To the devil with your metaphysics," bloated Barras said. "He was ordered to return with his army. His army is still out there. That is guillotinable enough. Desertion of his army in the face of the enemy."

"We must be accurate. That enemy has been defeated. Luck always goes with him. Flowers and fruit and wine at Saint-Raphael. The news of the Aboukir victory was a kind of fanfare arranged by fate or something."

"Where?"

"Saint-Raphael. Where he landed. Bernadotte recommends his arrest despite the popular acclaim. Let Bernadotte take over, it's a War Ministry matter. Court-martial, shot not guillotined. If not for desertion, for evading the quarantine regulations. He may have this bubo thing raging in France in a week or two."

"Shot for that?"

"Well, locked up. Till we decide what to do with him."

"We decide? We?"

O shake yourself awake and take your lance,
Triad of virtues shamelessly asleep,
For Bonaparte has kissed the soil of France.

Long languished in a treasonable trance,
Directory, in indirection deep,
O shake yourself awake and take your lance.

"And," Barras said, "how about *her*?"

"She was calm enough when the telegraph came through, calmer than I was. Nothing to fear, she kept saying, meaning herself. Meaning that she's been with my wife most of the time. Anyway, she has to get to Lyons before his brothers do."

"They'll mince her alive, those two. Behind her back."

Swifter and swifter, smoking wheels, advance!
Prepare a heart to plead, two eyes to weep,
For Bonaparte has kissed the soil of France.

"Look, mother," Hortense said, as they sped south. "More flowers and arches. Is it for what he's done or for what they think he'll do? I mean, what do they think he can do?"

Repeated and repeated in the clattering wheels: extraordinary man, extraordinary man. Madame de Montesson, was it? Never forget that you are married to an extraordinary man, my dear, an extraordinary man.

"I fear they will be there first, Hortense, I fear it. They cannot forgive either him or me, any of them. That whaleboned tigress. Well, you may soften him, if not I. He is very fond of you, as of Eugène. I may well have to plead through my children."

Corsican brothers, foes of dalliance,
Make vengeance spring, bid retribution reap:
O shake yourself awake and take your lance!

"A point you'll hear much of," Lucien said, "is this about the stigma of divorce. You change laws but you don't get rid of stigmas. They'll talk of divorce being no help to a public man with his way to make. But you know what *we* say." They were already approaching Paris. Flowers and arches, crowds waiting all night with torches. God bless you, General Bonaparte, savior of our suffering country. Give us work, give us bread. Give us money we can spend.

"She is what she is," Joseph said, "and will not change. Apart from this adulterous business, she's been involved in some very shady transactions. Army contracts. Bribes. She's been running heavily into debt."

"I loved her, loved her, no man knows how much."

Arches and flowers. Welcoming dirty hands groping at the carriage windows. Clean up our country, restore us to honor, dignity, solvency. Something like that.

"You'll never be able to look our mother in the face again unless you. It has to be. Painful, yes. Make a new start."

Your sun it is that flames, your waves that dance,
It is your children there that laugh and leap,
For Bonaparte has kissed the soil of France.

When she and Hortense returned, frustrated, throbbing with presentiments, to Paris, they found her trunks and boxes packed and stacked. His study door was locked. Eugène was there, his arms open to his sister. The distraught mother knocked and knocked, to no avail, till she lay prostrate in grief and weariness. The children's sobs penetrated. The servants listened, as to an enacted drama.

O GOD TO THINK THAT ONE TO WHOM I ENTRUSTED MY VERY INNERMOST HEART IN KEEPING but I swear it is all long over it was foolish but it is long done I have lived a life of solitary virtue there is evidence talk to Madame Gohier your whole family is against me they will say anything I WOULD HAVE DONE BETTER TO LISTEN TO MY FAMILY A MAN CAN TRUST ONLY HIS KIND O GOD GOD THE TREACHERY LET ME NEVER TRUST ANY WOMAN AGAIN I WHO SPENT SUCH TRUST ON A WORTHLESS WORTHLESS *let us speak for our mother let us speak for ourselves let us be a happy and united family she loves you we love you you love her* YES EUGÈNE YOU ARE A BRAVE A FINE YOUNG MAN AND YOU HORTENSE ARE O GOD GOD GOD I was foolish God knows I was foolish but I learned my lesson long before these calumnies spread IF ONLY I HAD NOT but you were bound to be KNOWN KNOWN *think of us think of* lied to since MY ISLAND BREEDS OTHELLOS your family hates me BUT I LACK THE they will do anything to KILLING SPIRIT blacken me in your I AM A MAN eyes as for black they talk of the tarbrush which is more WHO SEEKS BUT calumny PEACE PEACE and out of a mere peccadillo *oh you are breaking our* AND LOVE they wish to break all our AND A FAMILY OF LOVING *hearts* hearts HEARTS.

Marthe, oldest of the servants, nodded and nodded, toothlessly chewing every morsel, knowing that a strife of words meant communication, that no man could fight a woman's tears or resist a woman's white arms wreathing in anguish as in harp-playing, and a woman's white bosom heaving, no better solvent of a man's wrath than a décolletage, they would get to bed now in the gray dawn, some would get some sleep at last at 6 rue Chantereine, no, it was changed to rue de la Victoire, for him, *him*, he, he, he, la victoire. It was little Marie-Claire and the groom Antoine who were sent with the messages, that horrible black man he had brought from Africa guzzling in the kitchen and speaking little French. Lucien (head of the Five Hundred, big man now because of his brother there now at a lively peace conference in bed, big family, though only Corsicans) and Joseph (small head of the big family, they say it is his wife wearies and drags him down) arrived together as the day warmed. They were requested to go to the master bedroom.

"Murdered her in her bed?"

"Nonsense, he has not the murdering temperament."

"He is wearied out then, he has made his decision, where will he have sent her?"

The Mameluke on his master's mat growled, but Lucien, president of the Five Hundred, growled back and knocked. The *entrez* was tired but cheerful. They entered and saw him in bed with a naked woman. Well, he was entitled to seek consolation. They saw who the naked woman was.

"We have resolved all, *fratelli.* God knows, there is enough fighting to come without having it here in the family. Let us engage the corrupt state out of a happy fortress."

Fighting? Family? He did not mean the *real* family, the *famiglia.* He was being melted into the Beauharnais. Their glands meanwhile played an opposed music. Those shoulders, those breasts she was now covering. Well, there it was, our common manly weakness: lechery will undo us all. Lucien had a confused image of a lot of lechery ahead for everyone, the whole of Europe a big bed.

Love, linger in this brief cherubic chance trance glance;
The eagles soar to trumpet from the steep:
O shake yourself awake and take your lance,
For Bonaparte has kissed the soil of France.

"HONORED," he said. "Greatly." Sieyès's apartment smelled of bachelorhood, vaguely sour and dusty, with overtones of old apples that might really be the odor of his old books. The works of Voltaire, well aired, were in an alcove apart, under a flat wax effigy of the sage. As Sieyès sat down again he winced faintly. Bonaparte said:

"Hemorrhoids? I know about hemorrhoids. It is a varicosity that the application of chipped ice will reduce. As common in the field as in the er study."

Sieyès had the appearance of a minaret that had been capped with an overlarge onion dome. His voice, to match, had the thinness of an old wailing bilal. "So you saw our head director. And what did Gohier say? That you were too young? Undoubtedly. He is a stickler for the letter, very much a lawyer. No directors under forty. How old are you?"

"Coming up to thirty. The letter that kills, I told him. From your colleague Paul Barras I caught a whiff of metal polish. How much does he expect to be paid for cleaning up the crown?"

"Well," and Sieyès sniffled, "there seem to most to be two ways out only. Consider the condition of the country. Unemployment, thieves—"

"I was robbed of my baggage on the way north."

"There you are then. Religious fanatics in the west, a million francs barely enough to buy a decent dinner. Those who don't want the Bourbons back want a Reign of Terror, plenty of Jacobins in the two Councils—"

"And what do *you* want, Citizen Sieyès?"

"A new constitution, what else? We have no constitution."

"Just what I've been saying, ever since I returned. They threatened me with the law because I left Egypt without orders, but I told them they had no law." The two looked at each other with some warmth, and the grim profile of Voltaire looked out at a world of renewals. "You, sir, made our first constitution. Is not the time coming again?"

"Hardly the first, though my pamphlet on the Third Estate may be said to have started— What do you feel yourself to be, soldier or civilian? I see you are dressed as a civilian."

"I am both." Sieyès saw, with a sudden dyspeptic jab, what that might mean—general in one sphere its equivalent in the other—but let it pass. He allowed himself to take it to mean that this soldier was free to be politically persuaded. He said:

"We need a sword, we. I mean those of us who are agreed on the mode of action I will now outline. When I say a sword, I mean, shall I say, a show of force which shall be an emblem of order."

"I understand thoroughly, I quite understand, I see that very clearly."

"You will have had enough bloodshed already in your career. As I see it, the entire Directory must resign. This will mean panic in the two Councils, but I have already paved the way with certain of my friends among the Elders. We must have a meeting of the entire Assembly out of town. Paris is a panicky place, there is a mob, there are the unemployed. The palace at Saint-Cloud, I thought."

"I quite understand." He smiled in total sympathy as Sieyès winced again. "Chipped ice, remember. Leeches too are bloody but good. My brother, of course, will be useful in this conspiracy."

"I did not use that word. Erase that word from your mind. That word must not be launched into the public air. It is merely proposed that the Councils ratify the liquidation of the Directory and approve the establishment of a committee of three to make a new constitution."

"Establishment? That sounds like a permanent triumvirate."

"One cannot yet look ahead to any mode of permanency. First things first. Now my friend Cornet in the Elders is to inflame his colleagues with oratory about danger and, while they twitter in apprehension, to propose that you take over command of the Paris district—for the safety of both Councils, naturally. The proposition will be carried, no doubt about it, nem con."

"Good."

"I am leaving it to Talleyrand—"

"Can Talleyrand be trusted? It was proved that I could not trust him, he endangered the entire Egyptian—"

"—Talleyrand to secure Barras's resignation with a fair bribe—half-a-million, gold not paper. Gohier dithers, Gohier will give no trouble. That then will be the end of the Directory."

"Talleyrand," Bonaparte brooded. "Untrustworthy, slimy. Very much an unfrocked bishop."

"I, remember, am an unfrocked abbé. Leave that. Should things in the Tuileries not go quite as planned, should Barras or Moulins, say, give unexpected trouble, then you will leave three hundred of your men in Paris. As I see it, it is all a very simple matter. It is a *reasonable* matter, this liquidation of a weak executive. I anticipate no trouble at all."

"A triumvirate, eh? Very classical."

Sieyès pointed his long nose at Bonaparte like a toy gun. "I said nothing about a triumvirate. I mentioned only the formation of a committee of three. That is not the same thing, except in the matter of strict denotation, as a triumvirate."

"I quite understand, I see that thoroughly."

Augereau watched them march in while the string band played:

Let extortion and tyranny tremble
Now the blood-red flag is on high.

"Look at the bastards," he said, "in their togas like a lot of stage Romans. Lawyers, that's all they are. The more impotence the more show. What with the directors and their yard-long feathers nodding in the breeze. Bald-headed men fuck best. Well —so they say."

"You should have been with us at Gaza." Bonaparte was tricolor-sashed, gold-frogged, breeches a ripple of snow silk. They both stamped up and down for the circulation, it was a cold Brumaire they were having, no brume today though.

"I had enough dirty work to do here. In Paris, that is. That seems to be the lot. All those red togas and red squashy things on their heads and the tongues of the troops hanging out for a smoke and a drop of brandy. Not a pipeful of shag to a platoon.

Keep us waiting all morning while they have that stagy rubbish stuck up in there, honor and glory and the Sun-King shining on their napes, take their time marching in, four repeats of the *Marseillaise* I made it, and now it will be jabber jabber to no end without end."

"They'll be quick, I think."

Bourrienne came back with a report picked up from somebody just inside the door of the Apollo Gallery. "They're going to draw up a list of nominations."

"For the committee?"

"For a new Directory."

"For a— You sure you got that right?"

"Proposed and seconded they do that. Voted on. Nothing else on the agenda."

Bonaparte did a brief quarterdeck pace. Then he said to Bourrienne: "You and I are going in there. Berthier too. Get Berthier."

Augereau gaped. "You're going to drop yourself completely in the—"

"Remember Arcola? Think of Arcola. That was the real, ha, ordure. Nonsense, Augereau. They're a lot of stupid disobedient old men."

"Disobedient? *Disob—*"

The three clank-stamped in, but not before Bonaparte had noticed a ranker whom he insisted he knew. "Don't tell me, it's Carné, we were at Toulon together, drove the English out didn't we eh? Carry on smoking." Berthier performed a silent stutter at the louisine opulence, gold gold, the many-frescoed sun-god, cream pilasters, gold gold gold, magnificent no doubt about it, the elders like a bunch of women in scarlet toques and skirts, some clapping gently at the sight, unexpected, irregular really, of a frowning victorious general, others drawing their red skirts about them in fright or affront, a bunch of women. *Lui* wasted no time, he said:

"Liberty and equality in danger. Volcano's edge. Allow to

speak with blunt soldier's frankness. I am your sword, defender. Have already sacrificed so much for liberty and er equality. Must be saved."

"Am I to understand," a twisted man in steel spectacles said, "that the general is speaking against the Constitution?"

"In the name of the Constitution foul conspiracies are already at their deadly work. You, the people's representatives, are in grave danger. I am a soldier, I know these things." Over the cries of *who* and *what* and the deaf saying *what does he say about the people*, "I have myself been approached by the directors Barras and Moulins to assist them in the overthrow of the Republic and the reestablishment of the hated monarchy. You, gentlemen, our guardians, wise, just, moderate, have ever upheld our republican principles, loathing Bourbonism and Jacobinism alike. Dangers," he repeated. They all looked at him. "That is to say, I will protect you." They all looked at him. "From the dangers that threaten, I mean. Will not one who has founded republics protect the mother of republics? With arms, if need be. Old comrades, I see you standing behind me, bayonets ashine in the sun of victory, that is to say freedom." They all looked at him, except those who looked for the old comrades, who were not there.

"For Christ's sake," Bourrienne said low.

"Republics. Let me say this, just this. The god of victory and the goddess of fortune march with me. Let none try, let none attempt. I know I have enemies, some here perhaps, enemies of the state and of republicanism. Let them beware. Lightning, the lightning of drawn steel and the thunder of an army's anger will will—"

"General, for God's sake," Bourrienne said, "you don't know what you're—"

"The goddess of fortune and the god of victory march with me, remember that—" Then the Elders began to shout, thin arms waving in anger from under togas, the occasional very fat arm jelly-shaking. *The General would do well to leave oratory to the orators, how dare a mere soldier, such insolence, such pre-*

tentiousness, Monsieur President order him to. "All I wish to say, in all humility, is that the distinguished assembly consider the danger, take steps to obviate it, at once form a committee for the purpose of—" *Out out out out.* Berthier began to pull him, Bourrienne, with greater diffidence, to push. "That is all I ask."

Outside he did not seem too greatly discomfited. "Well, didn't do too well there, did we? You can blame Sieyès for this, he promised but he didn't fulfill. Now we're going to the Orangery."

"Ttto the—"

"Yes yes yes, we're going to approach the Five Hundred. Bourrienne, would you be good enough—"

"But the Five Hundred are swearing their loyalty to the Constitution, one by one. That's what they're here for. Believe me, you're courting exceptional danger."

"As always, as always. Be good enough to send a message to my wife, say I may be home a little later than I said but that everything is going well. Got that?"

Fifty thousand in the field, he thought, nothing compared to five hundred close-packed in a grim bare box of a meeting hall. He saw his brother Lucien on the dais, presiding, but no comfort there. *Out out out out* before he was properly in. *Sanctuary of the law profaned, out out at once, no right, OUTSIDE THE LAW.* Someone cried *dictator* and the word was taken up. Lucien was calling, gavel-banging: "My brave brother—his achievements in the field—at least a hearing—" Bonaparte saw the claws and fists looming, heard heavy breath, knew at once and for the first time what his only feared enemy was: the crowd, nails and teeth for weapons. He prepared to faint, recovered, turned to stumble out, found the enemy had blocked retreat, then the claws were onto him, tearing. The salt in his mouth was blood, he put fingers to his right cheek, unbelieving, but there, trickling to the palm, was wet red. Then came the blessed emblem of order—uniforms, strong soldiers shouldering and hitting out, himself thrust into the square of protective order, out, out, hitting out, out.

"Outside the law," Bourrienne said. "You know what it means—those were the words they spoke before Robespierre—"

"What's happening in there now?" They could hear roars and anger, a faint gavel. He did not wipe away the blood, he knew, sick as he was, the value of blood.

"You know what's happening. You know what happened to Robespierre. Your brother's trying to hold back the vote." A scribbled note came out with a panting usher. Bonaparte read it; he said:

"We have ten minutes. We must have Lucien out here. Get my horse. Get an escort for Lucien."

Drums, there was nothing so comforting as drums, a daddy-mammy in crescendo, a roll sustained, frightening the few birds of Brumaire. There were shouting faces at the open Orangery windows. Lucien spoke to the troops:

"That lawful assembly in there is being threatened—threatened physically, threatened with daggers, threatened with swords—by a handful of mad extremists. The army must rescue that lawful assembly, steel must answer steel."

The noise from the windows was confused, but the troops caught the words *outside the law*. The bloody-faced general spoke:

"Soldiers, have I not led you to victory again and again? Have I not again and again risked my life for France, our France, a France once again in danger from Frenchmen? I met danger at Toulon, in Italy, in Egypt, on the high seas, I meet worse danger now in a place of cunning assassins. You followed me before, will you not follow me again?"

Some shouted *Long live*, many were not sure. Lucien drew his sword and, Corsican luck, the dying sun pounced on it. He thrust it at his brother's chest, crying: "I swear, I swear that if ever he menaces the liberty of our dear land, I will—" Roars and roars and roars. It was fine drama—dying sun, brothers poised in tableau, a sword, blood. Bonaparte said to Lucien:

"All right now, I think. We have them now. Go with Leclerc and Murat, lead the way in, we'll clear that damned hall."

"Freedom, freedom, die for freedom!" Some of the Five Hundred were leaping out of the windows, as from a fire.

"Die, indeed," Augereau said. "Who the hell wants to kill those bastards?"

No trouble now about getting that committee.

"I'D much rather be," she shivered, "back at Number Six." They were walking at sunset in the Great Gallery of the Tuileries, big, cold, unhomelike, haunted especially at this hour by kings whose shining light had turned to dried blood. She herself, after all, was an aristocrat, had waited to join the democracy of the headless, shivered now not solely from the huge baroque cold but from the memory of the narrowness of her salvation. The First Consul slapped her rump, starting a chain of echoes, and said heartily:

"Courage, girl. A little bare now, true, and too many of the wrong ghosts—" He felt them too then, they were both from islands where the dead familiarly walked. "But we'll soon lay them with statues of the ever-living, men who became great, not puling inheritors of empty purple. A couple of dozen statues here, I think—Demosthenes, Alexander, Brutus and so on. Poor dead Washington, great general, great democrat. Cato, Julius Caesar—"

"Next to Brutus?"

"In the shades they are friends again, aware of each other's destiny. Marlborough, an Englishman but a very considerable, nay a towering, a gigantic—"

"Are *you*," she said, "a great democrat?"

He stopped their walk and looked at her. She looked at him, seeing his red velvet on fire. "Democrat?" It was strange to hear a political term from those languorous lips; perhaps she had, aware of her husband's new civil greatness, taken to reading A Child's Guide to Montesquieu or something. "Well, yes. Well, no. The whole process has been democratic, shall I say. A free vote and so on. The electorate knows nothing, God bless it, of constitutions, nor need it, nor should it. I believe in the obscurity of constitutions, but they should be short in order to appear simple."

"That sounds Machiavellian." She had been reading, no doubt about it. She walked on and he had to follow. "Poor Sieyès. I'm sure he had no idea that this would come about."

"The triumvirate—do you know that word?—was his idea. The term *consul* also. He knows all about constitutions but he knows little of rule. It's a matter of personality, of course. That piping little voice, those varicose veins—"

"Let me put it another way," she said. "Do you believe in the people?" He smiled indulgently; she knew that he was ready to say *I believe that the people exist if that's what you mean.* "I mean, do you like the people, do you *love* the people?"

"You can love only persons," he said, and put his arm vigorously about her breast. "When I see the people as a mob, and that's the only occasion when one really sees the people, then I know how I feel about them. They petrify me, like a nightmare. But give them the discipline they need and, at bottom, desire, place them under officers, put guns and not bricks in their paws, and then I don't fear them, even when they're marching toward me."

"But what are you going to *do*? You and the two others, I mean?"

"*Hic*, *haec* and *hoc* Talleyrand calls us. Witty and cruel. See that bloodstain on the wall there? That might be from poor Marie Antoinette. Must have it cleaned off. This isn't a museum. Do, you say, do? Take you to that great gilt bed for a quarter of an hour before dinner, bump a few royal ghosts out of the way."

"Be serious."

"I was never more. Come. What I'm going to do in the other er bed, a big weedy flower-bed you could call it, needs a gardener, to do is to rule. Stop the people being a mob." They strolled back, her silk slippers soundless, his boots firm and harsh. "Frederick the Great too. Cicero. Gustavus Adolphus.

Hannibal. He crossed the Alps," he said with regret. A civilian now, ready to grow pot-bellied in his country's service. The new Constitution said that the First Consul could not command in the field. Well, constitutions could be changed. No immediate hurry. "Scipio Africanus. Those poor devils in Egypt. Kléber and that fool of a general Menou. Became a Muslim, circumcision and all." He sighed. "There are some with no notion of moderation. Ah well, there's a lot to do."

In the name of Allah the Merciful the Most High. In that year of the Hijrah nothing of note occurred in the lands of the Nile except for the discontinuation of the annual pilgrimage to Mecca.

Germinal in the Year Seven, and if it is the spring of power it is no longer the spring of love. I would meet you honestly on this. And my seed will not work in you nor, as I now suspect, in any woman. Yet the scent of your body is in my nostrils as I sit here presiding, half-listening to nonsense that I will shatter in due time with a cannon-burst of sense. For my seed would not work in Egypt and it is as though I must seek the way of achievements and monuments and paragraphs in history tomes to secure the continuation of my name. Do we come now to what is called a mature love, nourished on wounds, as the flying life of Egypt was nourished, in which the death of the mad spring must not be regretted? And yet your scent maddens me now at this two-in-the-morning session, all dust and weariness, with some of the councillors dropping off, as it did when it arose from the maps of Piedmont and Tuscany. And with a start I see that I have written, over and over, in total automatism, *God how much I love you* on the order paper. It is my innermost heart speaking through my sleeping fingers and the innermost heart speaks tr—

"Citizens," he called, "for God's sake let's try to earn our salaries. It's only two-thirty-five." He banged his fist on the small table set on the consular platform. Old heads started awake around the green-baized horseshoe table below. Cambacérès, Second Consul, could doze with his eyes open, a great gift, but now he began to murmur something about truffles. Lebrun, Third and eldest, never slept. For an instant the First Consul saw himself in his ridiculous youth, set about by graybeards. He must cultivate humility, the appearance of being willing to learn.

"—the principles of the Revolution," Jodelet said. Somebody, a new councillor, stood up, inflating his chest for oratory. The First Consul said:

"Down, sir, down. No flourishes here. Impressed as we all must be by Councillor Jodelet's devotion to the principles of the Revolution, must we not admit that, whether there be a God or not, the widespread belief in a God is not a matter to which we may close our eyes—literally or otherwise, citizens?"

There were loud words, jumbled: *clergy corruption superstition monks.*

"I speak as a soldier," the First Consul cried. "We cannot have the flower of the army wasted in civil war. I refer to the Vendée. Too many martyrs there. I propose pacification. And if mass may be said there, why not elsewhere?" Too loud, too dictatorial. "I would be grateful, we would all be grateful for the considered views of the Council. Councillor Cathelineau?"

Outside, in the raw morning, Cambacérès and Lebrun went off looking for an early breakfast. Cambacérès knew of a small restaurant where they served an exquisite herb omelette. The bread would be smoking fresh about this time too. There was something to be said for staying up all night.

"What do you think?" Lebrun said.

"About *lui*? I think he keeps a damned bad table. I had him to dinner, you know, and he was actually *impatient*. An exquisite meal, Jean had exerted himself for the First Consul, and he wanted to know how much longer it was going to go on. A bit mannerless, you know. Said he'd be quite happy with a sausage and a swig of watered Chambertin."

"Stripped down to function." Pleased with the phrase, Lebrun tried it again. Pleased with the phrase, he said, "It may be a new kind of man. He's very young, of course, may change, become more human."

"Yes, something in that. He's not really human. Intellect and animality. A machine on top of an animal. He has a chest like an orangutan, have you seen him breathe in? Of course you have. He dances up and down like a monkey when he's in a rage. He should control those rages. Swives like a rattlesnake, so they tell me. Animal all right, and the brain isn't human."

They stood by the raw morning river a moment, seeing barges bringing dewy vegetables from the country. "Nice little turnips there. I like them cooked very slowly, for hours you know, to a kind of cream."

"But," Lebrun said, "where will this new kind of mechanical animal take us? Not to anything new. Religion coming back, and centralization, and favors for his friends."

Cambacérès looked through his lorgnette at some cabbages. "Very crisp, squeak under your fingers. Well, we're not his friends. No favoritism there. It's mad really, I suppose. I'm a regicide and you're a king's man, and here we both are, looking at celery together."

"I don't care much for celery. Well, very fresh perhaps with a nut of cheese. I'm not a big eater. What you say is true, and it means the Revolution's over. Jacobins and Bourbonites are packed together in lavender, memories of old times. It all feels like a new thing, and one can't define it if one's in the middle of it. But I'd say, at a venture, that the new thing is *lui*, Bonaparte. What I mean is, he doesn't express any separable idea—you understand me? He's not there to personify some new notion of absolutism or democracy or what you will. He's there to turn the age into himself."

"A machine married to an animal. He loves France, he says,

he's always talking of his love for France. Yet what does he mean by France? Certainly not any of the regional cuisines. The language? It's not primarily his. France, of course, may be just another name for Bonaparte."

"It frightens me a little."

"Nothing frightens me except overcooked beefsteak. But I see what you mean. A system based on a personality, the negation of a constitution. Not a paradigm but the verb itself. But there are enough checks. We're two of them."

"We don't have an army."

"*I* have an appetite. Some veal kidneys might be a good idea, simmered in butter, a touch of white wine." A lovely dawn of broken eggs and oyster shells began to rise over Paris.

The First Consul turned on the geyser again and let fresh boiling water gush into his tub. He lay hidden in steam. Constant the valet could hardly see to read. "It's no use, sir," he said at last. "It's like a fog."

A voice laughed godlike out of the billows. "Open the door then. Stand by the door." Constant took *Le Moniteur* to the light that came in to meet the steam and read seriously and loud in his Belgian accent:

" 'The First Consul ordered that more logs be brought in for the already blazing fires of the Tuileries. *These ladies must be cold*, he said, with a meaning look around the elegant assembly.' "

A roar came out of the clouds. "That will teach them, eh, Constant? Coming here with their tits showing and their navels peering through the silk. Too much silk being worn anyway, all from India, helping British trade. No, Constant, we'll have none of this Directory shamelessness so long as I'm around. Eh?"

"Sir."

"Elegant decency, decent elegance, They've all gone soft. Introduce a sterner motif, eh? Tents and drums and *marches militaires*."

"Shall I read more, sir?"

"Not from *Le Moniteur*. I write it all myself anyway. Anything scurrilous this morning? Pamphlets, broadsheets, anything?"

"It will make you angry, sir."

"Nonsense, man. Read it, whatever it is."

"Sir. Sir, it says:

Not satisfied with Barras's whore,
He sniffs around and looks for more,
But comes with haste that's quite unique.
He'd eff all Paris in a week."

"Hm. I don't think much of that, Constant." He was now out of his tub; broad low shapely compact nakedness, a rosy sculpture on an Alpine pass, wreathed around in draperies of shifting mist. "Some very low and envious minds about, but one must expect it. Position, Constant, the jealousy of little men. It will be worse yet."

"Sir."

Roustam held the shaving mirror while his master shaved himself with Birmingham steel, swift, neat, with never a nick. He had himself drenched in Cologne water, then pummeled back and front. Dressed in the green of a colonel of Chasseurs, tricorn in hand, snuffbox in one pocket, bonbonnière in the other, he went to work sucking a comfit of aniseed-zested licorice. Bourrienne was at the big mahogany desk that was deep in neatly stacked papers. "It's happened," he said. "A major offensive in North Italy. If only General Moreau—" He held out the dispatch.

"Let me see it, man." He read, sucking, then raised his head, big eyes seeing all, from Rhine to Danube and down to Po.

"If only the Rhine army—"

"Well, the Rhine's out of it now. It's Year Four all over again. No fool, this Melas. At a guess—no, at more than a guess— What would you do in his place, Bourrienne? You're the soldier here, I'm only the First Consul."

"I'd smash Massena, take Genoa, besiege Toulon. That means His Britannic Majesty's navy joining in."

"Not bad. Yes, Genoa's the key." He saw the map in his head.

"Poor Massena. Get this down, Bourrienne." He closed his eyes, opened them, began to pace. "This is for Massena. Right? The Rhine Army will start operations towards the beginning of Floréal. The right wing, under General Lecourbe, will occupy Switzerland and thus protect the right flank of the corps invading Swabia. Then Lecourbe will come under the orders of General Berthier and cross the St. Bernard Pass into Italy. At the same time part of the Army of the Reserve will occupy the Valais and cross into Italy by way of the Simplon or—what's the other?—yes, St. Gotthard Pass. When Berthier enters Italy, you, Citizen-General, must draw the enemy against you, forcing him to divide his army. Make a point of exaggerating your numbers, send the story about of large reinforcements on the way. Have you got that down?"

Knows all about it, has it all worked out.

"Hannibal, eh?" Bourrienne said. "Like Hannibal."

CITIZENS Carné, Thiriet, Blondy, Tireux, Hubert, Fossard, Teisseire, Carrère (Jacques), Carrère (Alexandre), Trauner, Barsacq, Gabutti, Mayo, Bonin, Borderie, Verne, Chaillot, Barrault, Brasseur, Dupont, Salou, eighteen thousand others, found themselves beaten back into Genoa in need of more supplies, especially food food, the food depots near empty, food. The fact is, lads, that those bastards in Marseilles did a fine fucking job of swindling the army, fat-arsed civilians who depend on us for their fucking lives, so get ready for starvation rations, horseflesh not too bad really as you already know, a bit sweetish but nourishing, we've got to hold out though, that's the point, and don't stand any nonsense from the Genoese. What's happened is that this General Melas has separated General Massena's lot, that's us, from General Suchet's lot and forced General Suchet's lot back to the Var. Well, you know where that is, lads, and you know what it all means. It means if we don't hold on here until General Berthier gets over the Alps and rams his bayonets up those bastards' arses, then the bastards will go marching into France and, as the song says, fucking our wives and sons and daughters. So we have to hold on. Any questions? Yes, when do we get some fucking leave, how about our back pay, I've got this pain in the balls citizen sergeant.

Drizzle fell coldly on Genoa, then thickened to proper rain.

Massena looked out to the rainy sea and saw through his telescope ships of the British Navy crammed in the Genoa roads. At his back, he knew, General Ott had some twenty-four thousand making a tight siege, so there it all was. I am trying to save France by sticking it out in Genoa. He read once more the cold dispatch that had come through—Lecourbe under orders of Berthier cross St. Bernard Pass Army of Reserve cross by way of Simplon—and felt lead encase his guts as he thought about poor stuttering Berthier, best man in the world for running a staff, but in the field, O my God. He thought with disgust and resentment of *lui* back there in Paris being a political man now, silk slippers on feet going soft with carpets, lying full-length on a carpet poring over his maps, nice hot coffee on the table nearby, yawning into bed with that chestnut wife of his, faithless bitch but he's forgiven her. Going soft, is that it? Well, he'd better not go soft on this issue. Smuggle a message through somehow: Citizen First Consul, I put the possibility of our continued resistance at a maximum of fifteen days. Let him sort that out.

"WHAT did you say?"

"First département pay taxes full has best Paris square named after it." Talking in his sleep. Cannot help thinking of poor little Fortuné, friend from the old days.

"War. War between Treasury and Finance Ministry. Opposition makes security. Sixteen percent interest too much, damned usury."

And what's happened to poor Hippolyte? Well, *lui* was fair, a man in his position could have ruined him. Poor Fortuné. I loathe this pitch-darkness.

"Country must live within its means. Family too. Disgusting

extravagance." And then, sighing in his sleep with a kind of satisfaction, he flopped over her. He breathed hard in her face.

Breath bad. Eats too quickly. Stomach pains.

"Strvgnce."

God, if he knew, but he will know. He'll come charging round the garde-robes, looking. Six hundred new hats in one month. And the army contracts, *cheating my army*. But everybody does it.

Poor little Fortuné's wet nose nuzzling in the dark. Am I happy now? Dull people coming to the Tuileries, little blue tickets in their hands, as to a museum. And Thérèse Tallien living with that man now, never see her. Everything changed.

"Change everything. Breed decent women, cook, sew, good wives. Fascination, charm—not enough. Solid Frenchwomen, fully clothed."

For me, is it, that? Let me see, it could be rather charming, mold the figure, puffed sleeves, suggest more, show less.

"Divorce? Ah no, too easy a way out. Too many divorces since the Revol. Solid marriages, tolerance."

He woke suddenly. If little Fortuné had been there, it would have started him barking. Pains. Ugh, arrrgh, ow.

"Damned partridges. What the, where the." He started bawling: "Eh, eh, eh!" A candle at the door. "Time is it?"

Her pressed watch said five, ghastly hour.

"Roustam, black devil, wake everybody. Hot bath. Work to do."

She went to sleep then, dreaming of Hippolyte, Fortuné licking her, saying woofing, "Happy now? Happy now, eh?"

"Not happy at all," Bourrienne said. "Not if they read this report of General Marescot." He handed it down to the First Consul who, on his belly, was swimming his way from map to map.

"Season of the year still early for the major passes. Snow, ice, glaciers. Thrilling, Bourrienne, yes? First time in history to cross them with artillery, caissons and so on. Avalanches bury whole battalions in an instant. Fire guns to bring them down, he says. March in moonshine. Effect of drinking snow water on troops' digestions. He recommends vinegar. A good man, Marescot. So." He sat back on his heels, grunting a little. Putting on weight, Bourrienne saw. Bourrienne waited, watching, seeming almost to hear the click of the balls of some hidden abacus. The First Consul crawled to a map, looked at it for five minutes unspeaking, then thrust his forefinger down among the blue veins and green blotches. "There, I'll engage him *there*. When we've crossed the Alps I'll engage him *there*." Bourrienne peered down.

"Marengo," he said. "Never heard of it." And then: "You, you say? You're going? But, with respect, think of all the work here. The estimate on art galleries to be gone through—"

"That will wait till I get back. What's the latest report from Genoa?"

"Nothing new. Fifteen days Massena said. That makes, as from now, let me see—"

"He must hang on longer. I'll need a month."

"They're shooting Genoese. Any grumbling group of four is shot on sight."

"Well, they're not eating Genoese, not yet. Poor devils," he said with no show of conviction. "Horse's guts and straw bread. Send a message telling Massena he must hang on. And add these words: *I leave at midnight.*"

"Midnight *tonight?*'"

"We'll see about that later. It's the *midnight* that's important. Gives a sense of urgency. Drama. A quick look now at that Bank of France prospectus."

CITIZENS Thiré, Carniet, Blondaux, Tiry and the rest, not forgetting the black-shock-headed giant Armoire, the great lake of Geneva in front of them, line after line after line of infantry and artillery and cavalry drawn up on the north shore, listened to him as he addressed them kindly from his nodding and bowing chestnut, riding up and down the ranks, the laky and glacial light making them squint (smell of ice ahead, there've been so many of these fucking rumors but now he's contradicting them and he should know). ". . . And I address you not as your commander-in-chief, but as a mere civilian adviser though I cannot recall my rank being removed. . . . Your task, soldiers, and I would whisper this if you could hear my whisper, lies closer to our own dear land of France than I would wish (I would whisper because the enemy is always listening). . . . The Austrians have crossed the River Var and so threaten the homeland. . . . How happy I would be if I could say to you that we intend to meet the enemy in Italy, but, alas, the *patrie* is in danger. . . . News came recently that your brave comrades starving in Genoa have reached the limit of their endurance . . . the way is open, the hordes will pour in. . . . Courage, defiance, defend France. . . ."

A good act, General Lannes thought, a good piece of untruth. The Austrians will be swilling it all down.

Some of the troops cried *vive vive*, others, more experienced, *you can't believe a fucking word they tell you.* The battalions marched off while the drums rattled and the flutes screamed *O come ye children of the motherland the sun of glory fills the sky*, and then it was back to GHQ for a mountain of paperwork, true orders. Message of encouragement for Massena's ADC to take back: army is all on the march, you are in difficult position but at least you're in Genoa not being hacked to pieces, give the men plenty of sleep, good solvent of hunger. And then:

"Good God, a letter from Desaix."

"Desaix, sir?"

"Old comrade from Egypt. Poor devils. He got through the British blockade, we could do with him here. Tell him to join us at Ivrea—No, wait, I'll write myself."

Fifty thousand men of the Army of the Reserve to be moved over the Alps. Position on Great St. Bernard? Steep, deep in snow. The guns are the problem. General Marmont? Drag the guns, one hundred men to a gun, in improvised trough-sleds—tree-trunks hollowed out. Sleds on rollers. Pull the carriages to pieces and transport them in sections. Mules and men for the mountings of the eight-pounders. Send the wagons empty ahead. Good. Nine days rations and forty rounds for each man. Start in moonlight.

It was a murderous climb to the Col, cold as hell, ice on your whiskers, breathing like snuffing up a pair of scissors, your spittle turned solid, the wind like a million little flutes, the moon looking down sort of surprised at seeing a huge fucking chunk of its own landscape stuck down there. But right at the top we came to a kind of monastery, three old miles above sea level, with monks, not a bit fat and not a woman in sight though they may have hid them all away specially, giving us a blessing but a bit of bread and cheese as well and a swig of wine, nothing in it for them you'd think, but there must be a catch in it it stands to reason, and there were these big fluffy dogs panting away with little barrels on their chests which made us laugh to see, brandy in them for those they track half-dead in the snow, what will they think of next? Anyway, after that it was all downhill and we got away from the snow but now it was all this raging fucking torrent and slippery stones and us slithering down on our arses, and there the bastards of Austrians were ready for us in this little fort at Bard, as it's called, right on top of a rock right at the narrowest point of the valley, four hundred grenadiers they reckoned and God knows how many guns, and we had to creep through in the night, but it did no good, they got some of us and we had to run yelling back, and then it was a matter of a mule track and us clinging to the side of the mountain with our fucking fingernails. Join the army and see life.

"No luck with Fort Bard at all, the garrison is evidently dislodgeable. Met the situation before, Berthier, as you know, in Syria. The days of reducing garrisons are gone, waste of time, have to creep round them somehow. Now, Lannes was right, you agree? The mule track, Monte Albaredo. Paving the other way for the other divisions. A good man, Lannes, you think Lannes a good man?"

"A vvv—"

Berthier had seen with wonder the First Consul sliding and rolling down on his bottom, with some NCOs pulling his mule after him. Torn and wet but cheerful as he approached the headquarters bonfire, six miles or so north of Bard, pulling his wringing wet gauntlets off. "Well, old friend, this is better than being a glorified office boy, yes? Command in the field, taken some weight off you already." And he had given Berthier a hearty and affectionate kick in the puddings.

"I know what you're wondering about, Berthier—how to get the cannon through. Well, look at it logically. Mule track impossible, right? Therefore it has to go through the village of Bard, right under the Austrians' snouts. How? Nighttime, obviously. There's not much moon and there's plenty of cloud. Drag the guns through the village at night."

"But the nnn—"

"Exactly, the noise. Get the men gathering horse-shit, cowshit, straw, plenty around, I've seen it. Spread it on the streets, Berthier. Muffle the wheels in old rags. Think of it." A visionary gleam. "The biggest army in history to cross the Alps. *With heavy artillery*." He gave Berthier's guts three finger-jabs, one for each word. Then he smiled at the staff, gathered round the map-table. "I always," he said simply, "wanted to cross the Alps."

It was a meager dinner—a bit of stewed mountain goat—but the wine was good. The First Consul drank it unwatered, alone with Berthier, and he monologuized about Egypt. "We've experienced the extremes, old friend, the desert, the mountains, all the degrees of the thermometer. Remember the little shrine you built, dedicated to your Giuseppina? At the time that my Giuseppina—" The great eyes darkened, the mouth drooped. "Oh, she was living a life of chastity then, it was just the disclosure, the belated horrid disclosure. Best to forget these things, Berthier," slapping him hard on the knee as though Berthier were insisting on remembering. "Desaix, you remember Desaix? A good man, yes?"

"A vvv—"

And if he was such a good man, why had he left him in Egypt? Berthier remembered that if they had called *lui* the Great Sultan they had called Desaix the Just Sultan—*Sultan El-Adel.* Never made much of himself, a conscientious and self-effacing harrier of Turks and Mamelukes, with never enough guns, never more than about three thousand men, brilliant really. Was he too good a man to have out of Egypt? Well, he was out now and was on his way to Italy. *Lui* was going to use him. A little bemused by the strong wine in this region of rare air, Berthier wondered if there were any difference, in the new language that *lui* was making, between *use* and *use up.*

"I shall be glad to use him, Berthier."

THE physician Corvisart walked with her in the garden at Malmaison. "A haven," he said, "I can see that. Here you must lose your Tuileries headaches."

"Oh, they persist. They drive me frantic sometimes. Your pills help a little." Corvisart nodded to himself: bread, that's all they are, bread. Hypochondria, melancholy, look for some malady of the mind. It was well-known that guilt could be at the root of twitches, pains in the joints, megrims.

"The scent of your roses is delicious."

"What we have to learn," she said, with sudden animation, "is how to combine scent and color with longevity."

"Yes yes, I see that—creative occupation, a great solvent of melancholy. And charming, yes. Rose is your true name, is it not? You perpetuate yourself, in a manner." She looked at him. "You can speak freely with me, madame, as you know well. You know, and I know, that there is no Lupercalian magic in the waters of Plombières—"

"Luper— What is that word?"

"The feast of Lupercal in Rome. The ritual whipping of the barren. The magical promotion of fertility. Caesar's wife, as you will know from your reading—"

It was a sky of most tender blue. She looked up at it, he admired the delicacy of the chin, the slenderness of the neck. A young woman still. A myriad blooms nodded in chorus.

"I know," she said, "all Paris knows, that I gave him cause for—"

"We ought not to use the word 'infidelity.' He is a man, a soldier, restless, importuned by the adoring. He loves you most dearly, he says this to all. What you, however, feel is that, with a child, his and yours—though, of course, he adores, as is well-known, his stepchildren—that if he should become a father—"

"I feel," she said, ceasing to walk, facing him in woman's gravity, "that he may be trying to find out if the fault, if the barrenness, is really his. He is in a position, as a poet might put it, to scatter his seed wildly."

Corvisart grinned inwardly at the image. The First Consul as fertility god, a wandering Priapus. But it was true: a great man was expected to scatter bastards abroad, very much abroad in this instance—Italy, Egypt. War, some mad philosopher had written, long since guillotined, reading one of his own little books with scholar's pleasure as he walked toward the impending blade, war might be an instrument of, what was his term?—of *exogamia*.

"You have proved, madame, the tangible and delightful proof is in your son and daughter—"

"I am still of childbearing age, am I not? I have, you say, no symptom of premature, premature—what is the word?"

"The term we use is 'menopausis,' a word of two Greek elements. No, if, as you tell me, the menses continue to be regular." Then he wondered how much more to say. The consequences of an infraction of the marital code could, as if morality resided in nature and not in the imposed and arbitrary decalogues of theocrats, be an unsuspected physical morbidity. Thou shalt not get drunk, said the crapula. Thou shalt not fall into the arms of the dashing hussar whose arms have been too often open, said the— Said the what? Said the lesser disease of love which, mere transitory agony in a man, could in a woman be the cause of an unseasonable sterility. Or so some hypothetized. He had best keep the hypothesis to himself. "The thing to do," he said, as he gently steered her by the elbow towards a blazing bed of carnations, "is to be cheerful and believe that all will be well. We know that the belief is not always, nor indeed often, fulfilled, but the optimistic stance is our best sustainer. I think, though, there is little point in your continuing your excursions to Plombières." Ironically, if the tales were true, and they were, of course they were, it was the road to and from Plombières that had brought her to this state.

"He's unfaithful to me, and it makes me unhappy. A husband should be faithful, whatever the loftiness of his rank in the state."

And a wife, and a wife, even in retrospect. "It is the animal in us, madame," he sighed. "It is nature, that Rousseau taught us was all good. He meant, presumably, for himself."

MILAN again: it seemed an age since those brazen and argent and aureate bells had crashed a welcome to this victor. Fallen like a thunderbolt, he had written to Joseph, and thunderbolts of sound (those humming particles, what was their scientific cause, the acoustic science had perhaps not been given its due in the *Institut*) fell and fell with a ponderousness mocked by the myriad blossoms thrown, the polychrome rain of petals. Well, a thunderbolt was right. Sixty-six thousand troops in Northern Italy now, having conquered the agonies of the Alpine passes, and the enemy was still incredulous. Melas's line was overspread, a fragile arc about Turin, and here we were thickening, concentrating, a lively bubbling broth ready to pour and scald. Why Milan, Berthier had wished to know. Why not proceed to the relief of Genoa? Because, dear old friend, the aim in war is not to comfort one's friends, however dear and old, but to harass one's enemies. And the Austrians would soon let Genoa free from the clamp when they knew that their line of communications along the Po's north bank was as good as slashed to ribbons. They had got out of Milan quickly enough, leaving only a small garrison in the citadel that Murat was prompt to start smoking out. And now such a treasury of abandoned guns and supplies. Indeed, everywhere in this sector: Lannes had found between three and four hundred cannon, siege and field, complete with carriages, in Pavia of all places. Four guns captured at Ivrea, those besieging the Fort of Bard ought to be here soon, surely that garrison has at last yielded. The First Consul set himself up in cool baroque splendor and poured the orders out till amanuensal pencils smoked, broke, wore down to a stub.

"—And Duhesme seizes the Lodi bridge—back to the bridge, it seems an age since—and Murat and Boudet proceed to Piacenza and make a bridgehead over the Po and Lannes marches to Belgiosi to find a suitable crossing-point for the army to move on Stradella, Stradella is the true key, and when Moncey's corps reaches us here it is to be incorporated in a division we shall newly form under Gardanne."

"News that Bard has fallen, sir."

"And about time too. Good, that means more artillery. Take a note to General Lannes, say I am convinced that the Austrians will move on Stradella, I will not be satisfied until I learn that there are at least twenty thousand men at Stradella."

"It is neary time, sir, for your conference with the Milanese clergy."

And, demure as a bishop's chaplain, he faced two hundred tough priests in a vaulted hall full of holy statues, saying:

"Our immediate mission, as you will understand, your reverences, is to protect our own homeland, forestalling an Austrian invasion of France here in this beautiful country whose language I may claim as my own. That you, like your fellow-citizens, have no love of the arrogant Austrian may be regarded as a matter of little relevance to the purpose of this, our informal assembly. As a child of the Revolution I must naturally come under suspicion as a votary of atheism or rationalism or pantisocracy or deism or some other upstart negation or perversion of the faith that I, like you, reverend fathers, sucked in at the maternal breast. Be it known, then, that the France I serve as its unworthy First Consul will soon see fully restored the entire apparatus of an organized Church, for man cannot live without God. Regard me as the friend of your faith, its earnest promoter—"

Applause applause applause. Encouraged, he continued:

"We are all the children of the one God. We in France have made many changes—erected a state in which privilege is outlawed, talent rewarded, science set to work for man's comfort and enlightenment—but we are not a new breed of beneficent monsters. We hold fast, after a period of understandable confusion, to the beliefs that—" A grave-faced aide appeared at the end of the hall, saluted, remained standing. Bad news, urgent. Bring this to a. "Respecting the holy prophet, worshipping Allah—" He caught puzzled looks. Wrong country, wrong religion. "—the pagan Egyptians may yet see the light." Got over that difficulty. "Think of us as missionaries. The armies of France will bring that light to the benighted. And here, in the country of light, we are all soldiers of Christ." Applause but also murmurs. He marched out, the aide preceding him to the malodorous Milanese day.

"General Murat has captured dispatches of General Melas. To the Aulic Council in Vienna. Genoa has fallen."

"Nonsense, a mistake. A mistranslation."

"General Massena requested negotiations at the very moment that General Melas decided to abandon the siege."

"O God, no no no. That fool Massena. He could have hung on. Cannibalism, anything. A traitorous act. O Jesus Christ." Some emerging priests nodded approval at the piety. "And now that means they'll use Genoa as an operating center. The fucking British navy out there. Get us at Stradella. God curse the fucking idiot." Aware of the priests, he kept that low.

AFTER her performance at La Scala, he took La Grassini to bed. A superbly fleshed woman, though perhaps a little more than four years ago when he, ardent bridegroom, had admired more or less or only, hard to remember now, ocularly, aurally. She said:

"*Ipocrita. L'ultima volta che eri a Milano combinavi l'ateismo con una riverenza superstiziosa per il sacramento del matrimonio.*" She repeated the last word in an improvised cadenza. She liked to try out odd words in song, even during a discussion about the price of meat. He felt the vibration possess the flesh under his arm. "*Adesso fai il pio, predichi ai preti e ti abbandoni agli adulteri del soldato. Ipocrita.*"

"*No, amore mio.*"

"*Ipocriiiiiiiiiiita!*" Portamento up to high mi-flat, then down again.

"*No,*" he said. "*Imparo a essere,*" smiling, "*politeista. A Parigi ho la mia dea ufficiale e qui qui qui—*" The *qui* meant first Milan, then the bed, then her person, a prodding forefinger for each. "*—l'oggetto vero della mia venerazione amorosa.*"

She pouted and snuggled into his armpit. "*Perché perdo il mio tempo con te? Con teeeeeeeee? A letto non vali molto.*" No whit abashed, he smiled onto her hair. "*Nessuna tenerezza, non un briciolo di pazienza. Sarà che raccolgo la sfida. Devo insegnarti a amare. Venere ha insegnato a Marte.*" A pleasant idea, though somewhat operatic. Or something for a painting, for that man David. "*Ma tu sei troppo instabile. Vattene pure a Stradella a sconfiggere gli austriaci, e subito dopo tornatene pure in Francia.*"

The cuckold always had a reward. A great man always had a mistress. Oh, many. He kissed her nape and said:

"*Tornarmene in Francia, sì, ma non senza di te.*" He would get Bourrienne to arrange everything, first thing in the morning. "*Non ti tenterebbe di andare a Parigi?*" She turned her face to his, great eyes searching great eyes. "*Un appartamentino in rue de la Victoire?*" For, after all, they weren't living there anymore: it was *made* for a mistress.

"*Accetto,*" she smiled and kissed him.

The act that followed took rather less time than sixteen bars of an aria in moderate tempo.

"Eat more," General Ott said in French. "Goulash. Fried chicken. Baked potatoes."

Massena said: "I cannot. The stomach shrinks. The stomach revolts. A little at a time. Some sugared water perhaps."

"You did well, I want you to know that. We know how to appreciate a brave enemy. You will find us generous."

"You're being generous now." And he surveyed again the loaded table, a dream to the starving man he still was. Also an old man now. Age, then, was like a revolution: it jumped on one. He had gone to bed with the hair of youth and awoken gray. But the men were worse, many of them now grotesque figures for a *Totentanz*, to use the enemy's word, crying with rage as the food they leapt on revolted in contact with very teeth and saliva and leapt out as if still alive. And then there were the true cadavers with vast stuffed bellies. The entering Austrians had been kindly cruel wheeling in their sides of beef and sacks of potatoes. One recovered but slowly from starvation. It was more needful to send in soothing orderlies bearing bouillon and weak syrup. He sipped some weak syrup. It stayed down without grumbling.

"*Zurückbeförderung in die Heimat*," Ott mumbled, reading from a dispatch. "*Repatriierung*. We place your force beyond the River Var."

"It will take some little time before my men are capable of — Such as are left." And he was thinking, weak as he was, that this was some help to that reserve army, wherever it should be, since Ott's forces would be held down here during the complex negotiations.

"You will think it ironic," Ott said, "that we permit you to resume combatant status when you are returned to the homeland. You have no combatants. You are weak as if you were prisoners."

"We're both soldiers," Massena said. "Tell me as a soldier what you think your chances are."

"You will have heard of this Reserve," Ott said, "as some great new force of salvation. Believe me, it is a disaster. Generals without talent—"

That would be poor Berthier.

"—Blunderbusses for artillery, bayonets stuck on poles, donkeys for cavalry. I am not now using to you the words of artful demoralization. France is beleaguered—British ships in the Channel, our own forces on the Rhine. You have no resources, you are bankrupt. All this must you know already."

"General Massena," Massena said bitterly, "in command of the Army of Italy. *Repatri—* Whatever your word was. It's the damned waste, we've just rolled back to things as they were five years ago."

"Oh, one never worries about that. We concentrate on operations, not policy. We take and lose the same town fifty times. It's a trade, no more."

They'll never learn, Massena thought, and then felt brighter. Sugar sparking gently through the blood.

A chief of men and not a chief of staff
Is what you need to wage successful battles.
If Bonaparte's the wheat, this man's the chaff:
No marble here but only clay and wattles.
A sort of wife, though not a better half,
He flusters fast, his reason rocks and rattles:
That's Louis Alexandre Berthier,
Who'll fight a war with paper any day.

To build a bridge upon the River Po,
He pores upon a map that's out of date,
Whereon each inch is sixteen miles or so—
Quite adequate for 1668.
The loaded sappers take their tools and go
And look upon a kind of Bering Strait.
Their language, uninhibited and horrent,
Is mercifully swallowed by the torrent.

Lannes and Murat moan about the rations
And wonder when the d———d things will arrive.
The lack of rounds arouses Boudet's passions:
There's thirty-two per man, not sixty-five.

The troops indulge in groans and dental gnashings
And wonder how in G——s name they'll survive.
Only the kindly calm of their First Consul
Quietens the stomach and deflames the tonsil.

THE rain was unseasonable and heavy on Stradella. The First Consul was red-nosed and tearful with a cold, chewing aniseed and licorice comfits to soothe his throat, leaving licorice fingerprints on dispatch after dispatch. His speech was somewhat denasalized as he greeted Desaix, thin, burnt, wearing the dark odor of Egypt as Dante had been said to wear that of Hell. "By dear friedd," or something like it, he said. "You are cobe id the dick of tibe." Roustam brought salt in, recognized the Just Sultan and showed him thirty-two teeth in greeting. The First Consul or merely Great Sultan mixed salt with water and snuffed some up, going aaarkh and waaaargh and spluttering. The nasals were shocked into reappearing.

"Egypt. Was it all then a waste of time and men and money and talent?" He had his own answer to give. "No, it was not. If nothing else comes out of Egypt there will be a beautiful book, many volumes, in a sense my child. And the whole of that past lost language recovered."

"By the British," Desaix said. "By the British."

"Well, scholarship knows no boundaries. And history will tell the truth."

"Whose history, whose? And," Desaix added, "does anyone want the whole truth? Whom does it ultimately profit?"

The First Consul knew what he was thinking of; he looked at him warily. "We must take our chance," he said. "For my part, I feel I control history. In a sense. I've been thinking of school curricula. In the reign of Charlemagne surely there is enough for any child to study—to gain an image, that is to say, of the true nature and destiny of France. Don't you agree?"

"Men crucified on a cartouche," Desaix said irrelevantly. It was a phrase which he now seemed to have been waiting to deal, a good phrase nursed through the blockades and the rocky journey to Stradella. The First Consul said:

"You've become a poet. A *bulbul* or whatever their word is. Well, you didn't become a Muslim. Not," he smiled, "like poor Menou."

"Abdullah they were calling him. He married a barber's daughter."

"Nothing wrong in that," the First Consul smiled. "He took everything a little too seriously perhaps—democracy as well as Islam."

"How seriously," and Desaix was stern, "is one to take things?"

The First Consul weighed that, his head inclined to a map, his eyes turned up to Desaix. "Generalship," he said. "One plays to win."

"Cheats? Lies?"

"*Well, of course!*" The First Consul was astounded. "All our strategy is based on lies. The enemy slumbers through a lie and then wakes up to the truth. The point in war is to say something, truth or lie. The Austrians are saying nothing. They should by now be attacking. I don't know Melas's intentions. This worries me."

"You will have to provoke him."

"*Provoke*—that's the word. Now, as to your place in our scheme. I'm giving you an army corps—Boudet's and Monnier's divisions. Victor will take over Gardanne's division to brigg his corps back to stredgth." The salt douche was wearing off. "Dabded code."

And damned rain rain rain as they advanced to the river Scrivia, then crossed it, the light cavalry finding no trace of the enemy, rain rain rain. "Avoiding action," he said. "Austrian swine." He had bullied his cold into being better. But the rain was dispiriting. He sent out a flurry of orders—Desaix to move with Boudet's division towards Rivalta and cut the main road from Genoa to Alessandria: Melas must not be allowed to fall back on Genoa; Monnier to come up into central reserve; Lapoype to be ready for a march on Valenza, join up with Chabran's force, prevent the enemy from cutting the French line of communication by pushing towards Milan. But no sign of Melas, Melas was avoiding a battle. At Marengo, only a few thousand of the Austrian rearguard quick, when Victor and Gardanne advanced on them, to yelp off towards Alessandria. He shouted, went into a spasm of coughing, shouted again:

"This damned plain is the only damned plain in Italy where he can put his cavalry to work. Why doesn't he come? Where the hell is he?"

He is here, said a bright Sunday morning after a night of peering for Austrian camp fires. The men heard guns in their sleep. They awoke: it was no dream. Guns hammered, larks soared. The First Consul, licoricing out a faint benignant indigestion (chicken, oil, crayfish, eggs: last night's dinner, bizarre multiple trophy of the foragers), was a flame at Torre-di-Garofoli. "Aggression, I asked for his aggression, a statement, a word, but I did not really expect it. The Austrians are not acting like Austrians." A hundred cannon, the galloping intelligence made it, three columns of some ten thousand each. Narrow bridgehead though on right bank of the Bormida, Melas following false report of French at Cantalupo, detaching cavalry. But five guns only for Gardanne and Chambarlhac of Victor's corps, shielding Marengo behind the Fontanove. "A bluff," he shouted, "a cover. Melas is withdrawing to Genoa."

"Or to the Po."

"Or to the. Lapoype's division to march north towards Valenza—"

"That drops us three-and-a-half thousand."

"I know what I'm doing, blast you. Send a quick message to Desaix. Boudet's division to make for for for Pozzolo Formigioso. Sounds like the smell of cheese when you say it quickly." Calmed them down: humor.

With the sun well up he rode to the scene and saw more

clearly the peril. Had his intuition then been wrong? Lannes and Murat were now supporting Victor's corps—fifteen thousand, about half the Austrian force. A division under Watrin, to the right of the village, was being hacked by Melas's own column. Ott, over from Genoa, was as good as in control of Castel Ceriolo to the northeast. So the only thing to do was to send ADCs after Lapoype and Desaix, calling them back. *For God's sake come up if you still can.* The Austrians regrouped, flexed, took breath. Watrin's division was in ribbons. The Consular Guard moved up, all nine hundred of it. The final reserve, a division under Monnier, moved on to Ott and Castel Ceriolo. A matter of time time time. The First Consul lashed his leg again and again with his whip. "Hold on, a matter of time." Twenty-three thousand Frenchmen were pushed staggering back to San Giuliano, miles east of Marengo. It was three in the afternoon.

"He must," he divined, "believe they have the victory. Who said he was wounded?"

"Melas, sir? It came through the lines. You know how these things get put about."

"They're regrouping. Columns. All this damned smoke."

"General Desaix, sir."

The massive breast of the First Consul took in and gave out a whole carboy of air. Desaix, panting, all mud. The relief.

"The river was swollen. I got your message at one o'clock. Three minutes to."

"Thank God the river was swollen. What do you think of it all?"

"Quiet. Ominously so. You've lost a battle."

"We," the First Consul said, "*we* have lost a battle."

"*We*," Desaix said, "have time to win another." And his stomach fell within him: *we* were what survived: he foresaw in an instant, and he could neither exactly formulate nor explain it to himself, *you* and *I* being silently removed from a marble field by weeping draped female figures. Was *we* merely the surviving ghost of *I*? Was *I* a brushed-off cell-flake or dead hair of *we*?

"No more retreating. I must address the troops." And he mounted, five-and-a-half feet of him, small, even dainty, that huge tank of air he bore above his ribs some extraneous property of myth, and rode off to dispense issues of charm, simple stirring rhetoric, words like *comrades, bravery, France, we.*

Lapoype, then, had not received his message, but it would not matter. Marmont thumped and tore with his eighteen cannon at the solid column Melas, tired, wounded, confident, had handed over to his chief of staff Zach, and the column groaned and staggered. Desaix led his brigades into the smoke to meet with shock a white-jacketed battalion of fresh and ready grenadiers. But Marmont hurled four salvoes, close range, and, an unhoped-for gift, a whole ammunition wagon exploded to yells and panic. Kellermann wheeled in with four hundred cavalry against the left flank of the column of six thousand. It wavered, shuddered, broke. Time, history, wavered, shuddered, *a minute sooner or three minutes later and it could not,* broke, *have succeeded.*

See it. Is that green smoke or are those trees?
In the right foreground the plumed generals prance,
While brassarded Lejeune leads prisoners.
The solid cruppers of the mounts are answered
By broken skeletons of limber wheels.
A cannon shoots its flower, and frozen smoke
Opens a horse's mouth in shock forever.
In graceful postures men lie wounded. There,
The Consul, in left foreground, shows his staff
The things it can already see: a forest
Of flustered enemy, of tangled horses,
Of shouts and totterings and crazed dismay.
High in the high left corner shadowy
But hideously substantial lines of French
Move in geometry, unwavering parallels
That meet at the horizon. But, there, see
Desaix already struck, a graceful fylfot
Who'll fall this second yet will never fall.

So cunning is the art that the substantial
Masses lead the eye to him, and he
Is nothing, the expendable, the faceless.
He needs no face, being about to die.

Germaine de Staël said, "Carnot? Moreau?" Her drawing room was delicious—honey and cream, but toothsome not melting.

"They fail somehow," Talleyrand said, "to capture the imagination." He limped restlessly about the room, his hands behind him. Suddenly, like a lizard's tongue, an arm would shoot out and long mobile fingers engage a bibelot. He would give it to his eyes for some seconds—a porcelain cherub, a silver Hermes—as though his eyes were a nose and it was a nosegay—and then put it by impatiently, as though the handling had been forced upon him.

"The Duc d'Orléans?"

"You see," he said, facing her squarely, though twisted, "the whole anomaly of the situation lies in the fact that France palpitates over his living or dying. The solidity of his allure lies in the insolidity of his physical future. Set a man on the throne and surround him with sweetmeats and mistresses—a fat hulk blessing everybody from his gold carriage, chewing— You see the problem?"

She saw herself in a gilt mirror an instant—handsome and thirty-four, the face fascinatingly tortured by the contrary tuggings of reason and passion—and, since the mirror was wide enough, set the First Consul's image beside hers. What a pair they would make, would have made. It was the way of such men, to fall for the swaying languor of such as that one, empty except for dreaming of flowers and lovers. She said:

"I see it all all too clearly," somewhat deep and cooing. "Intolerable. Everything set on the turn of a battle. But if he dies, if he is dead already—"

I mourn him as I mourn a brother. Brilliant in battle, good and just as a man, a most virtuous citizen. Had he lived, who knows what heights he might not have scaled?

Sieyès said, "The talk, you see, of his being made First Consul for life presupposes a disaffection with the republican philosophy. They are all reading of Cromwell these days. And then your Cromwell dies and you have an incompetent inheritor. Why not turn Bonaparte into General Monk while your, or their, hand is in? I tell you, we will come back to a kind of monarchy."

Those who listened, mostly men in old Enlightenment wigs, nodded and took more of his wine. There was the matter, for some of them still, of tracing the point at which his direct line to power had been somehow allowed to shift or deviate, so that he was, despite everything, now really nothing. One of them said:

"But if he is killed? In battle, that is?"

The highest position in the Army of the Republic and, who knows, with such virtue, such integrity as he displayed in Egypt, might not he have evinced a genius for civil rule second to none? Anyway, let it be set on record that I mourn him before proceeding to rejoice in the victory which he so signally helped to achieve, and, should any pictorial representation of this sad moment be ever effected, let tears be depicted rolling down my cheeks.

The telegraphs flashed and clanked across the summer skies of France and set the bells to clashing, such as had not become cannon. Marengomarengomarengomarengo. Across the meadows at Auteuil the message came in silvery hosannas almost drowned by the sunset swallows. Talleyrand grinned.

"All conditionals. If if if. And now he comes back trampling on our ifs."

"Fifteen Austrian colors captured," someone read from the *Moniteur*. "Forty guns."

"Eight thousand Austrian prisoners," over his shoulder. "Six thousand dead."

"Number of French dead?"

"Not stated here," smiling. "But undoubtedly infinitesimal."

"Let us not," said an exquisite, "fill a lady's drawing room with such gore and carnage. War really is disgusting."

"I foresee," Germaine said, "a period of repressive autocracy. The mob will just beg to be trodden on."

"Oh, the mob will do well," Talleyrand said. "It is the position of the intellectual that must be in doubt. Such," with a hint of smugness, "as have not rendered themselves in some way or another indispensable. Bluestockings," he said with open malice, "are in his view—" He was about to say *a sort of hermaphroditic anomaly*, but that would have been, considering the rumors about her *longitudo clitoralis*, to say the least indiscreet.

"He told me once," she said, "and loudly and defiantly too, that women are for the bedroom and the kitchen. I foresee for myself," she said, surveying her exquisite drawing room with regret, the exquisites that filled it with less regret, "a period of exile."

"Constructive exile one hopes," Talleyrand said.

"Switzerland is a pleasant enough country. Sanctified by the memories of Rousseau and Voltaire."

"I shall stay," Talleyrand said. "I shall outstay him. I find it hard to envisage a Bonaparte grown old."

WATER WAS THE ENEMY. IN HIS DREAM HE WAS CROSSING THAT Italian river in his carriage, and it was deeper than he had thought, and the horses slithered on the slimy bottom and panicked as they went deeper and the water had begun to fill the carriage (a sort of stupidly irrelevant annoyance as he foresaw the cushions made filthy with green slime and water-weeds) and his own panic rose. He fought his way up out of the dream now, finding himself in a dry and clean coach thundering across the

Place du Caroussel. César the coachman was reckless tonight, mad. Drunk, of course. The new calendar had never quite driven out the old. Everyone had always known tonight was, despite the Goddess of Reason, really Christmas Eve.

He remembered now where they were going. So damnably sleepy. A long day, a doze by the log-fire, early bed. But at the Opera House they were to perform Haydn's *Creation.* A religious oratorio, see how far they had come, able now to tolerate, unthinkable under the Jacobins, a celebration of God's making the world out of nothing. He had looked in one day, no activity beyond his interest or patronage, to hear the orchestra rehearsing what they called, with some justice, The Representation of Chaos. Modern music. He liked something with a tune. A clarinet or some such instrument snaked up out of the depths like life coming up out of the primordial slime. Well, she wanted to hear the work. And Hortense. "Oh come, sweetheart, don't always be dozing by the fire like an old old man. See how beautiful Hortense and I have made ourselves." He could not hear nor, looking now out of the rear window, see their carriage. It must be well behind. Woman-like, she had thought of some last-minute change of ornament or shawl. He, First Consul for Life, must gallop ahead, complete with retinue of grenadiers.

Rue Saint-Nicaise. Some recognized the coach, waved and cheered. He leaned out to smile and wave back. The street lighting could be better here, there must be some sort of estimate made out on the cost of improving street lighting. Good lighting deterred crime. Leaning out, he saw with surprise and annoyance a horse and cart set along the street, partly blocking free passage. What was needed was a sort of street or traffic police: streets and roads were arteries of civilized life. The drunk mad César did not, as he might have done, pull up and curse the owner of the horse and cart. Instead he dared the narrowness and rushed through to the rue de la Loi. Some sort of cask or barrel on the cart there.

The street exploded. *Representation of Chaos*: in a minute pellucid bubble of his brain the connection was made, the gross image of unity allowed to flash. If we have missed the opening we have had reality not art here. But the connection with battle after battle was not made, though this was artillery onslaughts made crude and raw. It was a matter of there not being space or air. The instant of impossible noise sealed his ears from the noises that followed—screams of women and children, a whole street turned to fuming rubble, that horse with its cart and cask commingling in the undifferentiability of chaos, splinters and bits of hot soft gut floating high in the smoke and reluctant to descend. He was firm, he noted, in his descending from the coach whose door had flown open, César miraculously unstruck, let me never preach against drunkenness again, to see much and hear nothing. The grenadiers were in their saddles still, pricking leaping mounts till the blood came. There was a woman alive screaming with a flat expanse of black blood where her breasts should be. The carriage behind was safe, thank God for the vanity that made women late, but the rabid horses had been released from their shafts and danced about the street as though it were a circus, soundless mouths whoaing them. She was dead, no, in a faint, unhurt, God bless and preserve her vanity. Hortense stared at blood welling from her hand. Caroline had then, at the last minute, joined them, big-bellied and near her time, pumping out sobs, holding her freight with desperation, think not only of the dead but of the yet unborn. Sound and control returned, the street bloomed into noise, he held out two unwavering arms to his wife, but then control was ousted by madness. He heard in great surprise his childhood dialect return and in that tongue he cursed and vowed with a terrible clarity. None understood yet all understood.

WITH a terrible clarity. Cambacérès and Lebrun listened. They knew it was the Corsican coming out, vendettas and so on, blood flowing anywhere so long as it flowed, terrible revenge, nine innocent dead, there must be nine known royalists or suspected royalists or known or suspected enemies of the Permanent First Consul executed summarily. Lebrun said:

"In our righteous anger let us not forget the Constitution—"

"To hell with the Constitution. And I see few enough signs of righteous anger in your your your. Like puddings, you sit like puddings in a shop."

"The courts will take care of the criminals," Cambacérès said. "They will be tried and guillotined. That is what the courts are for." Like puddings, indeed. "They," he explained patiently, "are the judiciary while we are the executive. The executive has no power under the Constitution to—"

"This is war. This is the Bourbons hitting at the Republic. On the field of battle there is no invoking of the Constitution. And there are generals tied up in it. How about this swine Pichegru? How about Moreau, lapdog of that bluestocking bitch who keeps plotting against me? What are we going to do with them all, eh? Wait till they kill a few more innocent women and children? Wait till they blow my family to pieces?" His fellow-consuls both noted that he did not think in terms of himself actually being assassinated; there would always be someone else in the way.

"If I may say this," Lebrun said, "there is a certain constitutional irregularity in your setting up what seems to be your own police force. One recognizes your anxiety—"

"Look, gentlemen—" He gave it to them fierce and hissing, swiveling his head from each to other, burning them each in rapid turn with his hot mad rational eyes. "The essence of a secret police organization is secrecy. They have to act fast without warrants. Call it irregularity if you wish, but what is that irregularity compared with the filthy murderous ingratitude of the Bourbons? I've done everything, everything. Forty thousand émigrés welcomed back, given money, my own money, my wife's money, anything for peace and amity. And what do they do? Look, gentlemen, I'll meet any of them fair and square, but I won't have this massacring of the innocents. I mean, I don't mind dying, but not yet, not just yet, the clock hasn't been properly wound yet. Five years, say, and they can have me if they want me. *But not now.*"

"English money," Cambacérès said. "Thousands of pounds involved. The English are financing these little—"

"Little? *Little?* Forty brigands loose in Paris. I'll make them shed tears of blood, the swine. I'll teach the bastards to legalize murder."

"We must sometime consider the question," Lebrun said, "of the succession. We must be realistic."

"Whose succession? What succession? This is a republic not a monarchy."

"Realistic," Lebrun repeated with greater firmness. "The First Consulate is no longer an elective office. The closest precedent to our governmental system is to be found in England—"

"England, always back to perfidious England."

"The England of Cromwell. An hereditary executive, not monarchical, a republic incarnated in a family. Think of the alternatives—the Bourbons back, a military coup, Jacobinism."

"You're thinking of me dead. You must not think of me dead. I'm erecting a preventive machine that will ensure my survival. As for the Bourbons, they'll never be back, be quite sure of that, gentlemen. The machine is going to strike. Wait. You'll see."

"Nevertheless," Cambacérès said, "there is always the chance. The chance, shall I say," smiling, "of your choking on a chicken bone."

The Permanent First Consul was good-humored again. "I thank you for the warning. No chicken bones. I'll instruct my cook to that effect. No, ha ha, chicken bones."

Louis Antoine, Duc d'Enghien, prince of the House of Bourbon, picked the last of the meat off a turkey bone and threw the bone to Max, one of his beagles. Then he walked about his dining room, glass of Rhine wine flashing in the candles, seeing occasionally an erect young officer, long-nosed, in the tarnished mirrors. The news he had received from Strasbourg did not greatly perturb him. Georges Cadoudal had been arrested in Paris, having first shot one of the arresting policemen dead. He had talked, whether under torture had not yet been ascertained, but one naturally presumed under torture. "My assignment was to assassinate the First Consul only when a prince of the House of Bourbon was actually present in Paris. No such prince has yet arrived." Well, that meant an indefinite putting-off, a lying-low. That suited him well enough. He liked this life of woodcock-shooting in the woods around Ettenheim, all at English expense, a plump *Mädchen* most evenings, a quiet read of a French romance in bed. He was safe here in Germany. When the time came to strike he would strike. Whenever that time should come. And it would not be a matter of striking Bonaparte, already killed by others, but of striking a paralyzed government into immediate acceptance of a Bourbon restoration. There was much to look forward to.

He went to bed and reread *Paul et Virginie*, one of his sentimental favorites. He slept and dreamt that an army had entered his room and he awoke smiling at the absurdity of it. By his bed a uniformed general stood, armed soldiers with him, the noise of other troops on the stairs. He looked many times, blinking in the newly lighted candles, and then the apparition spoke. "General Ordener, citizen." Enghien gaped. "Or your grace, if you prefer. Be so good as to prepare for a journey. Your valet is already awake and dressed."

"French? What are the French doing here? This is not French territory."

"We're aware of a slight irregularity. We were discreet. We will be equally discreet going back."

"Back? Where?" He still lay, as though fascinated, under the thick quilt.

"To Vincennes. The château there. You are, citizen your grace, to consider yourself under arrest."

When, dressed, he had been escorted downstairs, he found all his private papers neatly stacked, with a sort of sergeant-clerk tying red ribbon around them. There was no sign of any servant except his trembling valet. The papers were handed by a captain to a dispatch rider who saluted, pouched the documents, and strode out. General Ordener courteously led Enghien to a coach waiting in the drive. The grounds seemed to be full of dragoons.

"I see. Clever. You've muffled the horses' hoofs."

"Discreet, as I said."

In the coach, Enghien said: "I suppose I needn't ask what the charge is."

"Disturbing the state by civil war and arming the citizens against one another or against lawful authority. Article Two of the Conspiracy Act."

"This is nonsense, of course."

"The citizen duke is not obliged to say anything now. There will be opportunity enough when the military court is assembled."

"Military court?"

"A tribunal of seven colonels."

"This is nonsense."

"As you wish."

Later, very much later, nearing Vincennes, Enghien said: "How would you feel in my position, scion of a butchered royal house? I've sworn hatred against this Bonaparte, rightly. I would otherwise be a traitor to my own kind. The French must be made to see their error. If arms are the only way—"

"You may as well take that down," Ordener said to his ADC in the dark corner opposite. The ADC wrote: *Sworn implacable and undying enmity to the lawfully*

"Just reprisal," he shouted, leaving his dinner untouched.

"But he has not yet been tried," she said.

"You keep your stupid woman's nose out of this." He sucked a licorice and aniseed comfit for his heartburn, staining the papers he held with bold black thumb-whorls. He read about Strasbourg, where Enghien had had his net, and a certain Francis Drake (some British seaman was not that also?), agent in

Munich, and Moreau the darling of bluestocking bitches and salon plotters, disaffection and jealousy, *imperative you eliminate Bonaparte*, letters of exchange in English pounds, and the acids swirled in him and stuck knives in his throat. "Treachery treachery. Fucking ingrates."

"It is not right that you use such language in my—"

"Treachery everywhere. I have not forgotten yours, woman."

"We had agreed to. You will not let it go. That fat Italian opera singer in the rue de la Victoire."

"I will do what I have to do. I will do things my own way."

"The servants sniggering at me."

"You brought it on yourself. Well, she has gone now. Taking my child with her to be born for all I know."

"That is cruel. That is inexcusable. That is."

"I'm not firm enough, I've always been too soft, too compassionate, easily melted. Well, not this time."

elected executive also against the whole of the French people upon whom he proposed

"I understand you," Cambacérès said, "better than you think. You are impelled by a logic that your ancestors did not question but which you, who have risen above your, if I may term them so, narrow origins, must examine and see for what it is and, in the light of cold justice, endeavor to transcend and—"

"Don't throw these big words at me, Cambacérès. His family strikes at mine, I strike at his in just reprisal. Let him go and the factions will be encouraged. I will end by having to kill the whole world."

Cambacérès heard more in that than Corse rhetoric. He shuddered.

to make war whenever occasion offered.

"Occasion offered," the presiding colonel read out. It was a fine cold March day at Vincennes; Enghien's eyes, rarely closed these last nights, smarted in the huge sharp light that beat through the high windows of the dining hall of the château. The blue-clad tribunal swam and dissolved in eye-water, not tears, never those.

"I did not quite say that. You must consider my position, my birth—"

"Irrelevant. You are a conspirator like any other. We are especially charged with the duty of reminding you of this."

"Charged by whom?" There was no answer. "Since you pause, permit me to have set on record the total illegality of my arrest. Permit me to counteraccuse your master of wretched and despicable cowardice. To invade a territory is one thing, to sneak into it like a parcel of thieves is another." He knew the cause was lost. "The technique is in character. Your master is a cheat, a bully and a coward."

The statement went unrecorded, but a member of the tribunal, a young colonel with a squashed nose, barked that the prisoner must take care.

"I see. The head of the executive is beyond criticism. This sounds very like old-fashioned despotism to me."

"Irrelevant," the president said. "To resume. You received money from a foreign power, an inveterate enemy of France—"

"That does not make me, myself, an enemy. France is my dear country, I have no quarrel with France—"

"A declared enemy of the Republic. You received a salary of four thousand two hundred guineas a year. You admit this?"

"—Only with the present government."

"Democratically elected. You declared war on France."

"If that is so, I demand the rights of a prisoner of war."

"What makes you think you are not being given those rights?"

"Prisoners of war are not usually executed. No—wait—there have been, under this new régime, instances of the execution of, nay, the massacre of—"

"Under Article Two of the Conspiracy Act—"

"I defer to the pattern. History will vindicate. The injustice will be remembered." Outside, on the gravel path, a man sang a kind of bugle-tune, following it with a presumed fart that sounded like the rip of calico. Two or three of the colonels smiled.

"The order of this court is—"

Was that he be shot. The first day of spring, he told himself as he was marched out. The chaplain muttered prayers for his sinful soul but he hushed him. The hopelessness he felt as he faced the squad was, he was sure, of a new order. There was nothing after this. No martyr's crown. Heaven had been canceled by some act of the Year One. God had been put to sleep like an old dog. No history, no vindication. He willed himself into a zero, uniting his will with the order to fire, the annihilating spatter. The last thing he fully saw was a cloud intricately shaped, full of capes and inlets, like some map of a territory visited but almost wholly forgotten. A building swallow flew with a heavy twig and dropped it. That came just too late for him to hold and consider the image. Then he was shaken out of his dream and shot at two in the morning. The enemy was full of surprises.

"Let us," Councillor Regnault said, "consider the true meaning of the word *imperium*." There were some groans. "Or, better, the word *imperator*." He gave what looked like a little curtsey in the direction of the consular platform. Only Lebrun and Cambacérès were present today; the chair they flanked could, however, be addressed, one might fancifully think, like a tabernacle. A tabernacle was, was it not, etymologically the tent of a general officer or *imperator*? "What I am trying to say," Regnault said, "is that there is no contradiction beween the republican and the imperial notions. We are not talking of the restoration of a *rex* but of the establishment of an *imperator*. It is all there in Roman history. The *imperator* is entrusted with the *imperium* on behalf of the people."

"How about the contract?" shouted somebody not clearly seen. There was usually somebody concerned about the contract. The question was not answered, but Regnault said:

"As for the hereditary element in the imperial office, it is understood that the First Consul has insisted to the Tribunate that the transmission of the title must be effected by popular vote." There were some cheers (spoken like a good republican). "Here we may see the crux exhibited."

"Strong numinous flavor about everything today," muttered Lebrun to Cambacérès across the empty or perhaps not empty chair.

"The will of the people, not, as in the old discredited metaphysic, the will of God."

"Talking about God," Tronchet said, "I find it very hard to envisage a republican coronation. I mean, he has to be crowned by somebody, and who is this somebody to be? Hardly himself. There has to be some sort of priest, representative so to speak of the abiding spirit of the republic. But we have no hierarchy. We have freedom of worship."

Cambacérès said: "One thing at a time. Let us not eat all our courses at once. Chew slowly. Soon, ha, some honorable councillor will be taking it on himself to discourse on the content of the coronation banquet."

"Leave that to you," some honorable councillor muttered.

"Oh," Regnault said, "is it not now all a matter of procedure? The whole of France is agreed on the necessity of protecting the life of our *dux* or *imperator* by the simple act of conferring immortality on him." Well put, the murmurs said. "There are some intransigents still, admittedly, who need to have it demonstrated to them that an emperor is not necessarily a king. I ask them again to look at Roman history—"

"Crown him," an intransigent said, Barsac or somebody, a man from the West who had mended the left leg of his spectacles with a kind of puce-colored cotton thread, "and he becomes a king. What's needed is a mere matter of signing a paper, something severe and very republican."

"A contract," that voice said.

"You mark my words," the intransigent said, "it will soon be just as it was before. You can transmit rule but you can't transmit talent. You could have some gibbering idiot on the throne or some head-lopping womanizer, just because he has the right family name. He ought to have a son, by the way—"

"How do you know he hasn't?" said the councillor next to him.

"A lot of Corsicans squabbling over France as if it were a brass bedstead. You mark my words."

There were loud cries of *withdraw withdraw* and the Second Consul had to bring the meeting to order. Soon Cambacérès had something to say about the Pope. He consulted a slip of paper and it was evident that these were the notes of somebody else, somebody absent. "There has to be a coronation and there has to be a priest. We want the best priest or, if you wish, the *chef* of priests. Who could that be but the Pope? Also consider that the papacy thus seems to bless and sanction the Republic and that it will give the whole of Catholic monarchist Europe something to think about. England too, for that matter. A sort of French victory over England."

"But will the Pope come?"

"Of course. Since the Concordat he can hardly say no. He sincerely loves France, he says."

There were a number of murmurs against the Pope. A slow-witted councillor who was a confirmed atheist said:

"Does this mean then that the contract will be signed *in a church*?"

"A solemn oath, not a contract. Of course a church. Where else? In the Opera House? On the Field of Mars? And not a church either but a cathedral. Incense, music, massed choirs and trumpets, a Te Deum, a pontifical high mass, everything. We must beat these monarchies at their own game."

The older councillors chewed over their excited bewilderment, remembering when naked women representing Reason or some such reasonable abstraction had pranced (naked) in Notre Dame and people with crowns on had been decapitated. Well, new thrills now. Call it progress. The world had to move on.

THE consort of the Permanent First Consul pleaded a headache at the prospect of a dinner with the Bonaparte family, or such members of it as were willing to come. But the headache was genuine and even fierce: they had had a quarrel about his acceptance of the ultimate honor, she saying that he was wrong and he replying that she only spoke thus because she feared he would divorce her, going up in the world and taking a woman who had not been various men's mistress and perhaps having a son by her, well she need not fear divorce (giving her a couple of most painful loving tweaks on the lobes, dislodging an earring she could not later find, and then a pair of husky smacks on the buttocks, ha ha), he would stick with her, though he was now a great man, since he had an ordinary man's decent feelings, let us spend five minutes together on the bed. She pleaded a headache.

He did not wait for the coffee and cognac before getting down to business with the family. He was no Cambacérès, making a dinner into a sacred silent rite, and besides no cognac was served. They were an impatient and fairly mannerless family anyway, and the wrangle about the succession began with the soup (all too clear, like salty warm water). Most of the family, especially the males, were growing plump, the First Consul noticed with distaste. Waiting for the next course, they wolfed all the bread that was on the table.

"I'll tell you why not you," he said to Joseph, pointing at him with a fork. "Because all you have is a couple of daughters and I'm not having the empire ruled by a girl."

"You talk as if I'm going to die. You talk as if I'm not going to father any more children."

"If you do father more, they'll be girls. It's a matter of the stronger element, as has been scientifically proved. Madame Julie will see that you have daughters."

"You seem to forget I am the head of the family."

The First Consul beamed at that, lolling back in his chair an instant. "That won't stop you having daughters."

"What I mean is my rights."

"Rights? *Rights?* Under what law or system or contract or covenant do you have rights? Is there some old Corse tradition which says that if your younger brother is made emperor of the French you then—by *rights*—become his heir?"

Joseph looked thunder at that and Lucien grinned. The First Consul said:

"Oh, I know that you, Lucien, think yourself to be a very great man since Brumaire, but you know what I think about you and your so-called marriage and your so-called wife who is not here."

"My marriage is my own business."

"Oh is it? I'm not having these irregular relationships, I tell you. I had my own ideas on marriage for you, as you know perfectly well."

"With respect, sire, or whatever it is you're to be called, if our mother raised no objection—"

"This has nothing to do with mother, mother is not the emperor-designate of the French."

"You would not talk of her like that," Joseph said, "if she were sitting here now."

"Mother will toe the line like everybody else," shouting. He did not moderate his tone before the servants who had now brought in the main dish.

"Ergh, what is it?" Elisa made a child's vomity face. It was chicken sautéed in oil with crayfish and fried eggs bedded on croutons. "A horrible mixture, some soldier's sort of muck."

"That," the First Consul said with horrible sweetness, "was served at the battle of Marengo. That is already a great historical dish. *Eat it*," he cried. Lucien said:

"Well, for my part, I have little appetite. I beg to be excused."

"Stay where you are, sir, I haven't finished with you yet."

"Let me say this," Lucien said, "before I have finished with you, your majesty or whatever you are. Love is not a thing to be dictated. You have no right to tell a man where to place the affections of his heart. You denounced Jerome's marriage. Is it a crime to love?"

"Oh, very tenderly put, sir. Very Rousseau and so on. Sentimental horse-dung. See here, puppy, I will not have your insolence."

"I will not be called puppy."

"Very well, not puppy then. Sit down, eat your dinner. But I will not have your insolence."

"You shall not have my presence, then. There is one member of the family that does not feel obliged to attend your sickening masquerade. We fought to eliminate the monarchy, not to bring it back in a debased and hypocritical form." Being on his feet, he was ready to sail into a wide sound of oratory. The First Consul gaveled loudly with his knife-handle.

"You did not do much fighting, sir. Retract what you said or get out instanter."

"It is my intention to get out if the mangy yappers you call your secret police will let me."

"Ah, over the border, eh? Join the plotters, eh? Well, let me tell you—" There were hard words while Joseph and Louis ate their chicken sadly and the ladies picked at it with tentative forks. *Manigoldo—farabutto—mascalzone—ingrato—vigliacco—* Lucien knocked one of the heavy dining chairs over as he blazed out.

"Come back, sir! Pick up that chair, damn you!"

But the double doors closed behind him and all eyes kept to the plates before them. Joseph's plate was empty. To Louis the First Consul said:

"Well, I have nothing to say against your marriage, brother. I could not be happier. I am glad, though, our sweet Hortense is not here. She is a sensitive girl. That was not an outburst I should have cared for her to—she knows some Italian, of course."

Louis waited dumbly, a sliver of egg-white on his fork.

"It is, as you may have guessed, upon your dear son that I place my hopes. Scion of the two families most dear to me." Caroline sniffed at that. "You, dear Louis, are, as we all know, not very well."

"I am well enough."

"No no, you are not at all well. You have these fainting fits, you stagger sometimes, it would hardly be seemly— Besides, to be brutal about it—"

"*Brutal*, I would say, is the word."

"Oh, the whole of life is brutal." He glowed with health and ate some chicken. "The point is, brutal or not, that you must be passed over. You will all, of course, be made princes or dukes or something. Don't worry about that. But I have made up my mind that, in default of a legitimate child of my loins—" Julie, Joseph's wife, made a sour though ladylike face at that *legitimate*. "I mean, is it not logical?"

"I will not be passed over," Louis said, looking very pale. "It is as good as to advertise to the world that I am a dying man. Well, I am *not* a dying man."

"At the moment, no. But we have to look to the future."

"This is intolerable." And Louis began to cough into his napkin.

"You see what I mean," his brother said kindly.

"You mentioned princes," Elisa said. "You have said nothing about princesses."

"Well, naturally," he said with great kindness and reasonableness, "Hortense and Julie here, as consorts of my brothers, must bear the honorific of *highness*. As for our mother, she will just be Madame the Mother of the Emperor or something. She has no ambition in that line. It is money she is chiefly after, showing her usual good sense."

"Why shouldn't Elisa and I be princesses?" Caroline said.

"Well, why should you?" he asked, ready to be stormy again. "Since when has a woman had a title conferred direct on her? Use your common sense, read your history."

"Look," Louis said, having finished coughing, "I will not be passed over."

"Ah yes, you will."

"You cannot compel me to hand my son over to you as heir-presumptive or whatever the term is."

"You will do what I say."

"Ah no I will not."

"Caroline and I demand to be made princesses," Elisa said.

"Listen," he hissed, "little sisters. My own dear wife, who is prostrate at this moment with a headache—"

"With whom?" Caroline said pertly. The First Consul gave her a long glare and wondered whether to get up, go round, slap her. He decided instead to ignore her stupidity, saying:

"My own dear wife, alone among all others, has no desire for this imperial honor to be conferred on me. Bless her sweet heart, she is totally without ambition. She does not go around trying out terms like *your majesty* and *Empress of France*."

"I regard the whole business as an intolerable affront," Louis was saying.

"Well, she is to be Empress of France, and she is to be crowned by my own hand in Notre Dame. Will you be quiet," he shouted at his brother, "about intolerable affronts? Very well, then, I will have no heir, do you hear me, no heir? As for you," he turned back to his sisters, "you shall be princesses, for all the good it will do you. And my dear Hortense will teach you how to behave like princesses, and the four of you will carry the Empress's train. There, will that satisfy you?"

"You mean," Julie said, a fat purse-lipped homekeeping little body, "that I am to help carry the, your wife's train?"

"You have to have an heir," Louis said. "That is what the whole thing is about, what they call the hereditary principle."

"Well," he shouted, "I will think about it, do you hear me, think about it at leisure when I do not have a family of pouting sulking ingrates baying about me. But it won't be you, sir, or you, sir, so get that into your thick skulls."

"I shall find it somewhat painful," Julie said. "I mean, I have always been a virtuous woman. To carry the train. Well."

The First Consul bayed to the ceiling.

"Ah yes," Pius said. "A thoughtful touch, my son. It is as if I had not left the Quirinal at all. Why, when I woke this morning I was quite bewildered. I remembered a journey to France but could remember no journey back to Rome." He laughed somewhat sillily, a decent holy sort of cleric. "Every detail of the room exactly the same. Even some of the books. Though I noticed the *Zadig* of Voltaire there. Perhaps that was an oversight. My dear daughter," he said vaguely to the First Consul's consort.

"I am delighted Your Holiness is pleased," the First Consul said. There were a lot of cardinals about the luncheon table and they were disposed, in the Roman manner, to linger over their meal, asking for refills of the various monkish liqueurs that had been provided. One or two grumbled about the quality of the coffee. "I take it Your Holiness had time to look over the order of the service."

"It is a very mixed sort of service. I have, of course, taken advice. I have no lack of advisers." The First Consul nodded kindly. There were about a hundred of these advisers crawling over the Tuileries. "It is so strange a fusion of new and old, of religious and secular, my dear son. Strictly, I cannot be expected to crown an emperor who then proceeds to swear to maintain what is called, ha, freedom of worship."

"Oh, you don't have to worry about the crowning, Holy Father. I'll do that myself. First me and then her," pointing with his thumb towards his consort.

"No no no, my point was, is—"

"Yes, I see your point so well. How do you think I feel," and he opened up large sincere eyes on to Pius, "as a son of the True Church, forced, yes forced, by this rabble of deists and so on to allow tin chapels and wooden tabernacles and, yes, synagogues to subsist along with our traditional faith and the temples of our faith?"

"It means, in effect, that you swear to uphold the right to atheism."

"Yes, that too, unfortunately. I am not in your position, Holy Father. I am a mere man, a very ordinary and sinful one, charged with the thankless task of holding together a ramshackle empire. As for atheism, it has been presented to me as a sincere species of negative faith."

"Of neg of neg."

"It requires a certain devoutness, a kind of theological toughness, to hold, unseduced by the siren voices of doubt, to a belief that God does not exist. For my part—" He lowered his eyes in modesty, and Pius felt that the sun had been temporarily clouded. "—I see it as a divinely bestowed state of utter emptiness, a sort of dark night of the soul, into which the ultimate effulgence will rush unaware, and the unfaith become faith. I see it so, so I see it. Therefore, I consider in all humility, Holy Father, that it would be on your part an act of holy import if you would—"

But wary hard-eyed cardinals were quick to thrust themselves in. They feared that this Bonaparte would talk His Holiness into giving a coronation sermon on the virtues of tolerance, the advantages of Protestantism, the essential holiness of atheism. When Bonaparte later was heard discoursing to Pius in the Tuileries gardens on the aspective approach to the Trinity, they knew that, given time, Pius would innocently declare himself a Sabellian. Popes, they sighed, so rarely became popes because of their eminence in theology.

"Well," the First Consul smiled, at dinner on the eve of the coronation, "we are ready."

"Yes yes, ready," Pius said doubtfully.

"Nothing that has to be done has been left undone."

The wary cardinals nodded over their pasta. Pius said to the First Consul's consort:

"Are you nervous, my dear daughter?"

"I have a little headache, nothing more." She smiled sweetly in the ingenious way she had: hiding all her teeth but leaving the smiled-on with an after-image of a warm pearly flash.

"You'll have a big headache when the crown goes on those chestnut curls tomorrow, ha ha," the First Consul said with heavy humor. "The weight of imperial responsibility."

"Oh, but I understood that—"

"Yes yes yes, my little joke. Laurel wreaths in gold, very tasteful, good Parisian workmanship. Ah yes," he beamed round at all, "we're back to richness, to ceremony, and a good thing too. A nation needs ceremony, it needs the mystical, a ritual of dedication to the glories of its past, prefiguring the glories of its future." A fat cardinal paused, pasta writhing on his fork, to consider the possible meaning of that, if any.

"It is the sincere hope of us all," Pius said, "that a little prince, a future emperor—I pray," he added simply. A palpable cloud passed over the First Consul's chewing features. "How long is it now, my dear daughter, that you have been married?"

"Germinal, Year Four," the First Consul said. "I began badly. I was late. Kept them all waiting—the registrar, Tallien, Barras, that lawyer of yours, angel. And you, of course, my treasure. Still, we wasted no time once I was there. Got it over in a couple of minutes. Two squeaks of a pen—done."

Mouths began to open all down the long table, some showing unchewed food. Pius began to tremble. "I cannot," he said. "I cannot. A secular contract. You are not married. You are living in sin. Why," he asked the table, "did nobody think of this?"

Nobody knew why not. They had assumed. It was naturally taken for granted. Nobody had actually considered the possibility that. A natural actual considered assumption.

"The coronation ceremony," Pius said. "A sacrament. My participation. Unblessed by Mother Church."

The First Consul ate the few morsels left on his plate, considered his plate, wiped up what was left with bread, swallowed the bread, said:

"If you will excuse my wife and myself, Your Holiness, Your Eminences—"

He and she talked it all out in her boudoir. He lay on a sofa from Constantinople, she sat at her dressing-table mirror, all gilt putti. "You realize," she said, "that there can be no turning back once we have done it."

"Divorce, you mean, divorce. Yes yes, immense legal problems, the papal disaffection, the people."

"I have no wish to bind you further if you do not wish to be bound. I think it totally unlikely now that we will have children."

"The flaw is in me, the fault, but suppose it is not—"

"Be honest with me on that. This Italian woman, that little Egyptian kitten, others, I know there are others—"

"Not many. No. I am always honest, I think. I think I am always honest."

"The question should be a question of love, no more."

"Yes," he said with great firmness, "yes," getting up from the sofa. "Can you doubt that, eh? I love you. I adore you. You are my empress."

"Being empress is not the point."

"Love love love. Can you doubt it? Tomorrow the whole world shall be sure. It has never before been done in our age—except for Marie de Médicis I believe it was. I place the crown on your delicious head. It is a sanctified and solemn embrace." He attempted an embrace less solemn, certainly not sanctified. "We shall be married tonight, just before bedtime. Cardinal Fesch can do it."

"Don't we have to go to confession first?" She disengaged herself, a woman's sense of propriety.

"If you wish. It may be a relief for you to get those things off your conscience."

"Oh my God. And you?"

"My conscience is clear, I think. I think my conscience is clear. Venial sins, perhaps. No more."

December Sunday, clear and cold, saw them enter, Mars and Venus, in shining mantles, borne up by cheers and bell-clangor, the cathedral of Our Lady, he in purple adorned with his letter, an N embraced with branching oak and olive and laurel. Thirty-five years of age, he had come a long way in a short time (a long way? Ridiculous, *all the way*) and the best of life was yet to come. Citizens Carné, Thiriet, Blondy, Tireux, Hubert, Fossard, Teisseire, Carrère (Jacques), Carrère (Alexandre), Trauner,

Barsacq, Gabutti, Mayo, Bonin, Borderie, Verne, Chaillot, Barrault, Brasseur, Dupont, Salou and their wives and children or widows and orphans or quiet or unquiet ghosts, and thousands upon thousands more, had waited from dawn to see it all. Inside the vast forest of the cathedral the officers of the new empire waited, some with unquiet bladders, in the glory of a myriad candles that dissolved the Gothic shadows. Talleyrand, magnificent in his chamberlain's ermine, seeing N coming down the aisle, aware of hours of tedious magnificence to come, thought: his dysuria will serve him well. N saw them all, old companions-in-arms, now transmuted to a mythology glorious in plush, silk, satin, silver, gold, sky-blue, sea-blue, with palms and eagles and bees and doves and dogs and lions and leopards as emblems and mystic riddles, seeing too Corporal Gallimard in the crowd, who must really be told to do something about his drinking, and Sergeant Pichou, who he had intended should be promoted but things had got in the way (he made a note of it, advancing up the nave to where His Holiness waited among swords and ivories of office). To his consort, who shone like a goddess and walked with the pace of a goddess and would not be hurried up to the more martial step that seemed to him, *imperator*, more appropriate, he said:

"You remember that notary, Raguideau? The one who told you not to marry me?"

"What?" The coronation march, played on brass and drums and clarinets, was very loud. "Oh, Raguideau."

"Said I'd never own more than my cape and sword. I had him in this morning."

"What?"

"Asked him what he thought about that now. Eh? Eh?" Seeing N so merry, everybody smiled. A one-legged discharged sapper cried: "That's right, laugh, you little bugger," but it was drowned in shouts of "Long live the Emperor." And so N and J approached the high altar. It was the first Sunday in Advent, but the mass was a votive mass of the Blessed Virgin. Talleyrand said to the officer next to him:

"The feminine theme, you see. France is to be regarded as a sort of Blessed Virgin. *La patrie*. Fathermotherland. The Blessed Virgin," he chuckled, admiring the magnificent satiny J. "The spirit of the chevaliers. Poor Germaine would have loved all this." And then he saw that nobody, however emancipated or clever, really had room any more for laughter, unless initiated by N. A Corsican nothing had turned himself into a greater than Charlemagne.

N and his almost empress were bowed to golden thrones by a beaky cleric not unlike the custodian of the Louvre who (his brain had filed the fact away) opened twenty minutes late the day before yesterday.

"That parrot of yours. It has to go."

"Why?"

"I can't have it shrieking *Bonaparte* all the time." Her tears gushed. "There there, angel. It can live in the servants' quarters."

"I was thinking," she sniffed, "of poor little Fortuné."

The Carolingian ghosts attend him now.[1]
And hover o'er the new nobility.
Great Pepin's glory[2] *shines upon his brow*
And shining trumpets seek the vaulted sky.
Then Vivat imperator *is the*[3] *cry,*
The organ[4] *bids the massy*[5] *columns shake*[6]
While drums thud deep and martial flutes shriek high.[7]
An age is dead, a new age doth awake,[8]
See night roll back and see a glorious morning break.[9]

1. His Holiness blesses the imperial regalia then hands to N the sword, scepter, hand of justice, orb.
2. His Holiness prepares to crown him but N places on his own head the golden laurel.
3. J with hands joined proceeds to the steps of the altar but her trainbearers (Madame Julie replaced by Pauline) seem in deliberate clumsiness to seek to hobble her steps and make her trip. N frowns and whispers something harsh. They are subdued, with grace J kneels.

4. N crowns her with care, setting the featherweight gold on her curls with the deliberation of a Paris coiffeur.
5. Mass continues. Incense, lavation, osculation, sanctification.
6. The Emperor dozes off an instant. A Mameluke waddles towards him, bows, his head becomes detached, its owner catches it dexterously, pours blood from it into a cup shaped like a big hollow hand, bids him drink. The Emperor starts awake.
7. His Holiness gives the blessing and discreetly leaves.
8. The Emperor swears to maintain Liberty Equality etc and to rule for France's greater happiness and glory, seeing them, as momentarily the congregation, in terms of total compatibility.
9. The herald at arms takes a deep breath.

The herald at arms took a deep breath and cried with a main voice: "Now is he consecrated and enthroned, the most glorious and noble and august Napoleon, Emperor of the French Republic." Main voices of gold and bronze and nickel and silver gushed swung crashed in jubilant flame, cannon roared in public parks, the citizenry roared. The fetus in the womb heard, the tombs of the glorious and inglorious, those who had been lucky, those who had made mistakes, trembled minimally. But he came out modest and charming, Empress on arm, a republican, ready to start work again tomorrow morning at seven, a great deal to be done. *Te Deum laudamus.* I am sun and wind, I am your best solvent. The roaring open mouths seemed to be roaring for glory. Well he would give them glory, glory was very much on the agenda, plenty of glory *Te Deum laudamus* on its way.

II

There he lies
Ensanguinated tyrant
O bloody bloody tyrant
See
How the sin within
Doth incarnadine
His skin
From the shin to the chin

NONSENSE, OF COURSE. AND THIS WHOLE SITUATION WAS, IF NOT exactly nonsense in that sense of nonsense, to be recognized as the perpetration of an error that he himself would never have perpetrated. He knew, if anyone did, the difference between a live body and a dead one. The savants of the Empire knew much, but they were curiously ignorant of the special properties of god-blood, godflesh and so on. Such studies had been unaccountably neglected. A god could be struck down so that handkerchiefs might soak up the lavish holy blood and the more exiguous holy semen, but what followed was not death but a sleep of peculiar profundity. The sleeping god should be embowered amid ever-greens and then stretch and smile awake with the trumpeting of the violets.

They had all made a hardly credible mistake, and now he was waking (unseasonably, true, that had to be admitted) under a boiling sky, being jogged towards the source of a piercing wind. His body, clad in a loose and dirty cerement, was corded to a splintery board of, he thought, mahogany. His head could move hence his eyes could see that the board was set upon piles of what seemed to be loosely stuffed gunnysacks, secured to them by tarred ropes, one about his ankles, another above his navel, of the thickness roughly of a woman's wrist. The sacks were set upon a kind of farm tumbril, and this four asses drew. He remembered distinctly and irrelevantly how, as a cadet, he had read a poem too quickly and wondered for a second at the conceit of a soul braying. These souls merely plodded, patient in immemorial asininity, gray and shagged and unwhipped.

See
How the sin within
Doth incarnadine

Capering on the cobbles of a street he did not recognize, twanging large Jew's harps and blowing brass instruments that farted ragged military calls, though deeper in pitch than any bugle known to the Great Army, there were men who, he soon saw in shock, were caricatures of himself, live and yet flat, as if line and wash had become animated. They wore a mockery of the chasseur uniform. Sometimes they grew the third dimension required for organic reality, but only to thrust out cushion bellies in a parody of frotting. On either side of the narrow way were massed laughers and jeerers. He cried to them but none heard. He called to the seething sky. Surely at least his moving ball of a head could be seen, as also the eyes he knew to be enlarged with the chemicals of desperation, the calling lips? No. He was a corpse, so therefore the eyes and mouth and head were to be taken as frozen in corpsehood.

He lay back exhausted, aware of the steady strengthening of the acute wind. It tasted, for some reason, of fermentation—marc, stale beer, something. Then he raised his head in terror. He had been brought to the edge of some sea. Northern and chill, it seemed a sea he was sure he knew, but not (O Christ O God help us) from this shore. A quay with bollards, high-masted men-of-war riding at anchor.

Hee the seen witheen
Deeth eenc

That was a high fife piping somewhere. He saw the flag and screamed. Jeering boys, ship's monkeys, clambered barefoot yarely my hearties up the sacks and freed him from his knotty ropes with baccy-stained jackknives. Stiff as he was from the bonds and the terror, he was yet able to surprise them all by agitating his limbs in the manner of a monkey-up-a-stick he had once had as a boy in Ajaccio. Pushed toward the cobbles, he caught with his nails at a sack and grieved to see how ill-kept the fine hands had been allowed to become and nearly wept at the breaking of the nail of the right mercurial finger. The sack tore open, so that a mess of damp rubbishy newspapers, all French, was disclosed as stuffing. He read in a split instant: LA LUTTE ÉTAIT TERMINÉE. IL AVAIT REMPORTÉ LA VICTOIRE SUR LUI-MÊME. IL AIMAIT . . . He was now upright, in a boxing stance, on the slimy quayside, already shouting *I am come to set you free.* None understood the language he was speaking, and he himself was surprised that he knew it. It was some kind of ancient Mediterranean language, older than Latin. He mimed liberty (a man cheering and dancing); he mimed liberation (the tearing-off of chains and manacles) but the crowd seemed appalled. A gentleman who sneezed on a snufftake and looked like Talleyrand cried: *Un sorcier. Donnez-le au feu.* He was ready to agree with twenty nods, saying *Yes yes the fire I know fire I can control fire have I not always had the better of fire*, but brawny tars' arms, blue-tattooed MOTHER and ENGLAND HOME AND BEAUTY, grasped him, raised him, and with a heave ho me hearties thrust him to the dirty eager water that lapped the stones of the quay. As he hit in wretched panic and anger, teeth ready to bite it, the quaking roof of the Channel a single shout rang. He surfaced gasping from the filthy world of slobber and green ropes of slime. There was a rowboat there now with an ancient boatswain and callow midshipmen, and he thankfully grasped towards the oarlocks. But oars hit out at him, and he saw, callow grins beyond, his own blood stain, though in salt dilution, a sogged newspaper floating. ET À PROPOS PENDANT QUE NOUS EN SOMMES À CE SUJET VOICI UNE CHANDELLE POUR ALLER VOUS COUCHER VOICI UN COUPERET POUR COUPER VOTRE TÊTE. The massed guards bands from the quayside played and hallelujah choruses sang:

There he lies
Ensanguinated tyrant
O bloody bloody tyrant
See
How the sin within
Doth incarnadine
His skin
From the shin to the chin

He awoke in Moscow to resignation of a sort and also resentment. His heart was not pounding, as it should from nightmare, but kept calm time to the beat of the funeral march that had been in the dream, purged now however of its gross words. It was indeed a theme of great dignity played by the bands of his army but remote, pulsing out from some city many versts away over these frozen plains. But were they frozen? No, not yet. He was anticipating: there was still perhaps time. He stopped the sound in mid-measure. Resignation to the truth that he had not conquered that woman-element. That was all the dream meant. The sea was not his nor ever would be now. The sea was theirs. Water was treacherous and, in a certain mad sense, unnatural. It could not be shaped. It would, though grudgingly, be bridged. It would consent to play in fountains. It would consent, though coyly through a metal membrane, to agree to consent to agree to be coaxed to respond to the coaxing of fire. It could be seen as an aspect of land or as a servant of the body. But river, spring, bath had only the remotest kinship with the measureless pits of tigers with the salt teeth. What was the Empire? Children, what is the Empire? It is what sea can surround, sir. Sea defined it.

The resentment was a resentment that his own elements of earth and fire should now be, though temporarily, turning against him. Temporarily only though: mark that. Terrain refused to be battlefields and fire ramped through the Moscow streets. Fire, however, could always be doused. Tomorrow surely land would thud with battle or else yield on a map to new apportionments and containments. His fingers (clean, well-kept, nails untorn) itched to be at work with protractors as a pianist's (who was that pianist girl who had once giggled at him?) for a keyboard. He put his hands behind his head and lay thinking grimly in his nightshirt: a raft of fingers to hold him from sinking into the deep pillows after a dream of sinking. The bedroom was huge and still tropically hot from the fire that, itself now sinking, had begun as a roar of tree-trunks, leaves and all. The Kremlin fireplaces were grossly ornate, proscenium arches framing a *drame* of fire. There was no better play in the world than the performance of fire in a great fireplace. But not sinking, no. He got out of bed and trod many meters of white bear-rug and Italian marble. He manhandled a couple of pinelogs long as himself and thrust them on, panting. An apocalypse of sparks, a roar. In time he stopped himself from kicking the logs into a deeper engagement with the flames. He was barefoot.

Turning his back to the fire he felt that heat altogether friendly, protective as an army. But then, as he squinted at the picture over his bed, viewing it as it were from a cannoneer's angle, a far and obscure vision of an obscure Muscovite princess, there came the stab. The sudden mockery of a stab of fire behind the breastbone. Heartburn, a nervous bolting of ill-cooked venison, raw and burnt. Strange: raw and burnt were aspects of each other; the cooked was something altogether different. He clapped his spread left hand to the pain and noted, looking down at the gems of the rings which, having flared in firelight, now slept in the great shadow he threw, that this was the gesture he had first used when the image of what that failed assassin had willed burnt into his consciousness. The stab that had not been, and yet the very intent was an abiding pain which the dyspeptic pang now, as it were, clownishly seemed to wish to mime. That the liberated should wish to destroy the liberator: was not that altogether against reason? He heard a silly song somewhere on the Teutonic horizon; a damson sunset rung with it:

Wach' auf! Es nahet gen den Tag!
Ich hör' singen im grünen Hag
Ein' wonnigliche Nachtigall. . . .

Or some such yearning nonsense. He had been told the words and had them explained to him; he had known no German at all then, knew little enough now. A ridiculous language, rather like English though more raspingly and sorrowfully naïve, unfitted for hypocrisy.

At Schönbrunn during a review of the troops, after the Wagram victory, a student with hair on fire with the October sun. A petition, Sire. And then the fire of the dagger in the sun, and then Rapp's hand staying the dagger. The student's name had been Stapps. Stapps and Rapp. Destroyer and savior drawn into a foolish intimacy of rhyme. Rapp Stapps Rapp Stapps—the rhythm in his brain, so crass a rhythm, had become the thud on a funereal drum, muffled and snareless. General Rapp, a fine ADC but with a brain that could not think round corners. "To think that he's the son of a Lutheran minister. A Lutheran minister from Saxony. I cannot believe it." He had written to the Burgomaster of Schönbrunn to say: "He confessed all to His Majesty the Emperor. Tomorrow is fixed for his execution. To think that he is the son of a Lutheran minister from Saxony. I cannot believe it."

O Deutschland arise
Light is rising in the
Deutschlander skies.

More nonsense. Student songs. They ought to get on with their fucking studies.

"You are the son," N said, "of a Lutheran minister from Saxony." They were alone together in a small sitting room of the palace. He had insisted on this. He had to find out *why*. "You were brought up on good Christian doctrine. Thou shalt not kill, and so forth."

"Some things have to be killed. You know that. You, Bonaparte, have done enough killing." He spoke good slow French, straight out of books. Everything he said at first sounded too bookish to be offensive, like dialogue from some novel in French he had read earnestly to improve his French.

"You call me by my surname. That is, I suppose, refreshing. No nonsense about Sire or Your Majesty. You object to royalty, is that it? I too object to royalty. In a way. There is royalty and royalty, of course. You are a republican? I am a republican too. We have at least that in common." And he had let the great warmth, guaranteed to melt anything, beam out. The boy, stupid German fool, was not melted.

"I object to foreign rulers. Let Germany be ruled by her own princes. It is the presumption of foreign rulers I scorn and execrate."

"Ah. It is not just me?"

Stapps let the tip of his long nose twitch into a sneer. "You are a godsend to the patriotic assassin. With you out of the way at least one dynasty comes to an end. I have thought at times of killing the Austrian emperor. But his race goes on. He has heirs."

He would not sit. He would take no refreshment. He stood in the middle of the carpet, like a good erect little German toy soldier. But he was no soldier. N put him into uniform and then pulled him out. He wouldn't last a ten-kilometer march. Then N caught a swift vision of Josephine, smiling away at a whole adoring salon with her teeth hidden, elegant bitch, not doing her job, nothing kicking around in her belly. N restlessly stalked about thin upright scornful Stapps. He said, heeling the flowery carpet, his hands behind:

"I am presented to you as some sort of tyrant, yes? That will be the English with their lies. Not the English people, but the rulers of the English. What they are impotent to do by force they seek to do by the poison of misrepresentation. Be honest with me now." He addressed the thin straight back. The left sleeve of the dirty green jacket had been half-torn from the shoulder in the violence of the arrest. "What agent persuaded you? How many English pounds were you paid or promised?"

"None to both questions. It was for Germany. I failed. I am sorry I failed." The sorrow sounded so sincerely personal that N was absentmindedly fain to say *Not at all.* The boy said: "Now let me pay. Let us get it over with."

"I can see the attraction of martyrdom, yes yes. To cry Down with Tyranny as the guns are raised. It is a schoolboy dream that I have dreamed myself." He came round quickly to look up into Stapps's water-blue eyes. He felt himself small and tubby in this straight pared presence. A boy thinned down to a patriotic gas jet. "What I wish is to let you go. Let you leave this room and this palace and go free."

"So," another boy's sneer, "I can tell everyone of the magnanimity of the French emperor."

"Nothing wrong with magnanimity. Magnanimity is nothing to be ashamed of. I should be glad of your saying that. No, not for that reason. And don't think I'm scared of your martyrdom. Ah no, since there seems to be no cause here for which a man could worthily die. To be a martyr for the cause of belief in a flat earth or the right to eat cow-shit."

"Eat what? I do not know the expression. I have not before already met it." A bit confused now.

"Never mind. Can't you see that it is I who am the cause, I and what I stand for? I stand against old tyrannies, I stand for equality and decency and justice and mercy and forbearance. I stand for humanity. I don't want you to die. And why not? Because I want you to see the light. I want you to grow into the light. Can't you see that, German idiot that you are?" He had become too loud, he was growing irritable, there were many papers to sign and people to see, he wished to God this German idiot would be willing to sit down. "Why the hell," he yelled, "won't you sit down?"

"You are uneasy in yourself, Bonaparte," Stapps said kindly. "You are all nerves and irascibility. You are also a foreign tyrant. Down," he said conversationally, "with tyranny. Long live a free and united Germany."

"Such utter utter." N took in sourly a large canvas of some old Austrian victory on the wall, naked goddesses swimming down through the sky to fondle a monarch stern but with cat's eyes. "What's Germany to do with it? There's no such thing as Germany anyway. What's Austria or France or Corsica or any of the other false and foolish abstractions to do with it? I'm not France conquering Austria or these German states you're on fire about. I'm the spirit of the French Revolution, the American Revolution, any damned revolution you please. Nation is a false doctrine, you German idiot. It's a sin to want to die for a nation. What I want is a united Europe, not a bundle of yapping and farting little nations. There has to be a head of this united Europe. Well, perfectly simple, I happen to be the head. Not through blood but by election. By merit. I'm fit to be the head. Who else in Europe would you have, God blast you? One of these sweet-lipped little princes of yours, hunting by day and fucking by night, potbellied little tyrants—" Infelicitous, he saw that too late. "Real tyrants, though petty ones, grinding the faces of the—"

"Claptrap. You know it's claptrap. *Bobards, verbiage, phrases vides*," just to make all clear. "Your trouble, Bonaparte, is that you live in the past."

"Me? I? Live in the—I live in the—Oh God, oh sacred mother of our blessed Lord Jesus Christ, oh fucking buggery. I live in the—" He had to sit down. He chose a gilt bowlegged masterpiece of discomfort and gaped up at the clean proud young raised stupid chin. Stapps, he could see, could see himself in the blue cherub-encrusted mirror over the tiny fire, green wood slow to blaze; he was being posterity looking at Stapps giving bold talk to the French emperor. "I live in the past, eh?" N said, smiling. "Good good, the past. Now then, friend, all I want you to do is this. Give me a written statement, an apology, something of that sort. Say you were drunk or ill, temporarily deranged with fever, doing it for a student wager and you didn't mean it. Or, ah a good one, you were testing our security. Something like that, that's all. And then you're a free boy."

"You don't understand." The tone was of a good weary

patient provincial German schoolmaster. "I meant it and mean it and will go on meaning it in whatever piece of time I have left to me. I meant it and I mean it and I'm far from alone in meaning it. This is the nineteenth century, not the eighteenth. I don't mean the *old* past, though you're trying to teach French schoolchildren that not much happened in history between Charlemagne and you. Things are changing. Science."

"Knowledge? Learning? When you consider what we, I— *Are we not on the side of—?*"

"Your dreams are unsupported by the *right* knowledge. Communications between one wing and another of an army. Great centers of manufacture. Research. The English are good at these things."

"The English the English the." He was on his feet again, prepared to batter Stapps as if he were the English. Stapps nearly supported the fancy, saying:

"You forget that the English are a kind of German people."

N danced briefly in terrible rage behind Stapps's back, making noises. Stapps watched some of the dance indifferently in the mirror. He then said: "Change and science. The *Volk*."

N came round to Stapps's front, one eye closed, the other fierce enough for the two. "The what? What was that word?"

"The *Volk*. Untranslatable. The German people is becoming aware of its destiny."

"Oh my God."

"You don't understand. You're not German. You don't know our language and literature and folklore. You don't weep with joy at the smell of the German forest or the German sunrise over the German mountains."

"Oh my God. Oh my God."

Stapps went ecstatically into his own tongue for a space:

> "*Habt Acht. Uns dräuen übel Streich':*
> *Zerfallt erst deutsches Volk und Reich,*
> *In falscher wälscher Majestät*
> *Kein Fürst bald mehr sein Volk versteht. . . .*"

"Oh, for Christ's sake," N moaned, "shut up. Shut up," much louder, "that fucking gibberish, do you hear?"

"*Baragouin?*" The boy knew the word or guessed at its meaning. Very coldly he said: "You see what I am trying to say when I say you do not understand the *Volk*. We are the only pure race in Europe and must remain so. Our tongue is the old pure Aryan. France is a mongrel country full of Jews. We must keep ourselves clean. Once our blood is mixed with the lower races we become cursed of God, Jesus Christ turns his back on us."

"He was a Jew, man, what the hell do you think you are saying?"

"In him was the *echt* blood of the Aryans."

"You're mad," N said. "Really mad. Certifiable. I *can't* allow you to die mad. I shall send you to an institution somewhere."

"We don't want a united Europe," Stapps said, reasonable now. "We want a united Germany. You, Bonaparte, would fix us all in an immutable pattern made in Paris. Classical stagnation. Peace and calm. *Pax Gallica*. But the imposition of peace and calm are inimical to the evolution of the German, that is to say human, race. Stein said that."

"He did, did he? I know all about Stein, damned imitation Prussian. What sort of a name do you think *Stein* is, anyway?"

"Aryan."

"Yes yes, naturally, of course." Sarcastic. And yet Stein had freed the serfs and started a university in Berlin and reformed the Prussian Army. N had an intimation, announced as a gnawing desire for luncheon, that what he was doing for Europe was teaching it the most efficient techniques for rising against him. But could anyone really take seriously this nationalism business? What was that word again? *Folque* or something. Young men blinded by the light of what they called reason, actually a perversion of the true French commodity. Illuminism. He said:

"You are a student and hence willing to learn. Learn from me now what our modern history is all about. It is not about the struggle between nations. It is about the struggle within society itself. It began in '89 with the rising of the oppressed against the oppressor. That was in France, but there was no talk then about recovering some great golden age of a special French minting and everybody being made free to weep with joy in the glorious French forests and all that fucking nonsense. There was no talk of nation. It was a matter of making slaves free—not just French slaves but slaves everywhere. Because all over Europe the oppression was the same—gorging kings and princes and fat-bellied priests and the power and the glory theirs forever and ever amen. You talk about the destiny of this German *fouque* or whatever it is. Well, the destiny of the French was the destiny of a group of people who'd seen the light first, not a fucking resurgent nation. And this destiny was to set up and preserve the first model republic of free and equal men and at the same time to teach its principles to those who had not yet seen the light. We weren't fighting the Austrians and the Germans, man, we were fighting the armies of the oppressors of the Austrian and German people. Can't you get that into your thick German skull? And that glorious piece of modern history is still proceeding, friend. Europe has to be free of the dirty past."

"Some parts of Europe," Stapps said, resuming sneering, "seem to like the dirty past. Spain, for instance. England, for example."

"If I could land my armies in England tomorrow the oppressed English would feed us beef and beer and give us their women."

"And the oppressed Spanish?"

"They will see the light, given time. It's the damned English getting in the way."

Stapps did a surprising thing. He moved one pace to the left. Then he said: "Oh, fool fool fool. People don't want to be made to be given what the French think is good for them, they want to find out things for themselves in their own way. To the Spanish, Spain is a bigger thing than equality and liberty and down with the fat-bellied bishops. Don't you see, fool, Germany wants to be Germany first? The rest can follow later, if Germany wants it."

"I will not be called a fool," N said. "Calling me a fool is taking rebelliousness too far. You will retract that 'fool.' "

"I will retract nothing. I will say what I wish. I am going to die anyway."

"You are not going to die."

"Oh yes I am."

"Oh no you are not."

"Oh yes I am."

"Oh no you are damned well not," he said, moderately. "I am the one round here who says who will die and who will not die. Within reason, that is," still moderately. "You are not going to die."

"Oh yes I am."

"I tell you, puppy dog," N said, getting up and standing in front of the fire, "you are going to sign a document of retraction and apology and then walk out of here a free boy." But he was troubled. He took a pellet of licorice from his comfit-box to quieten his yapping stomach. "It may be a problem of language," he said. "French is not really your language. French is the language of reason."

"In any language I will speak to you good reason."

"There, you see. That did not sound quite like French. We'll have it all drawn up in German. Then you sign and off you go. Roustam!" he bawled, "Roustam, black bastard!" Roustam at once opened the door as though he had been eavesdropping. "My compliments to General Rapp and tell him to come here at once." Roustam went off. To Stapps N said: "This is the officer who stayed your assassin's hand. He speaks German."

"The truth is the truth and is above language."

"Ah, that's all German nonsense. Pure reason and all that sort of chopped-up dogmerd. Ach." He kicked the sluggish green logs viciously. "What you're saying is that I've gone wrong. I won't believe it, it's not common sense. It's not up to a mere boy to tell me I've gone wrong."

"There must always be somebody. However young or insignificant. There has to be somebody who comes from nowhere to say what others are too foolish or frightened to say. *Ich kann nichts anders.*"

"If you want to speak German wait for General Rapp."

"This is German that even a Corsican should know. That is what Luther said. I cannot do differently from what I now do."

"Ah, Luther, eh? You want to be Luther. If you only realized the trouble that that fucking man has caused." He spoke confidentially, as though Luther were out there, rampaging with a bible and farting against the rational truths of Latin Christianity. "Luther, indeed." And then, "Aaaaah." For Roustam was opening the door and General Rapp was entering hatless, with a bow and a heel-click. "Look here, Rapp," N said, "this boy wishes to die and be a martyr for what he calls Germany. What do we do with him?"

"Better him a martyr, Sire, than, with respect, you yourself."

"He says I've gone wrong, Rapp. Get him to speak to you in his own horrible language."

"Sire." At once Stapps entered a big murky German forest, full of yelps and cooings and sawyer's rasps. Rapp listened sadly and at length said: "He says that if you let him go he'll try and kill you again, in the name of the German soul or some such thing. He will not accept—with respect, mine, not his—pardon from a blood-soaked Caligula. He says that he knows that some other brave patriot who believes in the destiny of the German race will be successful in sticking the knife, with respect, into your guts bloated with the bloody flesh of the innocent, even if he failed. It is only, with respect, a matter of time."

"Yes yes yes, I know all about that, yes." N stamped once round the room as if roughly yarding it out for new carpets, mumbling. Then he took in a chestful of the smoky air by the fireplace and spent nearly thirty seconds letting it go, an imperial pint or sigh, making the smoke bluely waver. Stapps responded to this, as though it were a new tyrannical statement, by entering a sharp thicket of clauses and compounds and cadences of regretful-seeming assertion. Rapp paraphrased, saying:

"It is, with respect, the mark of a fool, he says, not to look into the future and see what it holds. With respect, Sire, you, he says, are not looking to the future. It is the Germanic races, such as the Germans and the English, that have the brains to build the future. While you, we, are leading big cumbersome armies all over Europe and talking of honor and glory, the English are developing steam engines and spinning machines. That is all he wishes to say except, respect again, down with tyranny and long live a free and united Germany and now he is tired of all this and wishes to be taken out and shot."

N grasped Stapps by the thin arms. "I am your father," he cried. "I am everybody's father."

"That," Stapps neatly said, "is because you are nobody's father, except illegitimately."

"The father does not kill the son," ignoring that remark, "however much the son wishes to kill the father."

"My father is a Lutheran minister of Saxony. He is a German and a patriot."

"Well, give me a month to learn German and then I'll be a German patriot too. And a Lutheran, if that's what you want. It's not difficult to be anything once you've been a Muslim. Well, a sort of Muslim and the Egyptians more or less accepted us as such. But first first first, mark this, first I'll be a European."

"You will never understand. Stop embracing me. You are like a Russian bear. It is the hateful embrace you are giving to all Germany."

"With respect, Sire," Rapp said, "you are stronger than you think."

N let go. "I feel responsible for you," he mumbled, "like a father."

Stapps, as in a parody of military drill, raised his right forearm and made the gesture of snuffing out a candle. He grinned sourly. "Show some respect, damn you," Rapp cried in French. N now stamped and screamed, frothing:

"Go on, then, you squareheaded idiot with your fucking stupid lingo of coughs and rasps and sausage-words, go on and be a fucking martyr for a nonexistent cause. But I tell you this this," hissing straight into his face, "this this, you cretin, that nobody will know about it, that a forged letter of regret and apology will be sent out, General Rapp will work on it at once won't you Rapp, also a forged medical certificate affirming your insanity, signed by the chief doctors of the Great Army, I'll forge their damned signatures myself, here and now, and that history will record the magnanimity that General Rapp himself has witnessed and has been thwarted by your damned stupid German obstinacy. Have him marched out," he told Rapp. "Have him shot. Get him out of everybody's way."

"Down with tyranny," Stapps said, as though quietly quoting a Lutheran text. "Long live a free and united Germany." And, as an afterthought, "Your breath is bad. It's a bad breath that is blowing over Europe."

Had, N wondered now in the Kremlin bedchamber, there been a funeral procession, or had he merely dreamt it? As one got older, the memory of a dream became hard to distinguish from a memory of fact. He put his two right middle fingers on his nose and cupped the rest of his hand round his open mouth, blowing and at the same time snuffing. Yes, breath bad. What did it profit a man if he gained the whole world and yet had bad breath? On the wall as wide as a stage a cortège moved, dead Stapps drawn by two Saxon drayhorses, a Lutheran minister reading some nonsense from the Lutheran bible, full of *geschlossen* and *unaufgeknöpft*, or some such obscene Nordic gibberish, students singing rawly *Ein Feste Burg*, a tune which N had to admit he rather liked. What in fact had happened to the body? He went baaaaah loudly at the vision and it vanished. As he had sounded aloud he now spoke aloud, barefoot-flapping from one end of the fireplace to the other: "We had to have the Continental System, didn't we? Even if it ruined the Russian timber trade, didn't we?" And then, ceasing pacing, up at the wedding-cake icing of the ceiling: "I had to get a divorce, didn't I?"

Roustam on the mat outside could be heard stirring in his light watchdog sleep. "Sleep, sleep, black bastard," N said with bitter affection.

Again a funeral, this time not a dreamt one, but whose? A lot of weeping women, some of his own family or Josephine's, a bright gritty windy day at some cemetery in some northern city. Whose? There had been so many funerals and there were many still to come. But a civilian in black, a red-eyed mourner, a thin man who limped, had been emboldened by what was undoubtedly familial loss to speak out and question the worth of a man's dying for his country. The cemetery path was a long one, N had had to suffer a long and grief-rambling disquisition.

He looked at his watch, read four-fifty-one, and sighed his way back into bed. A long day coming for all.

"Yes yes yes, believe me, I am not on the side of death either."

"Why cannot the wars cease? Every year more sons taken from us and for what purpose? It seems to me that a man should be allowed to grow comfortably and dully into age, drinking his real Indian tea or real Blue Mountain coffee, warm in his Yorkshire wool, good Northampton boots on his feet, exulting in his boredom, his *boredom*, yes yes yes."

"No no no!"

He willed himself to sleep, hearing nonsense: "And let him also wear galligaskins of Paisley purple and eat of the flesh of the fine lambs of the Sussex downs."

"No no no!"

But now he was back in that dream again, bound, bound for the enemy water, what time the sneering bands played and the exultant enemy sang:

There he lies
Ensanguinated tyrant
O bloody bloody tyrant
See
How the sin within

Doth incarn

See the re-
Incarnate Cleopatra,
Barge burning on the water.
Bare
Rowers row in rows.
Posied roses interpose
Twixt the rows and the rose.

Nonsense, naturally, but rather charming played on flutes and oboes. And everything here seemed very sweetly absurd yet completely natural and *decorous*, even her almost total nudity save for swaths of tulle agitated by the spicy breeze and the golden serpentine headdress that the fat so sweet little brown boys kept, at her request, showing her from all possible angles in their really beautiful ormolu mirrors. The question was, she supposed, whether she was being worshipped as a queen or as a goddess. Well, it must be the latter, for she knew, with the so subtle as it were *layered* knowledge of dreams, that she was in waking life actually an *empress*, and she would hardly have taken the trouble, however thrilling the arrangement of the details, to mount this particular complicated dream, with all its really ornate décor, unless there had been a certain desire—perhaps naughty, certainly self-indulgent, but really *quite harmless*—for as it were elevation to the next rank. So here she was as a goddess, stretching out a lovely long white arm in greeting and acknowledgment of the crowd's worship, smilingly reclining amid roses and the shrilling from the shore of trumpets and violins.

And yet, goddess as she was, there was nothing insubstantial or what was the word *ethereal* about the lucent flawlessness of the skin of the long fleshly languor that flowered into visibility (the visibility of herself *to* herself, that was) from just above her truly delightful breasts down. Ah, so delicately *solid* and not an ounce of flesh too much. And this, how miraculous, despite the banquet of last night in which an absolute *plethora* of delicate sweetmeats had been served after the truffled boar and the peacocks farced with a mixture of their own brains and livers pounded with mushroom and very sweet onion. Thus, for example, there had been a multicolored cake of pure butter and vanilla and chocolate *swamped* in Parma violets and redolent of a finely subtle Alexandrian resin wine, and she had taken slice after slice from the smiling intellectual Nubian slave who served.

Posied roses interpose
Twixt the rose and the

The rose, of course, was not really proper in this context of spicy *easternness*, but it was, after all, in her name. Marie-Josèphe-Rose, Marie-Rose Detascher—but at this point it was necessary to order to be hit away roughly with oars from the edge of the barge a really ugly dripping creature, a *satyr* she supposed, that kept trying to shout at her very unpleasant things which the flutes and oboes on board and the trumpets and violins on shore rather effectually drowned. The horrid *dirty* thing was soon to be seen dancing and gesturing from the shallow waters by the shore, belabored with reeds by brown tall men of *impeccable* musculature but still gibbering and really obscenely parodying the sacred act of love in swift jerks of his horrible *hirsute* body. He seemed, and this was very strange, to have the face of Tallien.

The nymphs, her serving ladies, who, also in almost *total* nudity, lay in smiling rose-strewn and rose-strewing languor all about her throne (whose arms were most intricately and really *magnificently* carved sphinxes), were the very rose-pink of beauty, and the rowing slaves whose black sweat gave off a delicious odor of concentrated rose could not keep their great rolling eyes off the *not excessive* opulence of their haunches and breasts.

Rayers ray in rays,
Paysied raises interpays

That was the very refined voice of Edmée Renaudin, wonderfully transformed into a slim shapely *odalisque* but, like all the attendant nymphs, minimally flawed in deference to her nonpareil mistress. Her flaw was a rosy mole on the left shoulder blade out of which grew a *tiny* filament that trembled in the cinnamon-breathing breeze. And Thérèse Tallien herself, at whose *utter* loveliness even a lovely woman could catch her breath and stare, had the tiniest tiniest tiniest downy growth on her truly delicious upper lip which, when stained with ferrous wine, could glitter like a real *mustache*. And now, as to confirm her own *divine* perfection, a little dimple-bottomed boy brought up his ormolu mirror again. To her surprise and annoyance her face, for some reason known only to the gods of mirrors, did not show in the flashing blue metal; instead there appeared a text of utter and silly and *impertinent* meaninglessness: LA LUTTE ÉTAIT TERMINÉE. IL AVAIT REMPORTÉ LA VICTOIRE SUR LUI-MÊME. IL AIMAIT . . . But then it faded, and her face was there deliciously frowning. And here, at her right side, was a Silenus who looked like Talleyrand and, naked as he otherwise was, had a sort of silkweave bandolier about him to which a porcelain snuffbox was attached. He had taken a pinch, unseen by her and certainly without her permission (it was a *dirty* habit, the sight of snufftaking made her cross), and he now sneezed, spraying her right forearm so that she was ready to be *really angry*, then said, without apology: *Une sorcière. Donnez-la au feu.* She pouted prettily: *Mais le feu ne me plaît point.*

At once she was lifted by her own delicious-smelling and smiling nymphs out of the imperial divine seat and, kicking and laughing and screaming, was thrust to the river. This, she saw as she plunged (and it was *totally* without fear), was the true elevation, despite what appeared to be its opposite! She could breathe quite easily in the lovely perfumed waters, and the fish that came to greet her all had the cold snout of poor little Fortuné. When she rose to the surface it was to find that everything had changed—no barge, no attendants, no spicy Egypt. *But she had become Aphrodite.* Her hair was a golden fire, and she felt that her body was now somehow so delectable that great pieces should be broken from it like cake and munched, since it would all grow again in a twinkling, she now being *truly* a goddess. She was poised on the surface of delicious iced champagne foam, and her lovely back was protected from the wind by a really beautiful shell-like pavilion which rested, miracle, on the wild but mild and cool but warm waters. From the shore, she saw, great-muscled men, their faces of a brilliantly intelligent somehow *animality*, were plunging in to swim avidly toward her, all to do her pleasure, that was to say worship. But a Triton came over the surface from behind the shell to blow a feeble *ugly* blast on his conch and then to sing raucously at her, while a beautiful white-robed choir got ready on the shore: ET À PROPOS PENDANT QUE NOUS SOMMES À CE SUJET VOICI UNE CHANDELLE POUR ALLER VOUS COUCHER VOICI UN COUPERET POUR COUPER VOTRE TÊTE. For all that, the shore choir sang to the flutes and oboes and trumpets and violins:

See the re-
Incarnate Aphrodite.
Hail queen of love almighty!
Flesh
Fresher than a rose,
And maddening that rose
Twixt her nose and her toes!

She awoke in Malmaison to see in the dimmed lamplight monsters creeping toward her, panting and whimpering. She strangled her scream before proper utterance: it was only the puppies that had got out of their basket while their (miniature

German wolfhound) parents slept. Pretty dears, tumbling and loving but apt to be incontinent with excitement on the rose counterpane. She had come out of that quite pleasant dream with a slight headache and was not in consequence (she kissed each in apology) ready for puppy-play. Besides, it was the unearthly hour, so the ormolu clock on the mantelpiece said, of four-thirty in the morning, a winter morning too. Claire had, before retiring, fed the little fire with small coal, so that the room was warm still. She wondered whether to call Claire, bid her make a tisane and sit and chat, but that chat would lead to *poor madame* and so on. She poured the puppies back into their basket in armfuls, a task likely, she sighed, to be never-ending, but then their mother awoke and rushed to siphon them off with a horrible noise of relish, then lay on her side to feed them. Their father, how like a male, never awoke. Her parrot, under its night cover, squawked a gnomic syllable or two: *lutte* and *couperet* and something that sounded like *pendantquenous*, and then *hahaha*.

The warmth of that dream water clung still to her limbs as she lay once more, the headache receding, in her silk. The pirogue from Les Trois-Îlets to Fort-Royal, the Convent of the Ladies of Providence, across the bay: how she had loved the journey. How she had loved the islands of perpetual summer, castles built on the shore with children's screams and tired-runner panting of waves contending, paddling in the warm blue, native drums in the evening afar as they reclined on the veranda after spiced (heresy, that fat official from Paris had said at first, but later he succumbed as they all did) *coq au vin*. The island life, and what could be lovelier than the island life, except of course the *dreamt of* and as it were *remembered from other people's memories* life of Paris? The sea had never been a big monstrous divider but rather a joiner of island and island, so it had seemed to her as a girl, and ultimately the sea, and the wind that rose from out of the sea, joined you to France, though not directly to Paris. To get to Paris meant that horrid jolting over land, somehow very *male* in its roughness. The sea, the warm spicy sea, she never feared the sea, the sea was her element, the sea was a woman, *la mère la mer*, and lapped round a man and enclosed him and made him yield, yes, yield all. And now the sea had failed her.

The headache began to return, and she could almost *fore-taste* its promised quiddity, that of a true migraine. It had been a migraine of spectacular almost *majestic* intensity that had struck that evening before dinner, and it had made its own strange poem, in which she was a sea that could *feel pain* from the plowing of the prow of an iron ship into her brow. Ah, those two horrid islands with a staircase between them, her boudoir, his study, and he never knocked, never never. At the sound of the dinner bell she had had one of her great white hats pinned and arranged to shade her sore eyes, and dinner had been a nightmare, only ten minutes but *endless*, neither of them had tasted more than a dribble of soup and a morsel of chicken, and then, when it had come to the coffee—

Oh, he took his cup himself from the tray, roughly pushing her aside, not waiting as he had always done for her to put sugar in for him and then taste it to see if it was to his taste not tasting too sweet or not sweet enough not that he ever really had much of a sense of taste sometimes not seeming to know even whether it was sweet or not and then he.

Waved the lackey out and Count de Bausset, who was prefect in attendance, went out too very quickly without being waved at, for he knew what was coming, everybody knew, and now here it was, coming. But it was not going to be easy for him either, as she could tell from the rattle of cup against saucer, like a sort of musical chattering of teeth she had thought madly, and now it came, and he trembled in front of the fire. Trembling he said:

"Your daughter. That is to say. Hortense will have said something."

"No. No. Hortense? Nothing."

"You understand? You *must* understand. Do you think I want this? Can you honestly sit there and think I want it?" Trembling.

"You mean. You are in love with. This. Christine de Mathis."

"No. No. No no no no no, whoever that is, who is that, oh yes, a friend of Pauline's, no no no, that is not it. Oh foolish woman, could you think that, oh ridic, no no, it is nobody."

"You are not in love with anybody?"

"With you, with you, woman, stupid bitch, owwwwww." And he howled and beat his brow with his left forearm, his right hand being thrust into his tunic, rubbing heartburn or some such pain, but *heartburn*, in what is it, metaphor, would be all too right a thing to say.

"Well then, if you are in love with me. All is well. But you should not call me what you."

"Oh, I meant by that that, and it is I who am being stupid now, made stupid by the pain of it, you should have been a Russian princess or an Austrian one, and you should have given me a son. The stupidity lies in in, where does the stupidity lie? Fate? Destiny? The force of history?" Those big words which were *abstract* were making him tremble less. "I had best say the word, had I not? Well, the word is, the word is. Oh my God. *Divorce*."

A terrible word. All the two of them could now do was to taste the word, like coffee to see if it was sweet enough, taste it to see what it tasted like. *Divorce*. It did not really taste too badly, for all that it was the most dreadful word in the world. Perhaps the dreadful thing was that it had a *kissing* sound in it if you lengthened it enough, as her Creole way of speaking made her do. *Divooooorce*. On him it had a strange effect, like an aphro aphrodis, for he began to move towards her, right arm released from tunic, both arms out, eyes flaring. His words belied.

"The national interest alliance attempt on my life at Schönbrunn a male heir you understand you *must* under."

And then it had seemed to her the proper thing to do, though her migraine had miraculously cleared and she felt madly in control, like the sea, to scream for the whole of the Tuileries to hear and then, with grace, everything with grace, *very* important, to collapse to the carpet. You *must* under. So she undered, eyes closed, hearing everything, hearing the whole of the Tuileries startled to movement like a flurry of bats in a cave if one screams by her scream. She could see his boots, very clean though agitated, then they flashed out of her sightline as he went, as its opening and his words then attested, to the door that led to the salon and she heard him say quite calmly:

"Come in, Bausset. Shut the door as you." With Bausset there (his sharp intake of breath) she now had to cry:

"No! No! I cannot! I will not!"

"Carry her. Her majesty. To her." He did not have much breath.

"Yes Sire I will." She went totally limp, eyelids fluttered to a close, as he grunted, lifting her, should have taken his sword off first. And, while she was being carried, Bausset kept grunting *Sire* in reply to what he was stiffly saying: "National welfare, Bausset, violence to my true feelings, considerations of state versus the dictates of the heart, Bausset, divorce a political necessity, dreadful but true, I had not realized quite, must confess, that the Empress would react so strongly, Bausset, I had assumed, falsely as it has turned out, that she had already been prepared for the news by her daughter, Bausset." Sire. Sire. Relishing the prospect of tattling it all, despite the difficulty of. He did not seem to have had much experience of carrying a woman. N must have been mad to entrust all this to a *hypocrite* and *eavesdropper* and *tattletale*, as he had always called Bausset, but the whole world would know it soon enough. She wondered whether to sigh deeply, but there was trouble in getting her down the narrow stairway and Bausset was evidently, she risked a glance, going to trip over his stupid sword, because he tightened his hold, in fright it must be, on her. She said quietly in his ear:

"*Crushing me.*"

And then she was on her ottoman in her bedroom and Hortense was there, and then Hortense was there again, having been *summoned* to him and now bringing it all back while it was still fresh.

"Yes yes dear, what did he say?"

"Oh mother, he was very stiff at first and said something about the irrevocability of his decision, big words, *you know*, and that neither tears nor entreaties nor threats would make him change his mind."

"What do you suppose he meant by *threats*?"

"That you might, I suppose, you know, do something—"

"Desperate? But that would be a terrible sin. Me do something *desperate*? He must have been extremely agitated."

"Oh he was. Anyway, I was very stiff back to him, saying that he was the master Sire, calling him *Sire* all the time, but reminding him that he had been very very cruel, all those parties which only really began when you had gone to bed, and his sister Pauline bringing women all the time like a—"

"Brothel. Let us not mince words. And she herself is precisely a."

"What I said was that the whole of France would see him as a heartless tyrant but that the Bonaparte family would be hugging itself with joy, and then tears came to his eyes."

"Ah."

"I said you would do what he and the Bonapartes wanted and what he thought France wanted, and that when we left him—you and me and Eugène I meant of course—we would take with us the memory of all the kindness he had shown us."

"And then I suppose he *really* wept."

"Sobbed and sobbed and went on sobbing about were we all going to abandon him and did no one love him anymore and if it had been just a matter of his own happiness he would have sacrificed it—"

"What did he mean by that I wonder?"

"But the happiness and security of France were at stake and then we all ought to feel sorry for him because he was going to give up all that meant most to him in the whole world. Then I said that we'd need courage too because we'd have to stop being his stepchildren—I changed that to just *children*—but that we'd never stand in the way of whatever plans he had."

"Oh Hortense, this is *really* sad, this is heartbreaking. Oh

Hortense, pass me that handkerchief, girl, no, the big one. You take the little one. Oh Hortense."

"He said that I mustn't leave him and that I had an obligation to my own children as well as to him, but I said my first obligation was to my mother who will need me so badly. He went on sobbing and I sobbed too."

"Oh, it really is too utterly sad, my poor child. Come and cry on your poor mother's shoulder." And then, later: "Why does he have to make things so *difficult* for himself? All men are the same, but he is worse than most."

"It's about France and alliances and so on. Even Monsieur Talleyrand is said to have said something earlier about it being a sad day for France when the time came for him to do what he seemed to have in mind."

"You mean they've *discussed* all this before?"

"They had to, mother, I suppose. It's a matter of the state and so on. After all, they told me, but I couldn't bring myself to to—"

"Without having the *decency* to breathe a word to me." And then: "*Talleyrand* said that? I never thought that Talleyrand liked me. I'm sure I put myself out to try and please him, but he was always so stern or so *sarcastic*."

"It comes of his having been a bishop, mother."

"Ah." And she dried her eyes, then, having the handkerchief in her hand, dried one of Hortense's. "I'm glad you mentioned that. There can't be a divorce, can there? The Pope wouldn't allow it."

"But isn't the Pope his prisoner or something?"

"That may be so, I don't follow these things closely, so much happening all the time and so much of it vindictive and *silly*, but I should have thought that it wouldn't make any difference to the rights and wrongs of it whether he's a prisoner *now*, since he wasn't a prisoner *then*. And, in any event, taking the Pope prisoner can't mean changing a truth to an untruth, it's like saying that if one of these chemists who proved that water is oxygen and that other thing mixed up together is put into prison, then water is no longer what he *proved* it was. Do you see what I mean, dear?"

"What he said to me was about the parish priest not being there, which he has to be according to law."

"Ah. So you *asked* him, did you? Well, there was a cardinal there, and the Pope himself was not very far away, but just because there's no parish priest? I see, and they'll all nod and say *that's right*, men sticking together. I suppose we could fight it."

"It wouldn't do any good, mother."

"And I loved him, Hortense, loved him, surely you must know that? I gave him my whole heart, but I see now it was only to break."

"You didn't give him. You know what you didn't give him, mother."

"What fault of mine was that? These things cannot be *ordered*, Hortense, as you know full well. You cannot order nature. The question is: what's to happen to us now?"

Later, when she was lying alone in bed, he himself came in, having knocked humbly. He was wearing a dressing gown and his great eyes brimmed. He stumbled over to the bed like a disabled veteran and sat heavily on it. "The horror of the whole thing," he began to sob. "And none of my purposing."

She was determined to be dry-eyed now. She had spent an hour of appalled cosmesis on her face's ravagement, all his fault. She was not going to let him make her cry again. For a man it was different, but of course everything was: crying just made them look younger. "If a man," she said, "loves his wife, he does not go looking for an excuse to leave her."

"It is no excuse, no excuse, oh God God God, God knows it is no excuse. It is urgent necessity, it is the future of France."

"Who," she said, "are you proposing to marry?"

"It isn't certain yet. It's a question of either Russia or Austria. And one or the other has to give me a son, an heir, a successor. They tried to kill me, damn it. Meanwhile, it's all to be a sort of limbo. It can't be announced yet, all we can do is to let the rumors circulate, see how the people take it. And we have the victory celebrations in a couple of days—"

"Am I supposed to join in the celebrating of a *victory*?"

"Well, you have to, haven't you, with all these German kings and grand dukes and princes and so on coming to Paris? You're the Empress still, remember, till we get started on the divorce."

"Divooooorce." She would not cry, she refused, not any more. But he cried enough for more than two. Stimulated by the word *divorce*, he was also on to her at once, kissing her face, feeding her whole spoonsful of fresh brine.

"This is not the way for a."

"Oh, what do they know about it, any of them, it doesn't alter anything, you cannot legislate for love and passion." His appetite for her was fiercer than she had known it in years, there was nothing like the word *divorce* for, it seemed, bringing a couple close, or perhaps it was some Corsican superstition about frightening, by mention of that word, the genetic process into at once starting work on a son, not that that could really help much, since she was neither Austrian nor Russian. Afterwards he lay panting and said: "In three days' time there is to be this Te Deum at Notre Dame." That made the tears flow again, and he tried to quench them by gritting out the terrible word. "And the city gives us a banquet and ball the following day."

"Terrible. What happens afterwards to me and Hortense and Eugène?"

"Well." He thought, wiping his eyes with his chubby fist. "You have many things to choose from, no limit really. How about an Italian principality, with Rome as your capital? Plenty of palaces there, a fine city really, I could have it cleaned up for you of course."

She could not quite understand why that should make her so angry. She beat on his chest with her fists and said: "I'm not going to be shut up in Rome, I'm to stay here in France, in Paris, or near Paris. You can give Italy to Eugène."

"Perhaps Eugène doesn't want Italy. Could I have one of those hothouse peaches over there?"

"Not until you. Oh, all right then."

He mumbled at the peach with relish, mixing its juice with a still steadily flowing brine, and said: "All right, you can have Malmaison and the Élysée Palace, and still be called Empress and Her Majesty and so on, and have the imperial livery on everything. And, yes, three million francs a year. These are good peaches, hungrier than I thought, of course it's in the heroic tradition for grief to produce hunger, and we had little enough dinner, God knows." Then: "*Grief*. Oh my dear God, the *grief* of it." She wondered for an instant if that word too was a, but then he went on to say, almost with the consideration proper to an enquiry about ill health, "Your debts. How are they these days?"

"And I want the carriage to be drawn by *eight horses*."

"Yes yes yes. No problem." Plenty of horses around. "Debts. I've had no time lately to examine your accounts, subjugating the Austrians and so on, but I should imagine they."

"About two million, I think. It has been an expensive time."

"Oh blessed lord Jesus Christ, what do you *do* with the money? Oh holy Mary mother of God, how do you manage to get through that amount? *What on*, by St. Joseph and all the martyrs? Oh God, I suppose I shall have to arrange for a loan on your future revenues." He seemed quite cheerful now, though still weeping a good deal. She was able to notice now, with a certain relief at being able to bring it into the main area of her mind, that his breath was bad enough for her to feel a certain relief at being relieved of it as an aspect of her life, though she *must* tell him to do something about it before marrying again. What did one do? Cachets and peppermint and so on, no. He bolted his food, he had terrible pains, poor man. No, it was something you had to have along with the imperial purple. He wanted the whole of Europe, and the whole of Europe had to have bad breath blowing over it.

Lying in silk in her Malmaison bedchamber, she squinted at the clock on the mantelpiece: four-fifty-one, December the something, 1809. He looked at his watch, read four-fifty-one,

October the something, 1812. A long day coming for all. A long day coming for all.

Who would he marry? Princesses and archduchesses all over Europe, and the rule of the silly game, very much a man's game, was that if he married one of them that would mean peace and friendship and all the rest of the stupid *abstract* nonsense with the country to which the stupid girl belonged. Because she was *bound* to be a stupid girl, and he would know it. One thing he would learn was that there was nobody in the entire world like her, now lying in silk in Malmaison and already willing herself out of her headache into sleep and a resumption of the roseate triumph down the Nile. Why did he not, some giggling demoniac voice calling down one of the obscurer corridors of her brain composing itself to roseate sleep madly suggested, marry the Emperor of all the Russias? Worshipped him, he had said, this Alexander, and such an attractive, such a *clean* young man. Soul mates, embraces, exchanges of gifts (my dear, how *exquisite*), oh such friends. The stupidity of men, playing their little games.

Unbidden, the memory of a funeral came to her, but whose? A lot of weeping women, some of her own family or his, a bright gritty windy day at some cemetery in some northern city. Whose? There had been so many funerals and there were many still to come. A man in black, not an officer, a red-eyed mourner, a thin man who limped, had spoken to her out of his grief:

"Why cannot the wars cease? Every year more sons taken from us and for what purpose? It seems to me that a man should be allowed to grow comfortably and dully into age, drinking his real Indian tea or real Blue Mountain coffee, warm in his Yorkshire wool, good Northampton boots on his feet, exulting in his boredom, his *boredom*, yes yes yes."

The boredom part she could not accept, but she thought she saw the rest of his point, though it was very much a man's point. And this man had later talked with N and must have said something of the same sort, for she had heard him booming out, stamping his foot:

"No no, no."

He willed himself to sleep, hearing nonsense. She too, hearing nonsense: "And let your new hats be embroidered with puffettes of Paisley purple and swing with tails of the fine lambs of the Sussex downs."

"Oh no no no."

But now he was back in that dream again, bound, but now she was back in that dream again, bound for the enemy water, floating down the roseate water, what time the sneering bands played, what time the loving choirs sang:

There he lies
Ensanguinated tyrant
O bloody bloody tyrant
See
How the sin within
Doth incarn

See the re-
Incarnate Cleopatra
Barge burning on the water.
Bare
Rowers row in rows.
Posied rose.

One, two, three, and he was in the boat, muscular marines of the Guard ready to row him. He looked across the Niemen, squinting in the huge river-silver June light across at what was happening on the opposite bank: one, two, three, and he was in the boat, not quite so muscular marines of his own Guard ready to row him. So. Now they were both off, being rowed towards the middle of the river, the exact middle, where they would meet. Hellish big crowds watching on the shores, naturally.

They had done the work well, N saw, squinting towards the pavilion set in the middle of the river. A great raft floated, and on it was a superstructure of exquisite workmanship designed and executed exquisitely to the imperial exquisite specifications. On the roof two weathercocks, each with a flag, each flag with an eagle, one for Russia, one for France. There was perhaps something a little farcical about the weathercocks, especially two, as if one should be forced, just because the weathercocks were there, to talk about the direction of the wind and each have to look out and check it with his own weathercock and then smile and say our weathercocks ha ha are in total agreement. Still, they were exquisitely made weathercocks.

N could see the outer door by which he would enter, and that had above it a well-carved French imperial eagle. N could see that A could see the outer door by which he would enter, and that had above it a well-carved Russian imperial eagle. They had embarked at exactly the same time, they should properly arrive at exactly the same time, but that, N realized, would be carrying symmetry too far. "Faster, you bastards," he said cheerily to his rowers. They cheerily grinned back, squinting in the huge river-silver June light, and, the bastards, rowed faster.

N climbed aboard the raft, disdaining aid with flapping hands. He opened his own eagled door and found himself in an exquisite little anteroom. He opened the door that now exquisitely presented itself and found himself in a really delightfully appointed saloon, square lights letting in the dancing river light but supplied with curtains rapidly but elegantly run up in Tilsit to shut the light out if need be. The Emperor Alexander of all the Russias might not be too fond of light, having been brought up in a gloomy lightless land of snow and muzhiks and samovars. Fetch in the samovar and, ah yes, Ivan Ivanovitch, I could fancy a buttered muzhik. Not funny, perhaps. He must watch this post-victorial euphoria. The Russians did not have much sense of humor. There were comfortable armchairs and a chaise longue and a sideboard laden with refreshments—French wine, white and red, in dancing decanters, a Tilsit ham, cold Niemen salmon, confectionery from the imperial military confectioner. A couple of military flunkeys bowed. "Today," N told them solemnly, "the Emperor of Russia and I are to decide the future of the whole civilized world. You're Joubert, aren't you?" he said to the fatter one. "I can tell from your fingernails."

"No, Sire, sorry, Sire, Prévost."

"Oh," he frowned, "I thought you were Joubert. Never mind," he said forgivingly, then strode to the other door, opened it, found himself in an exquisite little anteroom, opened the outer door, and stood smiling in river light, the imperial Russian eagle above him, waiting, even taking out his watch to look at, while the Emperor of all the Russias' boat drew up to the raftside. An exquisite little man in a very well-tailored uniform, rather effeminate perhaps, leaping up, disdaining assistance with flapping hands. N took one of the flapping hands. Alexander said:

"I could see what you were thinking. You were thinking that my uniform was tailored in London. Well, it was not. I hate the English as much as you do yourself."

He spoke really exquisite French, better than N's own in some ways, except of course that N could regard himself as the arbiter of French speech. N said:

"If that is so, then peace is already made. Come in, come in."

They went into the delightful saloon, which Alexander said was really exquisite, there was no people like the French for exquisite workmanship, and the flunkies stiffened and seemed ready to fire the refreshments like guns. N said: "Let us sit." For some reason he would have liked to see Alexander recline languorously on the chaise longue, an exquisite young man and he could see the glint of adoration in his eyes. Young, impressionable, somewhat effeminate. N was surprised but not altogether displeased to find a fire starting up in his groin: it always helped if one could feel *physically* drawn. Alexander took an armchair and said:

"His majesty of Prussia is in a mill. Just outside the town."

"A mill, eh? Perhaps contemplating the great grindstones, eh? Well well, it was a fine clean campaign. Of course, we shall have to get him out, his floury majesty eh?, and dust him off and then tell him no more nonsense ever again from Prussia. That queen of his," he said. "No flour on her, I should imagine. Formidable woman, formidable," he mumbled grudgingly.

"She is in no mill," the Tsar or Czar said.

N looked round from his armchair at the two orderlies still waiting for the command to fire Tilsit ham and Niemen salmon and said: "You two, thank you very much for all your help, you may now leave, I think," and fired into each a single bullet of charm. Staggering, they left. To Alexander he said: "This is essentially, I think, *personal*, is it not? Two men may put off rank and responsibility for a time and enjoy a delightful day on the river. Is not that how it should be occasionally, yes?"

"Yes yes, indeed yes. I need not say how much I admire. Oh, even in defeat I have so *admired*—"

"Let us not talk of defeat, dear friend. What have you or I to do with talk of defeat? Prussia is defeated, and that is enough. But who could ever talk of defeating Russia?" This young man though did not really seem to have much to do with Russia, cheating in a way, no gross-bearded giant in a greasy slop with black fingernails, screaming about sin and God, chopping heads off and fucking brutally, both with quite random victims. Elegant, exquisite, impressionable: the thing to do was to get as much as possible on paper as quickly as possible, before *real* gloomy Russia swallowed him up again and some bearded bastard in the Kremlin heard the voice of God. "Let us talk rather of our mission in Europe."

"In Europe? Our mission?" He started eyeing the chaise longue as if he felt that was the proper place to be for seduction, knowing he was to be seduced (our mission!), but he stayed where he was while N double-gimleted him with his great eyes.

"We enclose," N said, "Europe geographically, you and I. Your former friends the Prussians would have you think otherwise, seeing you as a sort of anteroom to real Europe, but then the Prussians were always great misleaders. They have certainly misled you. But, in a sense, they have done us a favor, since they have at last brought us together."

"Together, yes, I see that. One of our philosophers has said that the deeper purpose of war is nothing more terrifying than a need to communicate."

"Really? Interesting." N looked warily at Alexander, something of an intellectual then, a bit of a nuisance, might come up with other intellectual gobbets like *Who controls Poland controls the world.* He said: "You and I deal with realities, not with the theories of slippered bookmen."

"T. S. Zhevotnoye," Alexander said. "Oh yes, realities by all means."

"Well," N said, "with Prussia and Austria licking wounds which I would regard as essentially self-inflicted, you and I, whole and healthy and with eyes open to realities, may set about fashioning a really beautiful European tranquillity from both ends of the map. You, if I may say this without offense, the Bonaparte of the East and I the Alexander of the West." Unfortunately it did sound offensive, Alexander being a more *hallowed* name than Bonaparte. You could change history overnight, myth took longer. "Try some of this ham, it looks delicious."

"Later, perhaps. What precisely, my dear friend, do you include in Europe?"

"I know just what you have in mind," N laughed, slapping a roguish knee. "Our minds are attuned, so much is evident. Turkey, eh? You shall have Turkey, no trouble there." To hell with Turkish interests anyway, for now anyway. "Take possession of European Turkey any time you wish."

"Thank you," Alexander said. "And what is France going to take?"

"Well, nothing much," N said, patting his incipient heartburn. "The Ionian Islands perhaps. A chunk of the Dalmatian coastline possibly. Ah, my dear friend, this is how peace treaties should be made. A couple of friends on a raft, tidying the mess Europe seems to have got herself into." He saw Alexander's lips prepare to utter *Poland* so got in quickly with: "Did you mean what you said about England?"

"Hateful. A land of rogues and hypocrites. What have they to do with Asia? A remote western island, very foggy, that presumes to meddle in Asia."

"I have always said," N said, saying it for the first time, "that only Russia, geographically and shall I add *mystically*, is qualified to conceive of an Eastern mission. How happy France will be to see Russia fulfilling her Asian destiny."

"But we were talking of Europe," Alexander said, quite cunningly.

"We were talking of England, which is not quite Europe. We were talking of the two front paws of a mangy lion, one of which is in Asia and the other in southern Europe. Conceive of any sacred mission in either continent, and it is always this island of schemers and hypocrites getting in the way." Loudly.

"Well," Alexander said, "if it is a question of getting the English out of Gibraltar, the Russian Navy will be there."

"Ah, my dear friend, the indomitable Russian Navy. And no more Russian timber to build ships for fat George, eh? Russia the very *voice* of the Continental System, delightful. We will starve the swine into submission yet. Could I perhaps serve you with a tiny plateful of Niemen salmon?"

"A mouthful perhaps. I *am* just a little peckish."

N carved him some somewhat blindly, seeing, far more vividly than anything in this light-throbbing saloon, a map of the Baltic, with Russia bringing Denmark and Sweden to heel. "Finland," he said, handing the bit of fish over, "the Russian mission in Finland. How does that sound, my dear friend?"

"We ought really, you know—thank you, that looks delicious—to say something about Poland."

"It is not for *me* to say anything about Poland," N said, frowning, making flashing ringy play with dismissive hands. Oh wasn't it though by God. "Did I not say that it was the West that is from now on to be France's concern, the East being in the capable control of my dear friend?" He was prowling round the map that glowed inside his skull, every river and even the most inconsiderable township glinting obediently. "Spain. Portugal. You would have no objection, I take it, to the liquidation of the Bourbons, very ugly people by the way, in Spain and the removal of that quite useless Braganza family in Portugal, my friend? Of course not. My own people could, I think, take very adequate care of the whole Iberian peninsula."

Alexander took his emptied plate to the sideboard, where N was still standing, bringing a whiff of fresh linen and Paris perfume. A clean young man, really delectable. He poured, despite N's *let me let me I am your host my privilege*, a glass of white wine. He sipped. "Hm, rather a nutty flavor." Then he went to recline on the chaise longue. N was delighted to see that. He said:

"The loneliness of responsibility. You must feel that too. The lack of someone to trust. A true friend. Women, pah." He consigned all women to the Niemen. "This woman," he said. "She will use every art and wile in the female almanac. Tears, screams, cooings, décolletages. But you and I will be strong to resist, ah yes. To the limit. We will not be seduced, will we, by a mere woman, whether she call herself Queen of Prussia or not." He strode in a manly way over to the foot of the chaise longue and sat down on its edge almost distractedly, his face full of the past and to come batterings of unscrupulous women. "My dear friend," he growled.

"How do you do it?" Alexander asked. "Can it be taught? Could I, for instance, learn it? Your really *incredible* record of military achievement—"

"Well," N said modestly, "you have to have a certain talent for it. I do not doubt that you, dear friend, have a spark there that needs a very little nurturing. We shall have our long talks together, never fear. Over there, in Tilsit. But," and he clasped his hands in tough prayerfulness, "you must build your army on *love*. Does that word sound strange to you in a context of smoke and slaughter?"

"Oh no. Not really. I think I see what you might—"

"You must learn that there is no greater love than that between a general and his troops. It far surpasses the love of man and woman. It is a mystical bond, heavenly, above the vulgarity of the mere flesh. And it is a good thing for a military leader to have known the ecstasy of a relationship with a woman, but much much more to have known the deceitfulness and treachery of a woman, so that he can the better throw all his hot affections into his relationship with the men he leads." He briskly unclasped his hands and laid the right one on Alexander's knee. A bony knee, a boy's. "Do you see that, my friend, do you? You too, I doubt not, have been deceived by women."

"I do not think that they will ever love me for my self alone."

"Exactly." N pounded Alexander's leg above the knee as in congratulation on an exquisitely phrased enunciation of a truth not sufficiently commonly acknowledged. "But my men. What do I offer them but death or the glory that they themselves have earned? Such love is, how shall I put it, *disinterested.* Men and men. Love. Disinterested. Ah, how well you and I understand each other."

They went out about half an hour later and walked the perimeter of the raft, slapping each other on the back, though N doing more slapping than A, showing teeth to the sun, acknowledging across the wide water the plaudits of multitudes on bank and bank. A meeting of emperors and *friends.* Europe all set for them like a dainty tea-table, a tête-à-tête between *friends.* Do have a nice slice of the Adriatic coast. Hm. This Duchy of Magdeburg looks rather tempting. Cheers and cheers and cheers over the water. N had already filed a good week's load of letters in his skull; they merely now had to be transcribed and delivered. *To the Foreign Minister: tomorrow the Czar or Tsar is to present the King of Prussia to me. I have accordingly neutralized Tilsit. Get here as quickly as you can.* Guns went off, first on one bank, then on the other. *Arrange for one-hundred-gun salute tomorrow when Tsar or Czar lands in Tilsit. Imperial Guard drawn up in two lines three deep from landing stage to my quarters and from thence to Czar or Tsar's quarters. Seduce the bugger.*

The face of that bugger King Frederick William of Prussia was by nature very long, and daily it grew longer. His Queen, on the other hand, Louise, kept hers round and seductive. There was no doubt about it, she was a very dangerous woman and, paradoxically, the only real man in Prussia. She came to the first conference with her jaunty military shako on over her brown curls, her military belted tunic furred and ruched at the collar, a fair expanse of creamy neck promising more when it came to dressing up for dinner. N and Alexander sat as close together as N could decently contrive. N said heartily:

"Madam, what you have seen was only a beginning. We have quite a detailed program of maneuvers. Berthier here has it."

"Bbb—"

"Good. The Guard infantry tomorrow—four o'clock, a convenient time for all? Good good. Davout's corps, I see, Berthier, the day after. Ah, two days for Davout. Then the Guard artillery, then the Guard cavalry—"

"Ggg—"

"Do you not think," Queen Louise said in pretty French, "you have made it sufficiently clear to us the conquered how strong is the conqueror?" Tears came to her huge blue eyes. N saw that Alexander was ready to be affected and so grasped his right knee under the table. The King said:

"The question is the question is—"

"I know what the question is," N said brusquely. "Magdeburg. You want to keep Magdeburg. Now what I say to you is this: you wanted the war and I didn't. You saw what it was going to be like. Anspach and Eylau and so on. As my dear friend here the Emperor of all the Russias has said to me," though he had said nothing of the sort, "there are no punishments in war, only consequences. And one of the consequences of this war is that you lose Magdeburg."

"Oh Magdeburg," she cried. "The cruelty of it. You can have no conception, not being yourself a Prussian."

"Look, madam," N said, "I don't want any of this German mysticism, heard too much of that at Schönbrunn when they tried to kill me, about how nobody but a German, all right Prussian, the same thing, can understand the glory of the German sunrise and the sacred stones of Magdeburg and so on. I tell you now what we're going to do with you—correct me if I'm wrong, Talleyrand—you have it all down on paper there—we're going to let you have all of the Duchy of Magdeburg on the right side of the Elbe—"

"Oh," she said. "Oh," she breathed.

"But you're not going to have the fortress of Magdeburg. You can keep Silesia, Brandenburg, East Prussia—"

"Not all of it," Talleyrand said.

"That's right, not all of it. And you can have the other place, where the dogs come from."

"Pomerania," Talleyrand said.

"This means," the King said, "this means, does it not, back to the frontier of—"

"1772," Talleyrand said. "And very generous."

"Chew all that over," N said, "and we'll talk about the rest of it in the next meeting. Berthier here says that we have a band concert laid on for you—"

"Fff—"

"That's right. Some good loud music. Opera and so on."

"You have bad things in store for us, I know," Queen Louise panted. "Why do you torture me like this? Why does he, dear friend?" she said to Alexander. N gripped Alexander's knee again. Berthier stuttered everybody off to the band concert. N kept Queen Louise behind and gave her eye for big eye. He said:

"Madam, you're a handsome woman."

"Such beauty as many were good enough to concede I had," she faltered, "has been ravaged by this tragedy. I feel for my dear Prussia as other women feel for their children—"

"Very creditable. Have you had a great deal to do with the Tsar or Czar, madam?"

"Our friend, our ally—"

"No, I didn't mean that. Personal dealings. Have you found him a susceptible man?"

"I do not think, our conqueror though you may be, you have the right to enquire into—"

"Because what I say is that all this swimming-eyed pearly-bosomed stuff is a waste of time as far as he's concerned. No use in trying to get round me by trying to get round him, so don't waste everybody's time doing it."

"Sir, you are a monster."

"That's what they all say," he said comfortably. "Personally

I'm not averse to feminine charm, try as much as you like on me, but it won't get you the fortress of whatyoucall Magdeburg back. Our dear friend of all the Russias—I know him, I've spent time alone with him—he's not a lady's man at all. Quite different, if you know what I mean. If you got a little boy to put on some great act about the rape of glorious dear Prussia, then you might get some response. I hope you understand me, madam."

Her bosom heaved finely. "It is not just that you are a monster," she panted. "It is that you are *low*. A Corsican blackguard."

"Ah," N went, "you have to be a Corsican blackguard to appreciate the gorgeous Corsican blackguard sun going down over the mystical Corsican blackguard Jewish hills, madam."

"I do not have to stay to listen to your insolence," she said, staying. "I can go and leave it all to my husband. Unless, that is, I am your prisoner."

"Ah, you'd like that, wouldn't you? A good idea would be for you to insist on riding naked on a white horse before all the ranks, off to a nunnery or somewhere. Drum up pity for poor little Prussia. As for his majesty your husband, you'll let him get rid of things that don't even belong to him if you don't sit by him all the time. *We're taking Toulouse away from you, your majesty. Toulouse? Toulouse? I didn't even know Toulouse was ours.* Haha. Hahahaha."

"You are deliberately trying to make me angry now. But it would require a better man than you to make me angry."

"You've had it in for me for a long time, madam. Hatred, that's what it is. And the horror is that, with all this hatred, you'd use yourself like a *whore*. That's what happens when you let women get into politics and statesmanship and so on. Met them already. That Madame de Staël, if you've ever heard of her—"

Punctually she swooned, gasping first; "*Ich kann nicht—*" She lay, having swooned beautifully, on the thick enough carpet of the room in the castle they were using for their conferences. N stood there, smiling. On to all their tricks. "Come on," he said, "get up. Very impressive, but that will do very well." She seemed well out, what they called a dead faint. Of course, a woman was without doubt differently constituted. They took things to heart. Pregnant, perhaps? It would not do, of course, to be responsible for the damage of a royal fetus. The shako had fallen from her thick brown curls. "Come on, your majesty," he said, on his hunkers over her. "Perhaps I went a little too far. Too personal perhaps. Not enough of the graciousness of the true conqueror." She was dead out, beautiful long lashes on her. "Is there anybody out there?" he called, hands behind him, going to the door. In the corridor there were men with rifles on duty. "You'd better come in. The Queen of Prussia has fainted."

Two men, having first given N a glance of horror or was it reproach, none of their damned business, picked her up clumsily, like a grain-sack, and put her on a sofa in an anteroom, N first opening the door for them. A damned nuisance. Hard to get the better of a woman. One of the men went looking for her women, ladies-in-waiting they would be called, and found them honking away in German in a sort of cloakroom. They came running in with eyes of reproach for N, crying "*Die arme Königin*" and so on, and he left them and went looking for Alexander, his friend. He hadn't really come too well out of that.

Still, next day (she didn't come to the dinner he'd arranged), she behaved like a lady, as if nothing had happened, and they got on with the dismembering of Prussia. "Where's the map?" he said to Talleyrand, and it was unrolled on the mahogany table. He had just had to take a licorice pellet because of the twinges in his stomach, and he left a brown thumbprint on the margin of the map. Never mind. Corsican blackguard, eh? "West of the Elbe," he said. "Hesse-Cassel, yes, everything on that side of the river I propose we make into a new kingdom. Something for my brother Jerome, the Kingdom of Westphalia. I think they'll like him, he has a fine capacity for making himself popular."

"Oh my God," the King of Prussia moaned.

"My brother Jerome," N confided, "is an international man, one of the new kind. Married to an American lady but, of course, all that is being taken care of, there are limits, as the Pope himself has to realize, we are not now living in the eighteenth century. What's next, Talleyrand? Ah, yes," looking at the order paper, "my dear friend here, the Emperor Alexander of all the Russias, should, I consider, be given the great and flourishing province of Bialystock." Nobody seemed to have heard of it, and there was a good deal of head-craning over the map. "There it is," N said, stabbing his finger vaguely. "All the rest of the Prussian provinces in Poland must merge into a new concept. A new concept for a new age. The Grand Duchy of Warsaw. What do you think of that?" he beamed. He saw Murat at the table, looking strained and eager, what the hell was Murat doing there? Must have had something in mind for him, couldn't at the moment remember what, to seduce perhaps the Queen of Prussia, quieten her down? "It seems reasonable for the moment to assume that the King of Saxony could take care of this new Polish concept, and I know you will all join with me in saying a heartfelt *thank God* that the Polish question is for the moment resolved, a thorn in all our sides." He gunned them all with his eyes, fellows in past tribulation. Everybody seemed stunned, except for Murat, who was flashing brilliant fire from his own eyes in the noon sun. "You have something to say, Murat?"

"It will keep, Sire. A matter of a certain verbal promise respecting the Duchy of Warsaw."

"Promised you that, did I? Can't remember, should have made a note of it, I suppose. Plenty more, Murat, where that came from. Don't worry, my friend." And then, to Talleyrand: "Have we worked out the terms of the war indemnity?"

"I could, if desired, issue the tentative figures, but I feel that for the moment, Sire—"

"I understand you, Talleyrand, plenty to digest for the moment. Of course, French troops will have to occupy Prussia till full payment is effected, rather a nuisance, I hate to see troops idle, but our brother and sister of Prussia will, I know, cooperate to the full. We may as well deal now with what will be generally recognized as a mere formality, and then we can enjoy ourselves a little. Like myself, you will all be looking forward to the infantry maneuvers at four, and I think our good friend Berthier has arranged another concert of massed regimental bands for you immediately after luncheon. Is that not so, Berthier?"

"Fff—"

"Something vigorous and stirring to shake us all out of ourselves. A mere formality, I said. Ah yes, thank you, Talleyrand, your majesty of Prussia is to make formal recognition of what we, for want of a better term, term the Bonaparte kingdoms—Naples, Holland and of course our new one, brother Jerome's, Westphalia—and to accept the permanent reality of the Rhine Confederation. And, this goes without saying, you will once more join the Continental System."

The Queen of Prussia was today wearing something demure, nunlike, form-fitting. "It does no good," she said, "your Continental System. The English have found new markets in South America. And it is not being taken seriously by your own people. There are French buyers in Manchester and Huddersfield and the other place, Northampton. France cannot clothe her own armies, even. Am I not right, dear friend?" she added to Alexander.

"Lies," N growled, "is it not all lies, Talleyrand? It is all lies, my dear friend," he told Alexander, hand nearly crushing his knee.

"Is it lies too," she said, "of your selling surplus French grain to Great Britain?"

"That was a masterstroke of policy," Talleyrand said with sudden loyalty. "That was designed to drag gold out of London."

"Poor Magdeburg," the King said, to fill the pause that followed. The Queen looked sharply at him but then, loyal too in her way, began to fill her superb eyes with tears. Alexander's own eyes began to swim. He said:

"Ah yes. War. It is a terrible thing."

"Ggg—"

"Quite right, Berthier. We need to be taken out of ourselves. Come, all, the massed bands await."

The entire company, except for N, sat stunned at the final

banquet. As for noise, he throve on it: so he told them, beaming, while the eggs and chicken and crayfish were passed round. The King of Prussia, with hand cupped, said:

"Pardon, I did not quite—"

"*Noise. Thrive on it.*" Her evening dress was stunning, and he quite readily willed himself into being stunned by it. It recalled an earlier period, that of the Directory; it recalled early Josephine. There was no doubt about it, there was no getting the better of a handsome woman. A pair of female breasts was, so to speak, the ultimate and ineluctable dual argument. Well, he would prove himself not ungallant. He had something ready, had had it ready all along. "I take it," he said, raising a glass of Chambertin and water, "that none here will refuse to drink a toast to the Freedom of the Seas?"

"Of the what?"

"*The Seas*, dear."

They all obediently drank it. Drinking it, N felt the Chambertin and water strike his stomach like vinegar. The damned Seas, the accursed woman-element, the immutable boundaries of his Empire. "My dear friend here," he said, "has great gifts of persuasion." Alexander looked surprised. "He has, through his charm and his genuine magnanimity, prevailed upon me to grant a concession I would not otherwise have been willing to grant. Danzig," he cried, "is to be declared a free city." He swung his glass round, in a beaming invitation to toast Danzig's free citydom. As they were all still on their feet they had to drink to it. "Of course," N added, as they sat down again, "it will continue to be blessed with the calmative presence of a French garrison."

Later he talked to Talleyrand.

"I must be on my way to Königsberg," he said, "and then back to Paris. I think everything went pretty well. You can see that the Tsar or Czar positively worships me."

"I should not be too sure. Commercial interests in Moscow and St. Petersburg. Reactionary elements in the Kremlin. Beware of the impressionable, since anything is likely to impress them."

"I hinted to him at the possibility of my divorce. I sounded him on the feasibility of my marrying his sister. He seemed overawed at the prospect."

Talleyrand looked at him for a few seconds. "Overawed? Are you sure you interpreted his words or gestures or whatever it was aright?"

"He seemed overawed."

"Was that when you were drinking coffee with him in the corner?"

"Ah, you were watching, were you? You have a good head on your shoulders, Talleyrand."

"I thought you had just demanded some last-minute concession from Russia. Overawed, I see."

"Turkey, Talleyrand, this business of Turkey. You'd better let them know in Constantinople that my present policy as regards the Porte is—well, shall we say *shaky*? But Sébastiani must be expecting something new since the assassination of Sultan whatsisname Selim."

"So you just handed over Turkey, just like that." N.

"Can you not see," and his eyes glowed and expanded with persuasiveness, "that we are on the verge of great things? This year 1807 pulls back the curtain on the beginning of our last and glorious act. A neutralized Prussia—"

"That does not necessarily mean a quiescent Prussia." Ng.

"—Alexander the devoted friend of France, meaning of course of myself—why, the British will soon be screaming for peace. And think of those ultimate peace conferences in London, Talleyrand—Gibraltar ours, India, who shall we put in Buckingham Palace, Talleyrand? You see now one other urgent reason for divorce. The Romanoff girls have always been fertile, have they not, rich in sons? A little king of Corsican and Slavic stock, waiting to lash those puddingy English into *Europeanness*."

"What other things did you talk to him about?" Ngi.

"Alexander? He listened with mouth open and eyes large, starving to be taught. Techniques of leadership, the handling of large armies, the modern way of maintaining supplies. He was sincerely interested. The Russians are so much behind the times,

Talleyrand. One of our missions is, after all, to educate. Remember this, though: write it down somewhere: Women are totally ineducable. You cannot educate a woman."

"You are perhaps referring to Her Majesty of Prussia?" Ngis.

"There was a moment, Talleyrand—" He mused, amused, bemused. "She was sitting in her carriage, waiting, while the King was having a final word with young Alexander. Eyes full of tears, smiling bravely, so beautiful and so much *alone*—because that long-faced bastard she's married to is no good to man, beast, woman, Prussia or anything else. There was a moment, I say, when I nearly jumped in there and gave her what she so obviously needed—passionate kisses on mouth and neck and bosom, a pair of strong arms around her. And then, of course, she would have gone on about dear suffering Prussia, and then I would have said: Oh, have it all back, poor angel, what is a kingdom compared to a woman's tears? The world well lost, there's a play about that, I think. But I was strong, Talleyrand, I did not yield. Now you see what I mean when I say that *women are totally ineducable*." Ngise.

Ngiser. Resign.

See a fif
ty mile long column shuffle
through
Borovsk and Vereya

HE LAY WARM ENOUGH IN HIS CAMP-BED IN CAMP NEAR LOSHnitsa, hearing coughing from round the campfires without, but unable to will himself to the hour or so of sleep he had to have. It was not so much the weight of thought as the complication of its structure: creep round one hummock of it to find a bare corner inductive of sleep and there awaited another hummock of different color, shape and geologic formation. Borodino, for instance, back to Borodino, a fifty-mile-long column winding through, inspecting its own shame. There must have been thirty thousand corpses there, and the wolves had been at them. Their teeth, disdaining harder work, had gone for the soft portions, ripping open bellies to get to the rich bags where digestion had been abruptly halted, biting off genitalia and spitting them out again as too spongy, insufficiently nutritious. O Jesus Christ O Lord Jesus, a man tripping in a cannonball-furrow, hitting his head on a rusty helmet, unwilling, though his eyes were wide with a horror spelling life, to go on, for what did one go on to? To perhaps a remnant of time wholly filled with seeing Borodino again and again, forever. Now this would not do, and N, warm in his bed, nearly spoke the words aloud, for the quantitative view of death, misery and so on was built on illusion. Which is worse, he had once said to a subaltern in the Gendarmes de l'Ordonnance vomiting at his first sight of many dead, ten thousand bodies cleanly shot or a solitary child anally raped, throat slit, eyes pulled from their sockets and knotted neatly into a grotesque single diophthalm by a tugging and then twisting of their stalks? Do not be misled by number, my son.

See a fif
ty mile long column shuffle

There was far more horror, cause for suicide, say, in one man's act of defection than in the sight of a whole slaughtered brigade. In this clean Russian air he could smell the perfume Alexander had worn at Tilsit far more clearly than the wood-fires that burnt through the night. The boy, man rather for he saw himself now as a man, had submitted to bad teachers, and N had a notion that Talleyrand had been one of them (do not encourage grandiose notions in him, sir; there must be a limit to the Napoleonic ambition). Ah, Tilsit, and the Prussian monarch on his knees, and Alexander listening, watching, adoring. He, N, had been too kind, too accommodating. Why did one never learn the great lesson, that the whole aim of teaching was to convert the learner into a teacher in his own right, that the postures of worshipful discipleship were a bliss to the master as transient as spring or as youth itself? See, my son: here is your true sphere—the Eastern Baltic and the whole of the faceless and limitless East; my talk of a rôle in the Mediterranean was a mere gesture of grace, an exorbitant troubadour flourish. Did I not refrain from restoring the ancient kingdom of Poland, leaving a mere harmless Grand Duchy in your front garden; did I not choose to draw my troops into Iberia, there to suffer, as you well know, from obscurantism, superstition, the treachery of the British? Oh, but the ignominy of begging for an armistice, biting my nails through a Moscow autumn, waiting for a letter that never came. Why did you do this to me?

Single images supervened on that one of a kind of animated portrait of Caesar Alexander. His scent at Tilsit became the sweet stench of half-roasted horseflesh in the ravening teeth of an artilleryman with bleeding knuckles. The tens or twenties of thousands of horses dead on the road turned into a single platter of horse-shaped morsels of meat, canapés taken laughingly at some reception at the Tuileries. *Ach*, said Marie Louise, *es ist ein Pferdchen*, and she ate three in a row. That language, then, was now in his own bedchamber, the tongue of mystical dawns and mountains. The naked man whom the Cossacks had first stripped then ripped, from nose down, into two almost exactly symmetrical fascias, became the torn toy dog that his dear son, King of Rome, gurgling now in Paris, had ravaged in a tantrum. He saw the laughing cat-eyes of his wife, begging him to do it again, with no interim of convalescent peace. Under the blanket he was aware of a lifting phallus, the only one tonight surely, he sadly grinned, in the entire Great Army. Or what was left of it. Or what

What is left
is left of the Great Army
through
Borovsk and Vereya

Down, proud flesh. Choose, sleepless brain.

Force the line of the Berezina at Borisov, whip the army on to Minsk to join Schwarzenberg's forces for one last massive assault. And that was out now, for there was certainly no way of crossing the Berezina, not there, since Tshitshagov had captured and destroyed the bridges. There had been frantic riding along the Berezina's bank almost as far as Bobruisk, but no crossing-point offered. So there was then, and he spread the map in his head (at best an inaccurate picture of the terrain, at worst the ultimate and mythical hellmouth), so there was then the alternative of a drive to the north towards Wrede's positions, then a march on to Vilna. But Russia, that one dreamed of in childhood as a summer of plums and sweet william followed at once by snow, had its lengthy autumn and its mud. No real roads and much mud. Men falling in mud and not wishing to get up again. Mud.

He turned over onto his stomach, which nagged him, sniveling into the pillow with what he smelt was the return of his bad cold, and then he fell into a deep peace of mud which had the scent of summer Tilsit in it. He sank deeper and deeper into the deep peace and heard a quiet conference of insects that live in mud. *Not at all sure that total destruction of Bonaparte would be best thing for Russia. Vacuum would be at once filled by perfidious England, terror of the seas.* He saw Alexander lying on a chaise longue molded cunningly by exquisite French workmanship out of mud. "This mud is truly delightful," Alexander smiled, chewing a piece. "Who am I, my dear friend, to seek to prevail against nature? We will sit at home before our stoves with our muzhiks and samovars and let the winter rage outside. We will sing sad songs of poor men trying to get home through the raging blizzards. Go home, my dear friend. Nobody will *seriously* try to stop you."

He awoke in time to stop the dream of the funeral procession to the Channel beginning again. The grotesque band of combs-and-paper and Jew's harps had already struck up *There he lies ensanguinated tyrant*, and he was not going to have it, not death by water. He awoke aware of ridiculous confidence in an impending miracle, then saw that it was retrospectively concerned with Marshal Ney's unexpected arrival at Orsha with the sizeable remnant of the Third Corps that had been given up for lost. He had saved his eagles. And then, at this same Orsha, he had received the news of Dombrowski's loss of the Berezina bridgehead, and all the eagles of all the corps had to be destroyed, coaches burnt, a Sacred Squadron with generals as troop commanders formed, anything to lighten the burden of flight. A second lightening—first it had been convoys of booty but also, and who had allowed that to happen?, the pontoon train. It seemed to him that he had done his best and that now he deserved another miracle. He surprised himself by praying for one, very simply and humbly: "Please God grant the miracle of getting these men home safely to France, and then it will be enough to rule France and try no more mad adventures." This produced the miracle of taking the whole load off his mind and enabling him to sink at once to dreamless sleep.

Berthier shook him gently and stuttered something. "What? What?" N stared wildly and at first took the other officer present to be the Tsar or Czar of all the Russias. But it was Marshal Oudinot. "Oudinot. What is it, Oudinot?"

"Good news, I think, Sire. There seems to be a ford near Studienka, about eight miles north of—"

"Borisov, I know, I know. A *ford*, you say?"

"About three or four feet deep, Sire."

"*You* found this, Oudinot?"

"Brigadier-General Corbineau of the Second Corps light cavalry, attached to General Wredes' command, having received orders to rejoin his parent unit, found a peasant on the west bank of the Berezina who showed him the ford by Studienka. Sire." Oudinot had something of the policeman in him. "A stroke of luck. Sire."

"Indeed." He was wide awake, hugging his blanketed knees. "Get this down, Berthier. Diversions mounted at various points along the river—say, Stachov, Borisov and that place further south—"

"Uuucho—"

"Ucholodi, that's it. Draw Tshitshagov's attention away from Studienka. Get some cavalry and light infantry to cross on rafts or horseback and set up a covering position on the west bank opposite Studienka. Going to be a hell of a job."

"The bbbr—"

"Yes, it's the bridging I mean. Timber. Have to pull all the houses down in Studienka. I want to see the Engineers *now*. General Chasseloup. General Eblé. This is going to be *interesting*, Berthier. Human ingenuity, Oudinot. Oudinot, my compliments and thanks to this officer—"

"Corbineau, Sire?"

"That his name? And tell him he can command the cavalry and light infantry unit to be taken over the river. After all, he knows the way. Now, gentlemen, I'm getting up." And he got up, lalling:

La la laaaah
la la la la la LAH LAH
LAAAAH
Lilla lilla LAH LAH

Apprise the men of the inevitable difficulties of the constructive task that lies ahead, laying particular emphasis on the need for the utmost in improvisatory skill and stressing the importance of speed, General Eblé said, and the maintenance of sangfroid in the face of almost certain enemy harassment. Sergeant Rebour said: Right, lads, as you know, we lost the fucking pontoon train at Orsha, and all we have is a couple of field forges and a couple of wagons of charcoal and six truck-loads of nails. He says he wants three bridges but I don't see how we can make him more than two. The primary need,

General Eblé said, is to obtain the requisite structural materials and this will certainly entail the demolition of civilian housing in the adjacent township. Now the first job, Sergeant Rebour said, is to get planking, and the only way to get it is to pull down all those fucking houses. This place is called Studienka, if you want to know, but the name won't matter a bugger by the time you've done with it. I don't expect you'll find many in the houses, but those you do find just give a kick in the arse and send on their way, Russ bastards. There is a formidable concentration of infantry and artillery under the command, General Eblé said, of Admiral Tshitshagov. Now you can expect this Russ admiral (though what the fuck an admiral's doing in the army Christ alone knows) Shit Shag Off or whatever the bastard's name is to give trouble, but that's all being taken care of by the infantry and the gunners. I do not need to emphasize that the spirit of history is at this moment of time observing with the most concentrated of attention we're sappers, lads, and it's our job to get on with the job and let the other buggers get on with theirs indomitable courage and expertise of the Corps of Engineers.

It was already freezing at nightfall, not too much though, just enough to cake up the fucking mud, and it was at nightfall we got down to pulling this Studienka apart. The four hundred sappers available in a well-organized and rapidly executed operation demolished the wooden structures of the civilian housing, mostly already completely evacuated by the inhabitants. Hammer hammer hammer, and such as was left ran off shitscared, the place all dust and we coughed our bleeding lungs up, but we started laying the planks nice and neat to be laid on the carts. The next task was to construct the bridging trestles, it having been estimated that for the hundred yards to be doubly bridged something over twenty trestles would be necessary. The story got round and it turned out true for a change that Shitshagoff had got news that we were all going to cross at Bob whateveritwas, and the 25th was making a hell of a din, sounding like bridging, down towards Borisov, so off he goes down there. The Emperor was observed to indulge in gestures of exultation on receipt of the information that the enemy had been deceived by our subterfuge. Joy and cheers and dancing around and so on, but we had to get on with the fucking job.

The mixed assault force under the command of Brigadier-General Corbineau numbered somewhere in the region of four hundred men, and this effected the crossing without trouble and proceeded to repulse the Cossack rearguard patrols. We could hear them splashing over, going Jesus Christ my ballocks is gone all dead with the cold, because by now with the frost it was a bastard, and then it was the guns brought up to cover us. Some forty pieces of artillery deployed about the area of construction succeeded with a minimum of trouble in silencing the few enemy pieces that lingered in the vicinity. Bang bang bang and it soon shut the Russ bastards up. Well, we spent the whole of that fucking night hammering away at the trestles, warmed up by a drop of salty horse soup and of course we had the fires going hot and strong. The setting up of the initial bridging trestles on the bed of the Berezina was effected efficiently though not without evident discomfort. The fucking agony of wading into that water that was like liquid ice and right up to the fucking chin too doesn't bear talking of. There was me and Rastel and Lagrange and Perottin and Renault and Le Bellec and the other buggers, can't remember their names, manhandling the stuff with all nails sticking out that ripped the skin and meat off you but the bloody blood froze, but we got them stuck in there. I remember young Saytour going right under and couldn't get his footing and Frere got some water on the lung and cough cough cough. We lost Tissot and Guennec. Numerous problems were encountered but the perseverance and ingenuity of the gallant body of sappers speedily overcame them.

We'd been at it all night when dawn came up and were already getting the planks laid when he himself came along. The Emperor graciously encouraged the engineers with quip and relevant question, recalling his own earlier ambitions in the scientific and technical fields and showing himself adept in the use of the sappers' terminology. We could have got on with the job better if he hadn't been breathing down our fucking necks, but he meant well. Despite evidence of physical exhaustion the work proceeded with hardly a hitch until one of the afternoon, when the first bridge was announced completed by General Eblé and the men were encouraged to throw their caps in the air, though most were too exhausted to indulge in this gesture of well-merited self-congratulation. At once work on the second bridge, the larger of the two, was redoubled and arrangements were set in train for the initial crossings. It was a flimsy fucking structure and everybody's heart was in his mouth when Marshal Oudinot's lot started over, *break step* being called all the time. Eleven thousand men marched over, under Marshal Oudinot and General Dombrowski the Pole with a fucking pole in his pants and the division of cuirassiers commanded by General Dumerc. And then everybody went *Jesus Christ* and near merded his breeches when these two guns went across, but they got over, and then the structure was speedily inspected for signs of inevitable impairment and such repairs as were required were immediately put into we got down to patching them up hammer and nails bang bang bang.

The combat strength of the remnant of the Great Army at this juncture was estimated at some forty-nine thousand, with artillery of some three hundred guns and an incomputable supplement of baggage trains, but there had to be taken into account a body of some forty thousand unarmed stragglers, dispirited and disillusioned and demoralized and proceeding at the rear of the combatant body in something like total automatism. We got on the job in two working groups, one to do running repairs on Bridge N as some of us called it and the other to get Bridge J ready for the crossing of the artillery by three in the afternoon (J, why J, kind of in memoriam somebody said, I think it was Chabenat). It was estimated that the enemy had at its disposal at this juncture at least seventy-five thousand regular troops and Cossacks, all within reasonable striking distance of the Berezina. At three in the afternoon, as promised, Bridge J was ready, and from then on it was a business of keeping both going day and night, that being his intention though after he crossed over and set up his HQ on the west bank (*break step break step*, that was the Guards marching across) he sort of lost all fucking interest, leaving us and Eblé of course to get on with it, and one or two said (I remember Duvivier and Eglenne and Tixier spitting on his initial that they'd pissed in the snow—the snow came next morning, just before dawn—crown and all on top) that all we wanted was a bit of fucking appreciation, those bastards marching and galloping off to safety while we were left up to our fucking chins in the water that was crusting over fast with chunks of ice you could see floating towards you as you tried to get on with the job with hands that had no feeling left in them.

At four of the afternoon of November 27 there was an unfortunate accident, the passage of troops over both bridges having been up to that point smoothly maintained, when the structure reserved to the transfer of the artillery suddenly collapsed. We were standing by, watching for strains, not liking too much the look of the trestles under Bridge J, when Cornevin yelled out *O fucking Jesus*, him being first to notice one of them wobbling, then it was all panic and screaming and yelling as three of the fucking trestles went down splash and thud, and the lot up there pushed and clawed their way back, hitting and screaming *O Jesus Christ almighty* as they saw the planks in front going down, troops clawing at sergeants and even officers (that's when Captain Roeder nearly bought it forever, only his sergeant major thudded back at them) as they shoved back, thousands of the bastards, all arms and legs and screaming meatholes, trying to get to shore. And the guns trundling down the angled planks or over the sides, crashing into the ice, all of them clawing and screaming to shore. All discipline unfortunately failed at this juncture and there were some reprehensible gestures of insubordination which, granted the exceptional circumstances and the shock induced in personnel already in an advanced state of exhaustion, were, even when disciplinary action became a feasible consideration, taken no fucking notice of at all. Every bastard for himself. Hundreds of yelling bodies piling up on the east shore, the ones underneath squelched to buggery, you could see the blood pouring out and freezing at the same time, boots crunching into skulls and eyes popping out and one poor bastard trying to hold up both hands as a living witness to something or other, all the fingers broken, yelling as if he was the only one hurt.

What they were doing right away, those who didn't get rammed to bits in the crush, was to make for Bridge N, this being at the time fully operational, with the transit of infantry personnel proceeding at a smooth and rhythmical rate, yelling like war cries and thrashing about so that it soon looked just the same here as at the boarding-point of the other one. Not only bodies kicking and screams of *Jesus* but now horses snorting and neighing away, and carriages going over, wheels spinning in the air. But our job was not to watch but to the engineers with commendable promptitude and totally without panic at once commenced repairing the collapsed artillery bridge, restoring the fallen trestles and affixing the planks so that crossing might be resumed. The trouble was when it came to trying to get the First and Fourth Corps even into a position to start getting over, because everything was blocked up in front of both N and J, all these bodies piled up like the dirty washing of two whole regiments, as well as wheels and axles and carriage bodywork, horses, some of them not yet dead, only stupefied sort of with eyes blaring at you. What we had to do under General Eblé's orders was to General Eblé ordered not the removal of the obstructive dead personnel and impaired or ruined equipment, since the time required for such an operation would be excessive but the what we had to do was to hack. To hack. What we had to do was to hack. Hack, lads and keep on hacking, Sergeant Rebour kept on hacking out, so we hacked. Suppose you had a big plate of steaks and cutlets and fried eggs served up, and the whole mess was like ravenous, then instead of serving out an egg here and a bit of steak there, instead of that you'd just hack, meat juice and eggyolk flying, hacking away. Gontier screamed and said that he'd just hacked at somebody who opened his eyes at him and then nodded and died from the hack in his belly. So we hacked a couple of ways clear, the things we do for fucking France, and on either side of each clear way was like a wall of bone and flesh and guts and hacked uniform. Then the First and Fourth, a lot of them too sick to vomit, got through to N and J, and then over. There was a bit of a lull then, and along the east bank were these little fires lit by the stragglers who wouldn't go over, no will left in them, and then the ice came down like a great cold flat iron. Right down the east bank as far as your eye could see were this lot, all rags and shivers, who'd lit their little fires and crouched over them, without the nerve or the guts or the fucking brains to do a single fucking thing. They'd gone sort of quietly mad, that was about it. General Eblé, aware that neither bridge was at present in operational service, pending the arrival of the delayed Ninth Corps, endeavored to persuade and even to order under pain of dire punishment the noncombatant appendage of the Army to take advantage of the opportunity offered throughout the night to effect a passage to the western bank, but the personnel in question was apathetic and totally lacking in the moral fiber even to be able to perceive the necessity of undertaking such salvatory action. Quietly mad.

The engineers bivouacked and snow came down over the empty bridges just before daybreak. Look at all that snow, huddling round the fires they fed with boots, rags of uniform, perhaps a leg, a handful of teeth, anything, nobody really saw anything. Look at all that snow coming down. What is snow? What is the Ninth Corps? What does Ninth mean? Where are we? Russia. Where is Russia? What are we doing in Russia? We should be in France. Where or what is France? *France.* It woke something in some. If you go over those bridges there you get to France. Which bridge? Why two? Of the forty thousand odd some left their weak fires and dithered between the two bridges. Which one to take? Which one takes you to France? The Engineers said: We're waiting for the Ninth Corps. Noncombatant personnel had its chance during the night. We're expecting the Ninth Corps any moment now. No no, we're coming over, we want to go to France. The ragged stream began to push at N, then at J, it swelled, it began to go over.

Over away on the western bank, N, in his headquarters at Brilli, watched the snow fall. A rider, all iced up from his rapid fording, panted in with news of the Ninth Corps. Marshal Victor, Duke of Belluno, holding the rear there along the ridge near Studienka, has no left flank worth speaking of. Wittgenstein is moving in, a three-pronged assault.

"For God's sake, man, why hasn't he a left flank? Where's General Partonneaux's division?"

Took the wrong turning leaving Borisov with orders to fall back on Studienka, marched straight into the arms of the Russians, only one hundred and sixty men found their way to the Duke of Belluno's HQ.

"What sort of a divisional commander is that damned Partonneaux? Four thousand men being deballocked by the Cossacks at this very minute. Took the wrong turning, did he? How many turnings are there to take in a godforsaken hellhole like this? Did he think he was in the Place des Vosges?"

"Ggg—"

"How about that Baden brigade? Where is it?"

"Withdddr—"

"Well, who let me withdraw it? Didn't anybody have the sense to see that this is no time for withdrawing anything? Right, I want those Badeners back over those bridges and galloping like buggery for the left flank of the Ninth Corps. Infantry too galloping, no time to lose." Snow and sweat mingled on his nose.

I could practically feel my lower jaw dropping into my ball sack with the sheer fucking astonishment of it. There was this lot, artillery and all, trying to come back to where everybody had already come from, except for the Ninth Corps, and making us wonder why we'd had to build the fucking bridges at all, there's the army all over for you. It was a shitscaring astonishment for everybody including this brigade as it turned out to be, though their astonishment was in finding both N and J blocked with this ragged brainless whimpering load of bastards shambling over crying out for France as though it was a meat breakfast being served on the other side of the bridges. *Scheiss* and *Ach du lieber Gott* was coming out of this brigade, a German-speaking load, and they kicked and pushed and slammed, and then as we expected bodies started going over the sides, arms and legs and yells of mother mother and then down splash and crash and gurgurgurg into the ice and the icy water. It was a two-way push and scramble all the way, and they couldn't get the artillery pieces across. The story got round, and it turned out true again as though it was not possible for anything to be got wrong anymore, since whatever anybody invented had to be less fantastic than what this whole fucking fantastic campaign was capable of throwing up, that they were on the way to make the left flank of the Ninth which was acting as rear guard. Over on the west side there was a fair-sized set of battles going on too as we could hear thump crump and we heard that the cavalry was doing all right and old Shitshagoff was shagging off shitting himself. Snow coming down all the time and those that had time to notice it were fucking freezing to death.

At midday the enemy commenced a calculated artillery assault on the throng of unarmed refugees that was attempting to cross the bridges, the source of the fire evidently the position of the left flank of the Ninth Corps. This envelopment was speedily liquidated from the western bank by a withering storm of enfilading fire from batteries that the Emperor had speedily ordered to be drawn up there, as also from a notable cavalry charge led by General Fournier, the eventuality being that in the early evening the Ninth Corps was still maintaining its position and covering the bridges. But the fucking panic started off by the first salvo from the Russes started the crowd screaming and yelling and turning itself into a kind of fucking animal fighting itself with a million claws. It is estimated that the mass of would-be refugees formed itself into an indisciplined and maddened pack some two hundred yards deep and nearly a mile wide, the panic and indeed in effect suicidal behavior being compounded by the attempts by drivers of carriages to effect a passage through the press and inevitably crushing an incomputable number of the personnel in question under wheels and hooves. Many thousands were dislodged from the bridges and sent hurtling incontinently into the river, a certain number being lethally concussed rather than drowned by their striking of the increasing number of ice blocks that now clogged the waters.

I can't find the words, I just cannot find the cunting words for what happened when Bridge J broke down, it just sort of burst and collapsed, and there were still screamers and clawers and thumpers trying to push on over while it was breaking. Those that pushed the poor bastards in front over the edge got themselves pushed over the edge and so on all the way back. Never in my whole bleeding life. Those that could see what was happening from the J approach ran fighting and tumbling over and getting crushed trying to get to Bridge N and then it started all over again. When we started repairing both we were just standing on corpses that were like starting to dam the river, and later on the hack hack hack business had to be done like before on both the approaches because the Ninth Corps was already withdrawing and we could hear the bugles warning us they were on their way. Hack hack hack with hatchets and on living as well as dead to let the Ninth get through, they started crossing about half past nine and were still going across at one in the morning, and there was the rear guard of the Ninth to come at daybreak.

The funny thing was that as soon it was night the noncombatant mob got all dead and weak and couldn't move a muscle, as though France was only over there when it was day. There they were again with their bits of fires, huddling, some of them sitting on corpses as if they were chairs. General Eblé spent a great deal of the night attempting to clarify the situation to the apathetic and ragged companies, who did not appear to understand either plain language or gesture, namely that orders from Imperial Headquarters had been received for the firing of the bridges immediately after the transit to the western shore of the rearguard of the Ninth Corps. Arguing all fucking night with them and himself near dropping with the fatigue while the rest of us bivouacked down after we'd melted ice and made stews of the frozen horseflesh that we hacked hacked away at. It was hard for some of us to get any sleep at first because we'd had the figures about the Engineers, we were down from four hundred to about forty, no wonder the work had seemed to get tougher all the time. Forty of us, Jesus Christ.

When morning came, showing white white white as far as the fucking eye could see, the rest of the Ninth came shambling along and then over, and at about nine General Eblé ordered us to set fire to the bridges. As soon as the mob saw the flames licking they were all seized with a great fucking panic and they began to rush to both bridges and then to run over, pushing and clawing (those that had any claws left), screaming and cursing us for the flames, then a great number went over screaming, all outlined in fire. The bridges didn't take long to burn out, and down they went *covered* with burners and screamers, like fly-papers in summer you throw in the kitchen fire. The river was no longer ice and water but people, dead and dying, absolutely fucking blocked, a new kind of thing, a river made out of corpses. And that was the end of the crossing of the Berezina. Thus ended the episode of the evacuation of the remnant of the Great Army across the Berezina river, one of the most glorious chapters in the history of the Russian campaign. Glorious my arse, it was fucking murder. The Corps of Engineers in particular covered itself in glory. In shit.

In snow and snow and growing snow they go
So slow in woe the glowing snow their foe
Forego foreshow but oh foreknow the snow
The snow tableau and flow in vertigo
Rousseau and Diderot and frozen toe
Bestow or sow an Eskimo bravo
A tremolo fortissimo of snow

Fifth of December twenty-one below
Eighth of December twenty-six below
And throes of snow below and to and fro
And oh so slow to go and know the snow
To sow and hoe and grow and mow the snow
The groaning scarecrows moaning through the snow

Some died puzzled. Sergeant Huppe knew at odd intervals that they were evacuating Russia and had crossed a big river to do it and as soon as they saw the Niemen again they would be really on their way home, but he knew that the main enemy was England and why in God's name had they had to march into Russia in order to fight England? Because Russia was not supporting the Continental System. And what was the Continental System? It was everybody all being forced to band together to stop England exporting the things she manufactured into Europe, that was to say the French Empire. So you marched over half a million men into Russia to make the Czar or Tsar start supporting the Continental System again. But if supporting the Continental System was the most important thing in the world, then why was the Great Army not supporting it? Sergeant Huppe had had undeniable proof until very recently that army boots were coming from England—a tag in the inside of the boot said NOTTINGHAM, now disintegrated along with the boot, N and TT and NGH and M lowing like ghost-cows through the steppe winds. Sergeant Huppe composed himself for death inside the frozen shell of a horse. I am your little shuddering foal, give birth to me, huppe huppe, gee up, whoa, Continental System.

Lieutenant Ratiano saw his left leg, from the knee down, actually break off, no pain, like a rotten tree-limb, and then wept for it, seeing it in the snow: my baby, part of me, I have let you die. He prepared to die puzzled that God had not interfered in the huge agony of a dying army, but then saw the incredibly beautiful subtlety of the whole Universal System, God using the Emperor to bring about undeniable evidence of the immortality of the soul. It was so simple really: the one part of the Human

System that could not break off and lie there in the snow was the Human Spirit. Lieutenant Ratiano prepared in ecstasy to break everything off, including his brain, and then what would be left was the essential Lieutenant Ratiano, counting his broken-off parts invisibly, seeing that everything was there. Hallelujah hallelujah. And then he died puzzled that anybody had to be born in the first place.

Major Cordaillet was puzzled about too many things—the delay in leaving Moscow, the failure to use the warmer southern route home, the burning of the pontoon train (somebody had said that the rivers would be frozen, so the train would not be needed), but out of the manifold cloud of puzzlement flashed a maxim that he felt a dreadful hunger to be expounding in some military college somewhere to crop-headed cadets, lean as a bone and listening intently, just before the end of the morning session, then home to his quarters and onion soup and a small roast leg of veal with garlic: *Gentlemen, with Russia no army can win.* The winter was killing them, the summer had already killed them: they were dead before they saw the cupolas of Moscow, what with dysentery and malaria and starvation. It is Russia itself, gentlemen, that purveys death; Russia will find one form or another. But for God's sake expunge from your minds any romantic image of General Winter as the killer. He then dismissed his class and, saluting General Winter, grimly died.

Colonel Boutteau, who came of dairy farming stock in the Midi, wept for the cattle that had marched with the army into Russia, now all gone and mooing and grunting and bellowing forever in a sort of Homeric hell. For the horses he felt little pity: they had gone snorting in, willing extensions of man, saying ha ha among the trumpets. But the calves new-dropped had been cursed for not keeping a better pace. He died smiling, warmly nuzzled.

Senior Private Cornu was one of the men who did not drop away from the column between Smorgoni and Vilna. How many was it who had? Twenty thousand? Thirty forty? Figures meant nothing. Cornu had Grandjean on one side and Sauveur on the other when the story began to spread through the snow that Vilna was full of rations, the usual army fuckup, everybody starved on the way into Russia while the cunting rations were there all the time. Cornu said to his mates: Listen to the advice of an old soldier, don't fight, wait. They saw what he meant when they got to the town gates (town, gates, lamps, walls, streets, people in fur coats, *women*) because the raw and stupid began to clamor to be let in: open up, fuck it, we're fucking starving, if you knew what we'd been through you fucking bastards you'd fucking well open up. There, see, Cornu said, look. Fucking Jesus, Grandjean said. Men being crushed to death at the gates, hundreds going down, crushed and yelling. The fur-coated officers of the garrison, leading a small army with guns at the ready, would not open the gates, not until there's a semblance of order, who is in charge there? *There*—a big jet of steam out of his well-fed gob. The only way to stop the hammering and tearing at the gates was to let those in the front have it, right in the chest. See what I meant? Cornu said. That's quietened the stupid bastards down a bit. Then they opened up and let them trickle in. The trouble was that nobody could tell officers and NCO's from the rest of the mob, a ragged screaming lot as they were. Some got clobbered with rifle butts as soon as they got in, keep their fucking hysteria down. Get the bastards into billets, first job. Get the casualties into hospital, first job. NCO's barked away, sometimes cuffing, all right for those swine, they've been here guzzling while we've been fucking fighting. They got twenty thousand (or thirty or forty) into hospital, bundling them into beds or onto floors. They shoved the raving hungry noncasualties (but everybody was a casualty really) into big cold halls and barrack rooms and even into the houses of frightened civilians (all right missis we're not going to rape nobody we're just about ready to fucking drop). Then the quarter buggers started coming round, carrying blankets and new uniforms and rations.

Cornu and Grandjean and Sauveur started to cry when they saw bread and biscuit and sausage. Lads, lads, take it slowly, said one of the Q men, here, have a swig of this cognac here, but slowly slowly. You needn't be so eager to get it all down, there's God's fucking plenty in Vilna here. They reckon there's four million biscuit rations and the same of meat, just about. By the living lord Jesus, Sauveur breathed, his mouth stuffed. The usual army fuckup, the Q man said, nothing where it's needed, plenty where it's not. And liquid nourishment too? Cornu asked in a finicking manner, already near pissed on a glass of brandy. Cognac, the Q man said, and rum and vodka, vodka being this Russ stuff. We all know all about Russ stuff, Grandjean said, properly glazed. Take advice of old soldier, Cornu swayed, don't let bastards get hold of too mush liquizh nourizhnt.

When they woke up next noon, warm in twelve blankets each but with wooden mouths and coffin-makers hammering away in their skulls, Cornu and Grandjean and Sauveur heard from a sober bugger already dressed and going around the barrack room with the news, that there'd been a hell of a to-do in the night, some stupid bastards had broken into the Q stores and overpowered the NCO's in charge and broken the necks of bottles and started to get pissed. They got pissed and went raging round the streets shouting where is he?, meaning His Imperial Majesty, or looking for women, and a lot fell kalied in the streets and alleyways and have died of the cold and the exposure. Jesus Christ, Cornu said, isn't it what I was saying last night? Like fucking children, a lot of them. Where do we get breakfast.

For breakfast, sitting at a table with Camous, Matheron and an Austrian called Eichler, they had a lot of coffee with rum in it which cured the wooden-mouth nicely, and some boiled oatmeal with cream and syrup, and some cutlets and little beefsteaks with fried potatoes, a lot of hard-boiled eggs (stop you having the shits, Matheron said), very gamy sausage and bread, more bread with slabs of butter and raspberry jam, some cold roast chickens, a pint of red wine per man, more coffee with rum in it, some very nice creamy pastries, and a sort of rabbit and hare pie, followed by a glass or two of brandy and water. A bit of all right. There was also some pipe tobacco and clay pipes, so they lighted up, well-satisfied, and Eichler said: How long here we stay? Camous, who'd been around that morning in his new fur coat, watching them cart the bodies covered with frozen vomit from the streets, said that the orders were eight days' rest at least here in Vilna before pushing on. Whose orders, Cornu wanted to know. *His*, of course. He'd given the orders himself to Murat, King of Naples, man in charge. Well now, Cornu said, a good question might be: Where is His Imperial Fucking Majesty, God bless and save him and chew his ballocks off? Oh, he's gone, Matheron said. The whole of Paris is in an uproar because the rumor got round that he'd snuffed it in The Russian Snows, so now he's gone to say here I am, alive and kicking and ready to fuck the first thing on two legs that offers. He shouldn't have, Grandjean said, first rule of command is to stay with your men, that's laid down, one of the fundaments of army law. He makes the fucking laws, Sauveur said. I don't trust this Murat, Camous said, King of Naples indeed, big proud I-am of a bastard, he'll have us out in the fucking snowy wastes again just to show how cunting brave he is. That Eugène should have been put in charge, all right young Eugène is, son by first marriage of poor old Jojo. She was all right too, better than this one he's got now. Eichler said: You not say that, she Austrian lady. All right all right, keep your fucking Austrian shirt on, no offense meant, what time's dinner?

While they were all kipping down in the barrack room, wrapped in twelve blankets with the stove nicely going, the sober bugger with the early news about the drunk and dying feeding it with wood like a fucking madman, Sergeant Brincat came in, all smart and shaved and his belly full of grub, shouting: Right right lads, marching orders, pay attention, come on, show a leg. There were grumbles and disbelieving shouts of fuck off, pull the other one, get your head down until they saw that he meant it, and everybody sat up, a bit bleary with food and liquor and shut-eye. The Cossacks are coming, Sergeant Brincat said, and they'll be in here to slice everybody's balls off, you know what they're like, so draw rations and dress up warm and get fell in on the road. Jesus Christ, Grandjean said, isn't that the bleeding army all over? What did I tell you? Matheron said. Didn't I tell you that the first rule of the army is when in doubt fuck everything up?

So snow and snow and everything was snow
And slow in snowy woe the soldiers go
Groaning at snowy woe and moaning: oh.

We eventually came to Ponarskaia, where it was necessary to negotiate a great hill which was nothing more than a slithering obstacle course of polished frost (so Captain Gontier was to write to his old Latin master, Auguste Longevialle, in the lycée at Lyons). It was possible, with immense difficulties, for officers and men to claw their way, occasionally clinging at dead roots and stones and thorn-bushes, but the horses slipped continually, snorting in panic, and it became necessary, after hours of fruitless attempts, to abandon the wretched animals to snow and, it was to be hoped, a speedy death. The death, we knew, of the twenty thousand hospital casualties left behind in Vilna to the mercies of Cossack raiders would be less speedy and far more terrible. Nature is fierce, but not so fierce as man. The abandonment of the horses meant also the abandonment of carts, limbers, carriages, and hence all remaining artillery and supplies. There was a kind of relief in the recognition we all now conceived that we are at the total mercy of the pursuing forces.

But what will probably most interest you, sir, and, I should imagine, knowing you, incite you to a gust or so of Democritan laughter, is the fact that we had to abandon the entire remnant of the treasury of the Great Army on those inhospitable slopes. I, as the sole remaining representative of the department, was left with the decision. It was suggested by some of the greedier and stupider field officers that the money, which was all in gold, should be distributed among the personnel proportionately according to rank, but I had a vision of men tearing at each other in the icy blizzards of the hill-slopes for possession of mere dull metal, their pockets never full enough, and the survivors falling under the sheer weight of their greed. There were, by my computation, something over ten million francs in gold left there in the unmanageable coffers. Fr 10,000,000—now you have it in figures that dazzle the eye. Whatever became of that useless bounty I know not, but I am sure that, if found by our pursuers or by nomadic bands in the Russian spring, it will be a cause of dissension, death, and whatever other modes of misery gold, as we know, can breed. My compliments to madame. You will perhaps be pleased to know that I am rereading Juvenal.

And so, though slow, to snowy Kovno go
With pouch and pocket loaded low with snow

Forty-odd cannon sitting there grinning at us, but not a single horse to draw. Crammed with supplies, but how do you carry them? The town hardly to be defended, and the enemy closing in for the kill. Seven thousand only under arms now, gentlemen. Seven thousand under arms now, men. Under arms now, lads, they reckon about seven thousand. Seven thousand under arms, all that's left, Jesus Christ almighty. It is recommended that only such supplies as can reasonably be transported by nonvehicular means be taken, and that, in view of the danger of enemy harassment, the town be evacuated with all speed. Grab what you can and fuck off.

I'll sing you a song of Marshal Ney
Whose fame will liv for many a day
The scourge of Austria and Prussia
And the last man out of Russia

At Smolensk the Emperor had ordered him
When everything seemed gray and grim
To act as rear guard
While the rest of the army moved westward

But then in all the snow and sleet
The Emperor speeded up his retreat
But by oversight Ney never heard
One single solitary word

And so his Third Corps from Smolensk he led
When the rest of the army was well ahead
Along a ghastly road he went
With supplies near nonexistent

And a gap in front and a gap behind
Which the enemy was quick to find
So confronted him with huge forces
Men and guns and horses

The Russian general in charge of which
Was one named Miloradovitch
Who with no hesitation
Asked for Ney's capitulation

But for some strange reason the Russian forgot
To order cease-fire so shell and shot
Continued strong and unyielding
While parleying should be proceeding

So this reply brave Ney then tenders:
A Marshal never never surrenders
Under enemy fire no parleying sir
Consider yourself my prisoner

But he could not break through their shot and shell
And so as the freezing nighttime fell
Brave Marshal Ney drew his men over
To the village of Danikova

And many bivouac fires he ordered lit
The enemy laughed and thought that it
Was a camping down for the night
They would capture them at first light

But Marshal Ney's plan was cleverer and deeper
He nightmarched his men to the river Dnieper
And when the Cossacks got there
They found a fighting square

On Ney went only looking back
To parry another Cossack attack
His Gascon fire all kindled
Although his force steadily dwindled

A Polish officer with might and main
Galloped with a message for brave Eugène
Who sent troops out right away
To help the exhausted Ney

The Emperor believed that the Third Corps
Was finished and would be seen no more
Imagine his surprise
When on Ney he casts his eyes

Three hundred million from my treasury
I'd rather give than that such as he
Should go to an untimely grave
He is bravest of the brave

Hero of Russia and Prussia and Spain
Bravest of the brave he was again
When of all but two thousand bereft
All of our army that was left

He came at last to the Niemen's bank
He said brave boys it is God we thank
And his men cried May God save
Our bravest of the brave

Never again shall any see
A Marshal so courageous as he
His fame will live for aye
And we'll drink to Marshal Ney

A great raft floated, and on it was a superstructure of exquisite workmanship designed and executed exquisitely to the imperial exquisite specifications. An ice mirage, oh God God God. One bridge enough, shambling along and then over. Over.

Dumdy DUM
dee dum dee dumdy
DUM
DUM
DUM diddum diddum
DUM
DUM

He stopped his pacing and tuneless dumming as they began to troop into his quarters at Smorgoni. Murat, Eugène, Lefebvre, Bessières, Mortier, bravest of the brave Ney (but he *had* made a shambles at Tarragona), Davout. Berthier was already there, grinning as though good news was coming, getting fat. He said, amazingly without stuttering, life was always full of surprises, "Do please be seated, gentlemen." N said, while they were looking for chairs:

"I have dictated what in effect are the final orders of the campaign. I have also written this—" He waved it at them, what looked like the manuscript of a sizeable book. "The Twenty-ninth Bulletin of the Great Army, gentlemen." How the hell did he find the time? "This sets out, for the benefit of Paris, the present situation of the Great Army in the closing phases of what, as must freely be admitted, has not been the most successful of the various campaigns in which you and I have sought and found glory together." Lefebvre grinned at that humor but then saw, in the great gray lamps that turned on him, freezingly burning, that no humor was really intended. "Paris, gentlemen," N said. "Civilians, flighty, tremulous, panicky, disposed to believe the worst." And right too, Davout thought, right to believe the. "Alarmism," N said. "I trust none here have been sending alarmist letters." Not sending any letters at all, Lefebvre replied silently. No time for letters. "No time for letters, eh?" N said, looking straight at Lefebvre. "Quite right, too. They'd be censored anyway, be quite sure of that."

He paced, belched tinily though sourly, then said: "I tell the truth, naturally. One must always tell the truth. Some of it. Truth is a heady and dangerous brew for the common sort, but we have a duty to the truth. I speak frankly here of incompetence among the marshalate, for instance." He double-gunned them grayly. "Lack of initiative where initiative is called for, too much initiative where unquestioning execution of orders is, ah, in order. You know the sort of thing." He waved at them in a dismissive manner, as if they all accepted the necessity of being occasionally traduced. "But chiefly I blame the weather, gentlemen. The weather."

"Sire," Eugène said. N looked at him, sadly, fondly, his mother's eyes, poor bitch. "The bad weather only really began after the crossing of the Berezina." They could all hear the bad weather howling outside the commandeered nondescript dacha. N nodded kindly and said:

"You are brave, Eugène, it is altogether like you to wish to diminish the reality of hardship. Ah, listen to that gale, that blizzard. It is moving west, gentlemen." He looked at them frowning; they knew what he meant. "Bad weather all over Europe. Chimneys toppling, windows breaking, slates dislodged. The master of the house must see that all is in order within. The bulletin ends with these words: *His Majesty's health has never been better*." He agitated his body minimally and thinly smiled, as in a charade depicting good health. "You have heard, of course," he said, frowning anew, "of this damned Malet plot. A lunatic going round Paris saying I was dead. I," he repeated in contempt, "dead. And then the stupid panic, instead of at once proclaiming the King of Rome Emperor of the French." Ney kept well behind his eyes the horrible sad truth that that was one thing nobody was ever likely to do; for some reason they always forgot about the King of Rome and N kn[illegible] it. A family was not in charge of

Europe, only a man. Everybody knew this. Everybody knew, accordingly, what N was going to say next.

"I am going back to Paris," he said. "I cannot hold Europe together from a sleigh in the wilds of Russia. Europe has to be controlled from the Tuileries." He looked at them fiercely, daring them to respond as some had responded when, so many centuries ago, he had decided to walk out of Egypt. But the eyes of the marshals betrayed, a little too quickly, concern only with the question of who was to take over. "You see this?" he cried. "You see the necessity for my action?"

Oh yes yes certainly no doubt about it the best course certainly no possible doubt of it your place is in it is obviously the obvious thing obviously to—

"I want no shouts of *treachery*," he shouted. And then, reasonably: "You all know the way home. Vilna, Ponarskaia, Kovno, and then you're on the river Niemen. Tilsit," he darkened. "If there is to be talk of treachery," he cried in agony, "let the word be thundered in the proper area. You may all, crossing the Niemen near Tilsit, cry out that word *treachery*. Alexander," he whispered, as though at the invocation of spirits. "What right does he have to such a name? He has conquered nothing. We have been conquered by nature, gentlemen, not by the toy-soldiering of pouting pretty petty potentates. He has one skill, and that is treachery. Well, we may now expect his treachery to inspire the princelings of Austria and Prussia to conceive of new hope—hope doomed, need I say, at the outset. I go back to Paris to prepare our people for new glory, to form new armies, raise money. Watch," he said, looking at them all narrowly, "the treasury of the Great Army. Ten million francs in gold. You may have difficulty in getting it over the hump of Ponarskaia. Baron Caulaincourt was, as he would freely admit were he here, remiss about ice-shoeing."

Why the devil didn't he say who was going to take over?

"You are undoubtedly saying to yourselves," he said, pacing anew, "*why the devil does he not say who is going to take over?*" He smiled at them and it was as though a thaw had set in. "I will come to that in a moment. First, my departure. I shall leave at ten—that is, in approximately three hours' time—accompanied only by Caulaincourt, Duroc, Lobau and poor Roustam. Roustam looks positively purple in this snow, gentlemen. I shall take also somebody to help me to interpret when I come to the Duchy of Warsaw and, ah yes, I shall go incognito, as first secretary of Baron Caulaincourt. Two *calèches* and a sleeping coach—no more. And, as a tribute to His Majesty of Naples here, an escort of Neapolitan cavalry." He smiled long at Murat, and everybody then knew who was going to be in charge. A bad choice, too arrogant, all right in attack, hopeless in retreat, not liked by the men, everybody thought except Murat. "The news of imperial departure is to be kept secret for several days and then released along with the imperial decree to the effect that the King of Naples is appointed lieutenant-general and will command the Great Army in my, our, absence. It is not, of course, to be revealed that I am proceeding to Paris. Warsaw, gentlemen. No lie. I shall stop at Warsaw on my way home."

On my way home. Emotive phrase: some felt tears coming. Berthier sniffed quite loudly: probably expected to be taken back with him, *home*.

"Sire," Mortier said, raising a hand as if in school.

"I think that is all, gentlemen—princes, dukes, marshals I should say, nobility, soldiers. Yes?" with surprise to Mortier.

"What happens to us, sire?"

"Happens?" still with surprise. "You get the army home. Or you fall. You die. What happens to any soldier? A very strange question, my lord duke your grace."

"He didn't mean that," Ney said. "He meant what happens to the Empire. I admit, he will admit, that this is perhaps not the time to ask such a question—"

"Indeed not," N said. "But, gentlemen," he started to pace, "let me say this, something for you to think over while I jolt towards the center, the very heart, of the Empire—this: that we never sought anything, *anything*, but peace and security and prosperity at home. France is the Empire, France. We fought the enemies of France, and we will go on fighting them, but it was never our intention to do more than scare them off our territory —like big dogs, eh? We never sought aggrandizement, we sought only to be left alone, to implement, in peace, unmolested, the principles of the Revolution."

It was a long time since anybody had talked of the Revolution: the word struck strangely—an embarrassment, like an endearment pronounced in public, or an obscenity, or something very sentimental or old-fashioned.

"Is it our fault," N said, arms held out in pleading, "if the cursed English fail to see the light? God knows, the Eternal Spirit of Reason knows, that we have tried to make them see it. These crumbling tyrannies they more than any typify, these oppressive oligarchs—all have set their faces against the sacred principle of the equality of man. You ask of the future of the Empire. It will be like the past, like twenty years ago, if by Empire you mean, as I think you do, that Empire of Man which we endeavored to make replace the old foul tyrannous feudal Europe. We ask, gentlemen, so little, so very very little." His eyes went gradually out like lamps. Then they came, in a flash, full on again. "But that little is everything that history, with our help, has striven painfully to bring to birth. Fraternity." He mimed the concept: a Corsican brother greeting his brothers in a brotherly manner. "Equality." Arms down by his sides limply, a sudden inanity in his face. "And," he said, "the other thing." He strode briskly up and down, clomp clomp over the bare floor. "No, no, gentlemen, no." It was not quite clear what he was denying. "The work goes on. We have had a glimpse of the eternal forces of evil that militate against our simple pure and, yes, *Christian* doctrine. Antichrist is abroad, gentlemen. But, with God's help, Antichrist shall not prevail."

Everyone felt like applauding. He stood there an instant in a postperoration pose and then briskly made his farewells in the name of the sacred principles for which they all stood. He embraced Prince Eugène, Viceroy of Italy. He embraced Joachim Murat, King of Naples, Grand Duke of Clèves and Berg. He embraced François-Joseph Lefebvre, Duke of Danzig. He embraced Jean-Baptiste Bessières, Duke of Istria. He embraced Adolphe-Édouard-Casimir-Joseph Mortier, Duke of Treviso. He embraced Michel Ney, Duke of Elchingen, bravest of the brave, but still that showing in Spain gravely qualified much of the. He embraced Louis-Nicolas Davout, Duke of Auerstadt and Prince of Eckmühl. Brothers in republican arms, liberty's guardians. Finally he embraced Louis-Alexandre Berthier, Prince of Neuchâtel and Prince of Wagram, saying:

"I don't quite see why I'm doing this now, Berthier. Last minute, when I get into the coach. Still, never mind," embracing him.

"Bbb—"

"Let us all now sing together," Murat smiled, "an anthem appropiate to the occasion. Ready?" He started them off:

> "*Off he goes*
> *Ensanguinated tyrant*
> *O bloody* bloody *tyrant*—"

N awoke with a shock on hearing that. He was troubled that the bed was plunging and jolting, but then he realized where he was—in the sleeping coach trundling towards the Niemen through moonlit snow that the curtains shut out. He also knew that the fever had come on him at last after the stern months of being the iron man with the smile, and that these marshals and princes of the Empire were going to stay with him until the fever was spent. "The point is," Murat was saying, "that the legend is broken. The myth of invincibility is not invincible. The British rule the seas, the war in Spain drags on, and now look at this really incredibly remarkable showing in Russia." He smiled. They all smiled. Lefebvre said:

"Over-extension of resources. Damned bad strategy. But he wouldn't listen, oh no, he never listens."

"*You* listen to *me*," N panted, right index finger on left thumb ready to tick off points. "Always important to remember that a very narrow compartment indeed divides the sublime from the ridiculous. I remember distinctly being taught that as a cadet. One man is a man, six hundred and fifty-five thousand men are either a stellar sublimity or a joke. They march, they charge—they are the very movement of the heavens. They retreat, they all have dysentery—ah, how comic."

"Tell them that back home," Bessières said, coming very close and showing teeth that were decaying at the roots. "Get all the widows and orphans together and tell them how comic it was."

"But," N said sincerely, "widows and orphans wholesale, en masse, are themselves ha ha comic. Stage direction: Enter a chorus of widows and orphans. Laughter. You see what I mean?"

"Ah no," and Bessières spat out a fungoid tooth.

"Anyway," young Eugène said, reasonable as always, "it's always a smaller number in retreat. Enter left half a million, cross stage, then exeunt. Enter from right ten thousand, cross stage, exeunt. That is, I suppose, funny." He smiled without hope.

"Men at least have some idea of what they're doing," Ney said. "A man knows he may get his guts shot out. But how about the poor damned horses? By my reckoning, and I think Caulaincourt would agree with it, you've lost two hundred thousand of the poor damned beasts—trained all, cavalry, artillery, transport. That's why it's really the end: *no more horses*. Go and urge the mares in the fields of Europe to produce more foals to the greater glory of France. In any case, the bulk of your horse production is in the German-speaking lands, and they're going to be eager, aren't they, to foal out cavalry against themselves. *Ach ja ja Herr Kaiser hier gibt es tausend und tausend Pferdekräfte*. Sometimes you make me very very sick."

"Oh, I recognize all that," N said earnestly, "and I want to express really heartfelt gratitude for all your kindness in being so willing to be so exceptionally candid. Thank you *tausendmal*."

Lefebvre had started picking his forty-odd teeth with a sharp splinter of shell shard. "Tell me, my old one," he casually said, "what you propose to do when you get back to Paname."

"Well now." N smiled and folded pudgy hands on pudgy tum. "The first thing is to be gay and happy. To talk of the triumphant retreat, the great glory of a planned withdrawal. Moscow on fire, no need to tell them whose fire it was. Then balls and balls and balls. Dancing till the happy dawn, Christmas coming soon anyway. Get some gold paint on the Coupole, give the café-sitters something to talk about it. Organize a succulent scandal. Ah yes, revelations from Switzerland. Germaine de Staël of clitoral fame, bitch, always plotting, should not be in the least surprised if she is really behind all the defection. Pamphlets. A personal account of the impotence of Bonaparte. Why Bonaparte would not sleep with me. Well, the batteries of vengeance may now fire. The Imperial Bureau of Obscene Scandal has it on the highest authority that Madame de Staël conducts weekly black masses with human victim. Madame de Staël has gone so far in depravity that she is regularly pedicated by goats from the famous herd of the late Monsieur Voltaire. All that should, I consider, keep everybody more or less happy till the glorious year 1813 clangs in with bells of jubilation. And then," pudgy hands rolling drily round in each other, "we really get down to work."

"Alas, poor Yorick," Davout nervously ventured.

"Yorck, you mean? General Yorck? Nothing to worry about there, I can assure you. A loyal man, though a Prussian. How often do I have to tell you unbelieving bastards that the principles of Napoleonic revolutionary democracy are international? There are Prussian Bonapartists as there are Russian Bonapartists. It's all a question of time. Anything else, gentlemen?"

"Ooooooh," Lefebvre yawned voluminously, "such a long long funeral journey. Tell us a story, old one, to beguile the tedious time."

"Ah, I was always a one for stories," N smiled. "I could make them shiver round the winter fire in Ajaccio with my tales of specters and headless horsemen. Listen, then, all. It was a dark and stormy night in the bitter depths of winter, and the wind flailed and the hail hailed and the snow came hurtling down in the blizzard like furfur from the lousy locks of God. The young man Leo, whose full Corsican name meant Lion of the Valley, lay warm in his bed when he was shaken awake by an unearthly voice coming straight down the howling chimney. Revenge, the voice cried, revenge. Know, O you noble youth, that I did not fall from the cliff's edge in a howling storm like unto tonight's but was pushed therefrom by the villainous Count Paoli, who was unreasonably angry with me because I had dared to defile, as he put it, the chastity of his youngest sister when all I had done was initiate her into the arts of drunkenness and love. Revenge, revenge. The voice ceased and young Leo, Lion of the Valley, at once got out of his bed, wide-eyed, for the voice was of course the voice of his father. He dressed and went out as soon as the tempestuous dawn had arisen, seeking, as his dead father's voice had bidden him, to encompass revenge on his father's murderer. But as he left the hovel where he lived with his mother and brothers and sisters it dawned upon him that the villainous Count Paoli was no longer alive, having died drunk and swearing when his clothes caught fire as he was tottering to the hearth of his great hall to make a red-hot poker sizzle into his tankard of mulled wine. But revenge still had to be wreaked, so young Leo went to the castle of the Paoli family but found it locked and barred against all intruders."

Davout yawned. "Waaarsaaaaw."

"We'll be at Warsaw soon," N soothed. "Do please listen to the story. Poor brave Leo, try as he might, could not effect an entrance into the great castle, but he was able to go to the stables round the back, where the stableman was regularly, at early dawn, in a beery or vinous stupor. Without trouble he stole a fine piebald mare, but the other horses he ruined by knifing their tendons and, while his hand was in, he also knifed the sleeping stableman in the back. His revenge had begun. In the act of killing the stableman it suddenly dawned on him that, at the other end of the island, there dwelt a very poor third cousin of the villainous Count Paoli, a small clergyman with a tiny parish, a man given to books and praying. So, on the piebald mare, he rode and rode and rode till he reached the poor preacher's dwelling. Come in, come in, my son, you are tired after your journey. Let me prepare a basin of hot bread and milk, sit, sit, rest. And then, while the parson was busy at the little fire and had his back to Leo, the brave and pious boy drew his already bloodstained knife and stabbed the cousin of the villainous murderer of his father many times till he fell dead. Then Leo looked around the small parsonage and saw nothing but books. The better-bound of these books he stuffed into his saddlebag and then rode home, having first fortified himself with bread and milk."

"That's not much of a story," Eugène pouted. "Besides, it's horrible."

"Wait, I have not yet finished. He took, as I said, the books back to his mother and brothers and sisters, one for each. Thank you, thank you, Leo, they all said, but alas we cannot read. Never mind, says Leo. We will feed the fire with them. And he smiled, because he was a good boy and happy that his pious mission was accomplished. There. Do you not think it is a good story?" He beamed all round at them.

Some laughed, some protested, some spat. Caulaincourt, who had somehow got into the coach, said: "It's a Corsican story, anyhow."

Murat said: "The story you really ought to tell is about what that Austrian bitch of yours is doing back in Paname. By God, I wager she's being rogered, in faith. Shagged all ways and coming up screaming for more."

"It was the same with mother," Eugène said. "She was driven out of her mind by what she termed, neatly I always thought, Corsican ineptitude. Her theory was that most Corsicans are by nature homosexual but rarely willing to admit it."

"It would explain a great deal," Lefebvre said, nodding gravely and still teeth-picking. "The rage of the betrayed homosexual lover—him and Alexander, I mean. To fail in woman-water and then to fail on manland—what's truly left, faith, for him to do? He can't even make water, by the way, without getting into a foul temper, and then he pisses squirt squirt all over his breeches."

"Breeches bridges," Davout said. "He's done well enough, faith, so far with bridges, but you mark my words a bridge at the last will let him and all of us down."

N listened to this, panting hard, looking from face to face with growing first incredulity and then anger. "Faith," he breathed, "you talk of faith, all ye of little faith. INRI. Imperatorem Napoleonem Regem Interfaciamus. I know what's in the collective mind of the whole collection of you, traitors. I'll make sure your third cousins are safely knifed, never fear. It won't sink into your fat minds what I said about the wafer-thin membrane between the ridiculous and the sublime. Fat, yes, fattened on the kingdoms and duchies I've given to you as if you were my own brothers and cousins. I've a mind to replace the whole fat lot of you with young keen leaders who have their way to make. And then of course you'll cry *vendetta* and kill the King of Rome. My baby. My poor little boy."

"Of this you're sure?" Davout said seriously. He crossed one leg over the other and let the top one gently oscillate from the knee down, leaning forward seriously. "You know it's yours? You have proof?"

"Look at this," N said furiously quietly between his teeth, "and then talk to me of *proof*." He had some difficulty in lowering his breeches. Where was that black bastard to help him? "Have to cut them," he panted. "That knife," Murat said, "looks razor-sharp to me, vendetta-sharp so to speak. Do be careful."

The scream, muffled by the curtains of the sleeping coach and by the rattling jingling squeaking clopping was heard by the driver, who shrugged it off. Roustam, on the box, also heard it but he did not shrug. Instead he nodded with obscure Mameluke satisfaction. Kismet and so on. The hand of Fatmah. That town in the snowy distance there was called, apparently,

بارسوبي.

Napoleon Symphony-II

His Grace the Duke of Tarentum sang bitterly in the bitter cold one of the earlier of the Irish Melodies of Thomas Moore:

Sweet the groves
Where love and I lay dreaming
Swans on the waters gleaming

He, Étienne-Jacques-Joseph-Alexandre, was surnamed MacDonald, a name romantically exotic to some of the more literate of his fellow-officers, whom it had reminded of, during the time of the popularity of Ossian, Ossian. Scottish, yes, he had at first bothered to tell them, but Irish by persuasion. Still, they turned it into a sort of French name anyway and he had now for a long time been taken wholly for French. Marshal of the Empire with a fair duchy. A multiracial Empire anyway, and just look at the Great Army, what was left of it, now shambling home, whatever home meant. French mixed up with Poles, Dutch, Hessians, Swiss, Mecklenbergers, Croats, Bavarians, Württembergers, Portuguese, Illyrians, Italians, Saxons, Westphalians, Austrians, Neapolitans, Badeners, Prussians and again Prussians. His own Tenth Corps, Left Flank of the Army, had hardly a Frenchman in it—nearly all Poles, Bavarians and Westphalians. Until recently there had been Prussians. But now there were no Prussians.

He was riding, with half a corps only, through snow and ice toward Königsberg. The New Year had just about begun, and he had received his orders to retreat from the Riga area on December 18. Withdraw the flanks, we are evacuating. He had been a long time taking in the story that, in bits and pieces, got to him in Riga. Not possible, it just did not seem possible. He had always believed the Russians would come to terms, he had always rather liked the Russians, a people not unlike the Irish—drunken, lachrymose, manic, pious, unpredictable. Ah, but it was the unpredictability, was it not? Anyway, he had left the Riga area on December 19, making first for treacherous Tilsit in two columns. Not much of a Christmas, not much of a New Year. On Christmas Day the Russian Diebitsch had isolated the second column, the Prussian one under General Yorck—seventeen thousand Prussian troops, sixty French guns. General Yorck, a Prussian with an English-sounding name—he, MacDonald, had sometimes called him, for his pinkness and fatness, *Jambon de Yorck*—had made no secret of his resentment at being dragged, on the orders of his own timorous monarch, into a campaign he detested. So the Russians and the Prussians had looked at each other for a long time—from Christmas Day to New Year's Eve—and General Diebitsch had talked and talked with General Yorck, and now here it was, the Prussians turned into neutrals. For the time being neutrals. Seventeen thousand men and sixty guns. The Convention of Tauroggen. He, MacDonald, Duke of Tarentum, had known all along it was going to happen.

Yorck, at a senior officers' party in Riga, had spoken about three kinds of loyalty. There was, he said, soldier's loyalty—very easy, just a matter of obeying orders, yes my captain, no my general. Then there was loyalty to the monarch which, in his own instance, was agreeing, though with inner reluctance, to being loyal to an army chief whose political aims he execrated. Finally there was the only kind of loyalty that mattered—a loyalty beyond kings and emperors.

"Yes, I can see that," Marshal MacDonald had said, shuddering on the local firewater they were drinking. "Loyalty to an idea. To a philosophy, to a constitution."

"No, no and again no. Mystical loyalty. To country unpersonified in any particular reigning monarch or political constitution. To country as language. To country as the country's gods that dwell in the forests and rivers, in sunrise and sunset."

"A new idea, a dangerous idea."

"Dangerous? Dangerous to whom? Dangerous only to those

foreign powers that would seek to diminish or deride or destroy the mysticism of a nation."

"You mean Prussia. You mean Prussia before the King of Prussia. You mean that God is with Prussia."

"Much depends on the meaning you give to that word God. It is hard to think of a God who is a God of the Prussians at the same time as he is a God of the French. Or of course a God of the Jews."

"It is your own Prussian Jehovah you are thinking of?"

"*Jehovah*. You make a joke. And let us forget also this name Prussia. Let us think rather of the German *Volk*."

"The German what? *Folque*, you say?"

"It is Prussia that will lead the German-speaking peoples of Central Europe to awareness of their special destiny."

"And what of the other peoples of Europe? Will you perhaps decide to lead them too?"

Yorck's long blue-eyed somewhat tipsily unfocused look. Thinking it over. "Make no mistake about it," he said. "Some nations are men, others are dogs. If a nation can learn to glory in the unique mysteries of its blood and its gods and its language, then let it be so, but let it also beware of the *Volk*. Europe cannot be full of nations snarling at each other. There has to be peace and unity, and let the men impose this by kicking the dogs if need be. This is to be the age of the German *Volk*."

"And the French are to be dogs?"

"Do not talk of the French, you who are an Irishman. And being over there—" He stretched his left arm out suddenly and a couple of glasses smashed on to the hard floor. An orderly came running. "That's right," Yorck said, "whatever sort of dog you are, fulfill your destiny." And he gave the orderly's arse a gentle kick while he was gathering up the shards. "Over there, I say, a harmless island, get on with your own language and gods and sunsets and freeing yourselves from your English masters. The English are," he hiccuped, "not dogs."

"They see themselves as bulldogs, big-chested snappers. They are a hateful people."

"They are not dogs, but let them not get in the way of the destiny of the *Volk*."

"Was it not peace and unity we tried to give to Europe?" MacDonald somewhat sadly said. "The Napoleonic ideal. For Ireland, too. The French are on the sea, says the Shan Van Vocht. And the Orange will decay."

"I do not know what you mean by an orange that will *se délabrer*. And let me say this, that your glorious Emperor is living in the past. He believes that Europe is full of feudal monarchs. Well, it is not so. Europe is moving towards the revelation of the destiny of the *Volk*."

His Grace the Duke of Tarentum sadly rode on the treacherous ice. Horses behind him slithered and were cursed and whoaed. He had taken the precaution of having his own horses shod against ice. The horse he now rode was an Irish horse, the finest country in the world for horses, and the green grass and the soft brogue and the rich butter. Uprooted, a sort of Frenchman, with estates at Tarentum, whereof he had the duchy. His loyalty had once been to a Catholic monarchy, since the Church itself had been an empire of the spirit, with Ireland as a well-beloved and ancient province. But no: had not an English pope handed Ireland over to an English monarch? Yet at least beneath it all, in the Reformation time, a common faith. Well, His Holiness was now a prisoner of the Emperor, and how did the Irish feel about that? He knew well enough how the Spanish felt. Was his allegiance to be only to a temporal monarch who hated the English? More important, how now was *treachery* to be defined? Yorck had neutralized, but not forever, a cadre of armed Prussian revolt. On behalf of the destiny of the *folque*. Yorck had ended the party by tipsily singing some nonsense about

O Deutschland arise
Light is rising in the echt Deutschlander skies

Was he a traitor? In the narrowest sense, yes. He had broken his *sacramentum* or soldier's oath. But was a man who loved his country properly to be called a traitor? MacDonald tried hard to see himself back in Ireland, training armies that were themselves institutes of political education, driving the English out, wave after wave of snapping bulldogs, until there were no bulldogs to unleash, or the kennel-masters grew weary. Peace, a treaty, an independent Ireland. He was too old, and the time was not yet. He would die with the Napoleonic time, at ease he hoped in his duchy. But he feared the year that lay ahead. Ahead, he saw in the first sprawl of suburbs, lay Königsberg. One step at a time, dangerous to look too far. He wished he did not feel so desperately depressed.

"Yorck," N screamed, "is a traitor and a damned traitor. I will have the shooting of the traitor Yorck with my own hands." He stamped about the playroom for a time, crying *traitor traitor*, and his little son, the King of Rome, laughed. "You do well to laugh, my angel child," N said, eyes softening, "laugh indeed in your Eden of youthful innocence where there are no traitors. But the traitors will come, they come to us all, hissing in the green leaves, then striking, *striking*." He fisted the huge papier-mâché Europe he had had made and set up in the playroom and a group of lead cavalrymen fell over. Encouraged, the King of Rome fisted with both little fists, and grenadiers and infantrymen fell from the Tagus to the Urals.

The Empress, Marie-Louise, sat placidly in an armchair eating from a box of creamy sweetmeats that had come recently all the way from Vienna. She smiled with her cat-eyes at the Emperor her husband and said: "Sweetheart, rest, you must rest, to bed and I will rest with you, and do not cry out all the time about traitors. In your sleep you do it, for I have heard." Smiling winningly, winsomely, she put a big white powdery pepperminty sweet into her mouth. The family mouth, N thought, looking at it, the mouth that had been on a thousand portraits in Schönbrunn. N said:

"And what would you say if I said there is plenty of treachery going on at this very moment in Vienna? That English money is finding its way there, a million pounds I hear, and your own father is humming and hahing about the advisability of this and the imprudence of that, which means he will attack his own son-in-law tomorrow if the price is right? What do you think of that, eh?"

"Too fast sometimes you speak, beloved. If you are saying bad things about my father, then please do not say them."

"How in God's name can I say good things about your father when he is saying bad things about me? And do please stop stuffing yourself with those horrible nauseating gobbets of Viennese treachery."

"Again you say treachery. But this time it is funny."

"Confectionery I said, I meant. Oh God God God." His little son started going *goggoggog*. N turned tenderly towards him and the papier-mâché Europe, complete with mountains and rivers and horrible eastern plains. "You see now, my dear little one, what they will try to do. The Czar or Tsar of all the Russias and the Germans and the Swedes and the Austrians will all move like that towards daddy, and they will have lots and lots of gold from the treacherous English to help them to do it, but daddy will knock them all back, kick, smash, bang." And to his Empress he called in agony: "To whom are you loyal, to whom, to whom? I must know. What letters has your father been sending you, what advice or orders has he been giving, what has he been telling you to *do*?"

"Always my father says," and another powdery sticky round went in, "that a vahf boofy boo her hooboo."

"What did you say then? Stop eating that damned muck. I couldn't hear what you said, stuffing your gob like that."

"Gob? What is that word? It is funny. A wife's duty is to her husband, my father says."

"I put it to you," he said, one hand clutching his coattail, the other pointing forensically, his upper body hunched forward, "as a hypothesis. As a hypothesis only. If by any chance, and it won't happen, make quite sure of that, if by any chance your imperial Austrian father rolled haughtily into Paris with victorious troops behind him and said *Ach ja, dieser Napoleon muss ein* prisoner *sein*—"

"It is funny when you try to speak German."

"If, I say, they took your dear husband and sent him off somewhere out of harm's way so as not to be a nuisance to poor poor Europe anymore—"

"Too fast always you speak."

"Would you go with him—me, that is? Your husband. Through thick and thin, till death do us— Would you be *faithful*?"

"Faithful, oh yes. To you, beloved, always faithful. And to my little precious son too, always faithful." She radiantly but somehow mindlessly beamed at the King of Rome, making at the same time kissing and sucking noises. The King of Rome stared at her, fascinated.

"I don't believe it," N muttered to himself, marching over to the western flank of Europe and seeing the Iberian peninsula full of redcoats and treacherous Iberian mountain fighters. "I don't believe that anyone is really faithful."

"What do you say, beloved?"

"There's a lot of nonsense going round," he said, marching back to her, "about German self-determination. Do you understand that phrase? About the German destiny and all the German-speaking peoples banding together and down with Bonaparte and France. Do you hear such things?"

"I hear nothing, sweetheart."

"No, I don't suppose you do. Tell me this now—do you love Austria? A simple question even you ought to be able to understand. Do you love Austria? *Liebst du* Austria?"

She forgot about her Viennese sweetmeats and put her hands demurely in her green silk lap. "It is not like France. When I was a little girl we would run shouting through the green woods calling to each other, and there would be old songs when the sun was going down over the mountains. It was a beautiful time. The French people are very cold." N now saw tears in her cat-eyes. He groaned at that bit about the sunset and the mountains. He went back to his little son, the King of Rome, far too young to conceive of treachery, and saw him trying to drown the entire French army in the Atlantic.

"No," he said kindly, "no, my dear little boy. They must all go there, see, on land. Those there at that place there, you see, which is called Leipzig. It will be at Leipzig, yes, Leipzig, when the time comes." He became totally absorbed in working out on this juvenile Europe the basic plan of the ultimate punitive battle, each leaden soldier standing for a whole army corps. The King of Rome kept pulling at his sleeve for attention but the Emperor of France was too absorbed. The Empress sniveled out delicious *Heimweh* from her chair: *Schloss—Jagd—Morgenrot—wunderschön.* The King began to scream and then the Emperor (not too happy about that particular enfilade, frowning) ceased playing his solitary game. The King hit out and the Emperor took the child in his arms and kissed him again and again furiously. "They forgot you. Forgot to. Rally round. My little boy. King of Rome. When the bad wicked silly man. Said papa was dead. But we'll. Beat them all. Yet. The bastards."

Coffee and cakes were now brought in for the Empress by two liveried flunkies—delicate Meissen and steaming silver and a doilied dish of creamy *Kuchenbäcker.* There was also *Schlagsahne* or *Schlagobers* in a separate silver crock, and she took a ravening fingerful of it before the tray had properly been set down on her chairside table. N sniffed and sniffed, as for approaching battlefire. "That smells like real coffee," he sniffed. "Where did it come from?"

"From Wien. My father sent."

N took the lid off the pot and stuck his sniffing nose into the heady steam. Delicious. "Your father," he started to rave, "had no right. This coffee is real coffee. Hasn't he heard of the Continental System? Doesn't he know the law? Wasn't that the whole object of the whole damned punitive expedition? To make all the Germanic swine follow the Continental System?"

"Of my father you should not so speak."

"Hasn't he heard of it? By God, he'll have heard of it by the time I've done with him."

"You must not speak so of my dear father."

"I'll speak of him in any way I choose, madam. There's a damned hard day coming for the lot of them, I promise you." To the servants, who listened, making mental notes for memoirs, he said: "Take that aromatic muck out and bring some of the imitation stuff. And don't you drink it, because I'll know. Oh, here, nobody's to be trusted." He took the coffeepot and strode over to a potted palm, degging the soil with the hot rich brew. The Empress cried.

"You are cruel. A cruel man. Always my father said."

"Ach du bist gehässig." Charles-Maurice de Talleyrand-Périgord, formerly Bishop of Autun, now Prince of Benevento, Minister of Foreign Affairs till his master's Tilsit euphoria spoke, in some hardly audible upper partial, of the prudence of resignation, at present merely Grand Chamberlain of the Empire, made his little group roar with laughter as he improvised one of his famous parodies of the Emperor's domestic life. He did the gurgling Empress very well: "*Ach, du hast genug gesagt,*" and so on. He did not normally perform this act in the presence of the discarded Empress, his present hostess, but she was at the moment showing the Polish princess round the gardens. Women too, it appeared, were not averse to comparing notes about a common lover.

He stood in a corner of the great salon at Malmaison, enjoying the enjoyment of the ladies and the smiling crumb-spluttering of Cardinal Maury. "They do one very well here," Talleyrand said. "Far far better than one has ever been done at the Tuileries. Only a potentate with no palate could conceive of a perpetual Lent and call it a Continental System." Cardinal Maury, crammed with Ruccieri's gâteaux, sketched a sort of blessing over the exquisite buffet table, a work of art in itself, a shame really so to ravage it, full of succulent exotica from the Malmaison hothouses. At length he said, accepting an ice from a bowing flunky:

"Her Ruccieri is a great genius. Laguipière was a genius too but wasted. I coveted his services at one time. Poor man, one of the more regrettable casualties of the retreat from Moscow. Requiescat, and so on."

"Let us say Requies*cant*," Talleyrand said, "while we are so comfortably praying." He used a tone he had sometimes employed episcopally. "And the future tense may be made to cover the *morituri* as well as the *mortui*." The ladies, not much caring for this switch to piety—food or the fallen—were glad to be able to rush over and coo greetings at Henri de Guennec, handsome hero of Berezina, who had just arrived, left arm cleanly and somehow erotically bandaged. He was destined never to be one of the *mortui*—not, anyway, *in bello*.

"The *morituri*," Cardinal Maury said, "are as eager to salute their Caesar as ever. How much longer, my prince?"

"Not long, your eminence. When I saw him crown himself and our delightful hostess in 1804, I said to myself: *Ten years is enough*. And ten years, indeed, may be accounted more than enough for so bizarre an adventure. I remember—it was just after the Marengo victory—saying to poor Germaine de Staël—she must now, I should think, be preparing an end to her exile—saying, I say, that I could not visualize an Emperor Napoleon grown old. His imminent death in battle was a very large aspect of his glamour. I feared, at one time, a sempiternal martyrdom that would have shoved any number of fat and talentless Bonapartes on the throne, but I think the Bourbons will soon be back with us. Nay, I *know*. And I can see a comic Bonaparte gibbering behind bars, desperately wishing to die but unable to effect his own quietus. The reign is going to end in a mixture of absurdity and shame."

"Shame?"

"It will be a kind of shame to many to have to defer to victorious foreigners in the capital—Prussians, Cossacks and so forth. Perhaps the English too. But it is a kind of shame that his stubbornness and pride will ironically bring about. He will not accept compromise treaties and old boundaries. Everything or nothing. And so—the frog-dance and the goose-step in Paris. In the streets, not the cabarets." He grinned at Cardinal Maury, even while repeating: "Absurdity and shame."

"There was a time when you did not speak your treason so publicly." Cardinal Maury smiled, saying it. The term *treason* had ceased to have deadly harmonics. Once it had been applied to the hirelings of the Bourbons, but now the Bourbons evidently, logically, had to come back. Then one could start making *treason* clang like a dangerous bell again. For treason had to do only with the Lord's true anointed.

"I have never deviated, your eminence, from my initial loyalties. But a man must survive. Your eminence, if I may say so without disrespect, has practiced the art of survival as assiduously as I. It is the only art worth studying. Where," he grinned wickedly and with the shocking descent to sudden insolence for which he was becoming well-known, "has his holy squirrelship stowed his nuts? Has he, like so many patriots, a pseudonymous gold deposit in the central bank of the archenemy?"

"Ah—so you too? Well, the churchman, like the diplomatist, has to be a kind of international creature. Like those gray squirrels out there." He looked out to the garden, where a deposed Empress and the princess of a grand duchy were talking in womanly animation. Autumn was on its way. Cardinal Maury smiled at Talleyrand and then sketched a toast in ice cream. His Grace the Duke of Parma came over to join them, patting a belly well-satisfied, Arch-Chancellor of the Empire, formerly

Minister of Justice, still President of the Senate—Jean-Jacques Cambacérès, hale and chronically overfed. He said:

"The honey-hued hair of the Walewska lady—positively esculent. And our dear hostess so amical towards her: see, they practically *eat* each other. Women are strange creatures." He stared at them through the open window as though wondering how best they might be cooked.

"Women," Talleyrand said, "are *permanent* creatures."

"Eh?" Cambacérès did not understand but did not mind not understanding. "The strangeness, I would have thought, in this particular connection that is, lies in the fact that the Walewska lady provided the very tangible and visible proof of the fact that the— The root and occasion, in other ways, of—may we call it divorce, your eminence, or does Holy Church prefer some more er euphemistic, some more ecclesiastically acceptable er—"

"It's been called an annulment," Talleyrand said, the old bishop peeping out, "but I think most of us regard it as divorce, full-cream, undiluted. You refer, your grace, to the Walewska by-blow."

"One way of putting it, I wouldn't myself use that sort of— Well, yes, she is the golden-haired banner which proclaimed our poor Josephine's lamentable sterility."

"There had been others," the Cardinal said, in a worldly manner. "Hole-in-the-corner others. I still maintain that it is the hardest task in the world to prove paternity. There are people, I know," he primly worldlily added, "who would say *Deo gratias* to that."

"You say *poor*," Talleyrand said to Cambacérès. "*Poor* is what you said. I too, God help me, have said *poor* often enough—"

"Pardon me, I don't quite follow your reference— Oh, I see, yes, I see—" He nodded with vigor and his jowls shook like puddings. "Our poor— Yes."

"But where has our permanency lain? She has been the abiding myth, the goddess invoked by frozen soldiers limping back from Russia. She is the core of a whole national superstition. There is a very worrying quality about that family—"

"Worrying?"

"Yes yes, with her daughter Hortense the one shining genuinely aristocratic light at the Tuileries. With her son Eugène the only competent and loyal marshal he has left—well, very nearly. They will survive, and through no trickery. There is something in the blood."

"The Beauharnais blood was good blood," Cardinal Maury said. "Is, I should say. I was thinking of General Beauharnais, one of the nonsurvivors. Fifty heads a day at the Carmes." He shuddered. "Well, the days of Robespierre are far, thank God. We'll never see anything like that again."

"There is something in the blood," Talleyrand repeated. "I used to deride the notion of inheritable qualities of that kind. But now we are hearing a lot about the superiority of one kind of blood over another. The aristocratic principle has been expanded from the family to the nation. Not our nation. We have never spoken of great qualities in the French—only in particular Frenchmen."

"Including honorary ones," Cambacérès said. "A Frenchman is somebody who speaks French and lives in France. Like, say, poor tortured MacDonald."

"Tortured?" said Cardinal Maury in alarm. "Oh, I see. Mentally—"

"It was not his fault if Yorck made special arrangements with the Prussians. And it is, I think, my prince, the Prussians you have in mind when you talk of the new principle—what did you call it?"

"I had not yet got down to calling it anything," Talleyrand smiled, "but, since you press me, I will launch the term *master race*. It is the whole race, you see, and not just its exceptional representatives, that is to prevail. We may, in our post-Napoleonic crapula, be unable to meet the mad challenge of so preposterous a religion. But the German people, under the Prussians, are ready to shout its slogans. You'll be hearing them in Paris before long."

"Ah," Cambacérès said, "you too have suffered from this nightmare. I wake with it myself—often after stewed pike, for some reason—and it stays in the bedroom with me. Coarse sausage and beer by the kilo mug and national songs. There is a sobbing quality about the German language—the very lilt of the L in a word like, let me see, *kalt* or *alt* is an anthem of sentimental conviction. Gentlemen, I have eaten and eaten well—she does you very well here—but I am impelled to sample a few of those *biscuits glacés*. Her man Ruccieri is a genius of the lighter order."

"And your own genius?" the Cardinal smiled.

"Yes yes, it is time you came," munched Cambacérès. "It has been a long time since you honored my table. Tomorrow—why not? You too, my prince, if you can spare the time from weightier matters. I have a dinner for—no matter—somewhat complicated—a faceless gentleman from St. Petersburg. But ah, there is a fascinating problem. I have two really huge sturgeon—giants—brought live, in immense vats, now swimming in blissful nescience of their impending ah quietus. A gift, a gift but, a somewhat embarrassing one, since one fish is some fifty pounds—or ah twenty-three kilograms as we must say now, ridiculous really—bigger than the other. I may not serve the two at the one dinner, since the greater must shame the less. And how could I commit the solecism of serving two fish of identical breed on two successive days? I look to you, Prince Talleyrand, for a diplomatic solution."

"Hm." Talleyrand thought awhile. While he was thinking, his hostess and the Princess Walewska came in from the gardens. A little chilly, Josephine seemed to indicate by her delicate shoulder-rotating, her arms across her bosom. She said, smiling a radiant smile that hid her teeth and yet still left that traditional after-image of a margaric effulgence, "My apologies for being a neglectful hostess. But Her Highness really had to see the disposition of the beds before dark. And tomorrow she leaves early."

"Such displays," the honey-haired princess enthused, with a charming Slavic inflection. "Such richness and variety. It is something that Her Majesty has given to the whole world—this art of breeding the perfect rose."

"They are overblown, most of them," Josephine said. "You must come back in June, bringing your son with you." No whit embarrassed, the perfect rose, art of breeding. "Your Grace," she said to Cambacérès, "must find my buffet somewhat primitive—"

"It is a civilized innovation," the Arch-Chancellor bowed and bowed. "To talk and walk and pick such delicacies from this comestible Eden, counterpart of your bird-haunted paradise without." Smiles and smiles and bows and then she said, seeing the handsome wounded warrior:

"My dear Henri—"

The Arch-Chancellor had swept the dish clear of *biscuits glacés*. Talleyrand said: "Try this, sir. Bring in the lesser sturgeon. Bring it in in triumph, to the strains of flutes and strings. Make all exclaim on the majesty of it. Then arrange for a clumsy bearer of the dish to stumble. The lesser sturgeon will then go sliding to the floor in a flaky fishwreck. *Ichtyofrage*—may one use such a neologism? No matter. Cries of woe and distress. Then lo—the greater one is borne in in even larger triumph, with trumpets and drums. Imagine the rapture, the applause."

"You were always bound to go far," Cambacérès said, nodding in great gravity, as though Talleyrand had confessed to a major sin. "You always had this ingenuity, a kind of artistry of destruction. I admire you, sir. I cannot emulate you, not in a general way. But your *ichtyofrage*—brilliant, truly so."

"Are they Baltic sturgeon, sir?" the Cardinal asked.

"Yes, indeed. Sent overland in their huge vats, fresh now as the day they left their native waters."

"Do I descry, may I tentatively imagine, that the Czar or Tsar of all the Russias," Talleyrand said, "has been in, shall I say, a certain delicacy of communication? Do not answer if you choose not to do so." He smiled with immense charm.

"A certain gentleman—not one of these sausage-eating—or how might one neologize it—*panticivore*—Teuton beer-swillers —though his immediate destiny is bound up with theirs—a certain Slavonic gentleman— Do you follow me? Do you?"

"When the time comes," Talleyrand said, "it will be a civilized enough encounter. He has expressed a strong desire to come here to Malmaison. Here, you see, is a flavor of permanency. I wonder—a Romanoff-Beauharnais alliance—an interesting possibility, one involving annulments." He looked at the Cardinal, who shrugged comically. And then Talleyrand smiled and said: "Cossacks dancing among the late autumnal blooms."

"Charming." Cambacérès drank off a flute of exquisitely chilled champagne. "Exquisitely chilled," he said, "that champagne. There is much of interest lying ahead. After the slaughter. Poor young men. Poor poor young men. It is a pity that the Bourbons—well—"

"Oh, the quality of life," Talleyrand said, "is not to be legislated by the mere head of the executive. That is one thing we have learned. We must contrive our own patterns of existence. There are some most delicate tea-buds in Ceylon. I should prefer to have a London tailor. How one longs to drain a real cup of coffee, *without guilt.*"

"How very right," Cambacérès said with large sincerity. "That is a really astonishingly brilliant method of dealing with the sturgeon problem. I am deeply grateful. *Ichtyofrage*, indeed. You will see how it works out tomorrow."

There were sudden cries of rapture and amusement, the ladies especially going "Ah, too sweet."

"Charming, charming," Cardinal Maury said, squinting at the three little figures coming in from the garden. "I do not think," he said, very myopic, "I recognize that very peculiar— the one in the middle, I mean—now who would that—"

Talleyrand laughed. Napoleon-Louis and Charles-Louis-

Napoleon, the young princes, children of Hortense, were bringing in an especial favorite from their grandmother's private menagerie. It was a young orangutan, neatly dressed in muslin. "Oh really, my sweethearts," Josephine went, running toward them, not really annoyed, there was really something so very sweet about the tiny group. But the mawas saw the exotic display of fruit on the buffet table. It whimpered, half-barked a kind of apology to the little princes, then broke vigorously away from their little hands. Before any could prevent it, it had leapt onto the buffet table and was now swiftly plucking pineapples from the artificial tree. The servants, smiling, grasped at it vainly. It took a couple of hothouse peaches and then bounced away. It surveyed the chandelier, judged it too high, so went and sat placidly with its spoils on one of the Turkish sofas. Too sweet, really. The hostess did not have the heart to put it out. "Naughty Bobo," she kept laughing.

"Regard the massivity of that chest," Cambacérès said, almost like a poulterer. "And the eyes are remarkable—fierce, yet patient, closely watchful yet as though surveying great distances."

"The copious oxygen it inhales," Talleyrand said, "feeds no great engine of organization. The subhuman and the superhuman are alike in that neither is human."

Indulgently they all smiled at the charming bizarre tableau—a jungle exile in a pink and gold eminently civilized ambience.

Clop clop. Clop clop. Inside the plain unliveried one-horse carriage that jaunted down the immensely long drive of the Tuileries sat a solitary civilian—without title, without identity, without any name but a temporary and invented one: Monsieur Léon Laval. He was dressed in drab brown and the brim of a nondescript hat shaded his brow and eyes. In his hand he held a large red-spotted handkerchief which would serve, if need arose, to cover temporarily his lower features, turning him into a man with toothache. Clop clop. At the great gate the carriage stopped and a sentry had the temerity to look in. "It's me, you idiot," said M. Laval. "And I'm getting out here." The sentry, nearly dropping his rifle, opening the door for him, spluttering. M. Laval got out. He nodded at the solitary coachman and appraised the horse once again. No good horses left. The age of good horses was over. She had eight still, good ones, Arabs, to draw her imperial carriage out there at Malmaison. A terrible, terrible waste. Needed all the horses they could get. "I shall be away," he said, "for an hour or two. If anyone," he said to the captain of the guard, who now came spluttering and mustache-wiping out of the guardroom, "tries to follow me, from the Palace that is, stop them. I want to be *alone*. Everything perfectly clear?"

"Sire."

"Sire."

"All right then." And, brim well down over eyes and brow, handkerchief stuffed in backpocket, a few francs jingling in a side breeches-pocket, he made his way left right left right toward the Place de la Concorde. He noted the Seine to his left, *his* river, and watched unamiably ladies and gentlemen on foot, tasting the late afternoon's *fraîcheur*, coming over the Pont Royal. He saw inly sappers blowing it up, enemy flesh and rags going boom crack up into the air. He invented, for some reason, a stupid sapper ordered to blow up the bridge after the French had got across but, the fucking idiot, getting nervous and blowing it while they were still crossing. The army was not what it was. Too many young untrained idiots, rightly called Marie-Louises, meaning well but getting nervous.

Formations of the right wing. He walked, hands locked behind him, towards the Place de la Concorde. Third Corps. Fifteen thousand infantry, Eighth Division. Lefol? Thousand cavalry, the Tenth. Habert, yes. One hundred and fifty sappers, thirty-eight guns.

He had once regularly, as First Consul, made these quietly

listening and incognito ventures into the life of demotic Paris, finding out what was going on, good leadership, hear the voice of the people. Once he had gone without money, ordered coffee and been unable to pay for it. Hell of a row, holding on to his incognito. This is my city. I showed the bastards how to number the houses, for instance. Make your starting-point the river, everything springs from the river. Public fountains. Names. And yet it was possible, just about, that he would never see Paris again. Tomorrow into battle, not incognito then. Decisive campaign, ultimate campaign. By God, there would have to be brilliance, by Christ, there would, as never before. German-speaking bastards of Europe, unite against your common foe. There he goes, ensanguinated tyrant. O bloody bloody. He frowned over to his left at the Pont de la Concorde, a smart carriage coming across, two well-groomed prancers. He packed the charges, ordered ignition, stood back and waited. Rags and flesh and whalebone corset going up crash boom into the air.

Left right left right. He attracted no attention, though he had the impression that a lieutenant on crutches with half a leg looked with the sharpness of sudden recognition of somebody, don't quite know who, met him somewhere. M. Laval had a sudden spasm of toothache. He sat at a table outside a café called the Saint Dizier, strange name for a café, perhaps the owner was born there, and waited till someone should come to ask him his pleasure, which would be a small black coffee, no real pleasure. Meanwhile he listened and watched from great shadowed eyes. There were two rather silly youths lounging together at a table over *eau sucrée*, playing a stupid idle game which consisted of trying to slap each other's right hand as soon as it came down to the table before it flew off again. Idle young sods, why weren't they in the army, every man, every young imbecile even needed. A fat woman in black sat weeping over a large tumbler of red and a plate of cakes. Widow, war, probably. No, too old, if bereavement was recent, probably lost son. M. Laval was surprised to hear the woman say to herself:

"Wretched man, wretched wretched butcher of a man."

She said it though, though with wet eyes, with a kind of contentment, scoffing away. The waiter came up to M. Laval and asked him what his pleasure was. A small black coffee.

"A small cup of *diarrhée noire* for the gentleman, certainly."

So that's what they were calling it. M. Laval could not resist holding the waiter back by his dirty shirtsleeve and saying: "The Continental System, my friend. The filthy British and their filthy control of the seas." The waiter said:

"The Continental Arsehole, sir, if you will pardon the scatology. I would gladly give my left testicle for a cup of reasonable mocha."

Go and visit my wife, M. Laval felt like gloomily saying, and join her in a drop of illegal Viennese in one of the locked toilets of the Tuileries. "I will have instead," he said instead, "a glass of water and a small measure of red wine to mix with it." The waiter frowned at him, staring, M. Laval had a new twinge of toothache and warmed it against the mild winter with his spotted handkerchief, the waiter went off. M. Laval, his pain abated, saw with softening eyes a couple of scarred veterans totter to the table next to his. They waved at the departing waiter and one of them called hoarsely:

"Two balloons of blood." M. Laval said:

"Gentlemen, allow me to pay. It will be an inadequate but sincere expression of the heartfelt pride and gratitude any loyal Frenchman must feel in respect of your heroism, suffering and achievement."

"Well now, that's kind, sir," said the one with more nicotine on his moustache. "Make it two large cognacs instead," he called, but the waiter had already gone in. "And as for what we've done, sir, why, we'd be happy to do it again if we weren't all hacked to pieces like you see."

"That's right, sir," said the other hoarsely.

"What battle, gentlemen?" M. Laval asked.

"It was the battle of Borodino in Russia," the more nicotined one said, "and a right bastard it was, wasn't it, Jules, what with the Cossack horsemen hacking men's balls off for the joke of it.

And we were frozen with the snow and the whole battlefield was like all smoked up with the frozen breaths of the men. It was a terrible occasion, sir, and lucky you were to be safe and sound here in Paris while we were protecting the Emperor, God bless him, from his fierce Russian foes, more like beasts than men, isn't that right, Jules?"

"There was no snow then," M. Laval said. "The battle of Borodino took place in September."

"You're telling us, who was there? The snow starts in Russia very early and the fields was frozen in late August. Wolves howling round the bivouacs in the night, but the job had to be done for the Emperor, and by the little mother of the good God we did it. Right, Jules?"

"Right, Louis."

"And what was it all about?" M. Laval asked. "Forgive my ignorance, but I could never make any sense of the newspaper reports."

"Quite right, too. The papers are all a load of shitten lies put out by the Government." The drinks came. "Look, it was two cognacs we ordered, this gentleman being kind enough to be willing to pay."

"Make up your minds, soldiers, run off my feet as you can see."

"And how about us, friend, with our feet frozen and bleeding and the toes dropping off in the snows of Borodino? We'll have these but we'll have two cognacs as well when you've given your lilywhite tootsies a nice little bit of repose, friend. Health."

"Health," M. Laval responded in watered wine. "You were saying?"

"I was saying don't believe a word you read, sir. We marched into Russia a million strong to teach the Russes a bit of a lesson. The Emperor wanted to marry the King of Russia's sister and the King of Russia said: What, my blue-blooded kith and kin marry a Corsican nobody like you? So it had to be revenge, what the Corsicans call the vendetta. So we set fire to Moscow and off home we went, but the treacherous Russ bastards stole all our supplies and killed the cavalry. A great man the Emperor, sir, and we'll drink to him." M. Laval joined the others in drinking to him. M. Laval said:

"And what do you think will happen now?"

"In what lies ahead?" The nicotined one was content to do all the talking and the hoarse one, perhaps because of hoarseness, content to let him. "In what lies ahead." He liked the phrase. "What lies ahead is blue and bloody murder. It's not the Emperor's fault, it's these little boys they're drafting, some of them don't even have a razor in their kit, the good men being done for in the great Russian battles. The big days being over, sir, and we must take what's coming, having had our bit of fun. And no horses to pull the gun-limbers. I remember," he said, "the sad face of the Emperor—*Le Tondu* we used to call him, to his face sometimes when he was in a good mood, and he'd laugh till he near did peepee in his pantaloons—the sad face of the Emperor, and he spoke to me sadly—he knew my name, knew everybody's name near. 'Raybaut,' he said, that being my name, 'we're all getting old now, but by the Lord Jesus Christ and his Blessed Mother we've had good times together. Comrades-in-arms, fighting for the glory of France, but the good times can't last. So I'll shake hands with you, Raybaut, old comrade, and say God bless you.' " Tears came to his eyes and he wiped a snivel away with the back of his hand. "Loved his men, he did, even while he was sending off hundreds and thousands of them to be castrated by the Cossacks. So there it is, sir, and there's an old soldier's story for you. And here come the cognacs, so once again your very good health."

M. Laval now did a thing he knew he should not really do, but it was difficult to resist. He removed his wide-brimmed hat and showed his naked Bonaparte face to the veterans. They gazed at him wondering for a space, then the hoarse one said:

"A very nice and patriotic thing to do, sir. Taking your hat off like that to two old soldiers. Thank you, sir, and any time you'd like us to drink your health in return only too ready to oblige." Their glasses had become empty, in the manner of the vessels of the lower orders, without their apparently having touched them. M. Laval put his hat back on, threw a few sous on the table, and said:

"I wish to God I'd really had you at Borodino, scrimshankers and malingering bastards." He put a swift evil eye on them and went while they were preparing their whines and obscenities. He walked on left right left right. The whores were flaunting, early as it was, and one said: "Time for a short time, my old one?" A blind man led by a child plodded begging, a placard about his neck that said DISABLED AT AUSTERLITZ. He came left right to a café called The Wooden Horse of Troy. There were no tables outside—the customers here felt the mild winter more than those of the Saint Dizier—and, going into darkness and smoke, he saw nesh intellectuals and heard them giggling and bleating. That sort of café then. He ordered water flavored with peppermint essence and sat scowling. Five men at a table with four empty bottles and a full red one that was being glugged out shakily into all glasses went into intellectual screams and chortles at something that a sixth, pale-haired and chinless but otherwise acceptable cannon food, was reading aloud:

" 'As with all tyrannies, sexual license in high places went hand in hand with the suppression of free speech. When the tyrant met his end during the battle of Paris, occasion was found to ransack his secret drawers and other hiding-places, and a good deal of choice sodomitic fantasy was brought to light, some pictorial, some pseudo-literary. The true pornography, in his evident view, was any kind of writing that spoke the truth. Perverts love the dark, as is well-known—' "

"She's priceless," someone bleated.

"Listen—it goes on: 'The conduct of war was, to him, a highly extravagant mode of self-stimulation. It is conceivable that Austerlitz contrived for him a modest ejaculation, but the massive slaughter and suffering of the Russian campaign must, one hopes, have procured a truly satisfying orgasm—else, what waste.' "

"What," M. Laval said, "what," trying to get the word in through the screams and giggles and I-shall-expires, "What is this about the battle of Paris?" He calmed his breathing, smiled even, a fellow intellectual. "Of Paris?"

Wet eyes turned to him. The chinless pale-haired said, face broken with laughter: "I don't think we've had the pleasure, sir." Another, less formal, said: "A little piece of satirical history, set in the future." M. Laval said: "Mme de Staël?" Oh, most certainly dear Germaine, voice of witty common sense. Where, M. Laval, wondered, were the secret police these days? Why were not the frontiers better watched? Filth like that excreted out of Switzerland. He wondered for a delirious instant if it might be worthwhile to invade in order to capture her and make her, in public naturally, eat her own words, pulped up with the urine of selected members of the Old Guard. He said now, bravely:

"And what strategical ideas does she have for the defense of Paris?"

Oh, buy it yourself, sir, read it, banned of course, but there are copies on sale under the counter of the Librairie Clochard. Fools, M. Laval thought. Traitors to their own kind. Inviting a total stranger to call the police in. Intellectuals were always untrustworthy. They would sell their mothers for a witty quip. The intellectuals at the table now, in the stupid manner of intellectuals, turned their backs on M. Laval and began to talk about what he was very interested to know.

"But, my dear, Schnitzelbank is very good indeed on that particular theory. A civilization has to be *raped* occasionally for its own good. The forced feeding of new ideas, new modes of sensibility."

"I doubt that the Russians would have much to offer. I can foresee gloomy Ivans weeping in our cafés crying for muzhiks and samovars, whatever those might be."

"Oh, but the ikons, the Byzantine configurations. A new couture—imagine fur and boots on the ladies, *ravishing*—"

"Their cuisine is dull—"

"They have the best caviar in the world. I was given a remarkable recipe the other day for what are called, I think, blinis—"

"And the Germans?"

"A lumpish people, but they are starting to break up the lumps and reach friable soil. Have you heard of Jacob Grimm? Court librarian, so I hear, to silly old King Jerome Bonaparte in Westphalia. Tales of the *Volk*—Fayotte can read German, got a copy out of Berlin. The most incredible bloodthirsty myths —universal soul—exciting—"

M. Laval left his drink and a couple of sous and stood up. He had, he thought, perhaps better make a kind of ritual of this hat-doffing. Delayed reactions, eventual nightmares. He doffed his hat, saying:

"Thank you, gentlemen, for the er brief intellectual stimulation you have kindly given a man much cut-off from the great world. I will most certainly send someone round to the Librairie Clochard to collect all available copies." They all looked up at him. The pale-haired chinless one gave a giggle like a hiccup and said:

"You have, sir, but you must have been told this often, the most astonishing resemblance to the Ensanguinated Tyrant."

"He means our Senior Citizen," another said, grinning. "Pray forgive him, sir, he doesn't really mean to be insulting."

M. Laval went out, hearing intellectual laughter. Silly old oaf, out of his depth, out of his waters, this is a *literary* café. Left right left right. And suppose it did come to a matter of defending a city not worth defending? Well, one thought solely in terms of technique, holding one's reserve line up there, say, in Montmartre, stretching chains across the streets, fixing useful vantage-points for snipers, learning something from the Spaniards. The worth of the citizens was beside the point. He walked on left right and saw, with some satisfaction, the police at their work. In a sidestreet a ragged fanatic had been mounted on a box, now overturned, the man himself squirming in strong arms, crying out his thwarted peroration: "And so I say, citizens, that this is not what the good Lord intended when he gave men and women the gift of life. Is it to be all war, all specious glory, our sons led off like calves to the butchery, and for what *for what?*" The small squad of police grinned widely, beating him with truncheons, an old woman who screamed "And what's he said but the truth, are men to be beaten for telling the truth?" being truncheoned playfully on her old fat arse, the street being roughly cleared of the scant audience. M. Laval stood watching, and a policeman came up to him and said, "You, friend, don't loiter if you know what's good for you." He tickled his elbow with his truncheon, and M. Laval said to himself: No point in telling myself *if he only knew if he only knew*, since the law is the same for all men. "Sorry, constable," he muttered and went off, left right left right.

In a café called pretentiously The Fontainebleau, M. Laval sat amid gilt and glass while men of business, not grown noticeably thin on the Continental System, drank cognac and seltzer water and told scurrilous stories. "So old Nap says to this well-hung grenadier: Look, my old, how would you like to help your country get an heir to the throne and earn a thousand louis into the bargain? She's up there waiting, you go up and I'll wait down here. So he waits and waits and after three hours and a bit this grenadier staggers downstairs, shagged, and Nap says: Well, did you do it? Oh yes, Sire, says the grenadier, I did it ten times. Excellent excellent, says Nap. And I could have done it more, says the grenadier, if I hadn't run out of condoms." Laughter. "Wait, I've not done. So old Nap says: But I made it absolutely clear that it's an heir to the throne we're after. The grenadier looks a bit sheepish and says: Well, I know, Sire, but at the last minute I thought I'd better be careful. You never know what you're going to pick up from these foreign bints." Roars and coughs and backslaps.

M. Laval sat over his small black coffee-substitute and trembled. If he got up now and said Dirty swine, you're speaking of the Empress, that would be the best joke of all. Ah, filthy Paris, ingrate of a city, yawning over glory, deserving all the big stick the Allies could give her, palpitating with longing for her punition. Well then, remove the seat of government to, say, Orléans. But it would be the same there, they would be trembling with joy at the prospect of *the end*. Flighty, capricious, always easily bored, always ready for a change. By God, he had a mind to bring the Terror back, but they'd like that too, not boring anyway, always somebody to be informed on, the thrilling stuff of prospective anecdote. One of the laughing men in the drinking group saw his glumness and cried, "Cheer up, friend, it may never happen." Then he became immersed in a serious discussion about techniques of illegal importation. M. Laval left money on the table, got up, took off his hat, was lavishly unrecognized. No need for the disguise, he thought. I am your Emperor, gentlemen. Oh yes, and when are you going to stop this farting about with the Con Sys, no good for trade, you know. And how is your good lady the Austrian bint?

It was dusk when M. Laval left, and the whores were more numerous. A toothless drunk, gray-stubbled, waving an empty bottle, clawed at M. Laval for money, but M. Laval barked at him as if he were one of his marshals. He came to a café called La Jolie Brunette and found it full of students reading newspapers whose spines were wooden poles, the newspapers stacked on a rack like rifles. There were not many newspapers, and they were all government-controlled. M. Laval felt a sudden spasm of resentment at this—*why can't I read what I want to read*—but then he remembered that he was the government, *c'était lui*. A couple of students played a game of chess of arthritic slowness. That made M. Laval impatient. He liked games to be swift and full of cheating. A middle-aged man sat alone, cleaning his teeth with immense thoroughness—quill and floss—and he eyed M. Laval with what looked like professional suspicion. A government spy, then; good, the work went on. M. Laval ordered from the pretty brown-haired waitress a glass of wine and a glass of water and a piece of bread and a piece of sausage. Then he saw with shock, sitting at the next table, a man who should not be here anyway, should in fact be dead. A boy, rather, dressed in ragged green, earnest and bony. Rapp. No, Stapps. He sat with sugared water and a book. Stapps, the student who had tried to knife him and had refused to be let off. M. Laval said:

"Stapps. What the hell are you doing here?"

"How," said the boy, peering in myopic surprise, "do you know my." And then: "Good God, it can't be." He started a gesture of standing to attention but M. Laval said:

"Sit down, sit down, man. My name is Léon Laval, do you get that? Léon Laval. Come over here." There was one empty chair at M. Laval's table, and the boy took it, bringing over his water and what M. Laval now saw was a volume of Montaigne's essays. "You," M. Laval said, "are supposed to be dead." The boy stared. "Schönbrunn." The boy understood. He said:

"First cousin." And then: "This, of course, used to be quite common, rulers incognito listening to the vox pop. I approve. Piquant. I have a duty to show no deference. Do you have armed men stamping outside on the pavement? Did that spy over there get instructions to wait in here? Is he armed? He is acting well, look. He is giving you a full ocular load of concentrated suspicion."

"I am M. Laval," M. Laval said. "M. Laval is just a man wandering the cafés. His cousin, eh? Younger, naturally. You have grown up to be almost exactly as he was when he refused to be pardoned and had to be executed. Very regrettable. He wanted to be a martyr. A damned nuisance of a boy."

Sausage and bread and wine and water were brought. The girl simpered at Stapps. M. Laval bit hungrily into the garlicky sponge and went *ugh*. "Horse," Stapps said. "No, probably donkey. Even cat. The glorious Empire does not eat well these days." His French was very good, far better than the martyred cousin's. "Not even the glorious troops of the glorious Empire, so I hear. *Ichabod ichabod.*"

"You are a student here? What does a German think he can learn in Paris?"

Stapps shrugged, scratching an armpit, and said: "The French language is a good language for clear thought. German is heavy and so homegrown it smells of stale soup and cow-dung. Philosophy ought to be elegantly profound. Our native brand is profoundly inelegant. Thank you, by the way, for the scholarship."

"What scholarship?"

"Ah, of course, you cannot know everything. The Empire has carelessly cast these coins to the poor on its relentless passage through the Teutonic kingdoms. Thank you, anyway. I like Paris. The language and the women have a unique elegance."

"So," M. Laval said, having sipped watered wine, looking for pellets of licorice to quieten the lapdog of acid that was starting to yap in his stomach, finding none, M. Laval having a different stomach altogether, "you are not quite like your cousin. No nonsense about the fouque or whatever it is—"

"*Der Volk*."

"The glorious German dawn and the tearful sunsets and the ancient gods in the fucking German forests."

"Oh, that's good too, but limited. The future lies in synthesis."

"In what?"

"Binding things together. *Synthetisch zusammenfassen*."

"That sounds terrible, whatever it means."

"Yes, it does, doesn't it? Goethe, for instance. You know Goethe?"

"I have no time for reading these upstart cleverclever—"

"Oh, come. Goethe is, let me see, yes, just twenty years older than you are. He has the glorious German sunsets and mountains but he knows Greece and Italy too. I think I believe in a Goethean Europe, but I know I'll never live to see it."

"Is there," M. Laval half-sneered, "nothing you want to be martyrized for? Like your totally forgotten cousin, stupid boy."

"Oh," said Stapps in surprise, scratching the other armpit, "he's not forgotten at all. Nor will ever be forgotten. But, of course, he'll only be remembered because of you. Your first seedling of doubt or incomprehension or something. A pity, though. He wouldn't have had to die if you'd known more about history. You see, great generals have to become great despots—they conquer, and when they conquer they have to control what they've conquered. Improvisation. It's too late for them to be able to find time to study history. The Protestant nations didn't need the Revolution—you should have known that. France and Italy were anachronistically feudal, but in Spain Catholicism is an aspect of nationalism—they think the Pope's a sort of Spaniard living in Italy, it was stupid of you to start ordering the Pope about, you should have known that—and what's the other thing, yes, the Teutonic Reformation had got rid of feudalism already. Very simple, you see."

"To students," M. Laval wholly sneered, "everything is very simple. But what you students forget is that it was the monarchies that attacked the Revolution. What the hell were we supposed to do—just sit back and let them?"

"You French always go too far," Stapps said, altogether at his ease and wagging a finger with nail bitten down to the quick at his Emperor. "All right, all right, I know you're Corsican, but I mean the French before you came along. Cutting off the heads of the monarchy, that was stupid, especially when they had relatives all over Europe. The English managed their Revolution far better. They're not as clever as you, not so intellectual and logical and concerned with pushing things to the limit like your people are. They have a kind of inspired stupidity. A glorious Revolution without a guillotine, a king and queen on the throne, but the real power with the middle class. *Perfidious*," he said. "I've always wanted to know what you meant by that *perfidious*. What do you mean—*perfidious*?"

"Look," M. Laval said, "I know I'm here incognito, but I am what I am, and I'm not having this insolence."

"Get out then," Stapps said. "Drink up whatever it is you're drinking and throw that sausage to that cat there—cat-cannibalism it would be, probably—and off you go to your gorgeous palace where everybody says yes your supreme omnipotent nihiliscient majesty—"

"That word. What was that word?"

"A neologism. *Nichtswissend*. Nothingknowing. So why not do that and go?"

Before M. Laval could speak or act, or indeed decide how to, one or the other, the government spy said: "Don't think I'm not listening, because I am." He addressed, to M. Laval's annoyance, M. Laval alone. Students were perhaps dangerous meat, apt to prove in the police station that they had been speaking very high patriotism and that the spy had been too stupid to understand. Here was a middle-aged stranger who had not been in here before. "I heard you," the spy said, "say something about glorious German dawns and the monarchies attacking. You look to me to be a decent sort of man who shouldn't be in places like this, hot-blooded students who are only boys anyway, so I'm giving you fair warning for the moment, no more." He then got up, nodded quite pleasantly at Stapps, and went over to the chess-players, who had been long transfixed over a tricky pawn move. "Try blocking his queen," he said kindly, and then went out with a friendly wave to the company. The local spy, known to all, one of the community, quite harmless.

"Perfidious," Stapps said. "To whom?"

"To the cause of European unity, to new order and rational laws. They have this treacherous mastery of the seas."

"What was to stop you building a decent French navy?" Stapps asked. "And here's another thing. You were very nearly English yourself."

"*What?*"

"British, anyway. If the British had taken over Corsica when they could have done but weren't particularly interested. You might have become a British naval officer. A good one too, I should think," he added ungrudgingly. "And instead you're the Emperor of the French." He leaned back, as if visualizing M. Laval in his state regalia, letting his thin right arm swing loosely behind his chairback. "I have to go now," he said. "Forgive me, can't wait for the imperial dismissal. Meeting a little midinette in the Place des Vosges."

"I gave it that name," M. Laval said. "The Vosges people were the first to pay their taxes. *You blasted young seem to forget—*"

"History," Stapps said, putting out his left arm and opposing a spread dirty palm to M. Laval, as though he might propose denying that it was history. "An ever-moving stream. It's the time of the Germanic peoples now. Might be a good thing, might be a bad—who knows? But it's history. Here I am, one of the advance guard, already in the capital, might earn a few useful francs as an interpreter when the time comes. You see how it is, though? Synthesis. You have an Empress chosen from the Germanic peoples. You have a son, the King of Rome, without a milliliter of French blood in his arteries. Corsico-Austrian. Interesting, is it not? You yourself, part of the stream, impotent to change it except in minute particulars—"

"Life," M. Laval said, "is all minute particulars."

"That's good, that's really good. Yes. Nihiliscient, establishing Germanicity in the capital of the moribund French Empire. *Germanicité*. How the French hate the Germans. It's love, of course, love. Forgive me, I must go now." And he got up, nodding at M. Laval amicably, saying, "He wanted to die, you know. A very strong—how shall I put it?—*Todeswunschtraum?* Something like that, forgetting my German. *Vive la France*, and so on." He went, clutching his Montaigne.

He was no sooner out than an army officer came in, hale, sashed, sworded, probably never fired a shot in anger in his whole damned career, accompanied by an ailing limping sergeant with a limp mustache. "Papers, papers," the officer called. Papers began to be produced from inner pockets. "Papers. Eligibility for draft. Class of 1815. Any dodgers? Come on, my lad, let's have a look at it. Deferred, eh? Theological studies, eh? Lot of nonsense, lad, we want soldiers not sky-sailors. You, sir? Doesn't apply. You're past soldiering age." M. Laval took off his hat and let the two military have a good look at him.

"Know me, do you?" he said. "Know me?"

"Don't think I've seen you around," the officer said, his rank now clearly revealed as lieutenant, ridiculous, should be a colonel by now at that age. The sergeant's jaw fell and black and brown teeth showed. He said:

"Oh, my God, oh, my dear God, it's him, oh God."

"Something more active for you is called for, I think," M. Laval said, poking the lieutenant in a top button. "Report to your commanding officer tomorrow, request transfer to active service, mention my name. Don't try and get out of it, I shan't forget."

"Oh, my God, oh, my dear dear God."

"Carry on, sergeant." And, feeling much better, he left. He heard, left right left righting to the door:

"Oh, my God, do you know who that was? Oh, my dear dear God."

Not finished yet, not by a long chalk.

M. Laval sat in a gloomy backroom with a fortune-teller. She was a wheezing woman with masses of soiled gray hair, sack-bosomed in food-stained bombazine, breathing cheese, garlic and some undefined beverage with cloves and cinnamon in it but an overall gust of fetidity as she pored over the hills and plains and rivers of both palms and then finally over only the right. "It has been a hard life," she delivered, "hampered by lack of education. Self-instruction is no substitute for the professional training of a great college or university. Ups and downs by the look of it, but more downs than ups. Don't throw your money away, eat less. Things may be taking a turn for the better now, and you may look forward to a period of repose. A passionate nature—see the hump of Venus there—but no, if you will forgive me, real understanding of women. At the moment I divine you are living with a woman but not married to her. You have many enemies, rivals in business chiefly. Keep out of their way. Luck is on your side: when they come to Paris you will be somewhere else. Nothing to fear from water that I can see, at least not *big* water. Oh yes, I see a little bridge somewhere, be careful crossing little bridges. Do not be afraid of travel, see more of the great world. You can look forward to a pleasant retirement by the sea and there you will take up gardening. It is not easy to see how many children you have. That, sir, is all."

"AFTER THAT," N SAID, "I WENT TO A— WELL, A SORT OF DRINKing place. A soldier recognized me and came out of his— Look, I did nothing. All I did was to listen. This soldier was naked and started shouting about his Emperor, he had seen his Emperor. Later, going back to the Tuileries, three men attacked me and tried to rob me. There was nothing they could take except a couple of francs. Then I got a carriage and came here."

"On an impulse," she said. She yawned but really seemed to be smiling. "It *is* really very late, you know."

"I saw a funeral," he said, "an *evening* funeral, somewhat unusual. Plumed horses and weeping followers. Then a ragged old woman threw a stone at the hearse. And I saw a shop where they were selling white caps. Leftover carnival stock, they said, but I know damned well what it was. So," he said, "all I proved was what I always knew. That people are people. That a burnt beef stew is a bigger tragedy than a retreat from Moscow. It's different worlds. Look," he said urgently, "whatever happens, everything will be all right with you."

"I'm grateful, naturally. Some coffee?"

He laughed loudly, the loudest laughter that had been heard in Malmaison since Talleyrand had nearly choked on a plumstone. If he had been seated nearer to her he would have given her a couple of excruciating love-tweaks. "Real coffee, you little witch, I'll be bound. The Continental System doesn't apply here, the only place in the civilized world where it doesn't. Yes, I'll have some." As in former times she put sugar in it and tasted it before handing it over to him. "Hm, you can't beat a good cup of real coffee. I shouldn't have let you have those eight horses," he said. "We're short of horses."

"My eight surely will make little difference."

"I speak to you frankly," he said, "though I know you never listen to what I say, never have listened. Your head full of millinery and so on. It's going to be a hard business."

She smiled radiantly, meaning yawned, and said, "Oh, yes?"

"Germany and Austria and Russia and Sweden and English gold. And no more loyalty among the marshals. They want to sit unbuttoned in their principalities and dukedoms and so on and be drunk. I made a mistake. Pampered them. I'd be better off with some new men anxious to earn their batons. But it's too late now."

"Wouldn't it be better—" He listened with close attention. "—if you said no war and no battles and arranged treaties and so on? Old borders and everybody leaving everybody else alone."

"Talleyrand been here lately? Hm, I thought so. Snake of a man, used to be a bishop, you know, it comes out in him. No, that is not it. It's a question of métier. You remember those days when I was in Italy and kissing your portrait all the time and sending you letters that self-combusted, ha, so it seemed, under my very eye? That was the time. You didn't love me, you didn't care, but it didn't matter. I loved you, that was the point. Spring offensives and you my goddess of battles and the troops bootless and with one rusty rifle between ten. But I beat the humphing old bastards—forgive me, soldier's language, you've been a soldier's wife, all said and done—and showed them what war was. It's métier, trade, skill, art. Well, by God, I'm going to do it again. It's going to be *brilliant.* Have you such a thing as a map of Europe and a pencil around? Oh, never mind. But I tell you that this is going to be the most brilliant exhibition of campaigning that Europe's seen since the old days of the Directory. It will go into textbooks. Not enough horses and these Marie-Louises, as they call them—"

"The young conscripts? What a sweet idea. How is she, by the way? The little boy is charming. *What* a pity, *such* a shame—"

"She's all right," N said. "But one little flick of his little finger and her *pappi*, as she calls him, will have her back there saying *Ja ja er war ein* terrible *Mann, pappi.* Shame, yes. Pity, yes. I hope to God somebody puts a bullet through me if the time ever comes."

"Oh, no. You keep out of the way, don't you? Don't you have the Imperial Guard and the Household Cavalry and so on standing round you all the time?"

"I mean if it all goes the wrong way. Because it might. A good commander knows more than his enemy about the technique of his own defeat. If I have to go into exile—and I wonder where the hell it will be—Sardinia? No, too big. Corsica? I'd have an army raised there in five minutes. The Channel Islands? Never mind, think of that when, if, the time comes. What I'm saying is, who'll go with me?"

He lamped her, despite the lateness of the hour, with the luminosity of early morning. She lowered her lashes and poured more coffee.

"I had a visit," she said, "from your Polish friend. I liked her."

"Quite right, too. She's a remarkable woman. But what a damned mess it's all been. I'm sorry, I've always said *I'm sorry*, you'll admit. And now Austria doesn't give a damn about dynastic marriage, never taken it seriously, and it would have been the same with Russia. There's the child, yes, a good boy, but I had a good boy already."

"You mean Eugène."

"I mean Eugène. I have to be up early tomorrow. Back to the métier. You don't mind if I—"

"It's already early morning really."

"Yes yes. You realize I may never see you again? You realize I may never see Paris again? Our divorce was a sham and our first marriage was a sham—republican tomfoolery—and our second marriage was a sham—neither of us was in a state of grace—but we end up with things as God intended, whoever God is or was. I want to spend the night in your bed. No nonsense." He held up hands of shock. "No advantage taken. I just want to be where I think it's right to be. Before the big battles."

"Everybody will know. Everybody will talk."

"There'll be a lot of lies told in memoirs. Untrustworthy self-seeking bastards—forgive the term, soldier's language. Besides, I'm M. Laval. Bad choice of pseudonym, really. I should have used de la Vallée. Léon de la Vallée. That's the meaning of Nabuliune, you know. Valley lion. Why bad? Because the man who had this damned funeral this evening was called Laval. And they threw stones at his hearse. A man who saved fallen women, apparently. Curious coincidence."

"Why? Nobody's going to throw stones at *your* hearse. Oh, no, I shouldn't have said that, I didn't mean—"

"I suppose that's why they had his funeral in the evening. Darkness covering all. I could eat a bit of cold chicken. Is there any around? That black devil Roustam steals it, you know—a leg, anyway. I always have cold chicken at the end of the night's work. Had the damned impudence once to say that it was a one-legged chicken. Exploited, that's my trouble. People *eat* me. But I'm not finished yet, not by a long chalk."

Later they lay together in darkness. Her parrot, under his cloth, seemed to know who was there, for he kept trying out an old name—Brnpt Brrrrnprrrrte—until he settled to the blinking night-thoughts that served instead of sleep. Their bodies did not touch, but they held hands. Dreams started.

There he lies
Ensanguinated tyrant
O bloody bloody tyrant
See
How the sin within
Doth incarnadine
His skin
From the shin to the chin

He dreamt he was in Moscow, awaiting a reply to the letter he had sent to the Tsar or Czar Alexander, hugging friend of Tilsit, having just awakened from a dream in which massed choirs were singing and bands playing and he was being transported to a grotesque end in the English Channel. The dream did not possess the tones of terror or misery, for the dreamer knew it was a dream within a dream. The language of the anthem was far too literary to be taken seriously. It suggested Madame de Staël, Benjamin Constant, Talleyrand, and the rest of the failed and envious.

See the re-
Incarnate Cleopatra
Barge burning on the water
Bare
Rowers row in rows.
Posied roses interpose
Twixt the rows and the rose

She dreamt she was consoling herself with a dream, but what she had heard of Egypt, from *lui* and others, made her glad that she was not really that fat fly-bitten sallow Graeco-African, debilitated product of royal incest. It was better to be what she was, the dreamer unseduced by the dream, mother of a queen and a prince, grandmother of princes. And the royalty was no begrudged gift of the terrible Bonaparte family: it was in the blood. Moreover, she was an Empress by right, not by bestowed title, an Empress being woman raised to the ultimate power. To hell with the lot of them. To hell with the lot of them.

The funeral was quite an amusing affair, really. N sat up in his coffin, smiling gently, chin on fist, elbow on padded coffin's edge, and everybody except the funeral orators knew that he was still alive, young, plump, healthy, ready to conquer Asia now that he had done with Europe. Talleyrand, in purple senatorial robes, had lost many of his teeth and had difficulty in articulation. Moreover, "Moreover," he chumbled, "I seem to have mislaid my notes. A mere improvisation, my lords, ladies and gentlemen. Not forgetting Your Holiness, fellow dukes and princes. Here was a man. No one will doubt that. No one will doubt that for one minute he was a man that for one minute. His achievements were very considerable. Consider his considerable achievements. Consider the considerability of his considerably considerable considerations. Constellations too, for that matter. There they all are, up there, in the night sky considerately rendered available for this matutinal occasion. I now call upon my dear friend and colleague and whilom mistress, Madame Germaine de Staël, bluestocking extraordinary, to amplify these considerably unconstellated constatations."

Madame de Staël stood on the rostrum and her dress was billowed up by a great wind. The incredibly masculine sansculotted longitude of the clitoris was at once disclosed, to vocal amazement. "He lacked virility," she cried. "He rejected my overtures." There were catcalls. "He proclaimed an all-male empire," she shouted. "Spurious priapism. But, by God, what a pair we could have made."

Then the dream turned sour. The dream turned sour. N, touching her gently, knowing her to be awake, said: "You're not well, my dear."

"Oh, I'm well enough. As well as can be expected. I heard you groaning in your sleep. Are you in pain?"

"It's the mind that counts, the mind will prevail." The gray dawn was coming up. Coffee and the road and the battle of the nations. Twelfth Division—Pécheau. Fourteenth—Bourmont, but it might have to be Hulot. The parrot, though still artificially benighted, remembered the old name and announced it with glee:

"Bonaparte. Ahahahaha, Bonaparte. Booonapaaaaaaaahahah!"

III

From bivouac to bivouac to bivouac to bivouac to bivouac and all the way it was torches held aloft with Long Live The Emperor and It Is The Anniversary Of His Crowning and God Bless You Sire, rough soldiers in tears of love and joy as he walked, with straw torches blazing all about, from bivouac to bivouac to bivouac. He waved his hand in thanks, tears in his own eyes, God Bless You My Children, and came to the bivouacs of the artillery. Thank You Thank You he cried almost weeping at the soldiers' tears and the fiery blessing and then:

"Keep those fucking torches away from the artillery caissons."

And it was torches too, though not straw ones, lighting the way to the great ball at the Tuileries, where a hundred thousand million best sperm candles shone on the glory of Jerome Bonaparte, Prince of France and King of Westphalia; of Joseph Bonaparte, First Prince of the Blood, King of Naples, King of Spain; of Louis Bonaparte, King of Holland; of Lucien Bonaparte, Prince of Canino. And, carrying their own starlight with them, were Caroline Bonaparte, Grand Duchess of Berg and of Clèves, Queen of Naples; Élisa Bonaparte, Princess of Lucca and Grand Duchess of Tuscany; Pauline Bonaparte, Duchess of Guastalla and Princess Borghese; Madame Mère herself, the Dowager Empress Marie-Letizia Bonaparte. The Princes of the Empire swirled in a waltz with goddesses who were all pink flesh and diamonds—Bernadotte, Prince of Ponte-Corvo, yet to be Crown Prince of Sweden, yet to be King of Sweden; Berthier,

Prince of Neuchâtel and Prince of Wagram; Davout, Duke of Auerstadt and Prince of Eckmühl; Massena, Duke of Rivoli, Prince of Essling; Ney, Duke of Elchingen, not yet Prince of the Moskowa; Poniatowski the Polish Prince, still to be appointed Marshal of the Empire; Talleyrand-Périgord, once Bishop of Autun, now Prince of Benavente, Minister of Foreign Affairs and Grand Chamberlain of the Empire.

And then the Dukes—of Castiglione, Istria, Parma, Vicenza, Feltre, Frioul, Otranto, Gaeta, Abrantes, Valmy, Montebello, Danzig, Tarentum, Bassano, Ragusa, Conegliano, Treviso, Reggio, Rovigo, Dalmatia, Albufera, Belluno, the titles and gorgeousness of dress uniform clanging with stars and crosses hiding plain tough campaigner's flesh, except for Fouché the Great Policeman and Cambacérès, President of the Senate, and Gaudin and Maret, Ministers of State. The talk was not of art or of delicate amours but of how best to salt money and that bastard there has done well for himself I remember when he was a snotnosed ensign and Jesus what a pair she has on her and no no no you have it wrong it was just after Wagram he got this dose his prick so on fire you could see it in the dark anyway I could tell the husband guessed what was going on so I got the message to him that I'd had something shot off at Austerlitz and say what you like some spuds and onions fried in train-oil on a bivouac fire tastes better than all that muck they serve up at Nicalas's and charge you the earth for and good Christ I could have sworn that that bint over there was the one in the knocking-shop at Vicenza. And then, to a thousand trumpets and as many trombones and a hundred hundred thunders of drums, N himself came in, growing bald, growing paunched, Empress by his side. The cheers rose to the candelabra and made the million candle-flames dance, the floor rumbled with the stamping, the Seine heard the hosannas and tremor after tremor after tremor flowed over her bridged and conquered waters.

His Imperial Majesty Napoleon the First, formerly First Consul of the Republic, formerly First Consul for Life, Emperor of the French, King of Italy, sun and wind, everybody's best solvent, greeted and greeted the greeting greeters, grinning greetings, a word for everyone. Augereau, you old bastard, you've got that medal on upside down. Well, Bessières, you've come a long way. Hope the duck pâté's to your gourmet's liking, Cambacérès, you rotten old gourmandizer. It may be a good liniment for a strained hock, Caulaincourt, but it burns off the hair, man. You still owe me five sous, Clarke, that domino game, remember. How's my old Duroc, then, weak at the knees with shagging? Get your men to keep an eye on whatshisname, Fouché. Any money in the fisc, Gaudin? That's not your wife, whoever it is, Junot. Kellermann, I'd say you were too old for her. Hallo, Lannes, I'm not supposed to be on speaking terms with you, can't think quite why now. Got your Danzig pumps on, I see, Lefebvre. Top of the evening, MacDonald. Try peppermint cordial for heartburn, Maret. Stand closer to the razor in future, Marmont. Taking to little boys, Moncey? Sorry sorry, it's Mortier. Oudinot Oudinot, get that name set to music, Oudinot, Oudinooooooooot. Mademoiselle Savary, well, what else do you expect to be called with a first name like Anne-Jean-Marie-René, you old shitbag? How are the Dalmatians, Soult? God bless you, Suchet, you're pissed early. Claude-Victor Victor, the drummer-boy duke, ten quarts to the sitting and never a puke.

Dance dance dance! The orchestra struck up another waltz. Cohorts and caissons and case-shot and grapeshot and flankers and lancers and lines of retreat. Bar-shot and round shot and langridge and limbers and sabers and trail-chests and putrefied meat. Nothing to eat and no boots for their feet. But Mantua, Rivoli, Lodi, Legnano; Austerlitz, Jena, Caldiero, Milan. Auerstadt, Bautzen, Borghetto, Liebertwolkwitz, Shubra Khit, Walcheren, Cairo Divan. Six acres a man ran his promise and plan. But Jacobins, Royalists, ministers, bureaucrats, clergy and peasantry, new constitution, suppress those conspiracies, Codes and Concordat and Legion of Honor, reorganized army, colonial policy, state education, domestic security, public finance. Glance at the France that he taught how to dance. And advance. Assuming a stance leaving little to chance. La France.

The buffet was sumptuous. Truffled pigling Arcis-sur-Aube. Beef ribs Arcola. Spiced lamb Bassano. Duck pie Castiglione. Pâté Château Thierry. Garlic sausage Durrenstein. Quail Grössbeeren. Cold game soup Hohenlinden. Jugged hare Katzbach. Mille Fleurs Millesimo. Hash of saffron mutton Montebello. Pigeon eggs Mondovi. Ravioli Rivoli. Pyramidal chopped veal, onion, carrot and endive tart. Turkey drumsticks Mount Tabor. Chicken, inevitably, Marengo. Peppered stewed rabbits Sultan El Kebir. N roared genially:

"Rabbits! Rabbits, Berthier!"

Louis-Alexandre Berthier, Marshal of the Empire, Prince of Neuchâtel, Prince of Wagram, flushed. He had organized, as Imperial Hunt Master, a great Imperial Rabbit Shoot. He had made a mistake in the ordering of the rabbits, hundreds and hundreds and hundreds of them. Beaters and bearers, the buffet was sumptuous, glorious autumn weather. The rabbits, released, scampered about in joy. N took his gun and prepared to begin the slaughter. But the rabbits believed that they knew N well, an old friend. They were, that was the mistake, tame rabbits. They thought N was their keeper and feeder. They charged him, an army of hundreds and hundreds and hundreds. N was astonished. The equerries tried to beat the rabbits back. N was astonished. He retreated astonished to his coach. The rabbits, an act of strategic empathy, split into two wings and did a flanking movement on either side of the hunting party. They were into the coach along with N, supposed feeder and cherisher. The coach moved off in panic for Paris, furry bundle after furry bundle after furry bundle being flung out of the windows of the coach.

"Ignominious retreat," N said. "Defeated by a battalion of rabbits. Bad staff work, Berthier. You could have done better than that."

"But, wwwith respppect, it was not my fffault you shshshot Marshal Massena in the in the."

"Eye. What has that to do with it? That was a boar hunt or something. That was a different occasion."

"But I was bbblamed for that becccause of the rabbits."

"Are you feeling all right, Berthier?"

"You wwwounded Massena in the in the while I was in the luncheon tttt. I was nnnowhere nnnear. And yet you bbblamed me for it. Bbbecccause of the of the."

"Rabbits. I'm sick of hearing of these damned rabbits, Berthier."

"With resppppect, it was you who bbbrought the rabbits up."

"I don't want to hear any more about the rabbits. It was a shameful business, Berthier, and you ought to try to live it down."

"Bbb."

"Do I make myself clear, Berthier? Rabbits, indeed."

Sugared violets Vendémiaire. Peaches Montenotte. Petits fours Leoben. Coupe Stradella. Bombe Mombello. Pauline Bonaparte, Princess Borghese, breathed vanilla and caraway on the young man, Byronic without the limp, who stood by her, then, fixing her superb eyes on his, made a totally unambiguous rutting gesture. Candied pears Senatus Consultum. A fat duchess, rings and ringlets, was saying: "Can't let the bugger out of my sight one minute without he's getting his hand up some little bitch's skirt. And the more common the better." Raspberry soufflé Fructidor. Talleyrand was thinking: Is it, then, possible to make a new aristocracy? What is breeding? Is talent enough? It is certainly not a matter of good manners. The manners of the old court were often atrocious. It is perhaps, after all, the sense of divine right. There is no such sense here. Not even genius is enough. It cannot last. A smell of incipient decay comes off this table loaded with sweetmeats. Swiss tea is being served instead of Indian; chicory instead of coffee. It is a beleaguered culture. Its dynamic is sustained by war. Look at these dukes and princes, one-eyed or with nicked ears like tomcats, limping, scarred, loud and randy. Our furniture is gold-frogged, our beds look like tents, those stools there look like military drums. But let them dance, there is a time to dance.

Masse de décision, bataillon carré. Fantassins, fantassins, corps d'armée. Grosse-bottes, grognards, grenadiers à cheval. Corps d'observation, G-Q-Général. Voltigeurs, voltigeurs, levée-en-masse. Congé, une poule dans un hôtel de passe.

N was telling them, a drinking crowd away from the dancing, himself with nothing in his hands, hands indeed behind him, about art and politics and human greatness. Voltaire no poet? Nonsense, man. Best test of poetry is whether you can recite it without shame in the open air. *Caesar's Death*—you know the play? You should. After Marengo I remember saying the lines to the sunset: I have conquered forty years in service and command, Have seen unfold the destiny of a world held in my hand, And have known how each event, the trivial, the sublime, In the fate of states has hung on a single tick of time. But Voltaire didn't know the Oriental world, had to guess at it. Writing about camels and houris and muftis from Switzerland, can you imagine? The classical spirit rests on exactitude, on exact and accurate rendering of the world closely observed. Look at Gros's paintings (gave him his start really), five hundred horses on canvas and you can see the torn fetlock on one of them. Art, gentlemen. And why shouldn't I give the Iron Crown to Crescentini? I know, I know, he's a singer not a soldier, no bravery in battle there, I know, but, gentlemen, he's a castrato, isn't he? Been wounded, hasn't he? Eh *eh*? Opera. Nothing like opera. The only art that comes close to the art of war, don't laugh, gentlemen. Massing of choruses like troops, exact timing. My bands play operatic arias while the battle proceeds. Don't let me hear that term *tragedy* loosely used. Gods playing about with men, predetermination. Destiny is not up there but in here here here. Told that German that, poet, can't quite recall his. Politics is destiny—there, write that down, somebody. Not everybody, just somebody. Struggle, clash between strong personalities, idealist and cynic, disparity between the impossibly ideal and the really possible. And always, remember, told this to that fool Benjamin Constant, tragedy must never have chairs on the stage. Tragic characters never sit down. Sit down and they become comic. Think about it, gentlemen. Stand up to live and lie down to die. Yes yes, also lie down to make love if your tastes run that way, but we're talking now of the representable. Well, we've not done badly for tragedy in our age: Raynouard, Brifaut, Lancival. *Tippo-Saib* should last as long the Empire—yes, Jouy wrote that. *Les Templiers. Don Sanche.* As immortal as the spirit of man itself. Chateaubriand. That bitch de Staël with the outsize clitoris. Very unhealthy quality there, antirepublican, nonclassical. Putting themselves in their books, you know? As though human personalities were more important than society itself. Scotch mists, wishy-washy colors, nothing bold, positive. Where's the great splash of scarlet, the archangelic shout of gold? Don't like it, gentlemen, wide-eyed unruly unruled unrulable heroes. Don't like aquacity, tempestuous formlessness. Keep everything under control, set bounds to nature. Nature must not get the better of us. Greatness? A great man? Self-effacing, subordinating his own interests to those of the community he serves. Incorruptible, loving, even quixotic. And you start with the family, gentlemen. That is the basic community. If a man does not serve his family first, he is unlikely to serve the greater family of state, country, empire.

State country empire and. State country empire and. Madame Mère watched the dancing from her own gilt throne, fanning herself, thinking in dialect. All a big toy for them and they will wake up and grow up when it is too late, glad of their mother then, glad of the pieces of gold tucked away in mattresses and old socks. Jerome there, merry monarch, giving it all away to those Germans in Westphalia or whatever it is called, pockets full of jeromes as he calls them to give away. Give away to your mother, I say, while your hand is in, and he will be glad of it when the throne tumbles, for the game will not last forever. Pauline a disgrace sleeping with any pretty man she takes a fancy to, but it is the family fire, I know, they must learn to control it, nature should not get the better of them, the family beauty too is there. It has missed poor Elisa, married to that gutless fiddler, a great one for fiddles she is, what with that Paga something man at what she calls her court, Lucca, good for olive oil but not much else, Princess of Lucca, a lot of nonsense, still, a good businesswoman, though women should have nothing to do with business, all those busts of Nabuliune from Carrara marble. Four hundred fifty francs each is it they are fetching in Paris? And Louis become a proper Dutchman, King of Holland, all a big game, but poor Louis will not last with that weakness in the blood. Poor boy, he was in my dream last week, in his mother's arms. And Joseph giving the Spanish what he calls freedom of worship and conscience and they bang right back at him with only the Catholic faith, they're right, it doesn't do to play about with religion. I told His Holiness the Pope, just imagine, I told him they would all come back to it when they'd played their little games of being atheists and freethinkers and so on, they'll all come back to it on their deathbeds. Well, it will be pleasant enough back in Ajaccio, the whole family round me and Nabuliune a bit chastened, and talk about the great games they all played. For games it is and no more, all they're fit for perhaps, but that is the aristocratic blood coming out, too good for common work. And yet *honor*, which Nabuliune is telling them all about now, is not quite a game, for without honor we are nothing. Anything for honor. That was always said in both our families: the honor of a Corsican. And when as a little girl I would ask what it was this honor, they told me not to ask because if you try to see what honor is made of then you pull it to pieces and cannot put it back together again. You must merely honor honor, that being the only honorable thing in the world.

Honor: the trumpets said it. Honor: the drums. The winter night sky of Paris had fireworks in his honor imposed on it, streaking like signatures on black parchment or else stamped like fiery seals. He was in his coach with his Empress, drawn by eight bays, on his way to the theater, for the première of

Enuiluban's mythological heroic drama, written and performed in his honor. The coach passed fountains, water heroically tamed, with stone elephants trunking out great trumpeting jets, tigers snarling but at the same time vomiting water, bears hugging trees whose silver branches were water, goddesses of fecundity with the eternal milk of water gushing from their nipples. Holding torches aloft, the people of Paris did him honor, and his memory whirred like an oiled engine and dealt out names to attach to some of the faces split open with cheers. Montreuil, a discharged corporal with a wooden leg; Cambrai, a bowed tailor; Montdidier, a cheating quartermaster-sergeant who had been forgiven and pensioned-off; Vervins, whose bravery was an aspect of his stupidity; Vouziers, a craftsman good at delicate goldwork; Rouen, who could smell out water two miles off; Lisieux, whose teeth were like millstones and who could grind hay like a horse; Bernay, who once drank clinical alcohol and ran a mile in a straight line; Avranches, who had offered his pocked houri to give him comfort in the bad Egyptian time; Mortagne, with two hooks for hands; Fougères, a known bugger; St. Brieuc, a former lieutenant who could recite Horace by the yard; Morlaix, a pastry cook who did wonders with jam; Pontivy, who knew a horse as another man might know a machine, but whom horses hated; Laval the palindromedary, so once called in joke not understood at Cairo; La Flèche, short-sighted and blunt of speech; Cholet the cheeseman; Ancenis with the crude tattooed crucifixion on his back; Loches the sugar-lover; Romorantin the sycophantic banker, soon to be ruined; Veuve Auxerre, whose husband had been overcomplaisant; Montbard, who carried Dijon mustard in his haversack; Langres, who screamed in his dream that the Mamelukes were cutting his head off; Vesoul, author of a little tract on the possibility of developing mobile telegraphs for the use of the Great Army; Pontarlier, an undistinguished drummer-boy with a wart one inch above his navel; the whole family Charolles, drunk down to the eight-year-old daughter; thin wan Belley of the disgraced 69th; Montluçon the toymaker; Confolens, who was said to have killed a priest at Cognac (where, by the way, they had the best bottle-corks in the world); Montmorillon, seller of children's windmills not far from the Tuileries; Jonzac the joker—

A man in rags, evidently unarmed, broke through the hedge of soldiers and made for the imperial coach. Strong arms grasped him and drew him away, but he shouted:

"I'm in love with the Empress! I adore the Empress!"

"My friend," said N calmly, "you have chosen the wrong person in whom to confide."

Fontenay the poor man's lawyer; Sarlat, who in a charge would cry *Reculez pas, drollos!*; Parthenay, who swore he was a virgin; Dax, a clerk in the Department of Statistics; Bayonne, curator of a very small museum specializing in bees, founded by N; Condom-Mirande-Castelsarrasin, a man too trivial for his name; Florac, a cook whose ineptitude made him a sort of genius but who, when Indian tea had been available in France, had been able to make a really reviving strong dish of tea in the English manner; Tarbes the satirical poet, who had once written a sonnet on the imperial fart, in which appeared the lines: *That sweet efflation speaks as Memnon's statue speaks: Oceans of wisdom sound in one soft wind that breaks*; Draguignan, who loved to fish in the Var; Le Vigan with his eternal card tricks; big Albi and little Castres, inseparable friends; Limoux from Narbonne; Narbonne from Limoux; Céret, who had prophesied a successful invasion of England in the Year IX; Gourdon-Figeac, furniture-maker; Brive, fine silkman; Mauriac, who had conceivably the best singing voice in the 47th or was it the 74th, discharged now because of a gangrened foot; Isère, who swore his cousin owned half the property of Grenoble; Nyons, who was always Going To Die, but never did; Issoire, Ambert and Riom, who had a complex sexual relationship; St. Julien, who always talked of opening an *auberge* near Briançon, a great lover of the Alps; Brioude, a sergeant who saw ghosts at inconvenient times; Nérac the hatter; Montbrison, purveyor of fine wines mixed with fine well-water, found out and fined; Marmande, Gourdon, Vesoul, Saunier, others others, millions of others.

The rain struck some three minutes before the completion of the journey. It was exceptionally heavy and it sent many of the torches hissing out and the bearers scampering for shelter, showing their tails. Reinaus, Lousev, Nodruog, Ednamram. Rabbits, N was thinking, watching them. But no, those rabbits had run towards him and his gun in expectant joy, sweet innocents. Nosirbtnom, Eduoirb, Moir and Trebma and Eriossi. Helped out of the coach while the trumpets blared welcome, he insisted on standing bareheaded in the downpour. Snoyn, Erési, Cairuam. Lightning split the black sky, chiding the presumption of the fireworks. N saw himself standing there, upright in the presence of the lightning. A good picture for Gros perhaps. The thunder followed, chiding the presumption of the kettledrums. Some stood outside the theater still, cheering wetly, bearing blackened straw smoking up in weak defiance of the rain, and N thought that he did not know the names of any of these.

"Sire, with respect. You will be soaked."

"A big enemy, rain," he said, drinking it. "Mud. The bogging down of the artillery. Men cursing, slipping in it." And then he allowed himself to be persuaded to proceed within. Lights and obeisances. From group to group to group to group to group and all the way it was candles shining aloft with Long Live The Emperor and It Is The Anniversary Of His Crowning and God Bless You Sire, smooth courtiers in tears of love and joy as he walked, with best sperm candles blazing all about, from obeisance to obeisance to obeisance. He waved his hand in thanks, tears in his own eyes, God Bless You My Children, and was escorted to his glittering box. Thank You Thank You he cried from it weeping at the standing tiers who were doing him honor and then, quietly, to the inclined ear of his aide:

"Wake me up in good time. I have to lead the fucking applause."

After an overture in the classical style, the curtain rose upon a representation of Mount Olympus, with gauzy clouds floating convincingly, the wires which flew them scarcely visible. The gods in general synod stood about, statuesque, decrepit, angry, dressed in silver-powdered wigs and togas. Jupiter spoke first in wavering accents, the old and bent head of a doomed and discredited régime. In stately alexandrines he remarked irritably that these Titans were growing too bold, especially that son of Iapetus and Clymene, or was it Themis? Begotten on a remote island somewhere. Mnemosyne, one-time Jovian paramour, who had given birth all at once to the Muses nine, was herself growing crotchety and unreliable. He couldn't remember things as well as he used to. Forgotten even the name of the damned Titan who was especially demonstrating impious boldness. Mars, in battered armor and limping as with gout, said the name was Prometheus, Prometheus was the name, that was what it was, Prometheus. (Here the audience applauded. Smelling the possibility of dangerous satire somewhere, N stayed awake but did not applaud.) Ah yes, Prometheus. This Prometheus had taken it upon himself to make living creatures out of chunks of clay (more applause, more smell of danger) and was now teaching them the art of war—his own art, the Martian art, just imagine. War? said Jupiter. Fighting? Who was he teaching them to fight against? No doubt, said Mars, that the Promethean aim was to lead an army up the slopes of Olympus itself and do to death the deathless gods, so that he, a mere Titan, with his handmade soldiers, could take over the rule of the universe. Saturn, god of old age, shuffled downstage to ask how. Fire, how else? Mars rumbled. They have fire, fire. But that is the limit of impiety, shocked Jupiter said. Fire is divine, fire is sky-born, the gods' weapon. Where did they get the fire from? They made it, Mercury said. Or rather Prometheus discovered a way of making it, finding that the seed of fire inheres not merely in heaven but in the soul of crass heaven-shunning matter. Jupiter now delivered a set piece in praise of fire, the fire of the sun, all-consuming, the milder fire of the stars, the fire that strikes when divine thunderbolts are hurled. Fire is to strike lesser breeds, such as Titans, with; it is not, heaven forbid, even ever to be dreamt of as being used against the high thrones of the gods. Old the gods may be, but they still have divine power; they are by no manner of means to be minimally or maximally mocked. What then shall be done to Prome Prome—ah, Mnemosyne, why did you leave me? (Audience laughter. "Look," N said urgently, "what is this? A comedy? There are no chairs on the stage.")

Wipe out the entire race of Titans and, while your thunderbolt-hurling hand is in, the entire race of Titanic clockwork toys, men or whatever they are called. Thus spoke Uranus. But ah, Jupiter said, why wipe out what the torment of gives the gods pleasure? For it is not enough to carouse, it is not enough to sit long over the cenal or prandial ambrosia, it is not, for that matter, enough to swoop down on hapless nymphs in zoomorphic disguises. Power, gentlemen, power consists mainly in the power to hurt. (*La puissance, messieurs*—why, it was the very Aulic Council.) And so we will take away the fire-making faculty from these upstarts. But, to seem clement, nay to seem generous, we will send down a heavenly bride for this Titan—Prometheus is the name, Neptune said, scratching at his wig with a prong of his trident. We will send down Pandora. Bring in Pandora now. Mercury, in brave disdain of creaking joints, flew off lumpishly. Stay, Jupiter stayed him. She must not forget her box. ("See," N said, "if it is the Empress they are out to mock—") Mercury nodded and, with an exit-applause-provoking gesture which in fact provoked no applause, was off.

Neptune, to fill in the time of waiting for Mercury's return with Pandora, delivered a speech which N did not greatly like.

NEPTUNE

Let us admit, that age may come to birth
When a new rational race may win the earth,
May scale the mountains, drain the rivers dry,
Erect tall towers defiant of the sky,
May bid the deserts blossom like a flower,
May chart the year and calibrate the hour,
But yet remains and ever will remain
One kingdom over which they'll never gain
Of power's impiety the veriest grain.
The mighty billowing ocean stays exempt
From any would-be conqueror's attempt.
In nether caverns though I seem to sleep
Yet in an instant will I rouse and leap
And crash upon each bark that reckless rides,
Splitting its mainmast, stoving in its sides,
When, in my wisdom, it appears to me
I hear a claim to mastery of the sea.
Beware, ye island races yet unborn,
Divinity is in the power you scorn.
Rage you may reap whene'er you plow my plain:
The sea is mine, and mine it will remain.

(N chewed that over, not too sure who it was getting at. It was in bad taste somehow. And it was not true. History, like the gods, was not altogether mocked, try as one might. It did not fit in well with Trafalgar. Oh my God oh my God Trafalgar. Only civilians sneered at the enemy. N felt he would now like to nap a little, but he was apprehensive about what might be coming next.)

What came next was the entry of Pandora, accompanied by smirking Mercury. She was played by a pretty but, as N knew from backstage and backstairs visits, pert and buttock-shrugging girl from Châteauroux, a diaphanous gown pasted to her, bosom well on show, a reminiscence of the discredited Directory. Jupiter explained how she had been knocked together by Hephaestus, kneeded and molded, to be exact, out of clay, hence of a substance of those insolent creations of Prometheus, whom she was now (no magic involved; who could easily resist her? Were not the deathless gods now leering in senile concupiscence?) to wed. He, Jupiter himself, had given her a box as a kind of dowry. The bridegroom, curious as to its contents, would not be able to resist opening it, and then and then— Creaking stage machinery now made this box, or rather one of its sides or walls, trundle some way downstage from the skyey cyclorama, and the wall fell open to allow its living freight to be disgorged. This consisted of masked actors representing a rich selection of the causes of earthly woe—poverty, disease, superstition, famine, earthquake, tyranny and so on. They spoke each a long speech that made N nod. The gods in general, to whom N gave a bleary kind of attention, seemed to consider that Prometheus and his creation were being perhaps excessively punished for possessing fire (which they no longer possessed anyway, the gods having doused it for them) and cleverness—illiquidable by the gods, who could easily turn living beings into constellations, continents, or herbaria but not easily, the gods being ignorant of the nature of folly, into fools. Wait, said Jupiter, see how merciful we are. He clapped his hands and, to quiet music, a beautiful female figure sidled out, simpering in a kind of nun's costume, from the innermost shadows of the box. Hope, said Jupiter, her name is Hope. Tableau. The curtains closed to as much applause as the playwright and players could reasonably hope for.

Prometheus, acted by Beaumard, began the next part solo. Nothing Napoleonic about him, N decided, watching thin gesturing arms and the rise and fall of a prominent larynx. Prometheus told the audience that he had not liked the look of this allegedly conciliatory gift from heaven and given her to his brother Epimetheus to marry. Epimetheus, intrigued by the dotal box, had loosed on the earth a large horde of Ills and a very little

Hope. Still, he, Prometheus, was determined to emphasize the hopefulness of human life and so had sneaked up to Olympus and stolen fire. He showed the audience a sort of monstrance with the igneal semen cached in it like a eucharistic wafer. The journey hither had been terrible, what with all the Ills milling about, and the journey hence would be even more perilous, but he, Prometheus, had a responsibility to his creatures. (Applause.) Horns now sounded: the gods were giving chase. The horns wound louder, and from both left and right. Prometheus, hugging his monstrance like a priest during the Terror, sought to leave but found all ways cut off. And then the gods, some from left, others from right, Jupiter himself from up center, where he stood, pointing the finger, on a craggy peak, came on, terrible in controlled wrath. Prometheus, he. By what filthy trick of titanicity had he managed to mount Olympus and carry off sacred fire? Denunciatory speeches from the gods in turn, defiant ripostes from Prometheus. (N nodded, pleased mildly, guessing what would happen now, then home to a cold chicken and a warm bed. Prometheus would hurl fire at them, fire that, belonging to a new and vital race of beings, would wither the gods in a blinding flash of applied gunpowder, with strontium nitrate added.)

The monstrance was wrested from the Titan's hands, Mars supervised his pinioning and binding by a sort of godly bodyguard. Jupiter cried:

This frosty height is hight the Caucasus.
Here let this insolent and impious
Caitiff be punished for his simony.
Here let him howl forever to the sky,
A sky that hears not, so he howls in vain.
Bind limbs to craggy points with rustless chain
And let him live but live in deadly pain.
Eagles shall peck his liver for their food,
Nightly consume what daily is renewed.
I see their bulky shadows whirling now.

Eagles, I charge ye, do it. And I vow,
A vow divine, that equal punishment
Awaits each one who nurses the intent
Heretical of daring to aspire
To thieve our thunder and to filch our fire.

So the gods solemnly moved off, leaving Prometheus bound and moaning. He cried to the eagles, invisible above him, that he had thought they were his friends—mortal, aspirant, daring—but he saw now from their cruel eyes and beaks that they were friends no more, instead the ruthless consumers of his substance. Who will free me? he cried. Who help? The curtain came down to applause somewhat uncertain. N said to his Empress:

"I don't like it."

A flunky brought sorbets in, as well as champagne on ice and, for the Empress, a platter of canapés. She said: "The verse is very bad meseems, ah bad, yes."

"I don't mean the verse. I mean the story. I don't like it, Duroc," he said to Duroc. "I mean, I'm Prometheus, aren't I? Have you seen the text? What happens now?"

"He follows the myth," Duroc said. "Hercules comes to rescue Prometheus and then together they announce that the reign of the old gods is at an end."

"Who are they meant to be then?"

"It doesn't have to be allegorical really. But Prometheus is probably the spirit of man and Hercules is, with respect, yourself."

"Me Hercules? But Hercules is a god. I'm not a god. I'm a Titan," he said simply. "It would have been enough to have Prometheus sending them all off packing on his own. With perhaps the help of some of his clay creatures. I don't like it. It's a bad omen. That Caucasus bit too. It won't do, I tell you."

"Shall I arrange for the performance to be announced as over because of the indisposition of somebody or other in it? Ouvrard or Pécriaux or somebody?"

"No no no no, with Prometheus having his liver pecked like

that? Go backstage and tell them to get Prometheus to break his own chains—titanic strength, you see—and take the spell off the eagles. I don't like this playing around with eagles. They're mine, after all. And then he finds that the gods have inadvertently left that fire behind somewhere, so he fights them with it and burns them all up. And then the Imperial Hymn at the end."

"Improvise, you mean? They won't like that."

"God damn it, man, I've improvised victories, haven't I? You could go so far as to say that I've improvised a whole civilization. Surely they can improvise a last act. Liver." He rubbed his own, watching sourly his Empress bite at a kind of Torte. "Tell them it's the Emperor's command."

WHEN THE CURTAIN ROSE AGAIN PROMETHEUS WAS DISCLOSED still chained to the crags, but this time there was a vista of sea behind him. The audience jeered. Prometheus was baldish and had grown a morbid paunch. He kept going ow ow ow. "Liver," he explained to the audience. "Foie gras. Rotten. Decayed. Not even the eagles will touch it. Too much gross feeding. The Viennese cuisine, you know. Goulash. Bauernschmaus. Guglhupf mit Schlag. Topfenpalatschinken. Butterteigpastetchen mit Geflügelragout. Tafelspitz." His Austrian accent was not good. "Eagles, eagles," he called. "Do not desert me. You are the only company I have. They may as well desert me," he told the audience. "Everybody else has." The audience jeered. "The Dukes of Castiglione, Istria, Parma, Vicenza, Feltre, Frioul, Otranto, Gaeta, Abrantès—" Jeers and howls drowned the catalogue. "And me voici on a rocky island." He moved his arms and the chains fell off. "No need for these really. Can't get away. Too long a swim. Though I'd be buoyed up well enough, all this blubber. Bony become Fleshy, eh?" One of the lengths of chain was a string of sausages. "Wienerwurst. Sehr gut, ja ja.

And now a little song, petit chanson." The orchestra struck up a melody that, meant to be Corsican, was really Neapolitan. The Great Littlehampton beamed, swinging his sausages. He sang:

When my military career began
I gained a reputation as a good hard man.
At Lodi and Rivoli I trounced the Austry Ann
And I showed myself a very good Republy can.
I made a peace at Campo Formio
And taught the whole of Italy the way to go.
But the British lion took a great big bite
And said I could be Emperor
(Vive L'Empéreur)
Of an empire rather smaller than the Isle of Wight.

That was in London. In Vienna the gods in general synod stood about, statuesque sometimes but often ready to relax. Goulash. Bauernschmaus. Guglhupf mit Schlag. Topfenpalatschinken. Butterteigpastetchen mit Geflügelragout. Tafelspitz. Delicious, Cardinal Consalvi said, the Vatican delegate. He ate but, of course, did not dance. Well, Castlereagh said, our Titan had made a pretty pickle of Europe but now he was safely away on a remote island where he could do no harm. Wellington muttered to him about this damned fellow Talleyrand, not to be trusted, a Frenchman anyway, always on the winning side, knows which side his bread's buttered. Keep him out of the main sessions anyway. Britain, Austria, Russia, Prussia. Their task to make decisions. This Austrian wine's deceptive, Castlereagh. Silk-smooth but woke with a damned bad liver after it. Can never remember the name of that confounded Russian over there. Capodistrias, eh? Keep wanting to call him, ha, Aspidistras.

My reputation and my power increased
So I thought as how I'd tackle that ferocious beast.
But the Navy said no so I thought at least
I'd venture into Egypt for to prick him in the East.
But my wife proved faithless, the Directory too,
So I swam back to Paris to see what I could do.

I was made First Consul by my fellow frogs
And was on my way to Emperor
(Vive L'Empéreur)
Of an empire not much bigger than the Isle of Dogs.

The Prussian Friedrich von Gentz, Secretary-General, was quietly glad to see that Prussia was to get back Posen and Danzig, a good portion of Saxony, bits of Pomerania that had been ruled by the Swedes, and a very fair part of Westphalia. Let me speak, Talleyrand said, for the spirit of German unity. The proposal that there be thirty-nine German states in a confederation without a center must inevitably mean an eventual domination by Prussia. Not his affair, let him keep out of it. Leave all that till later, Hardenberg (Prussia) suggested. Settle the small apportionments first. United Kingdom of the Netherlands—Belgium, Holland, Luxembourg. That can do no harm. How about Cracow, somebody (Nesselrode?) said. Make Cracow a free city, Talleyrand proposed. Where is this damned Cracow, Wellington wanted to know. Wish that Frenchie would keep his impertinent nose out of it. Need him for the votes, Castlereagh said. Useful man when it comes to the votes. Put it to the meeting, said Stein, that we do now adjourn. Grand ball this evening. Cream of Viennese society. Need time to rest, dress, get ready. We are here to work, gentlemen, Metternich said, not to dance. The claims of Austria have so far received scant committee time.

I quickly forgave my adulterous wife
And soon I was created First Consul for Life.
I tried to quieten European strife
But, being a Corsican, I had to use the knife.
I beat two big coalitions down,
And made friends with His Holiness, who gave me
a crown.
But still I said I was Republy can,
Though on my way to Emperor
(Vive L'Empéreur)
Of an empire not much bigger than the Isle of Man.

Back where they were before—Spain, Naples, Piedmont, Tuscany, Modena. Restoration of legitimate dynasties. All a bit dull, thought Wellington. Permanent neutrality guaranteed for the Swiss. Nothing wrong with that, always a neutral sort of people, even Swiss cheese has a neutral sort of taste. Legitimate dynasties restored to Spain. Well, fought for that. Dull people, ugly, harmless. Norwegians united to Swedes. Nothing wrong with that either. Same sort of people, big-boned, light-haired, live off fish and aquavit. Languages sound the same, equally unintelligible. For ourselves, Castlereagh said, for the British Crown I would say, we ask little. To be confirmed in our possession of Malta, the cape of Good Hope, Heligoland, Ceylon, Tobago, Santa Lucia, Mauritius. We sit here, Talleyrand suddenly said, redistributing the civilized world. (Nobody asked him, damned French meddler. Turncoat too, very slippery.) We sit here assuming our safety, meaning the security of Elba as a prison. My intelligence agents (spies, he means, plain spies) inform me that he is ready to take advantage of the disaffection breeding among the disbanded army. Lot of damned nonsense. Bad dreams he's having. Knows he's a traitor and an ingrate. Guilt, that's what it is. Heard the last of old Bony.

The Continental System didn't work too well,
And the Spanish experience was concentrated hell.
Alexander promised friendship but decided to rebel
So I thought I'd quell the Russians with my shot and shell.
But we limped back from Moscow feeling sad and sore
And we had to meet Coalition Number Four.
We were trounced at Leipzig very very hard,
And now I am the Emperor
(Vive L'Empéreur)
Of an empire not much bigger than a knacker's yard.

A stronger prison is required, insisted Talleyrand, loud over the music of the waltz. I know the man (we know you know the man) and do not think for one moment he will resign himself forever to this ignominy (ah, ignominy, hear that? Giving himself away?) Metternich tapped his foot to the music, beaming (Austria would get the whole of Lombardy-Venetia, as well as Dalmatia, Carniola, Galicia, Salzburg).

Then the news came through and the orchestra stopped (heard the last of old) dead.

FROM CANNES (HAS KISSED THE SOIL OF FRANCE) TO GRASSE TO Séranon to Digne and there was no imperial eagle for the battalion from Elba to set winging from belfry to belfry to belfry all the way to the pinnacles of Notre Dame until they managed to knock a rough bird together from bits of an old four-poster bed. He did not touch Fréjus on this return journey since there had been no cries of Long Live The Emperor there or God Bless You Sire, no woman's weeping, man's too for that matter, when he was on his way to embark for Elba; instead there had been vulgar execration and even burning in effigy. Over the Alps then, with Thank You Thank You and God Bless You My Children to those who brought him, Father Violent, Violet one would say, Hope Of A Second French Spring, bunches of votive violets. To the peasant who said he would sell him his horse for one thousand francs (and there were only eighty thousand for the entire expedition) he said:

"Fuck you my friend and may your wretched nag be stricken with the bog spavin."

The news, relayed from Lyons by telegraph, reached the Tuileries where His Gallic Majesty King Louis XVIII dithered in bloat and gout. Talleyrand, he thought, should have warned him of this eventuality but perhaps he did, there was so much to think about, restoring France to its prerevolutionary stability and glory. Leave it to Soult, Minister of War, Soult would know what to do, probably a matter of scaring him off with a few cannon, perhaps even merely the truncheons of the rural constabulary. All about His Majesty were those who had come back from exile to enjoy their own again: the Duc de Grandejeuner, the Duc de Grandiner, the Duc d'Ivresse, the Duc de Droit-de-Seigneur, the Duc de Faireletour du Cadran, the Duc de Lever-une-Dîme, the Comte de Pressurer-les-Pauvres, the Comte de Veaudor, the Comte d'Ecraser-d'Impôts. Also there was the Comte d'Artois, heir-presumptive, who was confidently expected to bring back the really good old reactionary days, downing the peasants' uppishness and restoring the land to its rightful aristocratic owners, shamefully dispossessed. In the cafés twelve thousand ex-officers on half-pay drank their absinthe and said oh yes there was mud and spilled-out guts and bones crawling with maggots but it was a bit of life really a man's life you might say and if I see any bastard spitting at the mention of honor and glory I'll bite his balls off with what teeth I have left more teeth anyway than this fat-bellied Bourbon bastard (and I don't give a fuck if that is a spy sitting there behind that copy of the *Moniteur*, filthy lying rag as it is) all dropping out what with the syphilis in him and his guts hanging down to the floor with his filthy gourmandizing. Say what you like some spuds and onions fried in train-oil on a bivouac fire tasted better than all that muck they serve up at Nicalas's. Good Christ that bint over there might well be the daughter of that old bag in the knocking-shop at Vicenza. And it was a bit of life, say what you like, when the trumpets sounded and the drums did the old daddy-mammy and there he was, N himself, growing bald, growing paunched, with a word here and a word there, never forgot a face.

On over Alpine snow towards Grenoble. At Laffrey, fifteen miles south, the Fifth Regiment of the Line, seven hundred muskets loaded and waiting for the order to level. To the strains of the *Marseillaise* (forbidden under the restored Bourbons) played by his own small Guards band he left his carriage and marched. The muskets were leveled. He unbuttoned gray surcoat and blue tunic, baring his breast. Captain Randon of the Fifth called "Fire!" N said: "Soldiers of the Fifth. Do you not recognize your Emperor? Do you not see here your old General? Well, if you wish to kill me, why do you wait? If you wish to kill your Emperor, here I am." Captain Randon called "Fire!" N said: "If you believe I am come among you out of a desire to restore my own glory, to further new ambitions, then you are mistaken. Three of the major powers of Europe support my return from Elba. Forty-five of the best brains of the Government in Paris have called for me. France needs her Emperor again. Her Emperor is here, obedient to the wishes of the call of the land we all love." Captain Randon considered calling "Fire!" He called it and seven hundred muskets cracked. Pistol-shot range. The former Emperor Napoleon the First of France lay dead at their feet. Unthinkable. Yelling, the troops broke ranks. They waved caps that spun on their bayonet tips. Long live the Emperor! They pulled the old tricolor out of their haversacks. "We will march together to restore those principles for which so many of your comrades died. The Bourbons are ruling you without right, without popular election. Where is their contract, where are the plebiscites? Are they not ready to turn back the clock, to reimpose feudal injustice, to squeeze tithes from you? We will not allow it, never, never. We mock our dear dead comrades in permitting such tyranny. On on on to Grenoble, and then the road to Paris and victory and glory and." Wild cheers, caps in air, tricolor after tricolor after tricolor in the breeze.

A near thing, damned close run.

With a thrum and a thrum on the mettlesome drum and the Bourbons are scum and we'll soon overcome. The Seventh was sent down to intercept and capture but instead the colonel handed over the regimental colors and, as a token of surrender, stove in the drum. With a thrum to Grenoble we come and the Bourbons are glum. At Grenoble the commander of the garrison was unwilling to open the gates, but soldiers were leaping from the town walls into the arms of N. Peasants carried torches of lighted straw, night falling, and were ready with pitchforks to oppose military disloyalty. As for argument, that was easy: Where was Bourbon Louis's popular vote? The garrison commander still mustache-biting in indecision, sturdy artisans smashed the town gates open. N rode in on massive worker's shoulders. Darling of France again. Teach how to dance again.

The inn feast was hearty. Lettuce salad Marie Sarrazin with gratuitous earwig. Roast potatoes, an eye here and there, Jeanne-Louise Sautarel. Onions from the fire stern in burnt greatcoats, gift of the family Auque. A piece of beef. A cluster of golden though tough-thighed fowls. Dry cake from the grandmother of Maurice Lisnard, to be helped down with a slab of hairy butter. Peppered stewed rabbits.

"Rabbits," the Tuileries guardsmen sneered, seeing the packed bags loaded on to anonymous carts. "Scuttling off to Belgium."

His Majesty King Louis XVIII flushed yet again as he thought of that new indignity. Some Paris wit had nailed up a notice in a public place: "From Bonaparte to Louis: Dear Brother, do not bother to send any more troops. I have enough now." He had driven in the seasonable downpour to tell the two houses of assembly that the torches of civil war were being kindled by this incarnate devil, and the troops lining his route had shouted God Save The King, adding quietly *Of Rome*. He had heard, his hearing was alert enough. Ney had defected at Lyons, Ney. He could hear the jungle-snuffle all about him. Best to be off.

"Ignominious retreat," his ministers muttered. "Not to be thought of. Drive down in open carriage, face him. The divinity of true royalty. He'll look sick. He'll bow before it, scuttle off like a rabbit." It seemed very improbable really.

"Ignominy of my position," Ney was saying at Auxerre. "I admit I promised to bring you back in a cage. I considered my first duty was to France, sick, sore, weary, and to the physician who, however clumsy his fingers, was charged with restoring her to health."

"Yes yes yes, I understand, Ney. No recriminations, no punishments. Loyalty is a difficult commodity. You are to me as you were at Borodino. Nothing has changed."

It all gushed out now. "You have no conception. The haughtiness. We are tolerated because we are useful. The humiliation at court. My wife especially. Because of her humble origins. They sneered at her. How is the chambermaid's daughter your good lady? The King himself said that to me."

"All over now, Ney. Don't fret. The people of France are in the saddle again. I am not leading the way to Paris. They are leading me."

"The ignominy."

"No more of that, Ney."

Guglhupf mit Schlag. Bauernschmaus. Topfenpalatschinken. Marie-Louise, defecting wife, was at Schönbrunn with her one-eyed lover General Count Neipperg. So simple. One little holiday in the Oberland and there it was: a faithful, more or less, and certainly loving husband forgotten. Neipperg, black silk patch adding to his charm, singing his way into her bed. Talleyrand saw his own treachery as of a somewhat different order. A metaphysical treachery, austere, not like hers, which was to do with cooing flattery in her ears, praise of her Mongol cat's eyes, stroking hands on her arms. He, Talleyrand, had gone to the scabrous limit in denigrating N—incest with his sister Pauline, dropping with syphilis and a ravaged liver, Elba turned into a Sade cellar of wanton atrocity—but it had all been part of a chill and intellectual policy. Well, no further coat-turning was now possible. He must take the lead in denunciation: criminal act, unprecedented in the annals of infamy, enemy of civilization, the major powers must unite, sparing no cost, to drive this tigrine monster to his own perdition, hell as a punishment for creating hell. Funny thing though, Wellington had mused. Nobody told that Louis imbecile to get out. Got out of his own accord, scuttling off to Belgium like a rabbit. The people want old Bony back, no doubt of it. So we make war on the people of France. Has to be, though. Democracy can go too far.

They danced. United Kingdom of Benelux Benelux, Britain gets Malta and Cape of Good Hope. (Plenty for Austria, plenty for Prussia, but nothing at all in the paws of the Pope.) Santa Lucia, Mauritius, Tobago, Ionian Islands, also Ceylon. Swiss get neutrality, Russia gets Poland, so it goes on. But Russia and Prussia, England and Austria vow first to destroy him and never to yield. National banners but crusader's shield. Seven hundred thousand they'll put in the field.

N was telling them in the Tuileries, arranging the papers on his desk, finding odd prayer books and sets of rosary beads around and ordering them to be sent, with the Emperor's compliments, to the former King, properly styled Bourbon Usurper, about his recognition of the fact that times had changed. Change, gentlemen, is the very essence of life. So long as it is not backward change, the restoration of a cruel and unjust past. Liberty, equality and so on still belong to the future. We must work for them. A new constitution is what we first require, and I have asked this admirable young man Benjamin Constant to draw one up. France, our concern is with France. We are happy to keep to the frontiers agreed in 1814. No desire for territorial aggrandizement. Of course, we must recognize that there is an aggressive spirit abroad, fostered particularly at Vienna, and that any attempt on our national borders will call forth immediate retaliation, anticipatory if need be. But none, at the moment, can say I have not tried to sue for eternal friendship between France and her former enemies. I have sent Montrond to see Metternich, I have written a personal letter to the Prince Regent of England. I expect no word of conciliation from either. We must defend ourselves, gentlemen. I am happy to state that volunteers have swelled the army to over three hundred thousand. I have drawn up—see, here it is—a plan for the fortification of Paris. But our primal desire is for peace.

Peace, thought Madame Mère, on her way to join her son. Well, he has had his share of peace. Elba was after all much like Corsica, so that dream of a quiet old age for myself, away from court muck and bowing and scraping, came true. I am glad it did not go on longer. He said it was a matter of honor and he was right. He is doing the right thing. There are not many who are doing the right thing, especially that little Austrian bitch. Loves her still, he says, lonely for her, finds the Tuileries too big to live alone in, moved to the Elysée. Well, she gave him a son, did her duty there, which the other one, though God rest her soul, never could. They said it was when she fell that time, that balcony giving way, but it was loose living, a judgment from God. But now these Austrians will not let him see his son. What sort of a world is it they are building, when a man cannot see his own son? And so long as he is unable to see his own son then you can say that he is in a state of defeat and has lost honor. So it is a matter now of recovering honor and he has my blessing.

"Honor," N said, seeing the rain ease off. "What do they know or care about honor? It is not the pressures of the Manchester or Birmingham merchants that can inspire soldiers to victory. They have no fire in them, fire of honor. We will throw thunderbolts at them, we will pierce them with lightning. Good sailors I concede, but bad soldiers. The English are bad soldiers."

"Villainton," Bertrain said, "is an Irishman. We have had good Irishmen."

"He's a bad bad general leading bad bad troops. It will be nothing. It will be a summer picnic."

"I recommend," Drouot said, "that you start your picnic at midday. Give the ground a chance to dry out. We need firm ground for the twelve-pounders."

After midday. "That column on the right flank is Prussian. We can smash Villainton before the Prussians move up. What in God's name has happened to Grouchy? Where are those cavalry detachments I asked for? There has to be communication between him and HQ. What the hell does Grouchy think he's doing?"

Two o'clock. "News from Grouchy," Soult said. "He's still at Gembloux. He says one Prussian corps has withdrawn to Wavre."

"Direct movements on Wavre, tell him. And for Christ's sake establish communication with HQ."

Later, "That Grouchy is a fucking thaumaturge. Would you not say that only a man of miracles could fail to do something decisive with thirty-four thousand men and one hundred and eight fucking guns? This Blücher is nothing. This Blücher should be wiped out by now."

"With respect, Sire, don't underestimate—"

"I say this Blücher is nothing. And this Grouchy of ours is a milksop. Where's his initiative? Where's his energy?"

"With respect, Sire, he was only obeying orders." *Inspiration in war is appropriate only to the commander-in-chief.*

"Well, let's see how Ney gets on at the other place. And now we have the Guard artillery to worry about. Drouot should be there, but what can we do? Mortier is fucking idiot enough to be ill and who else but Drouot can command the Guard? It's a damned nuisance."

One-thirty. "Ney reports launching of first main attack."

Four massed columns of infantry thrown in, repulsed, losses heavy. No time to deploy. English volleys smack, smash. Lord Uxbridge's cavalry launch well-timed charge.

Three-thirty. "Ney says English line is in general retreat. He's sending in the cavalry alone."

"What?" N screamed. "First infantry without cavalry support, now cavalry without inf— He'll never break those squares. And now there's Bülow with his damned Prussians. We'll have to throw in the general reserve. Fourteen thousand men. That should do it."

Six-thirty. "Ney reports La Haye Sainte captured. Requests the Guard infantry be sent. Final assault on English center."

N danced with rage. "Troops? He wants me to send troops? Where the hell does he think I can find troops? Does he think I can make them out of this damned clay? Does he think I'm fucking Prom—"

Seven-thirty. Five battalions of the Guard sent to Ney for his final assault.

"They're retreating, Sire. It's over." Panic, rout. N was incredulous, then he could believe only too well. Everything could be explained, everything always could.

"I'm beat. I'm so tired I could drop." Helped him onto his horse. A thing never before seen. Helped onto his horse. Retreat to Charleroi. Riding to Charleroi he could explain everything. Strategy had never really changed, even from his first battle. Now well-known, now common knowledge. Now, in their reports, *Bonaparte predictably*— And growing old, though only in forties still, really growing old. Body fags, brain fags. We are not what we were. No initiative among the generals, but then I never wanted them to have it. Initiative was my monopoly. A rational explanation is, though, always a kind of victory. I reject superstition. All those double vees. To Soult he said:

"What's the meaning of the name? Waterloo, I mean?"

Soult told him. I reject superstition. All is not lost. I can still lay my hands on one hundred and fifty thousand men. To Paris quickly. I can guess what is happening in Paris. Dissolve the legislature? Reign by the axe? No. And by now the two Chambers will have announced that a decree of dissolution is treason. The National Guard will be protecting them. Another abdication. *I proclaim my son Napoleon II, Emperor of the French.* But the boy is a prisoner of the Austrians. I need a new great traitor, of Talleyrand's stamp. Fouché is well qualified for the post. He will be waiting in Paris, welcoming the victorious Allies.

The victorious Allies marched into Paris, firm pounding crotchets of battalion after battalion after battalion of infantry, the more skittish quarter-notes of the hoofs of cavalry on the cobbles. The sun of early July set the helmets and stirrups on fire and the brass of the horns and trumpets. Blücher looked murderous, the war not yet won until he could with his own hand shoot that outlaw and enemy of mankind. Wellington pointed his stern bony nose into a grim future. There were no flowers thrown. It was, for many reasons, no time of glory. The words of his own report, set to his mount's clatter, beat in the

Duke's ears. Most desperate business I ever was in ever was in. Never took trouble about any battle about any battle so much so much. Never so never so near being beat. Losses immense especially infantry. Specially infantry. After the infantry and cavalry and gunners and sappers the baggage train came.

After the baggage train, bloated, gouty, reclaiming his own again rode His Gallic Majesty Louis XVIII (would have preferred Louis Philippe, Duc d'Orléans, really, said Fouché, trusted Head of Police sliding into Talleyrand slot, but there was just no time to bargain), King of the French, restorer to France of whatever had to be restored. Horns and trumpets in hollow hunting harmonies, drums drums drums. All over.

IV

"NOT ALL OVER," HE CRIED TO THE SQUAWKING SEAS. "NOT IN THE least all over. I will not have these mad desperate rages." *Bastille tuiler massac swiss guaaaaaaar sept massac.* "You, Bertrand, must, I say it with appropriate er er, control your lady wife. I will not have her attempting to leap overboard." *Nat conven proclam 1st rpblc exec louis 16 reign terror marie antoin 9 thermidoooooor.*

"Marchand, Sire, said something of your intention to—"

"Kill myself, eh? Never take the word of a valet, Bertrand." *Robes fall pierre end of reign of 13 vendem coup estab directoooooory.* "I merely said that a man should always conduct himself as if every day was his last."

But he'd tried it. Rather than abdicate. The poison didn't work, though. Got stale or something.

"Gives savor to life. Come, who knows what the future may hold? I am removed from the European scene as a personage but now may enter the world scene as a *principle.* Read the Acts of the Apostles. Not, Bertrand, you understand, that I would commit the blasphemy of—"

"I did not think for one moment, Sire, that you would think—"

But all Judases, the whole lot. Even that Mameluke, pockets bulging with gold and silver.

"Nevertheless, the parallel is intriguing." *Marriage jsphn jsphn jsphn general buon bon campaign italy love.* "I showed them a resurrection was possible. And now it is the word that counts, Bertrand, the scripture. Besides, I may be called upon. Even England. Their Whigs want me. The people want me, you saw that on the *Bellerophon*, on the quay at Portsmouth or Plymouth or wherever it was." *Egypt 18 brumaire coup 3 cons 1st cons 1st cons for life exec of duc denghien.* "And even if I am not called upon, no prison is completely impregnable. As Elba showed. We may spend productive days planning, Bertrand." *Emperor emperor EMPEROOOOOOOOOR.* "It is by no means all over."

But this is going to be no Elba. A thousand leagues from nowhere. No prison walls like the sea. The British-held sea.

"Named after a great woman, Bertrand." *Coron empr empress coron king italy milan 3 coalition engl austr russ swed fren occup vien austerl peace pressburg.* "A lady of Britain, not at that time perfidious, mother moreover of a great emperor." *Confed of rhine 4 coalit pruss russ jena auerstadt eylau friedland tilsit tilsit TILSIT tlst tls tl t.* "According to the legend, it was she who found the true cross."

"It is not, all things considered," the Grand Marshal Bertrand said, "the most hopeful of associations."

True cross all right. No doubt of that.

"Come, Bertrand, consider instead that what was an engine of shameful execution to the pagan Romans became a symbol of glory. Again I do not wish to seem blasph—" *Fr occup rome penins war spain portug congr erfurt.*

"Of course not."

"But you may say that the four extremities represent those victorious allies that are hammering in the nails." *Alexander alxndr lxndr xnd x war austr fren occup vien 2nd time annex papal states pius vii excommun pius vii arrested.* "It is rather intriguing, poetic. But they dare not affix a mocking inscription. INTERFECIMUS NAPOLEONEM REGEM IMPERATOREM. The thought of my martyrdom frightens them." *Wagram schönbrunn div div divorce.* "I lost one crown." He chuckled. "Now I have gained another." *Marie louise KING OF ROME invade russ borodino retr moscow malet conspir cross berezina arriv paris 6 coalit leipzig leipzig lpzg.* He chuckled. "I am, as I say, not being bl—"

"Of course not of course not."

"The point I would make is that this too can be a conqueror's crown, Bertrand." *Capitu paris provis govt talleyrand snake abdic bourbon back count de provence louis xviii treaty fntnbleau exile to.*

"I quite see that."

Death death death of of. Escape Elba over water 100 days water 100 leau loo. And now.

And now he looked gloomily at that island bouncing on the southern ocean. Volcanic granite, a real rock for Prometheus. And this was, so that Irish doctor had said, a bad climate for livers.

"I know what you're thinking, Bertrand. Nothing seems to be growing here. Very rocky. Not even a thorn-bush, eh?" In good enough spirits, it seemed, robust despite everything, three months of sea air perhaps helped, he nudged Bertrand, so that Bertrand nearly fell on the deck. "We will make things grow here. We will get the island on our side, make it a tool, a weapon. Look what I did with Elba."

"You did much. Much."

Made the soil green with intensive cultivation, cleaned up the shit, bottled the mineral water, built the theater there, made the idle bastards work.

"This may yet be the center of the free world."

Bertrand looked doubtful. The island, now very close, its unpromising features clear in the sun pompous and bold as British brass, seemed an almost dementedly well-chosen negation of freedom. That British flag flapping there over gloomy cannon was three crosses, not one, one for each nail. T. N looked momentarily doubtful too. But then he began to sing. Tilsit tinrit. It was as if, after long years of exile, he were at last coming home. Titsil. He sang a song popular during the time of the Directory, all about the charms of someone's *tétons*. Poor bugger, not one woman willing to stay with him. Well, Rousseau had sanctified masturbation along with the social contract. Residuary reward of the imperial office. But she might have, she, had she not died untimely. Not more than six weeks after his first going into exile. She would have made it an outpost of French civilization, despite Sir this and Milord the other. They would have flocked from everywhere to see the roses.

I. N. R. I.
IMPERA
NAP
REGEM
INTERFEC
I. N. R. I.
TOREM
OLE
ONEM
IAMUS

SINCE SIXT WEEK I LEAVE THE ENGLISH AND Y DO NOT ANY PROGRESS. SO

I. N. R. R. I.

SIXT WEEK DO FOURTY AND TWO DAY. IF MIGHT HAVE LERN FIVTY WORD, FOR DAY, I COULD KNOW IT TWO THOUSANDS AND HUNDRED. SO

I. N. R. R. I.

If he would know what R.R. signifies,
(Not that the rustic *to raw rock applies),*
Regem Rusticatum *might well do*
It rustles, rustic, *rings with birdsong too.*

Irrelevant that connotative rust:
Nonferrous growls the grim volcanic dust,
Rich, though, the learned gardener assumes,
In potence, in potentia, *of blooms.*

A four-edged bed of agony? Inept!
A four-edged bed for Flora? Ah, accept!

In gardens the four warring elements
Nature and man to peaceable intents
Rein in, reign over, and to work inspire
Inaqueate air embracing terrene fire.

Ah we
Irishmen better than
Napoleoniform
Rusticant Corsican
Imperatores are
Inly equipped to be
Narrative poets of
Raw wounding exile:
Impressive, ah yes.
So let
Irish MacDonald and
Noble Kilmaine and the
Rest of the Celtic
Imperial Marshalate
Indicate now with a
Nod how we sympathize.
Rex Imperator,
In peace requiesce.

It was a cool and pleasant garden that he sat in, listening to the song of the birds, strange birds mostly, birds not known in Europe, and now and again looking sadly down at the sea far below. It was the garden of Mr. Bascombe, the East India Company agent of the island, and here, he sometimes fancied, he must find his only small paradise after the dirty inferno of Jamestown and before the eternal emptiness and loneliness of Longwood, still to come. The garden had, when he had first been introduced to it, been made especially pretty by the presence of two little English flowers, Betsy and Jane Bascombe, who had started with terror and then with a kind of joy at the unexpected sight of one whom they had only known previously as an ogre of the cartoons in the English journals. Here he was, strolling and even smiling, in a green uniform and a cocked hat, with one hand placed, just as in the drawings in the journals, inside his coat. The two pretty little romps were delighted to turn him into an uncle, our Uncle Napoleon yet still, and how delightfully, an *ogre*. For it is in the nature of children to be unafraid of evil and even, in their innocence, to wish well to those who practice or have practiced it. Little Jane had once, in church in Jamestown, prayed that Satan be made good and happy. So there he was, and his favorite was Betsy, who knew some French. As for his learning English, he swore that it was an impossible language. "A barren land," he had once put it, "full of thorn-bushes, and with birds with strange cries flying over it." And so it was that, this fine afternoon, he sat with Betsy, the two of them talking French together, she naturally not so well as he but, naturally too, improving all the time.

"I was," he told her, "a military cadet at Brienne. Do you know what that is? Do you know where Brienne is to be found?"

"It is no matter," said she with impatience. "Tell me the story, uncle."

"Each of us cadets," he continued, "was allotted a little square piece of land. In Corsica I had known much about farming and about the skill of growing things. The other boys at the military school cared little and knew little, so they willingly allowed me to annex their little plots of land to my own. I placed a wooden fence all about, and then I planted bushes. Bushes—do you know that word?" It was, of course, the French word he was referring to.

"Like little trees," said Betsy.

"Very good," he smiled. "I planted bushes and also vegetables and flowers. It was my own garden and none other's, and I would sit there peacefully dreaming of home or reading Tasso."

"What," asked Betsy, "is Tasso?"

"You ask such a question?" he exclaimed. "Ah, but of course you are English, and you English know nothing of the great Tasso. Know then that Torquato Tasso was a great Italian poet who wrote a very fine tale in verse, and the name of it is *Gerusalemme Liberata*. Many people said that Tasso was mad, but of course he was sane as you or I, if not saner. After all," he smiled sadly, "he did not have to spend his time on St. Helena."

"You read this poem in Italian?" exclaimed Betsy. "You must have been very clever."

"Ah, child, you forget," said he, "that my first language was Italian. I had to learn French just as you are learning it. Very well, then. In Corsica the soldiers and even the bandits sing verses from *Gerusalemme Liberata*. It is about the Christians fighting the pagans, and there is a magician who is the king of Damascus. He has a niece named Armida who lures—you know the word?—Christian knights into her magic garden."

"Tell me the story," says Betsy, as a child will.

"I will tell it some other time," he said with a kind of mock ferocity. "Now it is my own story I am trying to tell. My garden was, I suppose, a magic one, though magic in a way different from the wicked Armida's. For, you see, I could turn it into home whenever I so wished. And I always so wished. Whenever any other boy tried to intrude into my little garden, I would at once chase him out. Like that," he added, making with his hands the gesture that a henwife makes at her feathery charges.

"You were quite right to do so," said little Betsy, but, forgetting for the moment, she spoke it in English. But she nodded with vigor at the same time and he understood well enough.

"Now on the feast of St. Louis," he continued, "which we had as a holiday because it was the official birthday of the King—not real, but official, you understand—"

"Is it true," said Betsy, in her impertinent child's way, "that you saw the King's head cut off?"

"No. And it is not to the present point," said he. "Let me finish my story. Every cadet was allowed to make fireworks. He could buy some gunpowder and then pack it into cardboard tubes. Then he would attach a fuse and light it and make a great noise. To celebrate, you understand, the feast of St. Louis."

"I should think that must have been very dangerous."

"We were young soldiers, you must remember," he said, "so we had to know a great deal about gunpowder. Well, you see, what happened was that some of the cadets had built a great pyramid—"

"Peer a mead," she said. "What is that, uncle?"

"Pyramid, pyramid," he repeated, and he began to build one in the air with his very fine hands. "You will see them if you ever go to Egypt."

"Is it true," she asked, ever ready to divert him from his story with the hope of a better one, "that you dug the Sphinx out of the sand?"

"I will tell you another time. There is plenty of time. All I have, my dear child, is time." And his sad smile returned, one of the saddest and sweetest smiles, she thought in her young miss's way, that she had ever seen. "There was, as I say," he continued, "a great pyramid of fireworks. The cadets set fire to it, and there was so much light and smoke and noise, the sparks flying everywhere, that they grew frightened. So they came rushing away from it into my garden, trampling it all down."

"What a shame," she said, again relapsing into English, though her tone again spoke all her shock and sympathy.

"Fences, bushes, flowers, everything. So I picked up a *bêche* and with it I drove them out. I cared not at all whether I hurt or even killed them. When your garden is attacked, the thing that you have made with your own hands, remember, then you must be ready to do anything to protect it. I repeat: anything."

But Betsy was looking for the word *bêche* in her little dictionary of the French and English languages. "I do not know the word," she said. "What is a besh?"

"Why," said he, "the implement with which you dig." And with his white hands, that looked so softly gentle, he seemed to grasp an airy haft and to initiate the movement of digging. "*Bêche.*"

"Ah, it is a spade." And she showed him the two words together. "See the word *spade.*"

"*Spade*," he said in some surprise, giving the word two syllables. "Why, that is the Italian word for swords. Is not that interesting? So even the English see that a garden has something to do with fighting. Is not that a most interesting thing to find?"

"And in a game at cards," she said, "we have spades. But I was told that that was once swords."

"In cards we have swords still," he said, and he looked at her.

Looking at her from the rocky promontory of what she, a mere innocent English miss, must surely regard as the decrepitude of advanced age, he was powerfully aware of what might be, did he not guard feelings all too vulnerable and inflammatory in his enforced celibate loneliness, an affection not without possible danger to them both. How old was she then? Some fifteen summers, no more. And if Europe did not recall him to a destiny not yet, for all his aborted achievements, to be considered snipped by the Parcan shears, if, say, England did not, in its next change of government, install an oligarchy of Whigs inclined to Bonapartist sympathies, if, moreover or alternately, the papal appeal for his release did not prevail (though he cherished a hope that it would, since the Concordat had, despite many vicissitudes, been universally regarded as a shrewd stroke of policy), he might be forced, the agony flowering in his all too virile blood all too efficaciously fenced about, to observe her growth to an achieved beauty that now merely promised. Did his jailors then take him for a eunuch? Would he, who had enjoyed the frankest and most tender embraces from queens and princesses, be reduced to stammer protestations of shocking affection to an *English miss?* It was all an irony that might be regarded as the ultimate, however little purposed, in Britannic humiliation of a foe still hated though rendered almost zoologically harmless. Smiling now he said:

"We must cultivate our garden. You know who said that, little one? The great Voltaire said that."

"Voltaire?" said she, flushing in shock at the mention of a horrid name, yet intrigued, in a young girl's manner, at the *naughtiness* of it. "But Papa says he was a man without faith in the Supreme Being and was, moreover, the cause of all our troubles."

"What troubles?" he smiled with a touch of wryness.

"Oh, you know," she said, her eyes lowered in embarrassment. "The trouble in France and with France." She too frequently forgot that her kindly plump uncle in the garden here, staying indeed at the Briars until Longwood should be ready to accommodate him, was one with Nero and King Henry the Eighth and other fascinating horrors out of schoolroom history books. It was comical, and yet it was not comical, rather it was unbelievable, as if a picture had animated itself and stepped down from the wall, and it seemed to her possible, since she was still little more than a child, that the learned men who wrote history books could be mistaken in their judgments and presentations of the evil great, being in their way ignorant, never having left Oxford or Cambridge and certainly never having, as she had, dwelt in an outlandish zone such as these South Seas. Might it not be that Richard Crookback and the Emperor Caligula and Alexander the Great himself had been, in truth, kind avuncular men like her Uncle Bonaparte, and that they had been presented as historical ogres by men jealous of their incapacity to become themselves great tyrants and conquerors? These thoughts certainly passed through her young mind as she observed one held to be the greatest tyrant and conqueror of them all, now sitting at his ease in a wicker chair in the garden at the Briars, sipping lemonade and hitting at a fly that persisted in buzzing about his well, it was the correct word, was it not?, however little *lady-like*—perspiring nose. He was the nicest and most interesting of men and was, moreover, eminently teasable. It would appear that tyrants were, and she used the French word to herself, recognizing that there was no English word so apt, more *sympathique* than schoolmasters and clergymen, at least, for she was aware of the limitations of her childish experience, those she herself had any acquaintance of. She now smiled at him a little wickedly and said:

"Have you yet seen the new toy that Jane got in Jamestown? And do you promise not to be offended?"

"Goodness, must I answer both questions at once? Very well then: no, I have not and yes, I do. There. And what toy is this?"

"Wait," said she. She scampered up to the house, a pert English miss in white muslin over the lawn, wearing dancing slippers stained by the recently watered grass. She had come to see her Uncle Nap or Bony straight from practicing her waltz-steps. Tonight was her first ball.

The beautiful lady of seventeen, dressed for the midsummer Christmas ball, came out of the house and glided, her grotesquely elongated shadow truckling all the way as she went, a stately young queen, as fair as any he had known gracing the courts of Europe, towards her fat old uncle, who appeared to be not very well, since that stupid Sir Hudson had now forbidden him the healthful exercise of horse-riding, and she had neither a toy nor a word for him. He greeted her with courtly gravity.

"You are very beautiful, my dear," he said, and she flushed somewhat at the compliment, though her mirror had told her it was not undeserved. "It is, I think, Monsieur Montez-chez-nous who is causing all the trouble."

"What trouble? I know of no trouble."

"Ah, how our French Commissioner loves gossip and intrigue. He is still a part of those old wigged and scented days when, in high places, there was little else to beguile the idle hours. Our poor Montchenu refuses to accept in his heart of hearts that King Louis the Seventeenth was in truth guillotined, he seems to believe he is back there on the throne of France, having had that venerable seat thoroughly disinfested. Corsican fleas, you know. My dear sweet little Betsy, do you not know that you are in all the journals of the world, even your own English *Morning Chronicle*?"

Her flush now was deep and unhappy. "It is all a great stupidity," she said with some heat. "They are all being most silly."

"Ah," he said, shaking his great round head in humorous sadness. "They are talking of the fat dirty old Corsican adventurer. What they are saying is that he always had an eye for a pretty girl. That, dear Betsy, is your reward for being kind to the terrible tyrant Bonaparte. Keep away from tyrants, my dear, since good rarely comes from them."

"Papa," she said stoutly, "has said to take no notice. It is all French *bétises*, he says. He says it is a stupid game, with all their talk of *l'amour*."

He knew the English word, though he could not well pronounce it. The word *love* seemed to him to be a strange and cool word, much different in tone and meaning from the French, signifying also in tennis a score of nothing as well as a kind of game of euchre. No, it appeared that love and *l'amour* were far from being the same thing, a whole insulating channel flowing between them.

He smiled and said: "Cut off Monsieur Montez-chez-nous's pigtail. That will teach him a lesson." He made a snipping motion with his fingers, though at true tail-level, knowing that she was ever ready to pardon in him small coarsenesses of behavior, which she regarded as the harmless marks of foreigners who knew no better. And now she said:

"He will have to find someone else for his gossip. We are going back to England."

The pain he felt at that moment within him stabbed with a surprise for which he was not fully prepared, yet he knew well enough that such an event must sometime come and that it would entail an attendant emotion of loss; it was his prescience of the severity of the emotion that occasioned the surprise. Nor was there any real need for him to ask the question *why?*

"Papa received a letter from East India House in London. They require him to be back there. Nobody stays here forever."

"Except," he sighed, "your lonely old ogre."

"Oh," she said, "you will not stay here forever, for that would be too cruel." Somewhat heartless was the casualness of the tone in which she added: "Anyway, I shall think of you. And when anybody in England says that you are a cruel tyrant and a terrible ogre, then I shall shout at them and pinch them and perhaps even kick them."

"That would be not very ladylike behavior. But I thank you for being my only lady defender."

"Well," said she, and something of the old roguishness of the pert miss of fifteen appeared in her smile, "you have a Polish lady, do you not? She has great cause to be your defender, or so they say."

"Yes, yes, there is indeed she, and a very beautiful lady, though perhaps not so beautiful as my English lady dressed for the ball. You are my only friend among the enemy," he said, "and that is something to rejoice in and to wonder at."

"Oh, enemy, enemy," she cried. "It is all nonsense. Everybody is really your friend and loves you. It is only the stupid people who do not. Such as silly Sir Hudson and the men of politics and the rich people whom you have made a little poorer, which serves them right." And then she disclosed something she had hidden in her hand in the folds of her silk foulard. "See," she said, "I have this for you." And into his hand she placed a little snuffbox, a thing of cheap metal in blue and yellow, doubtless bought in Jamestown out of her scant spending money.

He took it with a grave bow and said: "Thank you. I will start to take snuff again, if Sir Hudson will allow me the indulgence."

"No, no, silly, you are to open it. I should really give it to you later, but I fear I may lose it first."

He opened it and found therein a lock of her hair. He was greatly touched and said, over and over: "Thank you, I thank you, I most sincerely thank you. Yes yes, we must exchange *boucles*. Alas, I have little enough to cut now, so I must cut it for you quickly. And then sometime you will find it and think of me. You will find it and think of me, if you do not lose it or give it away."

She stamped with her satin slipper on the lawn, but the soft sward yielded no noise. "Oh, fiddle on your stupidity," she cried. "I shall never forget you."

The tone was of a schoolmistress's firmness, and the promise seemed to hold the strength of a threat.

"I shall never forget you," she said again.

In his hand he held, not yet, a lock of her hair and a snuffbox.

In his hand he held the toy she had come running out with, the pert miss of fifteen years only. It was not, he considered, smiling and yet sighing over it, a toy in the best of taste: the toymakers, then, had reduced him to a monster merely meet for the play of infantile derision. For it consisted in a gross carven caricature of himself with characterizing military hat but the form else, and even the tail, of a monkey, clinging to a pole which the pulling of a string enabled his simian mock-majesty to climb to the top, whence he tumbled to a flat green-painted bed inscribed with the name *St. Helena.*

"Ah, yes," he sighed, working the silly model to see dourly the ridiculous parody of his rise and descent. "So then I am come to this."

"Do you not think it droll?" she asked, for certainly the little romp herself thought it comical enough. "Is not that really to be known and famous, to be turned into a toy, do you not think so?"

Before he could answer, or indeed even think of something wherewith to answer, there was a great commotion and certain loud angry cries from the direction of the house. It was Betsy's mother who had appeared, a trim English lady of the mercantile class, evidently wroth with her daughter and crying words which he could not well comprehend, though their import was lucid enough. Soon she was boxing the child's ears and poor Betsy was emitting cries of her own.

"Come," said he, "I am not offended. It is but the foolishness of children who know no better. Oh, is not this punishment too hard for so trivial a breach of courtesy?"

Mrs. Bascombe did not understand all his words, but in her halting French she made him to understand that the girl must grow up and out of her rudeness, Mr. Bonaparte being a guest when all was said and done, and that she must now be shut up in a room and go supperless while she meditated on her inexcusable behavior.

And so it was that, later in the day, Uncle Napoleon the Great Monster and Tyrant and Libertine of Europe stood outside the door of the room wherein blubbering Betsy was locked, and spoke soft words to her.

"You see to what it is come," he said to the door. "I liberated all Europe but you I cannot liberate. There is a great lesson in all this. It is for my sake, it would seem, that you are incarcerated thus, and yet I do not wish your incarceration. With all of us there are forces hardly to be controlled, whether with spade or *spada*. None of us is really free."

She could, as a mere child, not be expected to comprehend the deeper drift of his words, but she said: "I have said I am sorry and I can say no more," in a voice muffled both by the salt of her tears and by the intervening oak. "Except," she added, "once more to say that I am sorry."

"You are not to say you are sorry to me," he rejoined kindly. "Rather it is to some ancient law or tradition of what is due to a guest to which your good mother and father strictly adhere. Well, perhaps it is better to be made a prisoner for a breach of such than to be like myself, who am become a prisoner because of the greater guns and cavalry of envious kingdoms. And transformed also, as you have shown, into a monkey." This renewed her blubbering, though he swiftly quietened it with a paraphrase, with only the locked door as apparent listener, of the tale of *Gerusalemme Liberata*.

IN such encounters may we find
RIght contact between mind and mind.
INhuman to the larger sense,
RIch, though, in human innocence,
INto the little zone of light
RIdes the Archruler of the Night.

Napoleon Symphony-IV

Those of our readers who are prepared to seek occasional diversion in what may, for want of a more learned term, be described as *literal magic*, will perhaps be encouraged to ponder on the signification of the letter W in the truncated career of our incarcerated Corsican. We refer, naturally, to our own W, to W as a right English letter, that brief kissing melody that parts lips for the omission of a right English vowel, ignoring for the nonce the silent tombstone of earlier and barbarous modes of Saxon speech in *wrath* and *wreath* and the like, as also the ghost of an owl-call that terminates such words as *now* and *know*. For names like Warsaw and Wagram, extinguished stars in the sped constellation of his triumphs, carry the Continental V, and the vivving and vovving and vuvving that are attached in the tongues of Europe to our special and characteristic and, may we say, patriotic English letter are but a known part of the jibberjabber of his customary garlic-laden Gallic and coarse-grained Corsican speech.

He has had time enough to ponder on Wellington and Waterloo, and now, lo, he is presented with the empire of Longwood. We doubt not, also, that, finding in these three W's three coffin-nails for his boxed and buried reputation, and wondering at the lethal trinity in his Corsican superstitious way (for this propensity of his nature, as of his nation's, is well enough known), he will have made certain enquiries as to the meanings of the words so terrifyingly double-yewed. His downfall was as much water as land, for the British Navy deterred his huddle of a Channel army from the temerity of a foredoomed essay at crossing the narrow seas, save for a piteous ketchload that ran screaming for dear life from the scarlet shawls of Welsh fishwives, believing these to be doubtless a sort of Amazonian redcoats, just as the same undefeatable force made the world's oceans serve him in the office of a national prison wall. Nay, even in the fateful Leipzig encounter with the Allies, it was the waters of an inconsiderable river that indirectly spoke the word Defeat, when a scared pressed fledgling of a sapper blew the bridge with premature haste. He must know too by now, however unwilling to learn the tongue of exile, that Water comes from Wells and is ever Welling forth from the natural springs by the very Ton—and, for good measure, may we not add that his own *L'eau* was in orthographic bo-peep hiding in the Loo? But what now will our jailed general be making of Longwood? Nothing of a watery grave offers there, and we are happy that he is afforded that small onomastical comfort.

Yet if he avoids the blasphemous ring of one signification (and there are some of the Whig faction all too ready to apotheotize him to a degree that makes the sacrilege sufficiently explicit), he will be unavoidably confronted by the dire prolepsis of another, since a trio (we will not suggest another blasphemy) of Longwoods will escort him to his last end: one Longwood will creak beneath his extreme groans, on another Longwood will he be borne away, and in a subterranean casket of Longwood will his body at last disintegrate to its component atomies, what time his soul is experiencing the awfulness of the condign sentence. Meanwhile, each day at Longwood he will be reminded, in the name of his illustrious and gallant keeper Sir Hudson, that he has indeed been brought most Lowe, and find too, though humbly disposed in that cognomen, the persistent letter of his downfall, a Cassiopeia of retribution whose fiery original, by a strange irony, he will never see blazing in the southern firmament of his confinement.

The mutual frown with which the antagonists confronted each other was a kind of ocular thunder, while their eyes flashed levin enough. The British knight was no whit abashed by the eminence of rank of his opponent, nor of the terrific reputation which his exploits in arms had earned throughout the world. As for his imperial crown, this, following the dictate of his masters, he saw as a mere impudent and pretentious fiction; here was but a soldier and a captive one, and wholly at the mercy of Sir Hud, in whom, nevertheless, the chivalric blood ran strong and rendered him ill disposed to assume the vindictiveness of the captor. For all that, he was hard put to it to drive from his warrior's memory his previous encounters with the forces of his prisoner, whether in Egypt, Germany or France, and he smarted yet from the ignominy of his dislodgement of Capri. Nor did his intimate knowledge of the race, language and very birth-place of his captive dispose him to a compensative sympathy. In his eyes, then, shone the fire of one who would willingly dispense justice but in no wise admit the tempering of mercy; while the orbs of the other bespoke a grievous resentment above the common lot.

"So, Sir Knight," cried Lion of the Valley, "I am at last granted the overlong deferred favor of an interview with my jailor. I have much to say, and you will please to listen."

"I am not so bound," frowned the other. "My duty is fulfilled in overseeing the provision of what is meet, by the laws of my commission, for a captive taken fairly in war, and that duty I have been officious to perform. You have nothing further to ask and I nothing further to grant."

"Yet," said Lion of the Valley, "do I not descry in a gaze otherwise obdurate odd rays of misgiving, and is this granting of a parley between us itself not a concession beyond what you term your duty?"

"I perform a courtesy," the other replied, "and I satisfy myself that all goes as well as may be expected to. That you are in health I am able to observe, as also the adequacy of your lodging and of such other amenity as is fitting. And so, Sir General, there is no more to be either said or done."

"Ah, is there not?" exclaimed the prisoner. "And, for an apt beginning, I will pick you up on your mode of address. For I am not Sir General but Lord Emperor, and that address is the garment of a reality, and the reality's self persists despite the outer conditions to which I am subjected. Your prisoner I may be, Sir Knight—who indeed can deny it?—but I am in no wise a common prisoner, and it is your persistent and insolent treatment of myself as such that I most bitterly resent."

"If you are Lord Emperor," Sir Hud rejoined, not without the suggestion of a sneer, "then your documents and seals of abdication were but a dream that the whole world joins you in dreaming. Know too, and here I forbear to jest, that the greater part of mankind rejects even your retrospectual claim to the title. General you are, and General I must call you. For the condition of your servitude, it is approved by all the signatories of the Peace, and the *insolence* you prate of must be referred to higher authority than my own."

"*Insolent* I said," cried the other, and he strode threateningly a pace or so nearer to his adversary as he spoke. "I say also *tyrannical.* I further add *vindictive.* The defeats that I, or my marshals, inflicted upon you in the field rankle within and forbid the disposing of your mind to the forms of common justice. Yea, common justice I say, since you will have it that I am but a common prisoner."

Stung to the nerve, Sir Hud hissed: "Sir, I will not bandy words. But nor will I be impugned so, for it is my honor, as a soldier and as a knight, at which you hit. And so I challenge you to show in what manner I have assumed the posture of *vindictive tyrant.*"

"Ah," said Lion of the Valley, a smile playing on his lips, "so we have at least entered a region of converse. Well then, Sir Knight, I would ask you this one easy question: where is my prison?"

"Your prison, as you know well, is this island," said the other, and at once would fain have called back the words, for he perceived the trap into which he was like to fall. "Or," he added in haste, "shall I say that it is the manor of Longwood on this island."

"Nay, I take your first answer," smiled Lion of the Valley, "as true and sufficient, for the common prison of a common prisoner may be located indifferently in any place, since it is the walls that confine. But for this uncommon prisoner a most uncommon piece of topography has, I assume with care and reason, been selected. Are not the walls of my prison this entire Southern Ocean? Are they not? Answer me."

"In a manner that is true," responded the other with caution.

"Well, then," his prisoner continued, "if it be true, another thing is true, and that is, since I am not in chains, I may justly claim the liberty of passage from wall to wall of my dungeon. That is, I may have freedom of the island from shore to shore, and likewise freedom of converse with the inhabitants thereof. Why then," and he raised his powerful voice to a shout, "am I not granted such right? Why do I have your musketeers and your grenadiers peering in my very windows and even violating the sanctity of—I will not speak the word, in deference to your knightly delicacy. By what right and by what order?"

"Raise not your voice so," returned the other with an equal anger. "I am not one of your underlings to be railed at. To your uncivil rantings I will return a civil answer, and that is this: that once you are on the shore you may well be on the sea, and that we have ample precedent of that danger. In a manner," he said, and the sneer was now patent, "it is to protect yourself from another such signal defeat as you suffered at Waterloo."

"Puppy dog," raved Lion of the Valley, now near dancing in his rage, "how you dare taunt me thus I marvel at—"

"That you will retract and at once. You will take back between your insolent teeth that unseemly—"

"Aye," returned the other, sneering in his turn. "I could indeed swallow such as you at a breakfast, puppy dog. So," he continued, while Sir Hud chafed in the freshly self-imposed bonds of his habitual courtliness, "you fear, do you? You fear that the Ogre may scape your confines and, whatever the outcome in Europe, if outcome there might be, your head would roll on Tower Hill for negligence. And if I am not to wet my feet in your encompassing ocean, nor am I to set my feet at all beyond the limits of this pitiable manor, since feet once freed to walk may walk towards some phantom vessel of liberation. You are a fool, Sir Knight, and you are also a caitiff coward."

"I will no more of this," said the British knight with the calm of an inner strength to which the barbarian adventurer could not, either through training or through racial endowment, himself even remotely pretend. And he picked up his helmet from the table whereon he had put it, and prepared to take his leave. But the prisoner was swift to place himself between his jailor and the door.

"Not so swift, Sir Knight." And now the voice of Stentor was but a serpentine whisper in the leaves. "I know it is your will that I should die, and I guess that in your sleep your hands twitch on the coverlet in a mime of strangling, but your commission forbids, on pain of your disgrace and mayhap worse, the overt or even covert doing of the deed. But you have softer and slower and more insidious means of encompassing my dispatch than the knife in the dark or the poison in the cup. There is, for one ensample, the device of starvation."

"You do not," returned the good knight with a restored humor in his countenance, "seem to me to be dying of that malady. Your bones are as well hid under your flesh as the stumps of felled oaks under January snows."

"Aye, you say so? Well, and if I say that what your mean benison permits myself and my entourage is of a gross insufficiency and that I am forced, this very day, to send ancestral gold and silver to be sold in the markets of the island's capital—What say you then, O Knight of the Doubtful Countenance?"

"I say that it is but an act of gratuitous malice, to bring myself low in the world's eyes. You have no need to sell plate that you may eat, and well you know it." Sir Hud's eyes, which Lion of the Valley closely observed, betrayed unease and resentment of an injustice he could not scotch, since the members of his prisoner's household were not themselves prisoners and hence could not be barred from free access to the marts of the town. There would be talk and there would be calumny, and the malice, transformed to a mendacious image of his tyranny, would fly with the trade winds to the known corners of the earth. "This is," he said, "a traitorous and unworthy act."

"It is," rejoined the other, now disporting his small but ample body in the postures of a known triumph, "a fair return for your own cruelty, aye, unworthy and unknightly cruelty. For in confining me as you do to the wretched periphery of this estate, you deprive me of all exercise. Was I not at one time free to ride a-horseback over the island ridge? And now I, whose life was lived in the field, must nurse a liver swollen and a belly over-rounded with the neglect of bodily action. Is not this cruelty, is not this a manner of slow and contrived murder?"

"Ride the ridge and you will ride to the shore. I cannot allow of such dangerous liberty and well you know it." But the eyes of Sir Hud had still to recover the calm and light of one content in his judgment. Of the cunning of his adversary he had long known; he had not however conceived that such cunning might contrive a manner of victory through self-elected martyrdom.

"Oh aye," jeered his prisoner, "and your soldiers will shoot me if I ride too far afield. Or perchance they may not. In spite of the hatred of myself that the governors of your realm hug to their bosoms, it may well be that the governed are of a different heart. May it not then be," and his voice was low and musical, "that you nurse some inner fear of my cause being not yet lost, of your own men responding to my trumpet, of mutiny in the name of liberty, the jack hauled down and the tricolor raised? Is it not so, O Knight in whose knightly countenance glooms a whole night of doubt?"

"This alone is so," responded Sir Hud, and his look and his voice alike had recovered authority, "that your confinement to the boundaries of this estate of Longwood shall be reinforced with the greatest rigor, and that orders will be given in my name and thereby in the name of His Majesty of England that, should you essay trespass beyond them, then you will be shot at sight."

"Ah," returned Lion of the Valley all smiling and in a voice of honey, "this likes me well. Your enmity is declared and, believe me, Sir Knight, Knight of Blackness, it shall be chronicled forever in the annals of infamy. For when I am dead, and this cannot in the nature of things be long delayed, it will be known to all the world who was my murderer. I foresee a time," said he, and the light of the visionary shone in his countenance, "when the agonies of the Emperor shall be enacted upon the common stage, and the pusillanimity and rancor of his jailor, the unchivalric chevalier, shall call forth cries of outrage from them that see the foulness of it all, and, yea, the very comedians who enact your part shall fear for their lives. Was it such fame as this that your parents foresaw for their offspring in the unlucky hour of your begetting?"

Sir Hud now trembled with emotions he could not, in the moment of their arousal, well define. "This is unjust," said he in a choked voice, stressing the word with a trembling fist, "and before the Supreme Judge of all of us you know it. I do no more than my duty, and my duty is to oversee the security of your confinement, as is delegated to me by my masters. If you consider that you and your household are in want of the necessities of sheer life, that what is allowed for your and their provisioning is inadequate, then I will, as is my duty, convey your complaint to them best able to judge of whether it be well-founded. For the rest, I must set severe limits on the bounds of your freedom of movement, and before God I see not how I can do otherwise."

"And so," said Lion of the Valley, and he purred in rather a tigrine than a leonine manner, "I am to have armed men still patrolling about my walls and peering in at my casements. Well, this I promise, as the Almighty is my witness, that should any come too close I shall conceive of it as unlawful trespass and act accordingly. Aye, Sir Knight, I will fire a ball into the breast of the intruder."

"This is contrary to all the laws that govern the covenant," began the knight, still trembling, but the other at once struck in with:

"Covenant, say you? There is no covenant between enemies. You and I, Sir Lowe, are at war."

"This is the very cream of madness," said the knight, with a partial recovery of his equanimity. "By rights you should be unarmed."

"And if I were to say aye to that," responded Lion of the Valley, "there would still be the matter of my royal entourage, which is a body of free men bearing all the privileges of free men, though they have of their grace and loyalty joined me in my incarcerated state. And to be armed is their right, and it would be their bounden duty to use arms in the defense of their prince. So I say again: beware. And if you yourself, Sir Knight, seek entrance here as out of what you conceive to be your gubernatorial privilege, then you too will receive, before you thrust foot beyond the threshold, a ball in your breast. Are my words clear? Do you apprehend them?"

"I must seek instruction from my masters," said Sir Hud. "For the moment I will say that my men will, and this I grant of my grace, keep discreet distance, neither peering in nor unlawfully entering. Their limits shall be the borders of your gardens."

"Ah, you say so?" responded his prisoner in glee. "I have won so much. And is there some law that forbids my tending and working in my gardens?"

"There is no such law," said the knight, though unhappily, "and it may be regarded as the healthful exercise you seek, but I know well what you have in mind."

"Aye, you will have read of me. Aye, you will have been apprised of the time of my cadetship. For a garden is what a man must win from the wilderness, it is the order he seeks, with nature's own compliance, to impose upon the aimless growth of nature's germinating forces. And my gardens shall spread, sir, and my trees and bushes push back the bounds of your watchfulness. Once I sought to turn all Europe into a garden, nor, despite all, will the wilderness altogether reclaim it. And so it must suffice now, that in a smaller or microcosmic figure, I must resume the labors to which God called me. I will construct, while you will but constrict. Is that not the truest and briefest summation of our respective aims?" The knight said nothing, having nothing further to say. "So now," spoke the Emperor of Longwood as to an underling, "you may leave my presence and plan new stratagems. But I shall win, make no mistake of that."

The day was hot beneath that southern sun,
The time conspired to rest, though Nature's self,
Knowing no rest, was busily at work,
The bees about their task, the butterflies
Gilding the blue they sailed and skimmed along,
And all the hidden forces underground,
Inaudible to most but to the ear
Attuned to Nature's music live and loud.
Thus as I strolled, wiping with movement slow
The copious dew the sun called forth to film
My heated brow with the coarse handkerchief,
A sister's gift, that I had hither brought
Out of my gentler dales, I chanced upon
A sweating gardener, singing at his task,
Digging and hoeing, and with cheerful tones
Bidding his helpers, men less apt than he
And with no cheerful song upon their lips,
To work apace for soon the westering sun
Would sink apace, the southern stars rush out,
And in one stride the mantling dark descend.
His language was not mine, but I had once,
In those good days when Freedom was the cry,
And France was teaching Brotherhood, been fired
To speak it much and dwell some little time
Where it was spoke, and so I used it now
In cheerful greeting. "Good it is to see,"
Said I, "such happy industry, my friend,
And such fair promise of a myriad blooms
And saplings that, when you and I are dust,
Our souls recalled to Nature's bosom, may
Yield grateful shade which sunburned travelers,
Such as myself, will bless, as also bless

The good man who once placed them in the earth."
He smiled at me; he was of middle years
And corpulent, and something in his mien
Shone that was hardly of the common sort
As though, but reason thrust the fancy back,
He had been ruler of some little world,
A squire, or officer of revenues.
Smiling he said: "I do, sir, what I may
To enlarge my little kingdom, as of yore
I made a greater kingdom greater still."
And, saying thus, he plied his clodded spade,
Calling out "Spadé, spadé," *in a jest*
I could not comprehend, as though he thought
Our English "spade" was an Italian word.
This, and his earlier words, made dawn in me
A sense that he was what a happy trope
Terms one of Nature's naturals. So with a smile
But neither look nor word of unbelief,
I let him speak on gaily as he worked.
"Aye, sir," said he, "for all that wilderness
Which men call Europe, wherein noisome weeds
Did choke the flowers, and greedy hornets bred,
And fruit did rot upon the vine, I took
Once as my garden-plot, and with the help
Of Nature and my fortitude inborn
And the long gift of patience did I make
The greatest garden man has ever known,
With tended plots and avenues built fair,
And cool gazebos, glassed herbaria
And everything to glad the heart of men.
Now, as you see, I work a humbler plot,
But still my kingdom." Then his manner changed.
It seemed he had but now discerned the tones
Wherein I spoke his language, for he said:
"Are you of Albion's shore? Are you sent here

To spy and probe? Whether so sent or no,
You trespass on my kingdom—get you gone."
And then he offered with his spade to strike:
"I have no spada *but by heaven this spade*
Shall serve me," and I understood the word.
And so I got me gone, though smiling still,
For Nature is as various in the men
She breeds as in her fruits and flowers, I mused.
And to this day, when idle hours invite
The drawing from my memory's varied store
Of images extravagant, extreme,
Or pale and simple as the woodland blooms
Wherein I lie at summer ease, I see
That man again, of swollen dropsied frame,
Of swollen fancy too, and hear his voice
Speak of his garden-kingdom, and I smile,
But deg the smile withal with generous tears.

SERGEANT TROUNCER, of His Britannic Majesty's infantry, and as good and faithful a servant of His Britannic Majesty as His Britannic Majesty could hope to find, if His Britannic Majesty were disposed to look, lay at his ease, or at such ease as the broiling heat would permit, on the plain pallet of the guardroom, and removed his boots. Each fell to the stone floor in its turn with as much noise, within the limits of its booty capacity, as it could muster, as though aware of a kind of military responsibility to be noisy, and, for good measure, the hobnails of the soles flashed sparks against the stone, as though concerned to impress the crawling foreign blackbeetles with a sort of British firework display. Sergeant Trouncer observed his junior colleague, Private Slodge, admire the steam that arose from within the discarded leather, as though each boot were a fairy Vesuvius, or rather, since he was a young man of no large imagination, the boots were twin bakeries released from their task of roasting

Sergeant Trouncer's feet for some supper of delicate-stomached cannibals who must arrive soon if they were not to eat their pedal victuals lukewarm.

"I see you looking at them boots, young un," Sergeant Trouncer pronounced. His upper lip was adorned with an ample mustache whose looser fronds blew about when he spoke. If his statement were to be construed as being of the present tense, then it must be deemed inaccurate, since it was at the lively filaments of the aforesaid labial adornment that Private Slodge was now gazing. "Them boots," Sergeant Trouncer weightily repeated, making the very words sound like a soldier's feet coming to smart attention. "Them boots," he said, "has marched." He paused and looked fiercely at Private Slodge, as if the latter might be inclined to table a denial of that affirmation. "Yes, young un, them boots has marched from the Anterlantic Ocean to the Red Sea and all the way back again. Not that it's any more Red than what I am," he added somewhat inaccurately, for he had been baked as lobster-hued as his tunic by the tropic suns of service in the name of His Britannic Majesty, not that His Britannic Majesty was aware of this or, if aware, greatly concerned one way or the other. "It's just what they calls it—Red." He paused with the same ferocity as before, as though now ready for a new denial, this time in the realm of geographical nomenclature.

"Why do they call it that then?" asked Private Slodge, with the timidity which he considered that his sergeant might deem proper considering the gulf between their ranks. As for his mode of utterance, the meat of words, so to speak, to which his manner was but a bland sort of gravy, he had a habit of running his vocables together with great speed, as if speech was a painful process and had to be got over with in maximum haste. But to render his statement as veracity would require, would entail the setting down of some such monster of utterance as: "Wydthcawitaten?", which might weary the reader and would certainly fatigue the author.

"Why?" says Sergeant Trouncer. "*Why* you asks? You

might well ask why I am called of Trouncer and you of Slodge, though to me you looks not unlike a Slodge, whatever a Slodge might be." As there seemed no adequate reply to this statement, he of the alleged nominal aptness merely awaited further communication from his superior officer. This was at once forthcoming. "When I says," said the sergeant, "them boots has marched, I would not have you believe that they has marched of their own accord." The private soldier shook his head many times, as if very anxious to be acquitted of the suspicion that he might so have believed, though he had a sudden very clear picture of a pair of boots vigorously marching across a map of Europe, and would be ready enough to envisage a whole army of such tenantless footgear raising dust from Portugal to Egypt. "No," the sergeant elucidated, "them boots has had me inside of 'em, or rather they has had that portion of me which is called, and kindly correct me if I am in herror, by the name of feet." And he nodded twice, one nod for each of the anatomical portions mentioned. He then said: "Whiles we are on this topic, what could be better by way of a supper of a cold December evening than pig's feet done in a Dutch oven with a bit of toasted cheese as a side dish? I remember," he went on, and his mustache blew about as in a jig of joyful memory of the occasion, "it was that what I was eating of when the news was brought as how we was to be shipped here. Which," he added with exceptional force, "is not natural, young un."

"What's not natural, sergeant?" asked young Slodge, who was engaged, with a somewhat inadequate cleansing agent of spittle and a thumbnail, in removing a mustard-stain from the cuff of his tunic.

"Here," said his sergeant. "Here is not natural. There is stars in the sky here," he confided, "as was not seen by Hadam nor by Heve in the Garden of Heden. There is midsummer at Christmas, a season when by all human rights and by the talons of what is decent should have snow on the ground and skating on the ponds, as also, which is not demanding too much of a unreasonable favor, brandy served hot in the public houses.

I have wept," he confided further, "I have wept bitter to see the sun shining on the plum pudding. There," he added, in a tone which indicated that he had spread before his young colleague a veritable banquet of unreason, "what have you to say about that, young un?" But before the young soldier could drum up his brains to an appropriate response, his sergeant said, "I'm not a-going about denying that it is hard for him too, him not wishing to be here not no more than what we are or are not, as the case may be. And there is no denying of it, if the truth is told, whatever you or anybody else may be proned to say or to not say."

"You mean old Bony?" said Private Slodge with a sort of awe. "Old Nap, that is?"

"I am much of the opinion," pronounced Sergeant Trouncer, who was now peeling off his socks with a solemn motion, "that He is Not Well. He is being starved deliberate and I mentions no names, except to say that one of his names begins with a Haitch and the other with a Hell, and he is a Sir. And there is wholesome or wholesale deliberate starvation being issued with the rations, or rather the lack of. It is Ate, young un, and Ate is a ateful thing in a officer, carry he His Britannic Majesty's commission or, like me that you see lying here, not carry it, being more of a Non-Commissioned Officer, as you well know, and sometimes to your cost, eh, eh, eh?" He laughed raucously, as at the memory which he knew the young private must share of some transgression of the latter's which had been duly and Non-Commissionedly punished. And, to compound his merriment, he threw one of his socks at Slodge, so that it sailed through the lamplit air like a dispirited and elongated gray owlet.

"He don't look to be starved," said Private Slodge, catching the sock and then, in deference, carrying it over to his sergeant rather than throwing it back to him. "Not him he don't."

"Ah," said the sergeant sapiently, "happearances is not all, young un, and I would thank you to bear in mind that little ominy. I had a aunt that was twenty-five stone have her due poids if she was a fluid ounce troy weight. Aunt Flora she was called by all and sundry, that being her name, and had a tortoise-shell cat named Tiddles, besides being fond of the Hobitary Columns which she read every night with a stick of cinnamon in her hand. Well, that lady, young un, was plagued by a most cruel lack of appetite as you never saw. For breakfast, dinner, tea, supper and even Christmas Day it was always the same: one slice of bread and butter you could see through as if it was glass, being that thin to the eyes, and one cup of tea that you could count the number of stalks in if you was so minded. Fancied nothing more, and even a slice of somebody else's bacon at breakfast would turn her stomach with the mere sight of it. On the other hand, not to make too much of a song and dance of it, there was Mr. Creaklamb as kept the grocery in Rochester when I was a boy, and he was that thin he would have served as a lamppost, especially being very shining bald under a full moon, not that street lighting is needed then. Now that man, young un, would eat a roast ox for his breakfast and not turn an hair. All day they was pouring victuals into him for fear he'd starve, and that's why he was in the grocery, as there was dry goods on the spot and the butcher and the baker either side. I seen him," and Sergeant Trouncer's eyes turned somewhat glassy at the reminiscence, "I seen him eat for his dinner what you and I would be turned to stone to by the mere look of. He began with ten or twelve pork chops with tomato sauce in which he dipped his bread, a whole quartern loaf and of that day's batch too, and then he had a oyster stew with cowheels in for the thickening, then it was a cushion of veal very brown with potatoes done under, then two brace of Sussex fowl that he tore at with his teeth, these being strong, young un, as you will well imagine with the constant exercise of, like muscle as it were, and sucking the marry out of the bones for good measure, then he must have his bit of beef, as he called it, this being a fair round of topside with onions and cabbage with plenty of pepper, and he never sneezed no matter what the quantity what he shook from the pot, and then it was custards and jellies and crab-apple jelly tart, that being more of a jam than a jelly, then they'd bring the Stilton on for him, very maggoty as he liked it, and then bless and blow us all if he wasn't crying out for a cold leg of lamb which he would eat with his hands, dipping it into a big basin of mint sauce as he went along. Always left that till last, as his name was Creaklamb, and it was like putting his signature to it as he put it, being a laughing man in spite of his thinness. There's no food called Creak, or he would have had that along with it, him being a stickler."

Private Slodge's only comment was a noise indicative of awe that, indeed, sounded not unlike the word itself.

"Died, of course," said Sergeant Trouncer. "Died of starvation, if you can believe it. Couldn't earn enough to keep him in victuals, what with eating the shop-stock too. So as there's a great lesson in that, young un, and I hopes you'll hold that little ominy to art."

"Is He going to die?" Private Slodge nearly winded himself with the special effort of emphatic aspiration.

"We're all going to die someday," was the sagacious reply, "but He, as you call him, is not long for this world. If ever I see the Hand of Death in a man's face, in his I see it. Liver, I'd say it is, that being first to crumble when it's starvation. You see the yellow in him as it might be a Eathen Chinee. Liver, that is. Peck peck peck at it, goes Sir Haitch Hell, like any pecking bird that I see."

"Suppose," said the young private, "suppose he'd won. Just suppose."

"Old Nosey did for him, right enough," commented the sergeant, now absently tearing great strips of hard skin, like Nature's own bungling attempt at a sort of vegetable bootsole, from the underside of his left foot. "I wasn't there, but I heard all about it. Well, if he'd won it'd be Frenchies in Buckingham Palace and the Ouse of Lords, but it's Germans now, so what's the odds? It never makes but little difference," he said, surveying a strip of leathery foot-skin held on the palm of his hand, "to the likes of you and me, young un. But when he dies," he concluded, "and it won't be long, then it'll be back to Nature for you and me, lad, and proper stars in the sky, not these Happaritions, and snow and sliding at Christmas, and chestnuts popping on the fire, and hot rum, and no unnatural sun flaming on the plum pudding."

"Ah," said the young private, "well then, with no hard feelings and every kind of proper respect, as is only right and is required, let him get on with it and get it all over."

K. N. V. S.
KLEBA?
NIEMA.
VOTA?
SANA.
I. N. R. I.
Is there any bread?
None whatsoever.
River water, spring water, stagnant
water, water?
If there is, it must be looked for.
KI. NN. V. R. SI.

In profound fever and tortured by heat, thirst unquenchable, surrounded by the skeletons and hides of sucked shriveled lemons, he lay and transported himself to Poland. He lay naked in snow and kicked about in it until he shivered for sheer healthy animal want of heat: O let me be taken to some such torrid clime as that of the island of the cross that is named after the great woman who found the cross. He encased himself in an ice coffin and yelled to be hacked out of it and then be rushed to a roaring log fire in the barbaric hall of the hunting lodge of the Walewskas. He ate all the snow of the entire winter waste that stretched all about him in uncountable hectares, he crunched up the frozen ponds and rivers that a whole detail of the Imperial Guard hacked to crystalline gobbets with specially issued (Form GS59/AN237) hatchets. And then, cooled somewhat and his thirst partially slaked, he was able to give time to the smiling snow princess beside him, for they had suddenly become close-seated companions on a horse-sleigh, she with the reins and the whip, managing as well as any man, a single fur spread over their laps and lower limbs, whistle and creak and neigh and whinny, breath-smoke and laughter, over the lovely limitless snow wastes, now restored to the winter earth after his monstrous meal of them. But he was well again now and young again, and she was gold-locked and beautiful, and her voice that sang such charming Slavic French was wine-hued velvet to the white velvet over which they sped.

"*Kleba niema vota sana*," he laughed. "All the Polish the troops know, and God knows I know no more myself. I would that I could talk of love in the language of your people."

"The French tongue will do well enough," she smiled, and she, in her sudden concentration at keeping the bay steeds on the path, if path it could be called, protruded a millimeter of pink Polish tongue. And then she said: "So. Your army has suffered. No bread, no water. But now they have enough of both and more. My people are glad. And grateful."

"They were most reluctant to cross the Vistula," he mused. "But now it is crossed and they begin to be aware of my purpose."

"A noble purpose. My country has been too long a cake for Russia and Austria and Prussia to bite at. And now you will restore the ancient kingdom." She swiftly leaned sideways and, her lovely face glowing against his, swiftly kissed his own heated cheek. "I love you," she said.

"Ah, how I love you too, heart of my heart." But he did not tell her that the remaking of Poland's old glory was not at all his purpose. It was instead a matter of securing the eastern limits of the Empire. The Austrians and the Prussians were alike tremulous, but there remained Russia. And in the spring, with the Imperial Army secure in Warsaw, there would come the definitive thrust that would bring Prussia finally to her (very much her, oh how ironic) knees, frighten off her Russian ally, hold all Europe down, from Atlantic to the Niemen, in the salutary grip of the Continental System. The enemy of mankind would break at last, her Orders in Council dispersed in the gale, like the worthless mass of scrap paper they were, and the Empire rest secure forever. Meantime it was winter, and Warsaw was all light and music. As for the Poles, they must be turned into soldiers first and learn of their duty to the Imperial Concept; their rights, if they had any, could come later.

"Heart of my heart," he repeated. "My love is as candidly pure as this snow we speed across, as naked as the trees, and yet it howls with somewhat of savagery like those wolves we hear behind us."

"Far behind us," she smiled. "Nature's Cossacks." Her face darkened then, remembering those whooping forays, the bearded manic leers, the greasy barbaric tunics braided with looted gold thread, looted gold coins in their belts, the reek of goat, it was their pride never to wash, and her sudden vomiting that had made the lout desist, and her husband the prince, jeered at for his age, *filthy old one canst do it canst thrust it in,* then lashed with a knout stroke on the proud lined face that did not flinch, the burning of the ancestral portraits in a fire they made on the carpet, the floods of urine to loud laughter, anything to defile, and then, sick or not, they would have taken her had they not heard the clop of arriving cavalry without, Polish cavalry, and one beast tardy in leaving because he was defecating in the face of a stunned and supine manservant and could not in his stupidity decide between the claim of an emptying gut and the need to take horse, the horses were all there in the hall, fodder dragged in from the stables. . . .

"Far behind us, far far far."

He thought, but not for long, of a cuckolded prince. He had no pity for cuckolds, he, the most cuckolded man alive. But all in the past, true, and he was sure there was a faithful Empress in Mainz, anxious to join him in Warsaw, perhaps already having heard something, women were quick to scent other women, but he had written. "Your grief at our separation crucifies me with pain, but circumstances compel us both to a continuing agony of privation. Mainz is too far from Warsaw, the roads are wretched, the snow lies deep and blizzards howl, Paris calls you, Paris needs you, the Empress, you have duties to your people, Our Lady of Victories. Oh, how I chafe at our continued separation, oh, how I long to fold you in my arms, to warm and be warmed, giving and taking love, in these endless winter nights that endlessly continue, spring so far, your springlike beauty lost to me, Persephone Persephone." A good, he considered, and persuasive letter.

"Heart of my heart of my heart of my." He panted, riding hard, the goal in sight. Marie and he writhed naked in a tumble of bear-rugs before the great pine-fire of the lodge. "My kleba, my vota." And that was right: it was pure and honest water, which a man could drink without fear, in which a man could be cleansed, that mattered more than the wine. Deceitful wine that turned to vinegar. It was vinegar on a sponge they had handed up to him when it was the final kiss of his own element he had, in his final agony, begged. But not the sea, never that. All about their sanctuary of fire, where they rode in the act of life, the snow lay, *vota* turned to manna, a universal fall of white bread.

"Love of my."

Riding, riding. And at last the goal reached, the horses reined, the miracle of the gush that he knew, in the very revelation of the instant, not the imposed fancy of the later knowledge, to be ready to be transubstantiated to the bread of life. They slept, and he awoke to her kisses, her yellow hair all about him, as though it were he who was Danaë. He smiled, blinked, saw through the casement no snow, only sun-roasted earth and the sea beyond. This was Elba, and she had come to him in Elba, the bread and water of life, and their son was playing outside, calling in Italian: "*Cattivo cattivo*."

"What is that word he calls?" she said.

"It is the first word often a child will use when he comes to a place that speaks Italian. The Italian children say it to him and he learns to say it to them. *Cattivo*. It means *bad*." He sighed.

"But its older meaning is *prisoner*. Captive. He who is in chains and has lost everything—such a one is bad, bad. It is a very cruel kind of morality. I, my love, am *bad*."

"Well then," she smiled, and kissed him swiftly on his left eyebrow, "it is time for you to be good again. You are not in chains and you have not lost everything."

"I have lost everything except you. That means there is a little good left in me." He smiled, then his eyes grew sternly soft in passion, and the kiss he gave her was neither light nor swift. They writhed, their bodies dewed by the heat of the Elban afternoon, and then the child's voice from outside called:

"*Buono buono buono*."

They desisted, laughing. She knew what that word meant.

"*Bon, bon, bon*." They were in a horse-sleigh again, furred and rugged, riding embraced, the reins and whip this time in the hands of a Walewska coachman, snow in uncountable hectares all about, and the two of them were harrying Russia together.

"The Hospodars," she was saying.

"Yes yes, the Hospodars. I will write to the Sultan Selim and bid him drive out the Hospodars from Wallachia. And what sort of Russians are the Hospodars?"

"Just holy Russians living in Wallachia," she smiled.

"*Bon*. Being holy Russians, O Father of the Faithful, they will destroy your mosques in the name of their spurious Christianity, to them the very name of Mussulman is an abomination. Strike now, spit on the treacherous Serbians, march upon Choczim, butcher the—"

"Hospodars."

"*Bon, bon*. In the name of Allah, who is the Lord of all, I write to you as your dear and faithful and loving friend. Set the Balkans ablaze with the vengeful sword of Islam. There," he smiled. "I do this for Poland." And he kissed her heartily. "Then," he said, and his great eyes burned a huge map on the snow, "Persia. What shall we say to the Shah?"

"To the Shah say—let me see. Something about Allah again." It was mad, it was glorious. Love and snow and Poland and Islam. It was poetry.

"Ah, I will write this. The Russian infidel reels under the blows of your faithful friends of Frankistan, and the Ottoman Porte hacks him with the vengeful sword of Islam—"

"You have already used that phrase."

"Yes, but to the Sublime Porte, not to the Divine Shah. Perhaps the vengeful scimitar might be better."

"*Bon, bon.*"

"Ah, listen to this. Fortune has removed the bandage from her own eyes and placed them about the eyes of our common enemy. There is a power—God or Allah, but there is no God but Allah—who hovers over me, bidding me conquer in the name of Truth and Goodness, who sees the time as propitious for the new promotion of Persian Glory, and who smiles on the Empire of the Ottoman Porte. Three empires, dedicated to the spread of the Divine Word—let us go forward together."

"You go too far, I think."

"Forward together!"

"Too far!"

They tore at each other's furs, laughing, then tumbled out of the horse-sleigh, over and over in the gorgeous snow. The coachman drove on impassive, cracking his whip, not looking back, and disappeared over the ridge where bare blackthorns stood under the scimitar moon. Where they made love—

"Forward together!"

"Too fast!"

—naked, the snow melted and steamed. They lay side by side naked under the velvet heavens, and he said:

"What is that constellation?"

"Cassiopeia. My family initial."

"Not only yours." He grew gloomy and began to sweat. They were indoors, lying in a hot snow-tumble of sheets and blankets. Roustam came in and salaamed grinning at their nudity, then recharged the vast fire with fresh pine logs. "Too hot," his master complained, but Roustam turned and said: "*Cadeaux islamiques.*"

"God," he said, ignoring that, "how I hate the English."

"That's not very complimentary," pouted naked Betsy. He turned in shock to see that it was indeed she he had been riding, no more than a child, and said:

"You shouldn't be here, who let you in, who allowed me to—"

"Like all men, take what you want, and then say you hate me."

"But I don't hate, I love, I love—"

"Sweetheart," she said, bringing her thin whiteness closer to his fat, "remember what you said about gardens, hm? Well, we're a garden, you know, and we have our spades ready to stick into intruders."

"Quite right, quite right." He sighed heavily and looked down at his heaviness (that belly, the size of it). "But you should have left my garden alone."

"You should have left other people's gardens alone."

"But they weren't real gardens, they were more like wildernesses, a duty to reclaim, you know, and if they were gardens they were very badly kept gardens. God, it's so hot in here. God, I'm so thirsty."

"Oh, don't be so selfish all the time. Come on, do it again, I want it, you dig so vigorously, *komm' Süsser, wieder wieder.*"

"Now you're being like *her*. God, the thirst."

Roustam, who had silently and invisibly gone out, came in again by a different door. He was dressed as an English gentleman, a sort of pump-room beau, and he raised a disdainful quizzing-glass. "The friendship," he said haughtily, "subsisting between the Islamic peoples and the British is not to be broken by the clumsy machinations of a mere Corsican adventurer. You spoke of thirst. You require water? Note, in my language, the Cassiopeian initial. Water you shall have." He clapped his hands, as if about to announce a quadrille, and yet another door opened. Through it, whooping and whooshing and growling but undeniably very wet water, came the sea. "Drink that," said Beau Roustam. But the man who had called himself his master, by a supreme effort of the will of a sick man, manfully recollected his manly duty to resist, so, turning the water into Cassiopeia, he split it at its superior angle, so that the W fell apart into two V's, and a V thrust on either side of him as he lay otherwise helpless on his bed, piercing the wall behind in two separate places but entirely failing to transfix himself. That was the secret then, so simple once one had learned it. One V, of course, was quite enough. He smiled, but he was still thirsty. Roustam exploded with Britannico-Islamic rage.

"LET him drink that," said Dr. Arnott. "It is cow's milk. Highly nutritious, also refreshing." And he indicated smiling the crock to his medical colleague Antommarchi. But the latter did not smile; rather his face was full of thunder. He said:

"I must oppose most resolutely the proposal that he imbibe a beverage so heavy and indigestible. He requires a very much lighter diet. Even when he was in reasonably tolerable health he was unable to digest with any ease any species of milk—cow's, goat's, sheep's. Now to offer him milk would infallibly excite grave stomachic distress."

"But you do not quite understand," smiled Dr. Arnott. "It was Sir Hudson Lowe himself who suggested that he be given cow's milk. Sir Hudson ordered milk to be obtained and recommended its immediate ingestion."

"It would," cried the other, "be altogether characteristic of Sir Lowe to wish to cause the hero whom he hates and who now seems to lie totally at his mercy maximal pain and suffering. That is, naturally, presuming that Sir Lowe has sufficient medical knowledge to be aware of the ghastly consequences of lactary imbibition in the state to which the patient has, partially through Sir Lowe's own malice, been brought. It would, of course, be more charitable to see in this proposal, however misguided, a change of heart, a relenting, the blooming of an unwonted and uncharacteristic compassion. But his gift must be rejected. The patient may be given when he wakes a little orange-flower water mixed with ordinary water and sugar."

"You still do not seem to understand," still, though somewhat uneasily now, smiled Dr. Arnott. "It is Sir Hudson Lowe himself, the Governor of St. Helena, who makes both the recommendation and the offering. You see it here." And he once more indicated the crock. "Milk. The milk of a cow. Pure. Good. Nourishing. The milk of Sir Hudson Lowe."

"It would seem to me, sir," frowned Dr. Antommarchi, "that your clinical knowledge as well as your normal endowment of human compassion are alike being clouded by sycophancy. If Sir Lowe recommended and offered rosbif you would doubtless wish to force it down the throat of the sufferer. In order, if you understand me, that you reinforce Sir Lowe's good opinion of himself, both as a man of knowledge and a creature of compassion, and through that good opinion of yourself, his good opinion of you, who, against your better medical judgment, are totally prepared to corroborate that good opinion."

"Which good opinion?" smiled Dr. Arnott more uneasily still. "Of himself or of myself?"

"They are hardly extricable one from the other," cried Dr. Antommarchi. "It is all a matter of good opinions and not at all of what is clinically fitting."

"I do not think you have understood at all what I have been saying," said Dr. Arnott, with an easier smile. "Nor do you seem to appreciate the significance of this er present proffer. Here," he smiled, indicating the crock and its snowy content, "is cow's milk. Milk, a lactic or lactal substance obtained from the mammary glands of er vaccine quadrupeds. Forgive me if my technical terms are inept or inaccurate. I have been in this medical business a very long time and hence am become possibly somewhat ignorant. This is milk from Sir Hudson himself. It is for our patient. It is nourishing and highly digestible. Also refreshing." And he indicated once more the snowily brimming crock. "Let him therefore drink it."

"Must I reiterate yet again," cried Dr. Antommarchi, "my abhorrence of what is either calculated Britannic villainy or else uncalculated Britannic stupidity but, whatever its quiddity, most certainly reflects adversely to a degree hardly computable on the ethics and even professional qualifications of one whom I had deemed, perhaps, as I begin to see now, misguidedly, at least a disinterested colleague, but of whom I now, I must confess, entertain very considerable doubts."

"Ah," smiled Dr. Arnott, "that seems a little more reasonable. So I suggest we pour some into a glass or a cup, I leave the choice of the vessel of er imbibition entirely to you, and then wake the patient or prisoner or both, prisoner-patient really I suppose, make him imbibe the er beverage, sit back while he does so, and watch its immediate er beneficial er effects." He indicated the snow-white contents of the crock.

"No, sir," thundered Dr. Antommarchi, "we will do nothing of the kind, since as I have already said with, I should have presumed, sufficient clarity, that substance, however fit it may be for the digestive systems of British infants, is totally unsuitable for our patient in his present state. It is heavy and indigestible and will cause grave enteric distress."

"But," smiled Dr. Arnott, somewhat uneasily now, "this is proffered on the recommendation of Sir Hudson Lowe. Doubtless, though a foreigner here, you will have some notion of who Sir Hudson Lowe is. He is Governor of this island where our prisoner is a patient or, if you prefer, patient a prisoner. Now milk, as Sir Hudson considers, is an admirable and totally unsolid food, easily imbibed, supremely nourishing, bland to the inner organs and refreshing to the taste, also altogether digestible. And so he may, of his goodness and condescension, be regarded as the fount and original of this present er proffer." And he indicated with a smile the crock snowily brimming.

"It seems to me," cried the other, "that I must repeatedly raise my voice in opposition to a proposal that is redolent of most unprofessional malice or else nescience or even conceivably, since the British temperament is illogical enough to embrace totally incompatible elements, a combination of both. This *lac vaccae* is totally unsuitable for the patient in his present enfeebled state, and, even were he less enfeebled, were he, indeed, in normal health, it would be a totally inappropriate nutritive. More, it seems to me, I can hardly say."

"I am altogether delighted," smiled Dr. Arnott, "that you now propose to withdraw your admittedly eloquent but hardly rationally inferred opposition to the er galactic, meaning milky I believe, proffer of Sir Hudson. See it here," he smiled, indicating the niveal content of the crock. "Cow-milk, or as you somewhat polysyllabically put it *vac* er *laccae*, a candidly incolorated nutritive of gust inexpressibly bland, and all a freely and, may I say, magnanimously donated eleemosynous contribution of Sir Hudson Lowe, expressive of gubernatorial concern, towards the invalid diet of our er invalid." And he smilingly indicated. "Or perhaps you would like other opinions? Other opinions are, as you will be aware, freely available. Let us by all means call in other opinions."

"You know full well," responded the other in Corsico-Franco-Italianate gloom, "that they will be Britannic opinions, and that I shall hence be in the ignominious and impotent state of being in a minority of one. I protest most forcibly against the injustice of the arrangement. I consider that I, who more than any have the welfare of our imperial patient at heart—"

"As for the imperial epithet," smiled Dr. Arnott, "that has no significance as far as myself and my colleagues are concerned, nor, indeed, does it much signify in relation to his invalid status, since the organs of the human body are the same for all human bodies, for emperor and clown indeed, and the myth of the blue blood has, I fancy, been long exploded. So shall we, without more ado, and without feeling ourselves called upon to call on other opinions, help him imbibe of the gubernatorial eleemosynous—" And he smilingly.

"And that I have been regularly and exemplarily treated with the most scrupulous unfairness. This I regard, along with my imperial patient and master, alas alas moribund, I weep and will weep more, as very typical of Britannic hypocrisy and injustice, and I protest to posterity with every breath in my—"

"Ah, moribund, as you say," smiled the smiling British smiler, "and therefore it is a matter of little consequence whether or not he be fed with the gubernatorial gift, though the odds are that it might greatly nourish his moribundity, so let us therefore—" And he.

The moribund patient, from near-coma, smiled on marking the word *moribund.* The new device which enabled him to hear with exceptional clarity the conferences of the enemy was informing him of stupidity and strategic division and consequent paralysis. Of V on the morrow there could be no doubt.

From bivouac to bivouac to bivouac to bivouac to bivouac and all the way it was torches held aloft with Long Live The Emperor and It Is The Anniversary Of His Crowning and God Bless You Sire, rough soldiers in tears of love and joy as he walked, with straw torches blazing all about, from bivouac to bivouac to bivouac. He waved his hand in thanks, tears in his own eyes, God Bless You My Children, and came to the bivouacs of the artillery. Thank You Thank You he cried almost weeping at the soldiers' tears and the fiery blessing and then:

"Keep those fucking torches away from the artillery caissons."

Milk indeed, the very notion of feeding him milk. He dined with his officers on fried potatoes and onions, and there was good talk and much laughter.

"A fine phrase, Sire, that in the peroration of your Order of the Day."

"You could almost set it to music, Sire, ha ha, a new kind of hymn of hate."

"Ah, it is they who do the hating," he smilingly said, forkful of fried onion and potato ready for his lips. "For them we need have nothing but pity. Still," chewing hard and then gulping, and not even the promise of a stab of pain, "there's something in what you say. I fancied myself once, you know, in my distant youth—"

"Ha ha, Sire."

"—As something of a song-maker. Let us try, and then you can all join in." He raised his voice in a tuneful improvisation:

"England! England!
The paid lackeys of England!

Alas, gentlemen, I can for the present go no further. But perhaps it will serve. Come then. I will give you the recitative and then you will come in with the chorus.

Let every man be filled with the thought
That it is vitally necessary to overcome
These paid lackeys of—"

And over the camp the lusty song, of the Emperor's own making, boomed and rebounded, so that doubtless the engloomed enemy heard and trembled:

"England! England!
The paid lackeys of England!
A long incineration
For those who hate our nation.
England! England—"

It was the kind of song that could go on indefinitely, especially as the Emperor had not contrived a tonic ending, but he himself grew weary of it and talked of the East.

"The lure of Egypt, gentlemen, and the greater exotic lure of the lands beyond. The East—does not our way lie there? Europe shall, after tomorrow, be wholly ours. We do not wish America or Africa, shapeless savage continents with no future. But ah, the East. India, China, fabulous Japan. And, of course," with a fierce savagery replacing the mystic look, "we have the mission of striking at the enemy of mankind in that very East where he has so precarious a toehold—"

Some of the younger officers thought this was a cue for a reprise, so they lustily bellowed:

"England! England!
The paid lackeys of England!"

"Yes yes," said the Emperor sourly, "that will do very well." Then he brightened and said: "I hear that a comet—you know, a traveling star with a tail—has been seen over Paris. Any of you heard about that?"

"Sire."

"Sire."

"A good omen for the morrow, gentlemen, I have no doubt. Does it not presage the fall of princes? Well, they will fall—emperors of the blood, ha!—Russia and Austria, lackeys of—No, no, no," getting it in quickly. "No need to sing. Well," briskly, "we can't sit here all night chatting of orientology and astrology and the like, nor are we a musical society. There are things to be done. Any news yet of Marshal Davout's division?" Sad round eyes looked at him, heads gently signaled the negative. "Still on his way from Vienna, then. He'll be here, I doubt not, before dawn breaks."

"Sire."

He toured in torchlight, inspecting, inspecting. Long Live The Emperor It Is The Anniversary Of. "Thank you, men, and God bless you all. See," keenly looking south, "there are many enemy campfires around Augezd. I think, Savary, that a forward reconnaissance is called for. Find out their strength around Augezd."

"Sire. Sire, Marshal Davout has sent on ahead a report of his imminent arrival. Would you wish to see his dispatch rider?"

"I think not. I will see Davout himself when he comes. Now find out the strength round Augezd. I'd guess, hm, a whole corps."

"Sire."

"I'm going back to my quarters. An hour's rest is called for, Savary." And off he went, God Bless You Sire and so on, torches torches. Before he could lie down in the straw of the hut where he was lodged, Davout at last arrived, dusty, tired.

"How well you look, Davout, not an ounce of fatigue in your whole body I can see, you're remarkable, astonishing, eager for the fray, eh? Good, good. You know the position." He thumped the map in lantern-light. "You're on the right there. How soon can you be set up?"

"Sire. Cavalry and advance guard by nine in the morning. Infantry a little after."

"Eight, make it eight. Eight, Davout. By God, how *well* you look."

"Ten, make it ten," smiled Dr. Arnott. "You agree, Mitchell? Ten grams of calomel. Shortt, you agree?"

"I must protest with every breath in my body," cried Dr. Antommarchi. "The condition of the patient is far too enfeebled for a purgative. But I see it is three to one and that the claims of clinical reason and sheer human compassion are unlikely to prevail—"

"Good then," smiled Dr. Arnott, "we're all agreed on ten grams of calomel. Make him excrete beautifully."

News came in that a patrol of Austrian hussars had been driven off with ease at Zokolnitz, or just outside. "No need to wake me for that shit," growled the Emperor. "Wake me when Savary gets back."

Savary got back. "As you said, Sire. At least a corps round Augezd. What orders?"

"We'll have Marshal Soult in on this," the Emperor said, picking straw from his hair. "Slight change of emphasis necessary. No rewriting of the notes, if you understand my musical image, Savary, but the placing of a sforzando. Come. The time?"

"Three o'clock and a mist rising. Sire."

"We'll assume, Savary, that the corps you found there signifies a weakening of the enemy's forces to the north—their right center. So we'll shift our attack a bit to the north. And while we're at it we'll reinforce our own right with, oh, say another four thousand. I'm not too happy about getting Davout's lot in there on time. Davout looked very weary, Savary. Exhausted, you understand."

"Sire."

"You said something about a mist, Savary." He stepped out into the beautiful black (behold, gentlemen, the paradoxical etymology of our white calomel!) of the December foredawn and saw for himself the rising calomel exhalation of the frozen ground. "It should do us no harm, Savary."

"Sire."

"Vandamme and St. Hilaire will attack from Puntowitz, that spot to the right of my navel. Yes, that should take care of the enemy's, ha ha, debilitated right center. Come, let us visit Soult, wake him ourselves with an imperial shake-awake, a little surprise for him, eh, Savary?"

"Sire."

For if his body was lying at an angle northwest by southeast, then the Santon Hill nestled in his left armpit, and the Goldbach Heights were a little above his left elbow, and the stream called Golden, the Goldbach, with its tributary the Bosenitz, ran from left shoulder to down below the bottom right rib, and while his stomach was a hill with a peak called the Zurlan, his whole gloriously swollen belly was the Pratzen Heights. Puntowitz and Kobelnitz and Zokolnitz and Telnitz were moles about the silver scar of the Golden Stream, from navel down nearly to right hip bone.

"The distention is very considerable," smiled Dr. Arnott, prodding the Pratzen Heights.

"I protest with every breath in my body at this totally unnecessary and viciously inhumane palpation while the patient is at rest—"

"Very," agreed Dr. Mitchell, agreeing. "I agree."

At four in the morning the mist had thickened. The first troops groaned and cursed at the come-on-out-of-them-fucking-wanking-pits, yawned, cursed, gulped raw spirits, then moved.

"Well," he smiled from rising ground, "it is a good beginning. I would divine that the enemy is in some confusion beyond the Goldbach there, the mist intruding and hindering their formations."

At seven he stood with his staff, all enmisted up to the waist.

"Things going badly at Telnitz, Sire."

"Nonsense. Legrand can look after himself." But the massive

column of General Doktorov came lurching out of the mist of the dawn to join Kienmayer. The Third of the Line was being driven out of Telnitz, and Davout had to cover the retreat with his hussars and chasseurs. One village in the enemy's hands then. The Emperor began to dance up and down, though with legs hidden in the mist. Yet his face did not show rage. He was dancing with the cold.

North, at Zokolnitz, a garrison of eighteen hundred men and six guns, Merle's Light Brigade and Mangeron's Tirailleurs together, could not prevail against Langeron and Przbysewski's thirty cannon and eight thousand men and—

"Zokolnitz fallen to the enemy, Sire."

"General Heudelet will counterattack at Telnitz, the first thing is to get Telnitz back." But he spoke distractedly, his eyes on the Pratzen Heights. The mists were rising like a curtain to show its frosted rock and green, and towards it the Russian columns surged and frothed like a swollen river of spring. He smiled.

"I would say, would you not, my dear Soult, that something like let me see oh say forty thousand are massing against our right. Wait a little while, and their center will be as weak as water."

"Sire."

"Sire, a report has come in that the 108th Regiment has fired accidentally on General Merle's Light Brigade, Sire. Fog, smoke, Sire. Confusion, Sire."

"General Merde," he said cheerfully. "Now, Soult, how long will it take you to get your divisions moved to the top of the Pratzen Heights?"

"Sire, you see their present location, or rather you do not. They're hidden by fog and campfire smoke at the foot of the valley. I'd say thirty minutes."

"Make it twenty." He jammed his spyglass to his right eye, looked afar, grinned. "Two more of their columns moving south. So," he said cheerfully, "the enemy is in control of Telnitz and Zokolnitz. Well, well, well. The time?"

"Just on nine, Sire."

"And a very good time too. I think we may now, Soult, unleash your two divisions."

"Sire. *Pas de charge*," called Soult. And the drums thudded into it, all along the valley, ordering voices tore themselves apart, echo echo all along the valley, *pas de charge.*

"Ah, a gorgeous sight." Out of the valley mists arose the two divisions, bayonets agleam in the weak winter sun, moving up to the plateau, drums drums drums drumming.

The Emperor sang his own song softly: "England! England! the paid lackeys of England! Mister Pitt will be very very sick before this day is out, gentlemen." And then he made a kind of nursery chime-tune out of the names of the moles about the silver scar that ran from navel down nearly to right hip bone: "Puntowitz, Kobelnitz, Zokolnitz, Teeeeeelnitz."

"Sire. General St. Hilaire has taken the village of Pratzen and is now on the summit."

"And General Vandamme?"

"Some little trouble, Sire, at the village of Girzikowitz."

"All these witzes and nitzes, eh? Now let us consider Blasowitz up to the north there. Things going well?"

"Sire. There is an unsubstantiated report that the Russian Imperial Guard has taken the village."

He saw through his spyglass the messed-up Russian column to the south, a rapid and messed-up redirecting of the march, what looked like two mere battalions reaching, far too late, the village of Pratzen.

"We have it, gentlemen. We must now concentrate on the north."

"Nine-thirty, Sire."

"Thank you." An unwonted quiet courtesy. "Blasowitz, another of these damned itzes." Soult, Bernadotte, Lannes, Murat stirred into a soup of smoke, broken eardrums, eviscerated horses, four hundred of Cafarelli's division smashed and spattered in less than three minutes, the Seventeenth Regiment of the Line holding firm on the Santon Hill, cuirasse-flash and plume-tossing on a four-hundred-yard front as Murat's reserve plunged into left flank of enemy cavalry.

"Ten o'clock, Sire."

St. Hilaire's division was being attacked from three sides. A desperate bayonet charge while Soult's artillery reserve thudding up brought six twelve-pounder guns, Soult himself yelling orders. Vandamme, to the left of St. Hilaire, pushed like a madman at Kollowrath and Milorardovitch's God knew how many battalions.

"Those damned itzes."

Lochet stormed Zokolnitz with the 48th and the 111th, captured it and left the 48th as garrison, tried for the castle of Zokolnitz on the east bank of the Goldbach, the enemy hit back at the village and wiped out the 48th, the 111th had to be recalled, the Russians held on to Zokolnitz except for its south fringe the French gripped unwavering.

"Noon, Sire."

"The midday position, gentlemen. On the left and right alike the enemy seems sufficiently contained. In the center we hold the Pratzen Heights. Imperial Headquarters will now be transferred thither."

"Sire."

"The ten grams," smiled Dr. Arnott, "seems not to have been in the least efficacious. I think the dose must be increased. You agree, Mitchell?"

"Oh certainly I am agreeable," agreeing.

"I consider that the discourtesy of your continued refusal to pay attention to my strenuous objections should be set on record as a further example of Britannic treachery, and moreover—"

He looked down from the Pratzen Heights with hot coffee and a dish of beaten eggs, milk and sugar. His staff was busy about him, messages being rapidly penciled, messengers tearing off. "Masse de décision, gentlemen."

"Ah, Sire."

"I will have Bernadotte's corps moved from the north sector. I want the entire Imperial Guard stationed on the left bank of the Goldbach. The only trouble, as I see it, is the presence of the Imperial Guard of Russia, which, as is clearly visible, is moving up to fill in that broken center. But, gentlemen, I have great hopes of their excessive impetuosity." They didn't understand what he meant. "They have been in that reserve position too long. They lack action. They will be far too eager for action." They still didn't understand what he meant.

They understood when the Grand Duke Ferdinand attacked with four paint-fresh battalions the near-dead troops of General Vandamme. They charged, yelling, bayonets ready to gut, from a distance of three hundred yards. They were too much out of breath to achieve the exquisite slaughter they had envisaged. They broke through the forward line but then met the hard fire of the French rear. They fell back on Krzenowitz. Vandamme, receiving the Imperial order to right incline, opened up his rear and left flank. The Grand Duke Constantine crashed the flank with fifteen squadrons of Guard cavalry, and the grenadiers, re-formed, renewed their frontal charge. Vandamme moved up two battalions to cover his naked flank. The Russians—

"What in the name of Almighty God? What for Christ's sake do those bastards think they're— The fucking cowards I'll have their fucking balls—" He danced, punching the air, while the unarmed and diseagled battalion of the Fourth went speeding off in retreat, crazy, panicky, panting Long Live The Emperor as though that were a cantrip solvent of crazed panic and cowardice. "Now," he said, more quietly, the dance ended, the air unpunched, "we will have that Imperial Guard of theirs. Send Bessières with our own Imperial cavalry."

"Sire."

"We revert now," smiled Dr. Arnott, "to this matter of the gubernatorial directive that the patient be fed with this thoroughly wholesome nutritive which, on Sir Hudson's own orders, has been er delactated from thoroughly wholesome cows."

"I have said till I am thoroughly wearied out with the effort of saying it that I cannot endorse, either as a patriot or as a practitioner of the art which you and your colleagues patently desecrate, the administering of a beverage which the digestive system of the imperial patient—"

"The epithet is inapposite and irrelevant," smiled Dr. Arnott, indicating the brimming crock.

"Now that," the Emperor said, "was an example of initiative which I am disinclined to reprehend." For Bernadotte had detached General Drouet's division to support the hard-pressed five squadrons of the Imperial Guard. "So now we order General Rapp to administer the final— Two squadrons of chasseurs and one of the fellow-countrymen of Roustam here. How would you like to be out there, eh, Roustam, shouting *Allah chew their balls off* and so on?"

"Sire."

Oh, effective enough, very effective. Five hundred Russian grenadiers dead and two hundred officers of the crack and élite and nobly-born Chevaliers, personal escort of the Tsar or Czar, taken prisoner.

"Just after two o'clock, Sire."

"Well," smiled the Emperor, as Prince Repnine, Commander of the Holy Russian Imperial Chevalier Guard was presented to him, torn, dusty, cowed, but every inch a prince of the blood, "we gave you a run for your money, eh, my prince?" And then, brutally: "Some weeping and gnashing and so forth in St. Petersburg tonight or tomorrow, I should think. All these delectable aristocratic ladies bereft of aristocratic manly comfort. Very well, let our aristocratic guests be led away."

"Two-thirty, Sire."

"Very good. Final phase, I think, gentlemen."

The great supine body was cleansed of the infesting enemy. It was sluiced down, south of the belly of the Pratzen Heights, to a region of frozen lakes and marshlands. The west was clear of enemy, and the column that retreated east towards Austerlitz was harried, battered, clawed, bitten, chewed, spat out. General Doktorov faced the north with frozen lakeland behind him. Every man for himself. Five thousand scattered, many over the iced waters.

"Bombard," ordered the Emperor. "All available cannon." He looked south to the white sheets, already cracking here and there under the weight of retreating gun-teams. Cannonballs stoned the ice, and the ice starred and shived and men went screaming into the black water, horses too, terrified and threshing, and the great useless guns.

"News from the north?"

"Enemy retreat under way, Sire. Just after three o'clock."

"My two colleagues here," smiled Dr. Arnott, "are in total agreement with me on this matter. It would constitute a helpful conciliatory gesture towards Sir Hudson who, as you will know, has been rendered extremely despondent by the intransigent attitude of his prisoner." And he gestured towards the brimming crock.

"I am of a mind," cried Dr. Antommarchi, "to dash it to the ground."

"Tut," tutted Dr. Mitchell. "That is a typically southern attitude, far from helpful, I would say, and certainly, I would say, denotative of a somewhat unprofessional attitude of mind."

"So," smiled Dr. Arnott, "shall we agree to administer to the patient this bland and candid nutritive donated by Sir Hudson?" And he once more.

Cease fire sounded at five. Tentative figures were totted. 11,000 Russians dead. 4,000 Austrians dead. 12,000 from both forces taken prisoner. 1,300 French dead. 6,940 wounded. 573 taken prisoner.

"Let us revert," smiled Dr. Arnott, "to this question of a more efficient purgative. The ten grams of calomel have, as my colleagues will agree, proved totally inefficacious. I prescribe another ten grams."

"I must protest, protest and protest again. Britannic treachery."

Roll up that map, etc. My country, my country, how I leave my, etc. The patient, unheard, chuckled. Nitzes and witzes and litzes. No. Only one litz.

. . .

THE tempest that visited the island on the fourth day of May was of a violence unwonted even in those latitudes. Poets and demiphilosophers nurtured in the temperate zones, who make of Dame Nature a smiling and wholly benevolent mother, must be accounted guilty of building their fanciful systems, the law following the observation of phenomena, on an insufficiency of data, the mild matron of the Gulf Stream transforming herself in the Tropics to a harpy, a valkyr, a shrieking and essentially female embodiment of the eternal principle of destruction. The firmament of that tropical island, horrid with the swirling and shifting of unearthly colors, resembled nothing so much as the bubbling of oils of varying degrees of luridity in some vast witches' cauldron. The skies were cracked and shattered ever and again by lightning-knouts of immense length and terrifying contour, while thunders opposed each other from every point of the compass, as though whole army corps, composed merely of kettle-drummers, were cached in valleys over an infinitely large terrain. The rain fell passionately without respite, converting the air into an infinite lamination of vertical lakes, and the winds howled and screamed as though the entire sack of Aeolus had in malice been emptied upon the lower heavens. Many of the superstitious islanders believed that they had in their midst, in impending demise as it was bruited, a demon or else a demigod who was intent on speaking the puissance of the celestial or infernal abode whence he had come and whither he was returning, in a final flourish before quitting his terrestrial lodging forever, or until his next incarnation. They crossed themselves, chid each other with a variety of sins for which punishment now seemed imminent, and murmured prayers for the remission of this visitation, which prayers were slow in being answered. Meantime the demigod or demon, revealed to the watchers and weepers as all too human, lay still or in the convulsions of sudden spasms of agony, his pale visage—grown, as many remarked in wonder, young and comely again—intermittently lighted by the fires that flashed from the heavens.

The force of the winds and the rains was such that chaos seemed to have come again, and by what, to those who held to the demonic or demidivine persuasion, seemed an anomaly, it was that expanse of tamed Nature known as the Imperial Garden which was quickest to revert to a swamped and blasted wilderness. Another variety of superstition naturally spoke of the gods bellowing their ultimate rage at Prometheus, while it was left to the few coolly rational to remark on the Pathetic Fallacy. Nevertheless, it is an observed and well-attested fact that all the vegetative life started by his own hands or under his imperial orders was uprooted by rain and wind, while the great willow tree beneath whose shade he had been accustomed to savor a coolness in heat that reached its most agonizing intensity (by an irony to be pondered on by our specialists in sentimental exploitation of the feast) at Christmas, was, by those same two vindictive elements, gleefully plucked up and hurled away with horrific and insolent ease. A solitary gum tree for which he had an especial affection seemed likely to withstand the tempestuous disruption, but that too was at length deradicated and sent wildly hurling and thrashing like a dog maddened with the pain of the whip. Of all that he had made of green and grateful, of all that Nature, in her more complaisant dispositions, had afforded him of the same, nothing was to be left. There seemed to some to be a lesson here, and it was that a man may not make even a garden with impunity.

Impunity—I marked the word
Negate the fires of human dawn,
Ring out above the sleeves of lawn
In pomp but pity uninferred.

Is man and all his striving thus
Not but by moral terms assessed,
Reward and benison impressed
Implacably on each of us

Impelled to make what must be made,
Nor seeing in those forms of Good
Raw evidence of Shall and Should
In rusty moral arms arrayed?
I watched with lidless eyes that night,
Nailed to the all too punitive,
Racked on that gift to all who give,
Inching with him to dark or light.

In final sense his voice awoke,
Not babbling, kingly strong again;
Regal the words, the words were twain;
In pain I shook to what he spoke.

HEAD
ARMY

He spoke no more to those outside the garden and now considered that he was, if that term had any meaning in this given situation, free to walk through it and take pleasure in what, that year, seemed a singularly fine display of roses, while there was a curiously sensuous *élan* to be experienced in the yield of the plushy sward beneath his, so it came to him, sentient bootsole. Very beautiful was the melancholy that suffused him, of an autumnal old gold that belied the season of the roses but was altogether fitting to the season of his own life as he now, in a rapid conscient flash, recognized it to be. With a smile he looked down on his attire, a totally civilian "get-up," of a sobriety proper to his newly observed silver age, silver but for jubilee, yet nothing of the jubilant in the decent subfuse of the clothes, the broad-brimmed hat he carried in one hand while with a slender cane in the other he eased his way about the rosebeds. Brute beauty and valor and act here buckled with joints that, he knew with no great measure of regret, were now unmeet for straddling the charger or striding the conference room. It, he knew as well as he knew his name, whatever his name was—was the cognomen to be restored to the daily use of self-introduction or the filling in of forms or the signing of letters, together with a totally unpretentious honorific?—was all done with; he was, in a word, *hors de combat.*

The lady he saw approaching him, bearing a basket, was so light, was so fair that men, he thought, must wonder as she passed, as he now, in a very curious transport of not unpleasurable agitation, wondered, as also at the basket that she bore, which was charged with the glory of blooms of a really astonishing magnificence and none of them, very strangely as it seemed to him, at all represented in the garden where they both were. It was difficult, as it was also perhaps ungallant, to wish to speculate as to her age, half-hidden as her face was in the sieve of the straw of her plaited summer bonnet, but such considerations were after all not very much to the purpose. The liquid waist bespoke youth, and the broth of flue, sometimes goldish, sometimes dusky according to her passage through the pied summer light, which breathed round her bare arms, strangely recalled a visual notation of his early boyhood, when he had admired, with none of the admixture of *carnality* that would have hit him in a later and more intense phase of susceptibility, a similar delicacy of filament on the arms of his sister Pauline. He stood, smiling, somewhat undecided as to whether to give greeting, considering the niceties of behavior relevant to such chance, but none the less pleasant for that, garden encounters. It seemed to him that he would, in a word, decide to leave it to her.

It wasn't long before she addressed him in a voice friendly enough yet cool, of the coolness however of some friendly water, ever so promising of refreshment to the tired wanderer of a long summer day through Devon dene or Lancashire clough, rather than the conventional and indifferent coolness proper to the approach of a "correct" young woman to some male stranger's unexpectedly appearing. And it was with a very palpable astonishment that our friend caught from her address, through the veneer of its casualness, a sense, though hard to define, of his somehow being expected, of the encounter's not being entirely unpurposed, though, for his part, the purposing was non-existent, however much, now that it was actually "under way," he was able to reflect with the firm knowledge of retrospection that he would have been willing enough to purpose it. The fire that flashed from her, as she sauntered toward where he continently stood, was a billion times told lovelier, more dangerous.

"And so," she said, "it is very much *all over*, O my chevalier."

He wondered, smiling vaguely, at the plenitude of allusions which her words seemed to contain, and, for want of something more to the purpose, whatever this was, he replied to the effect that this appeared to be so, hoping from whatever she would come out with next to gain a degree or so of illumination.

"And what," she now said, "if posterity requires anything at all, would posterity be perhaps conceived of as requiring in the way of a summary?"

He thought he now began to get her drift, so, nodding and smiling amiably though with, he couldn't help thinking, some of that quite meaningless up-and-down agitation of the head which he had seen frequently in the old and now recognized, with some inner and motor sense, as emanating from the old man in himself, he ventured a reply that might, to such a one as she (he saw in the eyes, of a color not clearly definable, which would be the very deuce for a portrait painter to catch, an intelligent hardness which contrasted piquantly with the "willowiness," the softness, of the rest of her) be possibly considered satisfactory.

"Oh, well," he said, "there was a something to fulfill. I think one might say it was fulfilled—partially, I have to add, since what we term contemporary history has insisted on the truncation of that something. I mean, there was a thing I was told to do and I ventured to do it." And he agitated the cane in his left hand in a vague gesture of actions set oscillating.

"Told?" she picked him up. "Who tells?"

"Not *who* precisely," he replied, with an *oeillade* and a characteristic shrug. "Some force, some daemon, let us say, that impels to particular modes of action, for good or bad—the consideration doesn't apply—and which it is probably useless, even if one wished to, to attempt to oppose. We all have this indubitable embedding of a something." Shy or sly, he wasn't sure which, was the query he then commenced putting to her: "If I may be so bold as to ask, who—"

"Not *who*, then," she said, beginning, with a certain absence that could have been construed as unconscious cruelty, to depetal a particularly fine carnation that rested in her basket. "And so the moral consideration, the question of, to be blunt about it, the rights and the wrongs of the matter—" She did not continue. He waited, but it was evident that he was to take the ellipsis as the round.

"One cannot," he said with a triteness that surprised him only when it was too late to retreat from the locution, "make an omelette without breaking eggs." Then he added, with an unwonted flush, "I apologize."

"Much depends," she replied, with a coldness that could not be mistaken for her previous coolness: the palpable drop in temperature forbade it, "on whether one likes omelettes." Her smile was restored when she put in, before he could devise a reply, a remark that bespoke her learning. "We're concerned less with oology than herology, if there is such a term. And if there isn't," she said with a kind of young-miss bluntness, "there ought to be."

"Ah," and he felt he was on firmer ground now. As if to stake a claim to such ground, he planted his cane in a flower-border, put on his hat (he didn't have to seek her permission: this was the open air; he was much, he thought, her senior; she herself was hatted, and very prettily), folded his arms behind his back, and began to pace a little between two rosebeds. "The nature of the hero has to be made manifest. And what is the hero, you ask? The being of exceptional qualities, the man above men in the intensity and scope of thought and ability. The fields of heroism are, I think, manifold; mine was that of a *head of arms*, head of an army, head of an armed state."

"Why?" she asked. She possessed this quality of disconcertment, well able to brim it into that narrowest possible vessel of an *oh* or a *why*.

"Why? Why?" He gave back the word to her with something of his old vigor of the counterassault. "You mean to what end? That may be answered. To the end of disseminating the word of republican enlightenment. To the end of protecting *by arms* an already existing republic or, let me perhaps put it another way, of preserving the motherland, already, far ahead of the other nations of Europe (for we will leave, as we must, America out of it), blessed with the enlightenment of the republican principle, from the machinations—and in anticipation, if need be—of ancient, corrupt and jealously fearful monarchies. There," and he smiled at her much in the manner he had, it came back to him, used (a somewhat bizarre *mélange* of the triumphant and the ingratiating) in his extreme youth in the schoolroom when catechized on matters of Christian doctrine by the visiting bishop, in his voice a graciousness of answer, in his face displayed the plenitude of his whole handsome heart.

"Oh, as for that—" Then fingers that had been absently depetalling made a handsome, a graceful dismissal of what, he realized with the belatedness that was becoming characteristic of all his realizations *vis à vis* his responses to her so light-toned, so of a feathery delicacy, questionings, had been a decidedly jejune and at the same time positively elephantine, certainly demagogic, summation of the whole, so to put it, *tissage*.

"I know," and his eyes were examining the toes of his boots, where a certain minute quantity of summer dust had dulled the caps. "Kings and princes and dukes, even an emperor. But not, you understand, hereditary. Totally, but totally and in toto, earned. An aristocracy of sheer merit. Or," he was constrained to add in honesty, since he was aware of the sardonic quizzing of those eyes of hers, though he did not for the moment care much to meet them, "occasionally not of merit, but of family. There are, let us admit it, claims on one, of blood, sentiment and *tout ça*. But for ever so much the most part it was of merit.

The state much like the army, with merit rewarded, medals, pensions, duchies and principalities. Indeed, the state hardly to be distinguished from the army. Head. Arms. You will understand the whole of the, so to speak, *tremblement*."

"Oh, yes," and her response was swift, almost eager, and not at all unfriendly, as if she had at last decided to accept him on his merits, such as they were. "But none of that is quite what I meant." He descried then the true burden of condescension which the tone of amicable eagerness, like the ooze of oil, filmed over. "What we both have to agree upon," she continued, playing her little show of comradeliness to the limit, "is the essential *mestiére* or *métier*, the *métier* dressed to a dexterous and starlight order. To what purpose its practice?—this ought not to be asked, not, anyway, in terms of the larger and, so to speak, metaphysical aim. The royal cobbler may be said to make shoes not that the emperor may walk to the ultimate congress of the world, but that a pair of royal or imperial feet may be dexterously dressed. Would you not say that it might at least be thought of as conceivably being, within the small realm of possibility we concede to ourselves, so?" she said, with no diminution of the comradely-seeming eagerness.

He was quite ready to respond then with a warm look and some cautious enough inclinations of the head but not, as yet anyway, to respond more or less vocally, since he felt he must, she being what she was (who she was, who the dickens she was, was a question he was not now prepared to repeat), proceed quiet-padded and with all jungle senses alert.

"The *métier* of hero," she said in a now musing tone, "of the quite exceptionally endowed genius of action—how far it must be fulfilled in, and the term is *à propos*, action, is a question that may be put. The *métier* of Don Quixote or, indeed, of Don Juan—you will perhaps catch my more surface meaning."

"Ah." He smiled at the childishness of the collocation. With some confidence he said that the applicability wasn't particularly apparent, since the one Don was mere legend and the other Don certainly the creation of another Don—he smiled more broadly—and so, the one fiction and the other very nearly so, if not wholly so, the analogues to himself weren't all that aptly chosen.

"The point I am trying to make," she said with a coldness positively of a near-glacial order, "is that the hero doesn't have to have existed. To nourish the imagination with the heroic image—this can be as well done through some superior (and hence perhaps heroic) imagination. Oh, we don't have to call on the ultimate imaginer, if he may be called that, since all that he can add to the image is the corporeal and the spatial element and the time thing and so on, all of them limitations."

Her extreme coldness stung him, like a well-aimed snowball, into a more intelligent reply than perhaps, all things considered, he might be thought of as being in a position to give. "But without me," he cried, and he doffed his hat as though to wave huzzahs in his own honor, "this particular image couldn't have been. Modesty forbids the uttering of the name or the epithet available from it, but the imaginations of the yet unborn will, to use your own phrase, be nourished by it. So I had to, and how absurd this sounds, exist, quite apart from the tabled and achieved enactments which will change, which have changed, which are changing, the order of things." And he breathed somewhat stertorously, as with the labor of intellection required for the earnest, earthless, equal, attunable, vaulty, voluminous . . . stupendous utterance.

"Oh, as for that—" It was one of her phrases, the exordial something that preceded the larger dismissal, the more explicit pushing-by. "A man, a German he was, *ein* or *einer Mann*, I find the accidence of the language excessively, supererogatorily endowed with endings, says something somewhere about the German need to *oppose*, to struggle against that particular imposition, in the name of forests and sunsets and the like, which turned their romantic spirit political. No very creditable achievement, if I may say so." And in a strangely, he could only think of it as *sibylline*, tone she said, "*Our* evening is over us, *our* night whelms, whelms and will end us." And she shuddered in the large summer heat, as though foreseeing its premature and summary dismissal by some active force of cold, perhaps the cold that once blanketed the whole world come again. "And as for the other thing—" He could not for the moment recall what "the other thing" was, but he allowed her to proceed, hoping that words which he still expected uncomfortably to be sibylline would somehow jog his recollection of it. "You created, in your own Promethean manner, and I employ the term altogether without the disparagements of—"

"Yes, yes." For some reason he did not wish to hear the word upon her lips. "*Sarcasm.*"

"Very well." The day was indeed advancing, and the lovely behavior of the silk-sack clouds was being transformed into a cortège of unseemly haste with the rising of the wind (black, he was thinking involuntarily, ever so black on it, the night on its way). "You created your men out of clay, though to create women you had no power. You never had, and I must say everything now, if I can, without excessive circumlocution, much power over women. Bread and water." The sibylline pose was back. "Taken with the sword still in the scabbard. *Vota. Vuota.*" He flushed a deep crimson, the words being not all that sybilline. "But they had the clay about them even when they were made, since the creator must always maintain the sway of control and not brook the danger of the creation rising up and—"

"They were *made*," he interposed somewhat testily. "Who else could have made them?"

"The question rather is," she responded: "Who could have made" (the flowers in their straw basket had the look of flowers that were somehow aware, and the fancy has to be admitted, of an impending rapid shriveling) "*you*?" She twirled a blown Dieudonné by its stalk and watched with no observable emotion the loosening petals detach themselves centrifugally. "You could have been made, and made rather well, by some master of that kind of artifaction—in words, you know. Then there would not have to have been all that cauchemar of flesh and blood spilled about, and that notable cruelty to horses. I have always been particularly fond of horses." A fantasy of particular coarseness struck in on him, but he was quick to banish it. Besides, the properties of aristocratic Englishry represented only one of a positive zootrope of appearances under that shady hat; there were other masks capable of being rapidly imposed and then "whisked away" on and from the quintessential *herself*, and most of them he recognized with varying degrees of certainty; the voice too was a spectrum of voices, a basal auditory light, so to speak, capable of (in the same manner as the masks) the ever so rapid variant staining with colors which, despite his known daltonian affliction in this sphere of recognition, he was able to name with considerable exactitude. "The essence of the heroic," she went on, "herology, herography, heropoetics, with no one compelled to rise in the cold morning to go out and die. Or in music."

He tried to smile, though the chillness of the wind was intensifying, and it seemed to him that they ought both, or at least himself, to go indoors, or back indoors, although nothing that could be thought of as "indoors," the façade of it or, more aptly, door to it, for the moment proffered. The rosebeds, that had made so brave a flourish, were now not doing at all well. "Music? I know about music. Heartening, especially in battle, but unfortunately lacking in the precise content of—"

"You didn't do well there," she smiled with a tinge of young woman's malice. "It was all set up for you, you know, and he tore up the dedication. You know who I mean, I think. Still," she now smiled, her gold-flued arms apparently insensitive to the untimely winter, though it seemed more reasonable or seasonable to regard all this as some mere transitory tramontana, some boreal thrust, yet it was most unfortunate for the poor dear roses, "the more appropriate for being what you said it is. Heartening without content—the phrase is, though I truncate it a little, all yours."

"I had no skill in art," he shivered, "except that particular one."

"An art highly wasteful of its materials." She smiled still, and there was now a quality of near-finality about it, what time her countenance performed, so it *had* to be possible for him to think, a coda consisting in a sequence of appearances of the once known and the abandoned or abandoning. "Scarcely breathes that bliss." There was a quite certain incoherence now. "Now yields you with some sighs." *À propos* of what all this now was was not at all apparent. "Our explanation."

It was with an undoubted sensation of a, to look for no better word, detachment from what was, or certainly had been, a crowd of categories that had set about, punctuated, though not exclusively animated, the modes of being which had constituted what he had always habitually conceived of as, though not necessarily expressed as, interpretative of his own *essence*, that he now tried to give out, to "sing," not with the explicit vocality that might, on other planes, be predicated as of the primary necessity of the action or utterance (both terms could be regarded as apt: where, after all, does one draw the line?), but rather with the energy of sheer intent, in the manner of a distinctly spiritual *thrust*, the, as it were, melodic counterpart of what he had always seen his function to be, exclusively his, very much (because of the undoubted difficulty of separating out that same function and the before-mentioned essence) himself as he, though not he alone, very far from it, to do him justice, saw himself. But, so it dawned upon him in the giving out, there might be a means, and he thought there probably was, of conveying, of indeed distilling, into the particular fluidity of the form, more than the heart or essence of the function. After all, was there not, had there not been, a succession of actions that could look, and not in vain, to the sonorous panels of some great harmonious triptych or (and why on earth not?) even tetraptych for their generalized, though not too much so, harmonic and contrapuntal (though he shuddered at the connotations of fugue, *fuga*, until he saw how it might be construed less as a fleeing than as a kind of structured and multiple flying, intransitive or the other thing) expression. How not to generalize, though: there was the rub.

But in the generalized pouring forth, very loud or quite its opposite, the polarity of terms no longer seeming to apply in this sphere, an unvocal vocality not being at all out of the order of things as they now presented themselves, or rather as he was presented to himself through them, though *it* might be more applicable, the one true and entirely lovely thing, it did not appear in the least to be a diminution, but rather an augmentation, *the* augmentation (more properly to articulize), altogether very fine and grand and with trumpets, since to become not one's own essence (it had to be essence, since existing was now altogether out of it) but the one big final identification with the essential essence, so to put it, of which his own had to be accounted, in this unique retrospect, as a mere and very finite aspect, was of a glory, a dayspring to his former dimness, a crimson-cresseted east, entirely and satisfactorily enthroned and crowned, most quite definitely not to be gainsaid. Thus to *become* the thing was, and he could not forbear to flaw the great melodic surge with a momentary chuckle at the vulgarism, ever so much "one in the ear" for the intransigent, but undeniably a talented intransigent, who had balked so at the regretful necessity of that "taking off" that time (but stay: was not the locution bardic?) and at everything that had followed on after that, the sweetness of the orange in his hands of the true aromatic and zestful glory, in spite of it and so on, but of course *ce petit meinherr* had known, in his own way, and notwithstanding a disability that would not have gained him even the rank of plain *soldat*, all about the nature (the essence again!) of this particular glory, even though—and here was the deucedly queer thing—he evidently didn't go in at all much for that species of commodity. Thou mastering me. The chuckle, which had now become hard to control, went well enough with the music.

"Sir Hudson Lowe," smiled Dr. Arnott, "has consented to give his consent, but I see you already hard at it. A bit premature, wouldn't you say? A bit irregular, without the rest of your confrères present?" And he gestured toward the open corpse, in which Dr. Antommarchi was busily excavating.

"It was the imperial wish," cried Dr. Antommarchi, "that an

autopsy be conducted. It is in the imperial will, or in a codicil thereto, and there is nothing that your Sir Lowe can do to prevent it. Much, I know, as he would wish to. The costal cartilages," he said, in a tone more impersonal and professional, "are to a large degree ossified."

"No, no, you miss my point," smiled Dr. Arnott. "My point was to emphasize the entire willingness of Sir gubernatorial Hudson to have such an er operation conducted. Dr. Shortt and Dr. Mitchell will corroborate, I have no doubt." And he gestured toward them.

"Most willingly," willed willingly Dr. Mitchell.

"But his willingness is quite irrelevant and impertinent," cried Dr. Antommarchi. And then, more quietly, clinically: "This left pleural cavity is, as you see, filled with a citrous-colored fluid."

"That what you foreign fellows call it, eh?" said Dr. Shortt, peering in. "Bit of a stink, I'd say."

"It smells, if of anything," cried Dr. Antommarchi, "of violets."

"Ah, very good," smiled Dr. Arnott. "Very wholesome, is that it? A corpse in the very pink of health, what?" And he gestured towards the superior lobe of the lung.

"Tubercles," cried Dr. Antommarchi. "*Seminato di tubercoli.*"

"Oh, everybody has those," Dr. Shortt shortly snorted. "The main point is, as my colleague there," and he gestured towards him, "is implying or has already implied, that nobody can be blamed for anything, eh? That everybody's in the clear."

"I do not doubt," cried Dr. Antommarchi, looking at the right costal pleural sac, "that there will be evidence found of foul play."

"Not if it can possibly be avoided," smiled Dr. Arnott. "We will make every effort to avoid that."

"That Irish doctor spoke of neglect and persecution on the part of your Sir Lowe to the House of Lords in London," cried

Dr. Antommarchi. "And look what happened to him—court-martialed." Several bronchial ganglia were enlarged, degenerate, in suppuration.

"Oh, hardly to the House of Lords, not directly," munched Dr. Mitchell.

"An Irishman, note," smiled Dr. Arnott. "Not trustworthy, of course. All on the side of this one here." He gestured to the him that was now it. "A lot of Irish in his army. That man MacDonald, for instance, with some ridiculous title." And he gestured toward the right hand that had presumably bestowed it.

"A French Scot, I'd thought," said Dr. Shortt. "Joined the Irish Legion, though. And where are they all now, eh?"

"That *friend* of his, forget his name, reported him in good health and scrimshanking. Malingering, you understand," said Dr. Mitchell.

"Lies, lies, lies," cried Dr. Antommarchi. "You all know all too well of the conspiracy of hate. Your hateful Sir Lowe. The pericardium is in a normal state, but the heart, you observe, is fatty."

"He was generally fat, wasn't he?" sniffed Dr. Shortt. "It was remarked on, his fatness, as soon as he got here."

"No," cried Dr. Antommarchi. "A morbidity induced by the manner of life imposed on him by— And gaseous matter, not fat."

"You ought not to speak in that manner of the Governor of the Colony," smiled Dr. Arnott. "Your attitude however may, I suppose, be excused in a foreigner of your sort. By," he smilingly added, "a foreigner of your sort. You shouldn't really be here, anyway. The prisoner's dead and gone, and you should be at least, ha, gone."

"Distension of the peritoneum, a great quantity of gas. A soft, transparent and fluid transudation," Dr. Antommarchi said, making it sound rather poetical. Then he cried aloud: "I speak as a friend, a lover, a worshipper, and a man of science."

"Don't go well together, those," said Dr. Shortt, shaking his head as at a proposed supper menu. "Ah, let's have a look at that stomach, shall we? A good close look."

"There, you see," cried Dr. Antommarchi. "A certain engorgement that must be construed as cirrhotic."

"Nothing to do with anybody here," smiled Dr. Arnott. He gestured towards the peritoneal membrane, which was of a very beautiful though now purely morphological normality. "As for the stomach, gentlemen—ahhh. You know what we're after first, of course," he smiled.

"I know all too well," cried Dr. Antommarchi. And he almost seemed to make the gesture, with cupping hands, of trying to hide what he knew all too well they were after.

"A bit of a stink there," *ça pued* Dr. Shortt.

"The acridity and fetidity of the odor," now mumbled Dr. Antommarchi, "are self-evident and I do not attempt to mitigate them. Though to a more sympathetic, a more loving olfactory system—"

"No violets, certainly," smiled Dr. Arnott. "Rather violent if anything. Come now, you know what we want. Let's have a good look at it."

"With every breath in my body I protest," protested Dr. Antommarchi. "I protest at what you are lyingly proposing to find, or rather not to find, on the treacherous instructions of the archfiend Sir Lowe."

"Do try and get the name right," counterprotested Dr. Mitchell. "The sir bit goes with the first name. But you foreigners will insist upon having it your own way."

"A look at it," smiled Dr. Arnott, looking smilingly.

So there it was then: to Dr. Antommarchi the imperial liver; to the British medicals the general's, or general, liver. The liver. And they had a damned good look at the liver. "The situation is," cried Dr. Antommarchi, "and I will record it immediately in my notebook and request, nay demand, your countersignatures of confirmation, as follows." And he pronounced in Corsican pomposity, writing with a pencil: "The imperial liver, infected with chronic hepatitis, was intimately joined to the diaphragm on its convex surface. The adhesion—firm, cellular, very long-established—extended along the said surface all the way." And then, fixing them with fierce glowing Corsican eyes, "Hepatitis. Look at the abnormal enlargement, engorgement, elephantine hypertrophy. Now then, perfidious, I have you."

"Oooooh," smiled Dr. Arnott, like a little girl confronting her Christmas doll, and with a raised tone of little-girl ecstasy, "what a perfectly lovely liver. So normal, so unenlarged." And he gestured. The other two perfidious Albionites cooed in chorus, "Oooooh." A beautiful liver. A healthy liver. Not a bit, not to make a song and dance of it, enlarged. Dr. Antommarchi made a song and dance, and the others watched him. Then Dr. Antommarchi seized hold of the liver, as to auction it at a reserve appropriate to its enlargement, and said:

"At it. Look. At. It look."

"What we have always been chiefly concerned about," smiled Dr. Arnott, "is the stomach. *Look at it*, gentlemen," gesturing. "Clearly cancerous. Could one possibly have, in one's wildest dreams as a first-term student, any possible doubt as to the impossibility of its being anything other than cancerous?"

Most certainly (Dr. Antommarchi called on pre-Christian Corsican gods) cancerous, in a severely cancerous condition, there was no possibility of a reasonable clinician's entertaining the least possible doubt about that. Most clearly and patently, most classically cancerous.

"I know you all, I know your tricks," cried Dr. Antommarchi. "I know that you know that the Emperor's father died of a cancerous condition of the stomach, I know that you know that such things can be hereditary, but I know too that there is no cancerous condition here, it is the liver, the liver, he is dead of the liver, oh Castor and Pollux, the treachery, the lies, the cancer of perfidy."

"So," smiled Dr. Arnott, "we may sum up our autoptic findings to this effect: to wit, that the stomach is perforated by a hole large enough to admit a finger but adhering to the liver in such a manner as to effect a blockage of the perforation. Death due to a cancerous ulcer of the stomach, the same stomach (ha, I apologize: there is clearly no other stomach under postmortal examination) exhibiting signs of lesions about to become cancerous. Agreed?"

Agreed, agreed.

"Not agreed," fandangoed Dr. Antommarchi, screaming, "not and never to be agreed. Oh, the perfidy, oh the shame of the treacherous misrepresentation—"

"Wait," suddenly said Dr. Shortt. "I would say, you know, that that liver is after all abnormally enlarged." Drs. Arnott and Mitchell gave him the tribute of twenty seconds of staggering disbelief.

"Siding with him, are you?" smiled Dr. Arnott. "Going along with this Dr. Antimony or Dr. Antibody here?"

"No, no. On an independent view of it, I'd say that it was certainly abnormally enlarged. Nothing to do with what *he* says. Trust the judgment of my own—"

"It's a beautifully normal liver," smiled Dr. Arnott, "and you said so yourself. And this Dr. Antinomian here heard you say it, didn't you, my friend and colleague?"

"Treachery treachery treach—"

"I think," smiled Dr. Arnott, "that the Governor, that Sir Hudson Lowe, on behalf, remember, of Lord Bathurst back in London, would agree that there is no enlargement of the liver. Three to two, gentlemen."

"I'm surprised," sniffed Dr. Mitchell, "that you, Shortt, should be willing to go along with— Well, after all, certain loyalties, the claims of undoubted decencies. Damn it, man, whose side are you on?"

"He is on," cried Dr. Antommarchi, "the side of truth, the side of our great and good dead king and master."

"I wouldn't agree with that last bit," scowled Dr. Shortt. "Truth, if you like, but not the rest of the rigamarole. And if having truth means having to have all that, then I'm not too sure how I stand. Look," he said to his fellow-perfidalbionites,

"I'm not too sure either that I give a damn about Sir Hudson Lowe and that fool Bathurst back in London. No one's going to send me to the guillotine for having the courage of the conviction of my own eyesight. I say it's enlarged—"

"Abnormally, you said." Dr. Arnott smiled at him.

"Whatever that means—"

"Whatever *enlarged* means," twitched Dr. Mitchell. "Look, Shortt, do you know what the average size of a liver is?"

"I've seen enough livers in my time to know that this one is damnably enlarged. Sorry, don't want any trouble, as you know, but there it is, damn it."

"I heard that," cried Dr. Antommarchi, "about the guillotine. Have courage, man. His lovers and worshippers will be praying for you if that day should come."

"We don't have the guillotine in England," smiled Dr. Arnott. "We're civilized there. It was just a figure of speech. Nobody's going to send anyone to the guillotine. Except," he said, but his smile showed that this was no time for threats and insults and so on to this Dr. Auntie Margery here. "Now then," brisk, smiling, gesturing, "a cancerous condition of the stomach. Right, Shortt? Accept that as the cause of his taking off?"

"That liver's damnably enlarged. Funny thing I didn't notice it before. Very well, death through cancerous ulcer, I'll sign that, but I want that put in about the enlarged liver."

"Oh, I don't think we're going to have that," smiled Dr. Arnott. "We'll leave out the liver. An irrelevance, really."

"I'm having the liver in," snorted Shortt. "And I want it noted that Sir Hudson Lowe has suppressed the enlargement bit. And I don't care a damn."

"Friend to the truth and the cause," cried Dr. Antommarchi. "For my part, I will be no party. I will sign nothing."

"Couldn't be better," smiled Dr. Arnott. "Damned if I know really how you got into all this. It was his mother sent you, wasn't it? Along with those two damned snuffling priests. Madam Mayor or Mare or whatever they call her."

"Look," sourly said Dr. Shortt. "I don't want you breathing

garlic and *ami de la vérité* all over me. It'll sound as if I'm in on some damned foreign conspiracy. I go my own way, follow my own ocular testimony, so keep your garlicky breath out of it, do you understand?"

"I stand alone," cried Dr. Antommarchi. "Treachery, always treach."

"Oh, do shut up," smiled Dr. Arnott. "Can't you let the poor devil lie in peace?" And he gestured to the corpse, hacked open like a haggis. "Sew him up and have him made to look pretty. He won't keep long."

"It's a good face, you have to admit," admitted Dr. Shortt. "It's what I'd call a noble face. Compare it with Lowe's face, for instance. No damned comparison."

"Friend," cried Dr. Antommarchi. "The magic is working even from the shades of death." But Dr. Shortt looked at him in proper Britannic disgust, stupid hysterical foreigner.

Sir Hud abated none of the fierce sternness of his inveterate antagonism in the face he raised to the heavens. "He was my foe," he declared in an heroic voice, "and the foe of all mankind. He was the eternal enemy, but now he has passed away from the eyes of men. The forces of good have prevailed, and though no true heart may prate of forgiveness, yet what heart is this day so obdurate that it will not soften, yea, and liquefy to a brief dew-dropping of generous tears? Damned he is, damned he must be, the endless flames of perdition enfold him, but at the same time he reposes in the bosom of a just God, who knoweth better than any of us how the souls of the wicked shall justly be disposed. He is dead, which none may deny; he is buried, which none may deny either; he is gone from us, which the most skeptical must be ready to admit. Nevertheless, we must show true British generosity. His tombstone shall not bear the legend of imperial pretension, but nor neither shall it be inscribed with true and veracious, though in the circumstances ungenerous, accounts of his evil villainy and damnable dastardliness. Nay, blank it shall be; blank shall it rest; and the sun and the wind and the generous rain shall attest to the end of time to its blankness. So let us dry our eyes and pronounce Amen to that." And he spurred his charger and rode off, whither no man was much inclined to inquire.

"WELL, miss, as habit himpels me still to go on calling you of," said Sergeant Trouncer, as good a soldier of King George (though the Fourth now, not the Third, it making little odds however) as King George, if King George were disposed to look, could be expected to find, "them was his last words, as I have hevidence hof, and they is hinscribed ear hon this ear bit of paper, not to give it too rumbustious and overfacing hof a description." He sucked his ample mustache, which had been, together with the spacious orifice to which it was a curtain, amply laved with beer freely donated by the Bascombes. He sat with Betsy in their garden in London, listening to birdsong very straightforwardly British and no nonsense, none of your tropical ornithological melodic extravagances. In six more months they would all be celebrating a British Christmas (not these same birds, of course; they, having little of true Christmas or indeed of British feeling, would have winged their way to other climes), but now it was British summer and no whit the worse for that, God bless it.

Betsy read the scrap of paper, which bore evidence of long and arduous travel in the somewhat cramped diligence of Sergeant Trouncer's back trousers pocket, and wept a little as she read. "France. Army. Head of the Army. Josephine." She sniffed back a tear. "How very sad," she said in a muffled voice.

"Ha," said Sergeant Trouncer weightily. "So that's what it means, eh? I was never much of a one for the Frenchies and their lingo, miss, aving ad orrible hexperiences as I bitterly recall at Toulong." To her blankness he elucidated: "Toulong being by way of a seaside place, miss, in France, and terrible rumbustious goings hon there was—I takes my hoath hon it, hif you will forgive the circumloquaciousness, so to speak, miss."

"So he thought of her," sniffed Betsy, "at the very last. How sad, how really sad. And they all left him, Sergeant Trouncer, every one."

"I stayed," Sergeant Trouncer observed, teasing out like carded wool the left wing of his damp mustache. "But then, I ad to, in a manner of talking, me being in His Majesty's Forces, God bless im and them. Nor," he added sagaciously, "was I by way of being a Woman, miss, that being in your mind without a Doubt. But," he said mysteriously, "Eaven transposes all things in the long run, and whether we abide it or do not abide it makes but little difference to the houtcome of the ole boiling, miss, if you'll a pardon of the hobservance."

"And I left him too," Betsy said in a low and tremulous voice. "I deserted him with the others. How can I ever forgive myself?"

"The call of dooty, miss," pronounced Sergeant Trouncer, "and there is no going beyond of that, as is well detested by Them As Knows." And, as though this last word asked for it, he placed a great index finger against the side of his meaty nasal organ.

"I loved him, you see," murmured Betsy.

"Ah, love," said Sergeant Trouncer frowning, as though it were some military innovation of which he did not approve, "love we all as eard of, heven when we ave not been much deposed to it. So there it is, miss, so to speak."

"And now it's all over."

"Well," deliberated Sergeant Trouncer, "I wouldn't be too certain of that, miss. Them is very final words—Hall Hover. No, miss, I would think twice before deliverance of that there hutterance." Our military friend, though lacking in what the narrower world calls learning and refinement, was not devoid of a certain natural wisdom, and it was out of the depths of this that he repeated the words: "Hall Hover? No, miss, not in the least Hall Hover." And then he gladly accepted another glass of the Bascombes' good British ale.

359

. . .

Not *in the least all over.* It was a gorgeous spring morning as N rode out to inspect the troops. The words of the memoranda he had just dictated rang like a jingle of little bell-tunes. It was really a most beautiful morning. "The Louvre was five minutes late in opening yesterday. . . . That junior clerk in the Ministry of Works, Queval I seem to remember the name is, seems to me to be a sly tippler. How can he afford it on his salary? Irregularities there, and if in small, probably in high places too. Have it looked into. . . . The Egyptian fountain is in a very dirty state, have it cleaned out. . . . The rate of the bank loan must be raised one percent. . . . The time has come for a new school edition of the life of Charlemagne. . . . Corporal Masson has an inflamed eye, order him to report sick. . . . Some day we will have those bastards incorporated into the Great European Family. . . ."

With him rode his Chief of Staff, the Marshal of the Day, the Master of the Horse (sulking; some argument about shoeing techniques), two of his ADC's, two orderly officers, an equerry, a telescope-carrying page, a groom, an interpreter, a soldier of the escort bearing a map-portfolio and a pair of dividers fixed at the daily rate of march, Roustam, dear old black bastard. Ahead, twelve cavalry and two more orderly officers. Behind, the main escort of four squadrons of the Guard Cavalry (chasseurs, lancers, mounted grenadiers, dragoons). It suddenly struck him, with amusement, that he had forgotten entirely what, where—

"Sire." And he was told where they were, what the name of the coming victory was to be, who the enemy was. But, of course, there was really only one enemy.

"—Family sooner than they think, bastards."

"Sire."

The roar of loving greeting from the assembled troops scared the birds to mad uncoordinated circling. His birthday, the anniversary of a great victory, of his crowning? No, it was just him, he. He waved, tears of love in his eyes, marking at the same time the shocking turn-out of Sergeant Pécriaux, nearly on his knees and an upper button missing, must speak to the womanizing swine. Cheers of greeting and rejoicing. Everything and everybody joined in, far beyond this field. Animate and inanimate in general jubilation.

The muzzle-loading plugs, the last remaining stretch of the Zuyder Zee, the unleavened bread disk of the Eucharist, Wilhelm Richard and John Peter (Honus), the constellations Ursa Major and Auriga, the whole tribe of Motacilla, the widows and orphans, what was left of Solomon's temple in Jerusalem, the tongues of the Nootka, Bridges Creek, the Vaudois, the entire cavalry, camptosorus rhizophyllus, leucoma and strabismus, the tough wood of the gunstocks, witches' sabbaths, the brash and the buffalo, the salamanders, cowbane, plantain, purslane, diving beetles and wattlebirds, the snowberry, Mad Anthony, sea trout, meteors and meteorology, weave and lattice, gravitation, cisterns, canals, marine snails, Bengal, monsoons, the shark and the wheatear, the nematode worm, the knout and the vinegarroon, the gratuitously assumed mission of the Caucasoids, Pentecostal tongues, harlots and liars, islands and cutlets and physicists, the lily of the valley, the bellowing gnu, ships and clarinets and tempests, the Son of Sirach, hazel and witch moth, cuckolds and warlocks, sorrel and alexia, Sir Thomas and Breslau and all the flowing wine of the world rejoiced. Rejoice. And again I say rejoice. And I say aga INRI ng bells bells bells bells and rejoice. Rejoice.

I and III, Rome, 1972
II and IV, Rome, 1973

AN EPISTLE TO THE READER

Take then or leave this lump of minor art,
A novel on Napoleon Bonaparte
(In a Pickwickian sense, I ought to add).
Post-Tolstoy novelists are reckoned mad,
Presumptuous, temerarious, or all three,
To write about the Corsican, since he
Is brilliantly portrayed in Voina i Mir*:*
After that vodka, who wants British beer?
The two Leones met, the task was done;
Why seek the knout of vile comparison?
Our Thomas Hardy was aware of this
(Great in his way, though, as Count Leo is),
And so, when limning Bonaparte's career,
Eschewed the epic shape of Voina i Mir*,*
Choosing the Goethean super-closet-play
Instead or (daring prophecy, some say)
A filmscript with no dream of celluloid,
The firmament as screen, thus to avoid
Being, with those same knout-strokes, flogged and flayed.
Still the comparison is bluntly made
By all who ever read or tried to read
The Dynasts. *And* The Dynasts *is, indeed,*
A monstrous shocking failure. Nonetheless,
Malignity may munch but Muses bless
Failed boldness more than orthodox success.
As for my own flawed superficial thing,

Epistle

No critic would be fool enough to bring
In Tolstoy guns to blast me into dust.
This is a comic novel and it must
Be read as such, as such deemed good or bad—
A thousand versts away from Tolstoygrad.
Indeed, my working title used to be
This: The Napoleon Comic Symphony,
A name that reason forced me to reject,
Since comic *leads the reader to expect*
Contrivances of laughter: comic taste,
Like the term comedy, *has been debased.*
Arousing mirth—this is not what I'm at:
What's comedy? Not tragedy. That's that.
My Ogre, though heroic, is grotesque,
A sort of essay in the picaresque,
Who robs and rapes and lies and kills in fun
And does no lasting harm to anyone.
Standing behind him, though, or to one side,
Another, bigger, hero is implied,
Not comic and not tragic but divine,
Tugging Napoleon's strings, and also mine,
Controlling form, the story's ebb and flow—
Beethoven, yes: this you already know.
I was brought up on music and compose
Bad music still, but ever since I chose
The novelist's métier one mad idea
Has haunted me, and I fulfill it here
Or try to—it is this: somehow to give
Symphonic shape to verbal narrative,
Impose on life, though nerves scream and resist,
The abstract patterns of the symphonist.
I know that several works of literature
Have played the game already: these demur
(Point Counter Point, *the* Four Quartets) *at going*
Further than superficial fancy, showing
A literary fear of the whole hog,

Content with the most general analogue.
The most ambitious effort the world knows
Within this manic field—narrative prose
Made to behave like music—we can hear
When Joyce's Sirens captivate the ear,
Comic-pedantic fugal, *in* Ulysses,
Most brilliant, most ingenious. But this is
Really a piece of elephantine fun
Designed to show the thing cannot be done.
Nor can it. What for years has haunted me
Has been a like impossibility—
A novel where the horrible Marquis
De Sade comes up against Jane Austen and
They clash thematically, the whole thing planned
In four Mozartian movements: first, con brio;
Adagio *next; next, minuet and trio;*
A riotous allegro *at the end.*
I mentioned this to a film-making friend,
Quite casually. Uncasually he said
I ought to write on Bonaparte instead
(He thought of his own art: he wished to plan
An epic film about the Corsican
But lacked a script). At once there flashed in flame
A more ambitious notion—this: to frame
A novel on Napoleon Bonaparte
That followed Ludwig van, and not Mozart.
The symphony was there—Third, in E-Flat,
The Eroica. This novel, then, is that:
Napoleon's career, unteased, rewoven
Into a pattern borrowed from Beethoven.
The story is well-known: Count Bernadotte
Met Beethoven and said to him: "Why not
A Sinfonia Buonaparte?" —*"Yes:*
This great First Consul merits nothing less,"
Said Beethoven, and so he wrote the work.
But certain ogreish traits began to irk,

Then deeplier disturb, then fire to rage
Ludwig, who ripped the dedication page
To ribbons, crying: "Hero of the age?
Ach, nein—*another tyrant." He was right:*
The Duc d'Enghien shot at dead of night,
Without a trial; the Napoleonic line
Secured by regifaction. "Held? Ach nein!"
A generalized First Consul yet remains
Inside the symphony: heroic strains
In E-Flat, most heroic key, give out
The essential hero, not the Mafia lout.
My task as novelist? Restore that rogue ram,
That bad Colossus, to the symphonic program,
Dealing in hard particulars but still
Invoking what is always general
In music, the Napoleonic presence
And, contra punctum, *music's formal essence—*
As far as possible—if it can be done—
It can't, of course—, and so on, and so on.
The first two movements of the Eroica,
Although (but need I tell you this?) they are
Organized sound, no more, to awe the ear,
Yet do suggest some hero's brief career.
The Allegro*: see him live and vigorous,*
Striding the earth, stern but magnanimous,
In love with order, his regretful strife
Devoted to the ennobling of our life.
The Marcia Funebre*: already dead,*
The ironic laurels wilting round his head,
He's borne to burial; we weep, we hear
The purple orators about his bier—
That character, how noble; and how great
Those exploits in the service of the State.
He rests in peace beneath this hallowed shroud,
Quite dead, and resurrection's not allowed.
But stay—there are two movements still to run:

The subject's buried; what's then to be done?
The Scherzo—*how? The brisk* Finale—*who?*
Beethoven smiles: "What I propose to do
Is to invoke another noble creature,
No child of Nature, but of Supernature.
The vague historical—that's finished with;
Now the particularity of myth."
What myth? What hero? Aaaaah—Prometheus.
Beethoven makes it fiery-clear to us
In his Finale *who the hero is.*
He takes a bass and then a theme from his
Own ballet music on Prometheus, then
Builds variations till the count of ten.
The Scherzo—*is it fancy that hears roar*
The flames which from the gods the hero tore
To bring to man? Those horns—what are they doing?
The hunt is up, it is the gods pursuing.
In Plutarch's Lives *the heroes go in pairs—*
One fabulous and one historic. There's
The origin, one thinks, of this device:
The heroic is displayed not once but twice.
The novelist must deal in unity
Of character, so that was not for me—
Two slabs of prose about Napoleon
Followed by two (much lighter) based upon
Prometheus. You see, then, what I've done:
Forced mythic and historic into one.
The trio of my (sort of) Scherzo is
A play in verse the Emperor witnesses
Based on Prometheus, written by a man
Named, quite improbably, Enuiluban—
Nabuliune, him. In the last part
(Whose variations do not *dare the art*
Of parody, however it appears)
Another victim claims our tears or ears
Or eyes or fancy—three fused into one—

Epistle

Though basically Promethapoleon,
Chained to a rock, his liver eagled out,
This, then, is what the novel is about:
Its key E-Flat, its form pseudo-symphonic,
Ending upon a forte *major tonic,*
Napoleon triumphant—so he is,
Since, unfulfilled in life, that plan of his
Now operates at last: proud England, cowed
Back into Europe, humbled, silenced, bowed.
Let hell's or heaven's belfries clang out loud.